JSI

Michael Marshall is a novelist and screen-writer. Before becoming an internationally bestselling thriller writer with *The Straw Men* and its follow-ups, he had already established a successful career under the name Michael Marshall Smith.

He lives in North London with his wife, son and two cats.

BAD THINGS

On a summer's afternoon four-year-old Scott Henderson walked out onto a jetty over a lake in Black Ridge, Washington State. He never came back. John Henderson's world ended that day, but three years later he's still alive. Living a life, of sorts — until one night he receives an email from a stranger, claiming to know what happened to his son. Against his better judgement Henderson returns to Black Ridge, unleashing a terrifying sequence of events which threatens to destroy what remains of everything he once held dear. Bad things don't just happen to other people — they're waiting round the corner for you too. And when they make their way in through the cracks in your life, you won't know until it's too late.

Books by Michael Marshall
Published by The House of Ulverscroft:

THE STRAW MEN
THE LONELY DEAD
BLOOD OF ANGELS
THE INTRUDERS

MICHAEL MARSHALL

BAD THINGS

Complete and Unabridged

CHARNWOOD
Leicester

First published in Great Britain in 2009 by
HarperCollins*Publishers*
London

First Charnwood Edition
published 2010
by arrangement with
HarperCollins*Publishers*
London

British Library CIP Data

Marshall, Michael, *1965 May 3–*
  Bad things.
  1. Missing children- -Fiction. 2. Suspense fiction.
  3. Large type books.
  I. Title
  823.9'14–dc22

  ISBN 978–1–44480–006–7

Published by
F. A. Thorpe (Publishing)
Anstey, Leicestershire
Set by Words & Graphics Ltd.
Anstey, Leicestershire
Printed and bound in Great Britain by
T. J. International Ltd., Padstow, Cornwall

This book is printed on acid-free paper

For Stephen Jones
Who knows the darkest parts of the woods
— and the path from there to the pub.

Acknowledgements

Thank you to my editors, Jane Johnson and Jennifer Brehl, for helping me find the wood amongst these trees, to my agents Ralph Vicinanza and Jonny Geller, to Lisa Gallagher and Amanda Ridout for their support, to Carolyn Marino for her help over the last couple of years, and to the memory of Jean Baudrillard, for a decade of inspiration.

And for the hundredth year running, the award for Greatest Patience In The Face Of An Author goes to . . . Paula, my wife.

It is the practice of evil, and hence, in a sense, the inhuman, that is the distinctive mark of the human in the animal kingdom
Jean Baudrillard
Cool Memories V

Prologue

It is a beautiful afternoon in late summer, and there is a man standing on the deck of a house in the woods a fifteen-minute drive from Roslyn — a nice, small town in Washington State. It is a fine house, structured around oak beams and river rock and possessed of both cosy lateral spaces and cathedral ceilings where it counts. The deck is wide and deep, wrapping around the whole of the raised first storey, and points out over a slope where a woman sits in a rustic wooden chair, the product of semi-local artisanship. She is holding a baby who is nine months old, and at the moment, miraculously, peaceably quiet. The house and the five acres around it cost a little under two million dollars, and the man is happy to own it, and happy to be standing there. He has spent much of the day in his study, despite the fact it is a Saturday, but that's okay because it is precisely this willingness to work evenings and weekends that puts you in a house like this and confers the kind of life you may live in it. You reap, after all, what you sow.

The deck has a good view toward a very large, wooded lake the locals call Murdo Pond, sixty yards away down the wooded slope, and a little of which — the portion that lies within his property lines — the man guesses he owns too, if you can be said to own a lake. He is wearing a denim shirt and khaki shorts, and in his hand is

1

a tall, cold glass of beer, an unusual occurrence, as he seldom drinks at home — or much at all, unless business demands its shortcut to conviviality — but which feels deserved and appropriate now: what else do we strive for, after all, if not for such an indulgence, on the deck of such a house, at the end of such a day?

He can see that his wife is without a drink, and knows she would probably like one, and will in a short while call down to ask if he can fetch her something. But for a few minutes longer he stands there, feeling more or less at one with the world, or as close to that state as is possible given the complexities of quotidian existence and the intransigence of people and situations and things. Just then a breeze floats across the deck, bringing with it the faint, spicy smell of turning leaves, and for a moment the world is better still. Then it has gone, and it is time to move on.

The man opens his mouth to ask his wife what she'd like to drink, but then pauses, and frowns.

'Where's Scott?' he says.

His wife looks up, a little startled, having been unaware of his presence on the deck.

'I thought he was with you.'

'Working?'

'I mean, indoors.'

He turns and looks back through wide-open doors into the living room. Though there is evidence of his four-year-old son's passing — toys and books spread across the floor as if in the wake of a tiny hurricane — the boy is not visible.

The man goes back inside the house and walks

2

through it. Not quickly yet, but purposefully. His son is not in his room, or the kitchen, or the den. Nor is he hunkered down in the stretch of corridor near the main entrance on the other side of the house, a non-space which the boy has colonized and where he is sometimes to be found frowning in concentration over a self-imposed task of evident fascination but no clear purpose.

The man returns through the house and out onto the deck, and by now he's moving a little more quickly.

His wife is standing, the baby in her arms.

'Isn't he there?'

The man doesn't answer, judging his speed will answer the question. It does, and she turns to scan her eyes around the lawns, and into the woods. He meanwhile heads round to the far right extent of the deck. No sign of the boy from up there. He walks back to the other end and patters down the cedar steps.

'When did you last see him?'

'I don't know,' she says, looking flustered. He realizes briefly how tired she is. The baby, Scott's little brother, is still not sleeping through the night, and will only accept small hours' comfort from his mother. 'About half an hour ago?' she decides. 'Before I came out. He was in, you know, that place where he sits.'

He nods quickly, calls Scott's name again, glances back toward the house. His son still does not emerge onto the balcony. His wife does not seem overly concerned, and the man is not sure why he *does* feel anxious. Scott is a self-contained child, happy to entertain himself for long periods, to sit reading or playing or drawing without requiring an adult within earshot. He occasionally goes for walks around the house, too — though he keeps to the paths and doesn't stray deeper into the woods. He is a good child, occasionally boisterous, but mindful of rules.

So where is he?

Leaving his wife irresolute in the middle of the lawn, the man heads around the side of the house and trots down the nearest of the ornamental walkways that lead into the woods and toward the remains of the old cabin there, noticing the path could do with a sweep. He peers into the trees, calls out. He cannot see his son, and the call again receives no answer. Only when he turns back toward the house does he finally spot him.

Scott is standing fifty yards away, down at the lake.

Though the family is not the boating kind, the house came with a small structure for storing water craft. Next to this emerges a wooden jetty which protrudes sixty feet out into Murdo Pond, to where the water runs very deep. His son is standing at the end of this.

Right at the very end.

The man shouts his wife's name and starts to run. She sees where he is headed and starts to walk jerkily in the same direction, confused, as her view of the jetty is obscured by a copse of trees which stand out dark against water that is glinting white in the late afternoon sun.

When she finally sees her son, she screams, but still Scott doesn't react.

The man doesn't understand why she screams. Their boy is a strong swimmer. They would hardly live so close by a large body of water otherwise, even though the lake always feels far too cold for recreational swimming, even in summer. But he doesn't understand why he is sprinting, either, leaving the path and cutting straight through the trees, pushing through undergrowth heedless of the scratches, shouting his son's name.

Apart from the sounds he and his wife are making, the world seems utterly silent and heavy and still, as if it has become an inanimate stage for this moment, as if the leaves on the trees, the lapping of the lake's waters, the progress of worms within the earth, has halted.

When he reaches the jetty the man stops running. He doesn't want to startle the boy.

'Scott,' he says, trying to keep his voice level.

There is no response. The boy stands with his feet neatly together, his arms by his side. His head is lowered slightly, chin pointing down toward his chest, as if he is studying something in or just above the surface of the water, thirty feet beyond the end of the jetty.

The man takes a step onto the wooden surface.

His wife arrives, the baby now mewling in her arms, and he holds his hand up to forestall another shout from her.

'Scott, sweetie,' she says instead, with commendable evenness. 'What are you doing?'

The man is starting to relax, a little. Their son's whereabouts are now known, after all.

5

Even if he fell, he can swim. But other parts of the man's soul, held closer to his core, are twisted up and clamping tighter with each second that passes. Why is Scott not responding? Why is he just standing there?

The low panic the man feels has little to do with questions even such as these, however. It is merely present, in his guts, as if that soft breeze followed him down off the deck and through the woods, and has now grabbed his stomach like a fist, squeezing harder and harder. He thinks he can smell something now, too, as if a bubble of gas has come up to the surface of the water, releasing something dark and rich and sweet. He takes another step down the jetty.

'Scott,' he says, firmly. 'It's okay if you want to look in the lake. But take a step back, yeah?'

The man is relieved when his son does just that.

The boy takes a pace backward, and finally turns. He does this in several small steps, as if confused to find himself where he is, and taking ostensive care.

There is something wrong with the boy's face.

It takes his father a moment to realize that it's not physical, rather that the expression on it is one he has never seen there before. A kind of confusion, of utter dislocation. 'Scott — what's wrong?'

The boy's face clears, and he looks up at his father.

'*Daddy?*' he says, as if very surprised. 'Why . . . '

'Yes, of course, it's Daddy,' the man says. He starts to walk slowly toward Scott, the hairs rising on the back of his neck, though the temperature around the lake seems to have jumped twenty degrees. 'Look, I don't know what — '

But then the boy's mouth slowly opens, as he stares past or through his father, back toward the end of the jetty, at the woods. The look is so direct that his mother turns to glance back that way too, not knowing what to expect.

'No,' the boy says. '*No.*'

The first time he says it quietly. The second time is far louder. His expression changes again, too, in a way both parents will remember for the rest of their lives, turning in a moment from a face they know better than their own to a mask of dismay and heartbreak that is horrifying to see on a child.

'What's . . . '

And then he shouts. 'Run, Daddy. Run!'

The man starts to run toward him. He can hear his wife running too. But the boy topples sideways before they can get to him, falling awkwardly over the deck and flipping with slow grace down into the water.

★ ★ ★

The man is on the jetty in the last of the afternoon light. He stands with his child in his arms.

The police are there. A young one, and an older one, soon followed by many more. Four

7

hours later the coroner will tell the police, and then the parents, that it was not the fall into the water, nor to the deck, nor even anything before that, that did it.

The boy just died.

Part 1

It would be convenient if one could redesign
the past, change a few things here and there,
like certain acts of outrageous stupidity, but
if one could do that, the past would always be
in motion.
Richard Brautigan
An Unfortunate Woman

1

Ted came and found me a little after seven. I was behind the bar, assisting with a backlog of beer orders for the patrons out on deck while they waited to be seated. The Pelican's seasonal drinks station is tiny, an area in front of an opening in the wall through to the outside, and Mazy and I were moving around it with the grace of two old farts trying to reverse mobile homes into the same parking space. There's barely room for one, let alone two, but though Mazy is cute and cool and has as many piercings and tattoos as any young person could wish for, she's a little slow when it comes to grinding out margaritas and cold Budweisers and Diet Cokes, extra ice, no lime. I don't know what it is about the ocean, and sand, but it makes people want margaritas. Even in Oregon, in September.

'Can't get hold of the little asshole,' Ted muttered. His face was red and hot, and thinning grey hair was sticking to his pate, though the air conditioning was working just fine. 'You mind?'

'No problem,' I said.

I finished the order I was on and then headed through the main area of the restaurant, where old John Prine songs played quietly in the background and the ocean looked grey and cool through the big windows and it felt like Marion Beach always does.

11

★　★　★

The day had been unusually warm for the season but cut with a breeze from the southeast, and most of the patrons were hazy-eyed rather than bedraggled. Now that the sun was down the air had grown heavy, however, and I'd been glad to be waiting tables instead of hanging tough in front of the pizza oven, which is where I was now headed.

The oven is a relatively new addition at the Pelican, just installed when I started there nine months ago. It had controversially replaced a prime block of seating where customers had been accustomed to sitting themselves in front of seafood for nearly thirty years, and I knew Ted still lost sleep trying to calculate whether the cost of a wood-fired oven and the associated loss of twelve covers (multiplied by two or three sittings, on a good night) would soon, or ever, be outstripped by gains accruing from the fact you can sell a pizza to any child in America, whereas they can be notoriously picky with fish. His wife thought he'd got it wrong but she believed that about everything he did, so while he respected her opinion he wasn't prepared to take it as the final word. Ted is a decent guy but how he's managed to stay afloat in the restaurant business for so long is a mystery. A rambling shack overhanging the shallow and reedy water of a creek that wanders out to the sea — and tricked up inside with dusty nets, plastic buoys, and far more than one wooden representation of the seabird from which it takes its name — the Pelican has now bypassed fashion so conclusively as to become one of those places you go back to because you went there when you were a kid, or when the kids were young or, well, just because you do. And, to be fair, the food is actually pretty good.

I could have done the pizza math for Ted but it was not my place to do so. It wasn't my place to make the damned things, either, but over the last five months I'd sometimes wound up covering the station when Kyle, the official thin-base supremo, didn't make it in for the evening shift. Kyle is twenty-two and shacked up with Becki, the owner's youngest daughter (of five), a girl who went to a barely accredited college down in California to learn some strain of Human Resources bullshit but dropped out so fast that she bounced. She wound up back home not doing much except partying and smoking dope on the beach with a boyfriend who made pizza badly — the actual dough being forged by one of the back-room Ecuadorians in the morning — and couldn't even get his shit together to do *that* six nights a week. This drove Ted so insane that he couldn't even think about it (much less address the problem practically), and so Kyle was basically a fixture, regardless of how searching his exploration of the outer limits of being a pointless good-looking prick.

If he hadn't shown up by the time someone wanted pizza then I'd do the dough-spinning on his behalf, the other wait staff picking up the slack on the floor. I didn't mind. I'd found that I enjoyed smoothing the tomato sauce in meditative circles, judiciously adding mozzarella and

13

basil and chunks of pepperoni or crayfish or pesto chicken, then hefting the peel to slide them toward the wood fire. I didn't emulate Kyle's policy of adding other ingredients at random — allegedly a form of 'art' (which he'd studied for about a week, at a place where they'll accept dogs if they bring the tuition fees), more likely a legacy of being stoned 24/7 — but stuck to the toppings as described, and so the response from the tables tended to be positive. My pizzas were more circular than Kyle's too, but that wasn't the point either. He was Kyle, the pizza guy. I was John, the waiter guy.

Not even *the* waiter, in fact, just a waiter, amongst several. Indefinite article man.

And that's alright by me.

★ ★ ★

Wonderboy finally rolled up an hour later, delivered in an open-top car that fishtailed around the lot and then disappeared again in a cloud of dust. He went to the locker room to change, and came out twitching.

'Glad you could make it,' I said, taking off the special pizza apron. I didn't care one way or the other about Kyle being late. I was merely following form. You don't let fellow toilers at the bottom of the food-production chain get away with any shit, or they'll be doing it all the time.

'Yeah, well,' he said, confused. 'You know, like, it's my job.'

I didn't have an answer to that, so stepped out of his way and went back to waiting tables. I

14

established what people wanted, and pushed the specials. I conveyed orders back to the kitchen, instigating the production of breaded shrimp and grilled swordfish and blackened mahi mahi, and the celebrated side salad with honey apple vinaigrette. I brought the results back to the table, along with drinks and bonhomie. I returned twice to check that everything was okay, and refresh their iced water. I accepted payment via cash, cheque, or credit card, and reciprocated with little mints and a postcard of the restaurant. I told people it had been great seeing them, and to drive safe, and wiped the table down in preparation for the next family or young couple or trio of wizened oldsters celebrating sixty years of mutual dislike.

After two cycles of this, the evening ended and we cleared the place up, and everyone started for home.

It was dark by then. Unusually humid too, the air like the breath of a big, hot dog who'd been drinking sea water all afternoon. I nodded goodbye as rusty cars piloted by other staff crunkled past me, on the way up the pebbled slip road from the Pelican's location, to turn left or right along Highway 101.

The cooks left jammed together into one low-slung and battered station wagon, the driver giving me a pro-forma eye-fuck as he passed. I assumed they all boarded together in some house up in Astoria or Seaside, saving money to send back home, but as I'd never spoken to any of them, I didn't actually know.

As I reached the highway I realized Kyle was a

15

few yards behind me. I glanced back, surprised.

'You walking somewhere?'

'Yeah, right,' he smirked. 'Mission control's on the way. Big party up the road tonight. We're headed in your direction, if you want a ride.'

I hesitated. Normally I walked the two miles north. The other staff know this, and think I'm out of my mind. I look at their young, hopeful faces and consider asking what else I should be doing with the time, but I don't want to freak them out. I don't want to think of myself as not-young, either, but as a thirty-five year old amongst humans with training wheels, you can feel like the go-to guy for insider information on the formation of the tectonic plates.

The walk is pleasant enough. You head along the verge, the road on your right, the other side of which is twenty feet of scrubby grass and then rocky outcrops. On your left you pass the parking lots of very small, retro-style condos and resorts, three storey at most and rendered in pastel or white with accents in a variety of blues, called things like The Sandpiper and Waves and Trade Winds; or fifty-yard lots stretching to individual beach houses; or, for long stretches, just undergrowth and dunes.

But tonight my feet were tired and I wanted to be home, plus there's a difference between doing your own thing and merely looking unfriendly and perverse.

'That'd be great,' I said.

2

Within thirty seconds we realized we had squat to say to each other outside the confines of the restaurant, and Kyle reached in his T-shirt pocket and pulled out a joint. He lit it, hesitated, then offered it to me. To be sociable, I took a hit. Pretty much immediately I could tell why his pizzas were so dreadful: if this was his standard toke, it was amazing the guy could even stand up. We hung in silence for ten minutes, passing the joint back and forth, waiting for inspiration to strike. Before long I was beginning to wish I'd walked. At least that way I could have headed over the dunes down to the beach, where the waves would have cut the humidity a little.

'Gonna rain,' Kyle said suddenly, as if someone had given him a prompt via an earpiece.

I nodded. 'I'm thinking so.'

Five minutes later, thankfully, Becki's car came down the road as if hurled by a belligerent god. It decelerated within a shorter distance than I would have thought possible, though not without cost to the tyres.

'Hey,' she said, around a cigarette. 'Walking Dude's going to accept a ride? Well. I'm *honoured*.'

I smiled. 'Been a long day.'

'Word, my liege. Hop in.'

I got in back and held on tight as she returned

17

the vehicle to warp speed. Kyle seemed to know better than to try to talk to his woman while she was in charge of heavy machinery, and I followed his lead, enjoying the wind despite the significant G-forces that came with it.

The journey didn't take long at all. When we were a hundred yards from my destination, I tapped Becki on the shoulder. She wrenched her entire upper body around to see what I wanted.

'What?'

'Now,' I shouted, 'would be a good time to start *slowing down*.'

'Gotcha.'

She wrestled the car to a halt and I vaulted out over the side. The radio was on before I had both feet on the ground. Becki waved with a backward flip of the hand, and then the car was hell and gone down the road.

This coast is very quiet at night. Once in a while a pickup will roar past, trailing music or a meaningless bellow or ejecting an empty beer can to bounce clattering down the road. But mostly it's only the rustle of the surf on the other side of the dunes, and by the time I get home, when I've walked, the evening in the restaurant feels like it might have happened yesterday, or the week before, or to someone else. Everything settles into one long chain of events with little to connect the days except the fact that that's what they do.

Finally I turned and walked up to the house. One of the older vacation homes along this stretch, it has wide, overgrown lots either side and consists of two interlocked wooden octagons, which

18

must have seemed like a good idea to someone at some point — I'm guessing around 1973. In fact it just means there are more angles than usual for rain and sea air to work at — but it's got a good view and a walkway over the dunes down to the sand, and it costs me nothing. Not long after I came here I met a guy called Gary, in Ocean's, a bar half a mile down the road from the Pelican. He'd just gotten unmarried and was in Oregon trying to get his head together. One look told you he was becalmed on the internal sea of the recently divorced: distracted, only occasionally glancing at you directly enough to reveal the wild gaze of a captain alone on a lost ship, tied to the wheel and trying to stop its relentless spinning. Sometimes these men and women will lose control and you'll find them in bars drinking too loud and fast and with nothing like real merriment in their eyes; but mostly they simply hold on, bodies braced against the wind, gazing with a thousand-yard stare into what they assume must be their future.

It's a look I recognized. We bonded, bought each other beers, met up a few times before he shipped back east. Long and short of it is that I ended up being a kind of caretaker for his place, though it doesn't really need it. I stay there, leaving a light on once in a while and being seen in the yard, which presumably lessens the chances of some asshole breaking in. I patch the occasional leak in the roof, and am supposed to call Gary if the smaller octagon (which holds the two bedrooms) starts to sag any worse over the concrete pilings that hold it up on the dune. In heavy winds it's disconcertingly like being on

19

an actual ship, but it'll hold for now. In theory I have to move out if he decides to come out to stay, but in two years that's never happened. I last spoke to him three months ago to get his okay on replacing a screen door, and he was living with a new woman back in Boston and sounded cautiously content. I guess the beach house is a part of Gary's past he's not ready to divest, an investment in a future some part of his heart has not yet quite written off. It'll happen, sooner or later, and then I guess I'll live somewhere else.

Once inside, I opened the big sliding windows and went out on the deck, belatedly realizing it was a Friday night. I'd known this before, of course, sort of. The restaurant's always livelier, regardless of the season — but Friday-is-busy is different to hey-it's-Friday! Or it used to be. Perhaps it was this that made me grab a couple of beers from the fridge; could also have been the half-joint floating around my system, coupled with a feeling of restlessness I'd had all day; or merely that I was home a little earlier than usual and Becki and Kyle had, without trying, made me feel about a million years old.

I decided I'd take the beers down onto the beach. A one-man Friday night, watching the waves, listening to the music of the spheres. Party on.

★   ★   ★

I walked to within a few yards of the sea and sat down on the sand. Looked up along the coast for

20

a while, at the distant glow of windows in the darkness, listening to the sound of the waves coming up, and going back, as the sky grew lower and matt with gathering cloud.

I methodically drank my way through the first beer and felt calm, and empty, though not really at peace. To achieve that I would have needed to believe that I had a place in the world, instead of standing quietly to one side. I'd been in Oregon for nearly three years. Floating. Before the Pelican had been bar work up and down the coast, some odd jobs, plus periods working the door at nightclubs over in Portland. Service industry roustabout work, occupations that required little but the willingness to work cheaply, at night, and to risk occasional confrontations with one's fellow man. My possessions were limited to a few clothes, a laptop, and some books. I didn't even own a car any more, though I did have money in the bank. More than my co-workers would have imagined, I'm sure, but that's because all they know about me is I can hold my own in a busy service and produce approximately circular Italian food.

Finally it rained.

Irrevocably, and very hard, soaking me so quickly that there was no hurry to go inside. I sat out a little longer, as the rain bounced off the waves and pocked the sand. Eventually I finished the second beer and then stood up and started for home.

As Friday nights go, I couldn't claim this one had really caught fire.

★ ★ ★

Back inside I dried off and wandered into the living room. It was nearly two o'clock, but I couldn't seem to find my way to bed. I played on the web for a little while, the last refuge of the restless and clinically bored. As a last resort I checked my email — another of the existentially empty moments the Internet hands you on a plate.

Hey world, want to talk?

No? Well, maybe later.

Invitations to invest in Chinese industry, buy knock-off watches and stock up on Viagra. Some Barely Legal Teen Cuties had been in touch again, too. As was their custom, they were keen to spill the beans on how they'd got it on with their roommate or boss or a herd of broad-minded elk.

I declined the offers, also as usual, hoping they wouldn't be offended after the trouble they'd gone to for me, and me alone. I'd selected all the crap as a block and was about to throw it in the trash when a message near the bottom caught my eye.

The subject line said: PLEASE, PLEASE READ

Most likely more spam, of course. One of the Nigerian classics, perhaps, the wife/son/cat of a recently deceased oligarch who'd squirrelled away millions that some lucky randomer could have twenty per cent of, if they'd just send all their bank details to a stranger who'd spelt his own name three different ways in a single email.

If so, however, they'd titled it well. That combination of words is hard to ignore. I clicked on it, yawning, trying and failing to remember the last time I'd received a message from someone in particular. The email was short.

I know what happened

Nothing else. Not even a period at the end of the sentence. The name of the apparent sender of the email — Ellen Robertson — was not that of anyone I knew.

Just a piece of spam after all.

I hit delete and went to bed.

3

Next morning started with a walk up the beach, carrying a big cup of coffee. I've done that every day since I've been living in Gary's house. Far as I'm concerned, if the beach is right there and you don't kick off the day by walking along it, then you should move the hell inland and make way for someone who understands what the coast is for.

I was up early, and the sands were even more deserted than usual. I passed a couple of guys optimistically waving fishing rods at the sea, and a few people like me. Lone men and women in shorts and loose shirts, tracing their ritual walkways, smiling briefly at strangers. Sometimes when the sun is bright and the world holds no shadows at all I imagine what it would be like to have a smaller set of foot-prints keeping pace with mine. But not often, and not that morning.

I walked further than usual, but it was still only eight-thirty when I got back to the house. There was already a message on the machine. It was from Ted.

'Christ,' he'd said, without preamble. 'Look, I hate to call you like this. But could you come lend a hand? Someone's broken in. To the restaurant.'

His voice went muffled for a few moments, as he spoke brusquely to someone in the background.

Then he came back on, sounding even more pissed. 'Look, maybe you're out for the day already, but if not — '

★ ★ ★

I picked up the handset and called him back.

Rather than wait for me to walk, Ted came down, arriving outside the house ten minutes later. It's always been evident where Becki acquired her driving style. Ted turned the pickup around in the road without any notable decrease in speed, and drew level with me. I was leaning against the post at the top of my drive, waiting, having a cigarette. I leaned down to talk through the open passenger window.

'You need me to bring any tools?'

He shook his head. 'Got a bunch in the storeroom. Going to have to go buy glass and wood, but I'll get on to that later. Fucking day this is gonna be.'

I climbed into the truck and just about got the door shut before he dropped his foot on the pedal.

'When did you find it?'

Ted's face was even redder and more baggy-eyed than usual. 'One of the cooks. Raul, I think. Got there at seven with the rest of the crew, called me right away.'

'Which one's Raul?'

'You got me. I think they're all called Raul.'

'What happened to the alarm?'

'Nothing. It went off like it was supposed to. It was still going when I got there.'

25

'Isn't someone from the alarm company supposed to come check it out? Or phone you, at least?'

Ted looked embarrassed. 'Stopped paying for that service a while back. It's eight hundred a year, and we've never needed it before.'

By now we were decelerating toward the right-hand turn off the highway.

'How bad is the damage?'

Ted shrugged, raising both hands from the wheel in a gesture evoking the difficulty of describing degrees of misfortune, especially when however much 'bad' is still going to cause a day of fetching and form-filling and expense that a guy just doesn't fucking need.

'It's not so terrible, I guess. I just don't *get* it. There's signs on all three doors — front, back, kitchen — saying no money's left on the premises overnight. So what the hell? Huh? What kind of fuckhead comes all the way over here in the middle of the night, just to screw up someone else's day?'

'Maybe they didn't believe you about the money,' I said. 'Fuckheads can be strange like that.'

As the car slowed into the lot I saw Becki's car 'parked' down the end. 'Don't tell me Kyle's here already?'

Ted laughed, and for a moment looked less harried and disappointed with mankind in general.

'I had to call Becki to work out how to get your phone number off the database. I told her she didn't have to do anything, but she came right over.'

He pulled the pickup to come to rest next to his daughter's vehicle.

'You called the cops, I assume?'

'Been and gone. They sent their two best men, as I'm sure you can imagine. Not convinced either of them aced the 'How to pretend you give a shit' course, though. And I've comped a *lot* of appetizers and drinks for both those assholes in the past.'

We got out and I followed Ted to the restaurant. He led me around the side to the back door, the one you'd enter if you'd been out on deck with a drink before coming in for dinner.

The remains of the external door there was hanging open, most of the panes broken. The slats that once held the glass in place lay in splinters on the floor. Becki was hunkered down in the short corridor beyond the doorway, working a dustpan and hand brush.

'Hey,' she said.

'It doesn't look so bad.'

'Not any more,' she said, straightening up. She'd evidently been at the job a while, and a couple of blonde hairs were stuck to her forehead. She looked pissed off. 'The guys are still working in the back.'

I went through the second door — which had been more gently forced — and into the main area of the restaurant. The Pelican's register and reservations system runs on a newish Apple Mac with an external cash drawer. The latter had been unsuccessfully attacked with a chisel and/or crowbar. I looked at this for a while and then

27

headed into the back, where the brigade was tidying the kitchen.

'They messed it up some in here,' Ted said, unnecessarily, as he joined me. It looked like one or two people had really made a meal of throwing things around. 'And it seems like we got a machine missing.'

'Juicer,' confirmed one of the cooks — the guy who'd stared at me on the way out of the lot last night. He looked less moody now, and I could guess why. He and his fellow non-Americans would not have enjoyed the police visit earlier, most likely spending it on an extended cigarette break half a mile down the road. They would also be very aware of being high on most people's list of suspects — either for doing the job themselves, or passing the opportunity to an accomplice, along with the information that any alarm would go unanswered.

'Kind of a dumb break-in,' I said, directly to him. 'I mean, everybody knows there's no cash left here, right?'

'Yeah, of course,' the cook said, nodding quickly. 'We all know that. But some people, you know? They think it's fun, this kind of thing.'

'Probably just kids,' I said, looking past him to the anteroom off the side where staff changed and hung their coats. 'Anyone lose anything out of there?'

'Well, no,' Ted said. 'Nobody here in the middle of the night, right? The lockers were empty.'

'Duh,' I said. 'Of course.'

I turned, and saw Becki standing out in the restaurant looking at me.

28

★　★　★

I have no formal training in fixing things, but common sense and good measuring will get most of the job done. My dad had game at that kind of thing, and I spent long periods as a child watching him. Ted and I measured the broken panes and the wood that needed replacing, he listened to my instructions for a couple more items, then drove off to get it all from a hardware store in Astoria. Meanwhile Becki headed out to get a replacement cash drawer from a supplier over in Portland that she'd tracked down on the Net.

Ted was gone well over an hour. I sat on deck and slowly drank a Diet Coke. I was feeling an itch at the back of my head, but didn't want to yield to it. I knew that if I was back at the beach house, however, as normal at this time of day, then I'd already have done so. I also knew it would have been dumb, however, and that it was a box in my head I didn't want to open. The smart tactic with actions that don't make sense is to not do them the first time. Otherwise, after that, why not do them again?

Nonetheless I found myself, ten minutes later, at the till computer. The web browser Becki had been using was still up on screen. I navigated to my Internet provider's site and checked my email, quickly, before I could change my mind and fail to yield to impulse. There was nothing there.

That was good. I wouldn't be checking again.

★　★　★

Eventually Ted got back with the materials and I started work. The external door had been pretty solid, and so kicking the panes out had badly splintered the frame around the lock. I levered the damaged side off under Ted's watchful eye.

'You know what you're doing, right?'

'Kinda,' I said. 'More than you do, anyhow.'

'I get what you're saying,' he said, and went inside.

I worked slowly but methodically, which is the best way of dealing with the subversive ranks of inanimate objects. Ted proved to have a thorough selection of tools, which helped, as did having gone through the process of figuring out how to replace Gary's screen door a few months back. Security and good sense dictated replacing the door with something more robust, but Ted was adamant it needed to look the way it had, for tradition's sake. I'd specified that he at least buy super-toughened glass, also some metal strips that I intended using to strengthen the off-the-rack door.

While I was working through that portion of the job, Becki returned. I was ready for a break from hammering and sawing so I went to give her a hand with the cash drawer, which was not light. In the end she let me carry it by myself, though she hovered encouragingly in the background and went off to fetch me a soda as a reward, while I levered it into position and bolted it in place.

She got sidetracked with some issue in the kitchen, and I was back at work on the door by the time she returned with a Dr Pepper stacked with ice.

She stood around for a while and watched me working, without saying anything.

'That was a nice thing you did,' she said, after maybe five minutes.

'What's what?'

'You know. Signalling to the cooks that you thought they didn't have anything to do with it.'

'They didn't.'

I concentrated on manoeuvring a pane of glass, making sure it was bedded properly before screwing a piece of the metal brace-work securely into place. When I turned round, Becki was still looking at me, one eyebrow slightly raised.

I smiled. 'What?'

'You haven't always been a waiter, have you?'

'No,' I said. 'But it's what I am now.'

She nodded slowly, and walked back inside.

★   ★   ★

Midway through the day, the guy from the kitchen brought out a plate of food. I hadn't asked for this, or expected it. It was very good, too, a selection of handmade empanada-style things filled with spicy shrimp and fish.

'That was great,' I said, when he came back for the plate. 'You should get Ted to put those on the menu.'

The cook smiled, shrugged, and I guess I

31

knew what he meant. I stuck out my hand. 'John,' I said.

He shook it. 'Eduardo.'

'Got the dough ready for the young maestro yet?'

He laughed, and went back inside.

It took over six hours, but eventually everything was done. By four o'clock I'd replaced the frames on inner and outer doors, and fixed the other damage. Becki had the register back up and running, something I was surprised she was capable of doing. Her entire demeanour during the day had been something of an eye-opener. I hadn't figured her for capable and businesslike. The guys in back had meanwhile returned the kitchen to its spotless and socked-away state.

Ted came on an inspection tour, pronounced it good, grabbed a couple of handfuls of beers and took them out on deck. We all sat together, Ted, Becki and me with the guys out of the kitchen — and Mazy too, when she wandered in as if fresh out of some flower-scented fairy realm — and drank slowly in the sun, which wasn't very warm, but still pleasant. Fairly soon Ted got his head around the fact that though more than one of the cooks was called Eduardo, none was actually called Raul.

After a while Becki got up and went and fetched some more beers. She dispersed them around the crew and then offered one to me. I looked at my watch, realized it was coming up on five. I'd been working in direct sunlight half the day and my shirt was sticking to my back.

'I need to get back to my place to change,' I said. 'Pretty soon, in fact.'

'I'll give you a ride,' she said, as I stood up.

'This is good of you,' I said, as we walked together to her car. She didn't say anything.

★   ★   ★

She waited out on deck while I took a shower. As I came out into the living room, I saw she'd taken a beer from my fridge and was sitting drinking it, looking out to sea. I sat in the other chair.

'Going to have to head back soon,' I said.

She nodded, looking down at her hands. I offered her a cigarette, which she took, and we lit up and sat smoking in silence for a moment.

'How much trouble is he in?' I asked, eventually.

She glanced up. The skin around her eyes looked tight. 'How did you know?'

'Why steal a battered juicer and leave a computer? The mess in the kitchen was overdone, and the cash drawer looked like it was attacked by a chimp. No one came there last night looking for money. So where was it? In the locker room?'

She nodded.

'Dope, or powder?'

'Not dope.'

'How much?'

'About ten thousand dollars' worth.' Her voice was very quiet.

'*Jesus*, Becki. How stupid do you have to be,

to stash that much cocaine in your father's restaurant?'

'I didn't know it was *there*,' she said, angrily. 'This is Kyle's fucking thing.'

'*Kyle?* How did he even get that much capital? Please don't tell me you gave it to him.'

'He got a loan. From . . . some guys he knows.'

It was all I could do not to laugh. 'Oh, smart move. So now he's *royally* fucked, owing not just the back end of drugs he no longer has to sell, but the money he used to buy them in the first place. Perfect.'

'That about covers it.' She breathed out heavily, drained the rest of her beer in one swallow. 'And if you're thinking of getting heavy about drugs, I don't need to hear it.'

'No, drugs are way cool,' I said. 'Moral imbeciles making fortunes from fucking up other people's lives, staying out of sight while wannabes like your idiot boyfriend take all the risks.'

'Better get you back. Going to be a busy night.'

'Take it I'm going to be on pizzas?'

She smiled briefly, crooked and sad, and I realized how much I liked her, and also how close she was to seeing her life veer down a bad track into the woods. 'I'm not sure where he even is right now.'

We stood together.

'And you can't just walk away from this?'

'I love him,' she said, in the way only twenty year olds can.

★ ★ ★

She drove me back to the restaurant, letting me out at the top of the access road.

'Go find him,' I said. 'Get the names of anyone he might have told where he stashed his gear.'

She looked up at me. 'And then?'

'And then,' I said. I tapped the car twice with the flat of my hand, and she drove away.

The front door to the restaurant was open, other front-of-house staff busily arranging chairs out on deck, but I walked around the other way and went in through the portal I'd spent most of the day replacing. I reached out as I walked through, and gave it a shove. It felt very firm.

There's something good about having rebuilt a door. It makes you feel like you've done something. It makes you believe things are fixable, even when you know that generally they are not.

4

What can you do, when things start to fall apart?
Let us count the ways . . .

Not panic, of course, that's the main thing.
Once you start, it's impossible to stop. Panic is
immune to debate, to analysis, to earnest and
cognitively therapeutic bullet points. Panic isn't
listening. Panic has no ears, only a voice. Panic is
wildfire in the soul, vaulting the narrow paths of
reason in search of fresh wood and brush on the
other side, borne into every corner of the mind
by the winds of anxiety.

Carol wasn't even sure when it had started, or
why. The last couple of months had been *good*.
For the first time she'd started to feel settled.
The apartment began to feel like a home. She
got a part-time job helping at the library under
the dread Miss Williams, tidying chairs and
putting up posters and helping organize reading
groups. Work more suited to some game oldster
or slack-jawed teen, admittedly, but gainful
employment all the same. She walked to the
library and back and yet still managed to put on
a few pounds, having regained something of an
appetite. She made acquaintances, even put
tentative emotional down-payments on a couple
of potential friends, and generally quit acting like
someone in a Witness Protection Program.

Sometimes, she even just . . . forgot. That had
been best of all, the times when she suddenly

remembered — because it proved there had been a period, however short, when she had not.

At some point in the last few days this had started to change. She woke feeling as if she had sunk a couple of inches into the bed overnight. Instead of vigorously soaping herself in the shower she stood bowed under the water, noticing flecks of mildew between a pair of tiles and wondering how she could have missed them before, and if she'd get around to doing something about it — or if it would just get worse and worse until she was the kind of woman who had grubby tiles and nothing could be done about that or the state of the yard or her clothes or hair. Chaos stalks us all, gaining entrance through cracks in trivial maintenance, the things left undone. As soon as you realize how much there is to *do* to keep presenting a front, it becomes horribly easy to stop believing, and start counting again instead.

It was better when she got out into the world, but still it felt as if her momentum was faltering. Books slipped from her hands, and she could not find things in stores. A bruise appeared on her hip from some minor collision she couldn't recall. Annoyingly, this reminded her of something her ex-husband used to say: that you can always tell when your mood is failing, because the world of objects turns mutinous, as if the growing storm in your head unsettles the lower ranks outside.

And then, three evenings before, she had found herself returning to the front door after locking it for the night.

She knew it was shut. She could see it was shut, that the bolt was drawn. She remembered doing it, for God's sake, could recall the chill of the chain's metal against her fingertips. That night, these memories were enough. The next, they were not, and she returned twice to make sure.

And last night she'd done it eight times, furiously, eyes wide as she watched herself draw and redraw the chain, turning the key in the lock until it wouldn't turn any further, over and over, before finally withdrawing it. It wouldn't be nine times tonight. That wasn't how counting worked. If it didn't stop now, it would escalate to *sets* of eight.

Sixteen times, twenty-four . . .

To understand how much a person can mistrust reality and themselves, you need to stand in a cold hallway, fighting back tears of self-hatred and frustration, as you watch your own hands check a simple bolt over twenty times.

She knew the walls of your skull were not a bastion. That thoughts could get in through the cracks, and did. That, in fact, if you felt in certain ways, it was a pretty sure sign they already had. The more she opened her mind to panic, the more likely she'd start slipping down that road again. So she wasn't going to panic.

Not yet.

★ ★ ★

These thoughts occupied her most of the way home from the library, under skies that were a

38

smooth and unbroken grey. Once indoors she made a pot of strong coffee. She had an hour before he got back. Once he was home it would be easier. She'd have plenty to keep her mind off things. It also meant she wouldn't actually be able to *do* anything, however.

For a moment, thinking of Tyler, she felt a little better. Dinner could wait. Neither of them was a fussy eater. She could whip something up later. So . . .

She fetched her laptop from the living room and brought it to the kitchen table. When her browser was up she hesitated, hands over the keyboard.

She felt driven to do something, but . . . *what?*

She had thousands of words saved onto her hard disk, innumerable pdfs, two hundred bookmarked sites. The problem was none of the creators of these sites *knew* they were relevant. They were like people wandering the streets, blithely observing that portions of the sidewalk seemed to become white once in a while, without having the faintest understanding of snow. You needed to comprehend the system to place these reports in context. She *did* understand, had glimpsed it, at least. She was smart, too, though it seemed to her now that she'd never really capitalized on this.

There had been times when she'd experienced a glimpse of freedom, especially during the last couple of months. When it had occurred to her that the whole thing could be nonsense, a cloud on her vision that had never been more than a speck of dust in her eye. It didn't matter how many metaphors she conjured, however — and English had been one of her best subjects in high school; in the end, she knew she *believed*. Her faith was dark and unshakable. The knowledge did not make her feel better, and her faith didn't make her feel anything except afraid.

Faith/afraid: funny how similar the two words are. When we make ourselves believe things, how often is it just an attempt to hold back the fear?

She refocused on the screen, checking the sites with RSS feeds that automatically alerted her to additions, edits, new blog entries. Nothing. So she went for a trawl through some of her other bookmarks instead. Sites on mythology, folklore, local ephemera, anomalies. Still nothing.

Which made perfect sense. Her emotions didn't betoken a disturbance in the ether. She was not the micro- to the world's macrocosm, one half of a pathetic fallacy (God, high school English again!). It was personal. Each time she went looking and found nothing new, it diminished the comfort she'd once found there. What had previously made her feel that she was not alone, now increasingly confirmed that she was. So what next? When you know something's wrong, but not how or why, what exactly can you do?

Not panic. That's all.

★   ★   ★

Some time later she was roused by a knocking sound.

She blinked, realized the sound was someone

knocking on the front door. Of course. She hauled herself up from the chair and trudged out of the kitchen. She was disquieted to realize that she'd spent at least some of the time in thoughts she believed had left her: the idea of killing herself.

She opened the front door to see Rona smiling at her, looking teenage and wholesome as all get-out.

'Mommmeeeee!' a voice shrieked from below, and she squatted down to let Tyler give her a hug. He gave good hugs. She straightened up with her son in her arms, and smiled broadly at his occasional sitter.

'Thanks, honey,' she said, as the four year old in her grasp wriggled for the door catch. Locks and light switches were catnip to this kid. Pockets of the world on which he could exert an influence, Carol supposed, first steps in controlling the chaos. She hoped he never learned how they could turn on you.

'Oh, he's a peach,' Rona said.

Her cheer was unassailable. Tyler's mother knew that, on occasion, her son was perfectly capable of not being a peach, but you'd never know it from Rona's reports. 'So, Friday morning next, right?'

'Yep,' Carol said, her attention caught by the lock her son was manhandling. Thinking: *I'll be seeing you later.*

'You . . . okay, Mrs Ransom?'

Carol looked round to see her neighbour's daughter looking at her curiously. 'I'm great,' she said with a big fake smile, and shut the door.

41

While she fixed him a small holding snack in the kitchen she submitted her son to a forensic interrogation as to how he had spent his day. You needed to extract this information quickly. What had happened at kindergarten seemed to become unreal or uninteresting within a couple of hours, as if events were ephemeral, and the past lost its charge like a battery. Carol envied this a great deal.

It appeared that he had 'done things' and that it had been 'fine'.

They sat on the sofa together with a children's book — one perk of working at the library was an inexhaustible supply of these — and within fifteen minutes Carol felt herself relaxing. They could do that to you, sometimes, children. They were so much themselves that if you let yourself be pulled fully into their orbit, you could forget your own world for a time.

Then the phone rang. They looked up at it together. Their phone rang very seldom.

'Someone's calling,' Tyler said.

'I know, sweetie.' She got up and went over to the table, picked up the handset. 'Yes?'

'Hello, my dear.'

It was a woman's voice.

Carol knew immediately who it was. It was a moment before she could say anything in reply, and it came out as a brittle whisper.

'How did you get this number?'

'A little bird told me. Time to come home,' the woman said. 'We can help.'

42

Carol put down the phone.

'Who was that?' her son asked.

'Nobody, honey.'

'Can nobody talk, then?'

'Yes,' she said. 'Sometimes.'

She asked him to count up the number of cows on the page of the book in front of him, and managed to walk to the bathroom and close the door before she threw up.

That night she checked the bolt thirty-two times when she went to bed, though she knew it was too late. Nobody was already inside the gates, and that's what panic *actually* was, she realized. It was the noise of the world whispering in your ear, when your life was ruled by something that wasn't there.

It was the sound of nobody talking, all the time.

5

It was a busy night in the restaurant. I didn't give Ted a heads-up that we wouldn't be seeing his pizza guy, as he'd have wondered where I'd got my information, but waited until he came asking for me to fill in — and acted like it was business as usual. I alternated between the oven, the floor and the bar as we went through two half-full sets of covers. Unusually good for that time of year, and you could see Ted relax a little as he realized it was all going to help cover part of the day's costs and appease the dark gods of cash flow.

I was the last member of staff to leave the restaurant, and on hand when Ted gave the outside door a final looking-over before locking it for the night. He grunted approvingly.

'Nice job,' he said. 'I should really give you something for all that work.'

'You already do,' I said.

He looked at me for a moment. 'Want a lift?'

'I'm good,' I said. 'Looking forward to the walk.'

'You're a weird guy,' he said. When he got to his truck he looked back. 'Thanks, John.'

'All part of the service.'

He shook his head and got in the pickup, a man looking forward to a beer on his home turf and putting his feet up in front of late-night television with no idea that — for reasons of which he was entirely ignorant — his world

44

stood a little more fragile tonight. But I guess none of us ever do know that, until after the fact.

★ ★ ★

I waited until he'd driven away, then got a chair down from the stacks. I'd told myself I'd wait half an hour, forty minutes tops, but it was only twenty before I heard a vehicle turn into the access road.

I felt my heart sink as Becki's car came into the lot, but got up and walked over. If I didn't want to be here now, I shouldn't have said the things I had earlier. This happens because of that, and words are actions too. A lesson that mankind in general — and me in particular — seems to find hard to get through their heads.

Kyle was in the passenger seat. He looked up, then away, and didn't say anything. His hands lay on his thighs, the fingers of both drumming constantly.

'Hey, Captain Stupid,' I said. 'Having a good day?'

'I've been there already,' Becki said.

'So what does he have for me?'

She turned and stared at her boyfriend. He spoke quietly. 'Rick. And maybe Doug.'

'Who would be?'

'Assholes,' Becki said, bitterly. 'They're on the beach sometimes. They were at the party last night.'

I turned back to Kyle. 'So how'd they come to know where you were keeping your stash?'

'They just *know*, okay? I — '

'Kyle, listen to me. I can tell you've got the message. But I need to know whether these guys found out because they're smart and know how to play people like you, or if it's one of those things that just happens and they decided to make something of it on their way home. I'm assuming it's the latter, because of the amateur-night break-in, but I'd like to be sure.'

'I told them,' he said. 'I just kind of . . . said it.'

Becki rolled her eyes and muttered something under her breath.

'Good. You know where these people live?'

'Yeah.'

I opened the car door. 'So let's go.'

'What's this to you, anyhow?' Kyle asked. 'This is *my* problem. Becki already told me that.'

'Where'd you get the coke from?'

'Just some guys in Portland.'

'And ten thousand is not huge in the scale of these things. But they're still going to want their money. There are no acceptable losses to these people, Kyle. Losses make them look bad, and looking bad is something they will not countenance. If they can't get what they're owed from you then they'll branch out, with you as the fly in the centre of the web. That means Becki next. She doesn't have what they want. So that means they'll move on to her dad, and his place of business.'

He blinked.

'No man is an island,' I said. 'You get now what you've done?'

I knew I was pushing him, and that his pride was already hurt, but either this had to serve as

46

an object lesson or it would be even worse next time.

'Yeah,' he said, very quietly.

'Excellent,' I said, getting in the car. 'So let's go see if we can't get things straightened out.'

★ ★ ★

The house was on the northwest of Seaside, the town that lay between Marion Beach and Astoria. It took forty minutes to get there. I got Kyle to call ahead, acting like everything was cool — and arranging to meet the two guys the next day. This went smoothly, establishing they were home and further strengthening my impression that we weren't dealing with master criminals. Also, assuming they were the people who had staged the break-in, that they were assholes who were prepared to lie to a guy's face and snigger about it afterwards.

I asked Becki to park fifty yards down the street. I got out and opened the trunk, looked around until I found something I could use.

'Okay,' I said. 'Kyle, you're coming with me.'

Becki started in quickly. 'What about — '

'Trust me,' I said. 'Comes to a fight I'd bet on you any day. It's just in case we feel like leaving quickly. That happens, I believe you're the best person to be ready behind the wheel, don't you?'

She subsided. Kyle got out of the car and looked at me dubiously. 'So . . . what now?'

'Come with me. And do what I say.'

We walked up the side of the street opposite the house. There were enough lights on to imply people were home, but nothing to suggest a windfall-driven debauch in full swing.

'Stay here,' I said.

I crossed and went around the house, quietly, to see what I could glimpse through the windows. Not much. Music coming from somewhere, still not party-loud. A room that looked like someone had upended a junk store into it and then taken back anything worth more than five dollars. The living room, with two ratty couches at right angles to a battered television playing MTV. Another room with a single mattress on a floor strewn with dirty clothes and empty soda cans.

Around the back, the kitchen, lit by hanging bulbs fighting cigarette smoke. Two young guys hanging at a table: emo playing off an iPod with extension speakers, a few wine bottles, big bags of Doritos and an ashtray full of white power on the side. Heaven on earth, slacker-style. And on the side counter, a battered industrial-style juicer.

I walked backward from the house until Kyle could see me, and mimed him ringing the house bell. He hesitated but then started across the street.

I went to the back door and waited until I heard the bell go. The two guys inside looked at each other, and then one of them got up and left the room. The other slipped the ashtray full of drugs into one of the Doritos bags.

I gently turned the handle on the back door. It was locked. You build some, you break some. I raised my foot and kicked it in.

The guy at the table was nowhere near his feet before I got in range. I grabbed him by the hair and shoved him down onto his chair, let him see the tyre iron I was holding in the other hand.

'You Rick or Doug?'

'Who the hell — ?'

'Nope,' I said, and rapped him on the kneecap with the iron. He yelped. 'That's not how this is going to play. Want to try again?'

'Rick,' he said.

'Better. Where are the drugs, Rick?'

'What the *fuck?*'

A new voice. I glanced up to see Kyle and the other guy — Doug, I assumed — standing in the doorway. Doug's pupils were pinned even worse than his friend's, and he was looking at me as if I was a commercial for a cancer charity in an evening that had otherwise featured very mellow programming.

'Here's the thing,' I said, to Doug. It had been his idea to visit the Pelican in the middle of the night. You can always tell the difference between the big dogs and the little dogs, even when the bigger ones are still damned small. 'I'm the person who supplied your friend Kyle with his drugs.'

'Shit,' he said, urgently.

'Yeah.' I pushed Rick to the side, making sure he stayed tangled with the chair and wound up falling heavily into the corner.

'*Shit*,' Doug said again, blinking fast. Dumb and high though he was, he was smart enough to realize that the evening had taken a very poor turn.

49

I left a beat and then lashed hard right with the tyre iron, smashing the nearest light fitting and sending a shower of glass fragments around the room.

Kyle and Doug leapt back, arms over their heads. Rick meanwhile was trying to fight free of the chair so he could regain his feet.

I rested my own foot — pretty gently — on his chest. He went back down almost gratefully.

'Tell me you've still got it,' I said. 'Except, of course, for what you've sucked up into your faces already.'

Doug nodded quickly, compulsively. He hadn't been hit yet. He'd be valuing that position a great deal, and ready to do pretty much anything to protect it.

'I'm waiting,' I said.

He didn't hesitate. Ran straight to the fridge and dug in the vegetable drawer. Out came a brown bag. He thrust it at me like it was on fire.

I looked inside, threw it to Kyle. Then took a step closer to Doug, and looked him in the eyes.

'Do you understand how lucky you've been?'

He nodded feverishly.

'I hope so,' I said. 'Ordinarily this would go some whole other way. Kyle assures me you're decent people, despite appearances, and so I'm hoping you're not going to wake up tomorrow feeling pissed off and like you should have been more assertive about this, and decide to take it out on Kyle instead.'

'No way,' Doug said, quickly.

'Good. You do, then I'll come burn your house down. Understand? And I don't mean this

50

shitheap you're living in.'
'Honestly, man,' he said. 'W — we're cool.'
I nodded to Kyle, and we walked out the door.

★   ★   ★

Halfway back to the car I stopped and put my hand on Kyle's arm. He turned warily. He looked about twelve years old.

'I don't need to talk this through with you in the same way, do I?'

He shook his head quickly.

'Get rid of that shit, fast. Pay back the people you got it from, then pay back the loan. And *do not do this ever again*. You are simply not up to this way of life. You piss off someone just *one* step higher up the food chain and you're going to wind up fucked or dead. I mean you no disrespect, Kyle — this is just career advice from someone who knows.'

He was nodding almost continually now, his chin twitching.

'Okay.'

'Here's how this business works. At the top are the guys who make the stuff and run the top-level distribution: the shadows who make the real money and never get caught. Then there's the next tier, the guys you bought your drugs from. They make a bunch of cash too, though once in a while they go down or get shot when the next wave rolls over them. At the bottom there's the guy *you're* trying to be, the street grunts. Who make a little cash in the beginning but *always* wind up junkies, or in jail, or dead,

51

about which the guys above do not give a fuck.'

I grabbed his chin and made sure I had his full attention. 'You really want to be that guy? Bitch for some asshole who right now is sitting on a yacht bigger than any house you'll ever own?'

He shook his head, as best he could. 'No.'

'Well then.' I let go and clapped him on the shoulder. 'We're done. Let's go home.'

We walked the rest of the way back to Becki's car. She slumped with relief when she saw the bag.

'*How?*' she said. 'Is everything — ?'

'It's all done,' I said. 'And your boy did good.'

I rode in the back. I should have felt okay about what had just happened, but I did not. I watched the town as we passed through, then down at the river as we went south over the bridge, then the dunes and the dark sea beyond.

Becki stopped the car outside my house, a lot more gently than the night before.

'Thank you,' she said, but she said it like someone who'd been done a favour.

Then she shook her head, added, 'See you tomorrow,' and the feeling backed off a little.

When I got to the top of the path I looked back. The car was still there. Becki and Kyle were holding each other, their foreheads pressed together, her hand stroking the back of his head, the top of his neck. There's nothing to beat that. Nothing in the world.

I let myself into the house, feeling tired and wrong and like I could walk a thousand miles in any direction and have no reason to ever turn back.

★ ★ ★

I felt better after a shower, and took a Coke and cigarette out onto the balcony. I wanted a beer, too, but I know better than that.

No big deal, I'd decided, as the hot water coursed over my head. Not doing anything would have led to a worse situation for people I cared about. Isn't that as good a justification for action as any? And hadn't I been staring at the waves the previous night, feeling too much to one side of the world?

I shook my head, dismissed the train of thought. I know how much difference a night's sleep can make, that what seems ungovernable and world-breaking at one a.m. can be made to feel like someone else's dream if you put seven hours of unconsciousness between it and you. Tomorrow's not just another day, another person lives it — and every time you go to sleep, you say goodbye. Amen.

I went back indoors and got a glass of water to take to bed. As I passed the laptop I hesitated, then decided I could put the day properly to rest by checking my email one last time.

There wasn't even much spam and I was already moving away before I realized a final message had just come in.

Subject line: !! INTERRUPTED!!

I swore, wishing I hadn't checked. Now I had no choice but to read it. Staying on my feet, I clicked on the email and watched as it came up on screen.

Please email me.
I know what happened to your son.

53

6

I saw the sun come up the next morning, though I hadn't been awake for all that time.

For an hour after reading the email I'd alternated between the laptop and the deck, trying to work out what to do. My first impulse was to throw the email away, empty the trash, and pretend it had never happened.

But I couldn't just erase it. After a while I understood this, and had to work out what to do instead. The first question was how this person had got my email address. This address in particular, in fact, as I have several. My main, and most current, which receives nothing but infrequent missives from my ex-wife. Then a Google web mail address, set up for a specific purpose and not even checked in three years, but which presumably/maybe still existed. Finally a corporate address, legacy of a place I once worked. It had become a dead line long ago, but had evidently never been actually deactivated.

The email had come into this last one. The person sending it had either known or found out I had once been associated with the company in question. It *was* a she, presumably, though I couldn't take that for granted — you can be anyone you want on the Net. It didn't look as though this person was calling upon previous acquaintanceship, and I had no recollection of the name. I typed it into a web search engine

54

and found the usual randomers on their own or other people's personal sites, a few others on the staff lists or minutes of libraries and girl scout troops, and a handful referenced on genealogical sites.

In the end I did the only thing I could think of. I hit REPLY and typed:

Who are you?

I looked at this for a while, unable for once to even hear the surf, aware only of the low, churning feeling in my stomach. Should I send it, or not? For the moment I still had the option of walking away, not checking my mail, carrying on as I had.

But eventually I pressed SEND, and then stood up and went outside.

★   ★   ★

I drank glass after glass of bottled water, sitting out on deck, going back in to check the mail every fifteen minutes. It was very late. I knew there was little chance that a reply, were it ever to be forthcoming, was going to arrive tonight. But however different they may be in reality, we carry into email conversations a vestige of the expectations implicit in the more old-fashioned kind. We think that if we say something, then the other guy will say something right back.

She (or he) did not.

At three o'clock I locked the doors and turned the computer off. As I undressed I realized that, however it might feel during the day, the year was turning. The room felt cold.

I got into a bed that seemed very wide and lay listening to the blood in my ears, and trying to remember nothing, until I was no longer myself.

★　★　★

No reply at dawn, nor by mid-morning, nor four-thirty, when I changed into my work clothes and set off for the restaurant. There had been a lot of rain in the night, and on my early morning walk the sand had been dull and pockmarked, the beach strewn with seaweed. As I walked up the road toward the Pelican it seemed likely the same was going to happen again tonight. A couple of hours from now it would be raining with the sullen persistence for which Oregon is justly celebrated, which meant a quiet night in the restaurant. It was likely to have been anyhow, and Ted wouldn't be staying open on Sunday evenings much longer. The season was done.

As I walked, I talked myself down. The email was likely just the work of an opportunistic lunatic who worked on a slow news cycle. If there had been anything meaningful behind it, I believed the sender would have been in touch again quickly. What do you do if you've sent an email like that, and it's real? You expect a reply, and then you get on the case quickly. Once the mark is hooked you don't give them the chance to wriggle off again.

So I was back to the idea that it never meant anything in the first place. I worked the sequence

56

back and forth in my head for about ten minutes, and kept coming to the same conclusion. I tried to make it stick, and move on.

Two miles is enough to get a lot of thinking done. It's also enough to work out that you're not in the best of moods. I was one of the first to get to the restaurant, however, so I got busy helping set up. Eduardo walked by outside the window at one stage, saw me, and held up his pack of Marlboro. I went out back to have a smoke with him and two of the other cooks — which was pleasant enough but also kind of weird to do after all this time, as if I'd slipped into a parallel but not-very-different existence. Eduardo's English was decent but the others' wasn't, and my Spanish is lousy. The experience boiled down to: so, here we all are, smoking, in an atmosphere of vague goodwill.

As I headed inside I was surprised, and yet also not surprised, to see Becki's car entering the lot. Kyle got out, putting his arrival a good forty minutes ahead of service. I watched him head into the restaurant, and glanced across at Becki in the driver's seat of the car.

She gave me a smile and I realized things were going to be okay with her after all. Also that I'd probably seen the end of my nascent pizza-making career, at least for now.

★   ★   ★

We got a reasonable sitting for the early bird slot, but after that it went real slow until there was just one family left at a table in the middle of the

57

room, eating in a silence so murderous it almost seemed to drown out the music playing in the background. Ted sent Mazy home after an hour. The rest of the staff floated like abandoned sailboats on calm seas, hands clasped behind their backs, coming to rest in corners of the restaurant to stand and watch as the sky grew lower and heavier and more purple outside.

'Gonna be a big one,' said a voice. 'Like, kaboom.'

I turned to see Kyle standing behind me. He had strong opinions on the weather, evidently. We looked out at the clouds together for a while.

'You okay?' I asked, eventually.

He nodded. Could be my imagination, but he actually looked a little older than he had the day before, albeit somewhat wired. He glanced around, and spoke more quietly.

'Working on closing out the . . . you know,' he said. 'And then, well, I heard what you said. And Becki has sure as hell told me the same thing.' He looked down. 'Thanks, by the way. I didn't say that last night, and I should of.'

'You'd had a bad day,' I said.

It was quiet for a while, but I knew he had something else to say. Eventually he got to it.

'So how come you know how to do . . . that stuff?'

'Didn't do anything. Just talked to a couple guys.'

'Yeah, right. 'Talked' to them.'

'That's how I remember it.'

'But you didn't even know what they were going to be like. You just walked right in and let rip.'

58

'I'd asked what your impression of them was.'

'But I could have fucked up. Got it wrong. It's been known to happen, right?'

'It all turned out fine, Kyle.'

'But — '

'What does Becki think about this?'

'She thinks you helped us out, and we should leave it at that and go on like it never happened.'

'You could do worse than listen to Becki, on this and pretty much everything else. She's a good person to have in your life. You're a lucky guy.'

'Yeah,' he said, wearily. 'I know that.'

'Of course, being lucky can sometimes be a total pain in the ass. It's one of life's major trade-offs.'

He thought about this, smiled, and drifted back toward the oven. Half an hour later a cheerful English couple rolled up, got bounced by Ted on account of being falling-down drunk, and that was pretty much it for the night. We shut up early, a little after nine o'clock.

I shared a joint with Kyle on deck as he waited for Becki, and then I started for home.

★   ★   ★

I got home bare minutes before all the water in creation started dropping out of the sky. I rolled the canopy down over the deck and took a beer and a cigarette out to watch it coming down, listening to wood and canvas taking it like a barrage of incoming small-arms fire. But I knew I was just killing time.

59

I went indoors when I finished the beer. As I opened the laptop I realized it was possible this might be the night when I would be *glad* to only receive messages from shysters and pill-pushers, leavened with the revolving after-effects of viruses unleashed on the world by kids who didn't realize how frustrated they were at not being able to make genuine contact with the world, in the shape of a proper kiss with a real live girl.

I hit the key combination, and waited.

They were there, these email shadows of the void, with their usual empty offers and demands.

But that wasn't all.

7

The message was short.

If I don't answer please leave a message.
We need to talk.
Ellen Robertson.

And there was a phone number.

I was thrown by this, and stared at the digits as if they were a door marked 'Danger'. An email address says that if you type something to this person, they will (barring server crash, over-zealous spam filters or random strangeness) get it pretty soon. At some undetermined point in the future they will read it, and at a time subsequent to that, they may reply. It is time- and chance-buffered communication. A phone number is different. It's old school. If you call a phone number there's a real chance you're suddenly going to be talking to a real person, in real time.

The email had been sent at 7.12. The clock on the laptop said it was now 10.24. Was that too late to call? Did I care? If this person was determined to throw a hand grenade into my life, did she have the right to choose the terms of my reaction? The digits changed to 25, and then 26. The longer I thought about it, the later it was going to get. I picked up my phone and dialled.

It rang five or six times, and then picked up.

'Hello?' A woman's voice.

'This is John Henderson,' I said.

There was silence for three, maybe four seconds. 'I'll call you back,' the woman muttered, the words running into one. Then the line went dead.

I grabbed my cigarettes and went out onto the deck. I couldn't sit, so I stood, watching the rain.

And waited.

★ ★ ★

I don't smoke inside any more, or drink alcohol under a roof. It's one of the ways I've learned to stop myself from doing things all the time. I'd had two cigarettes out on deck before the phone buzzed in my hand.

'Yes,' I said, heading quickly back indoors, away from the noise of the storm.

'I've only got a couple of minutes,' the woman's voice said. It sounded as though she was walking.

'Who are you?'

'My name's Ellen Robertson.'

'I got that. But — '

'I need your help.'

'What do you mean, 'help'?'

She paused. 'I'm afraid.'

'Of what?'

'I think the same thing's going to happen to me.'

'Look, I've got no idea what you think you know about — '

'I live near Black Ridge,' she continued,

calmly, as if I hadn't spoken at all. 'Twenty miles from where you used to live.'

For a moment this derailed me, but then I thought — so what? What happened was in the local papers. Available from district libraries, and doubtless on the Internet.

'So?'

'Wait a moment,' she said.

Again I heard a noise like the swishing of a coat worn by someone who was walking quickly. It lasted maybe twenty seconds, and then I heard her breathing harder, her mouth back at the phone.

'I have to go,' she said, and the quality of her voice had changed. She sounded apprehensive, nervous. Maybe more than that. 'I'm sorry, but — '

'Look,' I said, finding a tone of voice I hadn't used in a long time, except perhaps to Kyle the night before. 'Help me out here. I don't know who the hell you are. You're telling me things that don't make sense.'

'I'm the one who needs *help*,' she said, her voice abruptly strong again — too firm, as if held right up against the brink of hysteria. 'There's no one who's going to believe except maybe you, and now I realize you won't either. I thought perhaps you knew but evidently you don't and I can't risk emailing again because he's scanning the Wi-Fi now. If I tell you on the phone you're going to think I'm crazy and . . . '

She stopped suddenly. There were two seconds of nothing. Then she said 'Goodbye' very quickly, and I was listening to the roaring silence of a dead line.

★ ★ ★

The obvious thing was to call right back, but the 'goodbye' had been smeared, as if the phone had been jerked from her mouth on its way to being stuffed in a pocket. I could pretend she was a lunatic trying to take advantage of me in a way I hadn't yet determined, but I know how people sound when they're scared and freaked out. By the end of the call, the woman I'd been talking to was at least one of these, possibly both. I couldn't just throw a ringing phone into her world.

It sounded like an email wouldn't be a good idea either. The idea that 'he' — whoever 'he' was supposed to be, a husband presumably — was pulling her messages out of the ether sounded paranoid (it's not as easy as people think), but an email is an irrevocable act. Call someone, and if the wrong voice appears at the end of the line you can claim a wrong number or put the phone straight down and take your chances with Caller ID. Once an email's sent, it's gone. It paints what you've said on the wall and no amount of scrubbing will get it off again.

'*Fuck*,' I shouted. It was the loudest sound the house had heard since I'd been living there. I had no idea I was going to shout before the sound had already echoed flatly off the walls. I did not like to hear a noise that loud coming from inside me.

I stuffed the phone in my jeans pocket and stormed out onto the deck, down the external stairs and along the walkway over the dune. It was still raining, but I didn't know where else to go, or what else to do.

★ ★ ★

At eight the next morning I called the restaurant. It rang and rang. I gave up, tried again half an hour later. Finally I heard it being picked up.

'Pelican?' An unfamiliar voice.

'Who's that?'

'Eduardo.' The cook sounded cautious. Addressing the public didn't come under his brief. 'Who is it, please?'

'It's John,' I said. 'I need you to find something on the computer.'

'I don't know,' he said, doubtful again. 'I don't think Ted is happy if I was fooling around on there.'

'There's no reason for him to hear about it.'

'I don't know computers.'

I forced myself to keep a level tone. 'Eduardo, it's no big deal. I'll tell you exactly what to do. I just need to get a number off the database.'

'Whose number?'

'Becki's.'

'Ah, it's easy,' he said, sounding much happier. 'She print it off, leave it here, after the burglary. Everybody's is here. Is okay.'

'Great,' I said, relieved at not having to lean any more heavily on him. 'Give me hers, and while you're at it, Ted's home phone too.'

He recited them, slowly and painstakingly. I thanked him, and was halfway to putting the phone down before he asked something.

65

'You okay?'

'I'm fine,' I said.

I called Becki first. I wasn't banking on her to be up, certainly not to sound so businesslike at that time of the morning. She listened without interruption, and immediately agreed to the two things I asked of her. So finally I called Ted.

'Don't tell me it's happened again,' he said, straight away.

'Nothing's wrong with the restaurant. I'm at home.'

'So . . .'

I told him that I would be gone a day, maybe two. That Becki had agreed to cover for me on the floor, if reservations merited it. The truth was they probably wouldn't.

Ted listened as I laid it out for him. 'What's this about?' he asked, finally.

'Family business,' I said.

'Didn't realize you even had one. A family, I mean.'

'Well, I did,' I said. 'I do.'

'Anything I can help with?'

'I appreciate it, but no.'

'You let me know if that changes.'

He was being kind but I wanted this over with. 'I will, Ted. It's no big deal. Just, it has to be now.'

'I hear what you're saying,' he said.

I'd packed a small bag and locked the place down half an hour later, and ten minutes after that Becki arrived to drive me over to Portland.

★   ★   ★

66

I was on a plane at 12.40, business class, which is all I'd been able to get at short notice. I spent the bulk of the flight staring at the back of the seat in front, trying to concentrate on how strange it felt to be in the air again. I'd flown a lot in the past. For work, and longer ago for other reasons and under different circumstances and in planes that did not offer hot beverages. Sitting on the flight to Yakima, I realized it must be the first time I'd been on an aircraft in over three years.

Yet my hands strapped me in without conscious thought. I passed my eyes dutifully over the laminated 'Let's pretend a crash isn't going to finish us all in a shrieking fireball of death' sheet, and accepted a coffee from the stewardess with the frequent flier's casual indifference.

The distance between then and now is always far shorter than you think. By the time the plane had reached its cruising height, I was cradled in the past's unyielding embrace, and listening as it told me the same old story again.

That I'd once had a son, and he died.

8

Kristina watched through the coffee store window as her mother started walking up Kelly Street back toward her lair. She took a deep breath, and let it out very slowly.

Children, huh. Again. For God's *sake*.

It was actually kind of amazing how her mom kept going on about it — 'amazing' in the limited sense of 'unbelievably annoying'. It was her sole subject matter, apparently. She never pitched in about her daughter not having a husband, or a boyfriend . . . but a *child* — that was the only story in town. As if *she'd* been this perfect Earth Mother figure, a *Good Housekeeping* bake-and-nurture paragon, and was just dying to see the maternal genius bearing fruit in the next generation. As if the whole of male-kind was a sideshow or distraction, the unending line of women the only thing that ever mattered (because a grand*daughter* was what her mom wanted, let's face it, not just any flavour of grandchild) — and her own not-much-lamented husband had not been father to someone who'd loved him.

As if she honestly didn't realize there had been occasions when her own daughter had fervently — though unsuccessfully — wished her dead.

★ ★ ★

She ordered more coffee. Might as well. Her shift didn't start until five, so why not while away another Fairtrade, kind-to-all-God's-creatures hot beverage, savouring the rich pageant of a Black Ridge afternoon?

After a few minutes a car trundled past, its tyres making sticky sounds on the wet surface. A little later, a different car went by in the other direction. Hold the front fucking page.

Five minutes after that a girl whom she'd known back in school waddled diagonally across the street, toward the hair salon. By the look of it this girl had successfully made it to motherhood, at least six or seven times. Either that or she needed to seriously rein back on the snacks.

The sight of the salon triggered the thought that Kristina should/could/might as well get her own hair attended to, and so she called and made an appointment for a couple of days' time. Then she put the phone back in her bag, and returned to staring out of the window. A few more minutes passed, as though on their way to somewhere they'd already been told wasn't worth the visit.

★ ★ ★

What bugged her most was she didn't even know why she'd come back, and in truth this was probably part of why conversations with her mother tended to start scrappy and go downhill from there. She knew that her mother regarded her return as a moral victory, and Kristina wanted to be able to explain and defend it in some way other than pure laziness or worse. She didn't want to believe it had been inevitable.

That her mom had won, basically.

But why *do* you go back to where you and your parents and their parents and grandparents were born, after a decade away? Friends? Nope — all moved away, either geographically or into the snug dens of parenthood. Father? Dead. Dear mother herself? God, no. There's plenty room in a Christmas card to be reminded of your alleged responsibilities, and/or be given a hard time about the only important thing in life, spawning a child.

She'd left town less than a week after her eighteenth birthday. *Goodbye, thanks for not much, I'm done here.* Worked, paid taxes and leased apartments in five different states and three foreign countries, including a whacky six months in Thailand as the weird tall chick tending bar: by all means buy her a drink but please understand it isn't getting you anywhere. Some of it had been interesting, some of it fun, a lot of it day-to-day and hard to remember in detail — even the high times and hair-raising scrapes. She could have kept doing it, though, or things like it. Could have stuck it out in Vermont or Chicago or Barcelona, dug herself a life or just committed properly to the ones she'd tried, rather than leaving a series of men staring bemusedly at brief notes left on kitchen counters.

Yet here she was, back where she came from, under her own steam and with no one else to blame. And she had been here — she was

70

horrified to realize — almost nine months now. She didn't *want* to be here.

And yet (and the words were beginning to feel like a spike in her brain, banged deeper and deeper by a hammer she held in her own hand), here she was.

$$\star \quad \star \quad \star$$

She accepted a refill from the server, a girl who — despite nose ring and turquoise hair — was so bovine it made you want to set fire to her (and not just because she so obviously resented her sole customer for being thin: well, sweetie, newsflash — your hips are what happens if you won't eat anything except nut loaf and cheese). She wondered briefly where the girl had caught her counter-culture vibe from. Some two-years-ago crush who'd entranced a teen, flipped her world, and moved on? The uncle who always seemed cooler than Mom and Dad, while quietly tapping them for money on the side? Or the girl's own parents, dragging her hither and yon as a baby, borne on Mom's fleshy hip from festival to protest and back. Not that Kristina was so different, she supposed. You think you're being yourself and then one day you realize you're in beta testing for turning into Mom 2.0, the worst of it being that the observation is *so* fucking trite you get no points for having hacked your way to it the long way around.

And had she finally got down to the point? Was she back in town because part of her knew being elsewhere would never make a difference, that these mountains and trees and the scratchy pattern of these streets were where she came from?

She didn't think so. And yet . . .

Oh, fuck it.

She stood before she could complete the sentence yet again, left a large tip just to fuck with the hippy's head, and went out onto the street.

★   ★   ★

It was cold outside. Winter was knocking on the windows, and she knew she basically wouldn't get her shit together now to ship out before Christmas. She'd always liked fall and winter here anyway — the land was made for it, so long as you didn't mind snow and the somewhat oppressive company of trees — so maybe that could serve as an excuse. Perhaps she was proving you *could* come home again, and then leave for good. She hoped so.

People came and went up and down the sidewalk, some nodding at her, most not. She walked slowly up the street, in search of something to do until it was time to go to work. It was as if she'd been awake for ten years and then allowed herself to fall asleep again. Or maybe the other way around, she wasn't sure.

There was nothing for her here. Nothing she wanted, at least.

And yet here she was.

9

We touched down a little after three o'clock. Driving up into the foothills of the Cascade Mountains took an hour, and then I turned north off 90 and through thirty miles of trees before reaching the outskirts of Black Ridge itself. It would be easy to imagine the town only has outskirts, on first meeting. Even if you know better, and where to find what counts as the main attractions, driving too fast will still have you out the other side before you know it.

Black Ridge is a place of small wooden houses on lots through which you can see the next street, and stands at an altitude of about three thousand feet. It stretches twenty disorganized blocks in one direction, twelve in the other, before blending back into the forest which climbs into the mountains toward the two major lakes of the area, Cle Elum and Kachess. There are off-kilter crossroads holding hardware and liquor stores, a few diners where no one's bothering to string up fishing nets or kidding themselves as to the quality of what's on offer, and a couple of car-hire places. Presumably to help people leave. The older part of town — an eighty-yard street at the western end, offers a short run of wooden-fronted buildings holding an antique/junk emporium, a coffee shop/second-hand bookstore, a burger place, a pizza place, a couple of bars, and not a great deal else.

As I'd driven up into the mountains I'd refined my plan. Finding a motel was the first step. I'd passed up a Super 7 and a couple of tired-looking B & Bs before suddenly finding myself confronted by a place I recognized. I'd known it would be there — I had lived in it for nearly a month — but it remained strange to see this particular motel still in business, looking the same as when everything had been very different. I didn't consider turning into the entrance.

On the road out the northwest side of town I found somewhere called Marie's Resort, an old-fashioned, single-storeyed motel that had cars parked outside all but three of its twelve rooms. It was clad in rust-red shingles and stood right up to the woods on all sides except the front. I vaguely recognized it from the old days and thought it would do.

Marie — assuming it was she — was a short, husky, sour-faced woman who looked like she'd seen most of what life in these parts had to offer and hadn't enjoyed much of it except the shouting. Her skin was the colour of old milk and the pale red hair piled on her head looked like it had last been washed in a previous life. Other than telling me the rate and asking how long I wanted to stay, she kept her own counsel throughout the entire transaction. I told her I'd be there one night, maybe two. From a back room I heard a television relaying an episode of *Cops*. The woman kept glancing back toward it, perhaps expecting to hear the voice of a

friend or relative as they objected unconvinc-
ingly to being hauled away to jail. Finally she
pulled a key out of a drawer and held it out to
me, looking me in the eye for the first time.

She frowned, the movement sluggish.

'I know you?'

'No,' I said. 'Just passing through.'

I moved the car to sit outside Room 9 and
took my bag inside. It was cold. There was a pair
of double beds, an unloved chair, a small side
table and a prehistoric television, all standing on
a carpet whose texture suggested it was cleaned
— if ever — by rubbing it with a bar of soap. I
didn't even check the bathroom, accessed via a
stubby corridor at the back of the room, on the
grounds that it would only depress me. Other
than a badly framed list of the things occupants
weren't allowed to do, the room offered little
diversion and no incentive to remain in it. I
scrolled through the call log on my phone and
clicked CALL when I found the number I'd been
sent via email the day before. It rang six times,
and then went to answering service.

'Hey, Ms Robertson,' I said, with bland cheer.
'It's John, from the Henderson Bookstore?
Wanted to let you know that item you ordered
has arrived. It's here waiting for you. You have a
good day.'

I cut the connection, feeling absurd. For
engaging in *Hardy-Boys*-level subterfuge to hide
the nature of a call to the woman's cell phone.
For being in Black Ridge in the first place. For
being, period.

I left the motel. If you have no idea where

75

you're supposed to be, movement is always the best policy.

★ ★ ★

For the next hour I walked the town. It had evidently rained hard in the morning, and it wouldn't be too long before the locals could start expecting the first snow. Black Ridge was never a place in which I'd killed much time. The town wasn't familiar and did not go out of its way to welcome me. Pickups trundled past down wet streets. People entered and left their houses. Teenage boys slouched along the sidewalks as if three-dimensional space itself was an imposition. The few realtor signs I saw in yards looked like they had been in residence for some time, and more businesses seemed to be folding than opening. From the outside, Black Ridge looked as if it was in the middle of a poorly motivated closing-down sale.

As soon as you raised your eyes above house level you saw the ranks of trees waiting only a few streets away, and the clouds thickening, coming down off the mountains to remind people who ran things around here. There are places where man has convincingly claimed the planet, making it feel little more than a support mechanism for our kind. Washington State is not one of them, and mountains everywhere have never given much thought to us. After nearly three years on the coast, it was nice to see them again.

My phone, meanwhile, did not ring.

I found myself glancing at the few women on the streets, wondering if any was the person I'd come to look for. It was impossible to tell, naturally. Usually strangers look like extras — background texture in your life. As soon as you start to look more closely, everyone looks like they might be someone in particular.

Eventually I found myself becalmed on Kelly Street, the only place that might cause a tourist to hang around for longer than it takes to fill up with gas or a burger. I bought a coffee and a sturdily homemade granola bar in a place called The Write Sisters, served by a cheerful girl with remarkably blue hair. I sat outside on a bench with it, sipping the coffee and watching the streets. Nowhere seemed to be doing much business except the Mountain View Tavern, which stood almost opposite. Even the bar's patrons seemed lacklustre, men and women breezing in and out with the stiff-legged gait of the mildly shit-faced, walking down slopes only they could see.

Black Ridge was, as it had always been, kind of a dump. Carol and I hardly ever came down here — getting our groceries from Roslyn or Sheffer (the closest communities to our house) or Cle Elum (bigger than Black Ridge, but still hardly the excitement capital of the world). Once in a while we'd saddle up and drive over the Snoqualmie Pass and thence to Seattle, about three hours away. There were a couple of other small towns en route — Snoqualmie Falls, Snohomish, Birch Crossing — which were just about worth the trip if you are open-minded about what constitutes a good time.

Black Ridge wasn't one of our places, which is among the reasons why, two and a half years ago, I'd wound up in a motel here for a while. I'd spent almost all of that time holed up in my room, not sober, or else out the back in a chair, overlooking the disused swimming pool — also not-sober. It was a condition that I'd specialized in at the time. This lay in the past, however, and so I had little patience with the people I saw drifting in and out of the Mountain View. I didn't know whether Ellen Robertson was the kind of woman who might find herself in bars of an afternoon, however, and so I vaguely kept an eye out anyhow.

Or so I told myself. The truth was I had no clue what to do, or where to go, and no idea of what she looked like. Until Ellen called me, I was just an idiot sitting on a bench. I stretched the Americano as long as I could but as the light began to change it started to get cold and finally I stood up.

As I did so I noticed a young woman walking down the other side of the street, tall with dark hair and bundled into a black coat, the effect overall being somewhat like a lanky crow. She walked straight into the Tavern without hesitating, revealing a flash of pale cheek and forehead as she reached out for the door.

Was that Ellen? No, probably not.

Just after she'd disappeared, I heard a shout from behind and turned to see a large man bearing down on me. I froze for a moment, wondering what was about to happen next.

'For the love of God!' the guy said. 'What the hell are *you* doing here?'

'Well, that's a sort of a greeting, I guess.'

'Jesus H, John. It's been . . . You lost weight.'

'Yeah,' I said, as I braced myself to submit to one of Bill Raines's trademark hugs. Bill sure as hell hadn't lost any pounds. When I'd first met him he was big but rangy. There'd been an even larger guy waiting to get out, however, and Bill had usually done his best to help him. He'd always been this huge, affable guy, who used his surname to make dumb but disarming jokes about the weather in the Pacific Northwest.

We disengaged. 'Well, shit on a brick,' he said. 'How the hell have you been?'

I shrugged.

'Yeah. Carol with you?'

'No. I'm really just passing through.'

We talked for a couple of minutes, establishing that Bill still lived out the north end of town, still worked at the family law firm down in Yakima, and was on his way to visit a client whose case he was affably confident of losing. I said I was living and working down in Oregon, without being more specific. I didn't proffer a reason for being here in town. I asked about his wife, because you do.

'She's great,' he said, glancing at his watch. 'Well, you know Jenny. Always got something on the boil. Look, shoot, I'm sorry, John — but I gotta run. Stupid fucking late as it is. You free this evening?'

'Probably not,' I said.

'Shoot. That changes, give me a call. Jen's out

79

of town. We'll get wasted like old times, man. It's been too long. It needs to happen.'

'You got it,' I said.

'Well, okay then,' he said. He seemed becalmed for a moment, then clapped me on the shoulder. 'Shit, I really have to go. Later, yeah, maybe?'

'Right.'

I watched him hustle across the street to his car, wave, and drive away. Then I walked back to the motel, climbed in my own vehicle, and got on with doing what had been in the back of my mind all afternoon, had perhaps even been the real reason I'd being willing to fly up here in the first place.

Maybe I'd never make contact with Ms Robertson, and probably it didn't matter anyhow. But there was one thing I could do, and it was about time.

10

When I was a hundred yards short of the gate I started to slow down, and eventually let the car roll to a halt. For the last ten minutes of the drive it had felt as if I was shaking, gently and invisibly at first — but growing in intensity until I had to grip the wheel hard to stay in control. As soon as the noise of the engine died away, I was still. When I was sure the shaking wasn't going to start again, I opened the door and got out.

I was now fifteen minutes northeast of Black Ridge. I'd taken the Sheffer road, climbing gradually higher, then turned off onto the country road which doubled back up into the mountains. A few miles from here it all but ran out, narrowing to a perennially muddy track under the aegis of the forestry management service. I walked up to the padlocked gate and stood looking over it, up the driveway.

Was this enough?

Over the last two years I had many times imagined being where I now stood, but in those morbid daydreams the gate had always been open and I had been there by prior arrangement. I had been possessed, too, of a keen sense of rightness, of a meaningful deed being under-taken. As is so often the case, life had failed to mirror fantasy.

I took out my phone. I knew the house

number, assuming it had not been changed. Perhaps . . .

I turned at the sound of a car coming down the road, slowing as it approached. It was a spruce-looking SUV of the light and elegant type owned by people who have no genuine need for a rugged vehicle, but know their lifestyle requires accessorizing.

It stopped a few yards past me and the driver's side window whirred down to reveal a cheerful-looking man in his fifties.

'Bob let you down?'

'Excuse me?'

The man smiled. 'He's a super realtor, don't get me wrong. Sold us our place — we're up the road a mile? Moved over from Black Ridge a year ago and Bob was great with, you know, the process. But timekeeping really isn't his core field of excellence.'

'No big deal,' I said. 'I'm only here on a whim.'

The man nodded as though he understood all about that kind of thing, though he looked like someone who last acted on a whim around five or six years ago, most likely a statistically sound whim concerning moving non-critical cash reserves from one low-risk portfolio to another.

'Had a look at that property ourselves, in fact,' he said. 'Not quite big enough for us, but beautiful. Has direct access to Murdo Pond. But I'm sure Bob told you that already.'

'It's been on the market that long?'

'You don't know?' he said, sticking his elbow out of the window to settle into what he was about to say. He was wearing a thick black sweater with roll-neck, and looked like he'd never been cold in his life. 'Okay, I'm sure Bob would be getting around to telling you, he's very straightforward, but it's actually been mainly empty a couple-three years now. There was kind of a thing that happened, apparently, and some new people moved in for a while, didn't take to it, and they're still trying to shift the place two years later.' He winked. 'So I'm saying Bob's likely to have a little wriggle room over the price — though you didn't hear that from me.'

'What kind of thing?'

'Pardon me?'

'What kind of thing happened? Before the current owners bought the house?'

'Well,' the guy said. He hesitated, perhaps suspecting he'd said too much and was in danger of compromising his acquaintanceship with Bob-the-realtor, with whom he doubtless exchanged banter once in a while at the grocery market in Sheffer; but also knowing that he couldn't back out now without looking rude. 'Basically, some-body died. A kid. A young kid.'

I nodded, not understanding why I'd pushed myself into having this conversation. 'Really.'

'Uh-huh. And, you know, from what I gather . . . nobody's too clear on what actually happened. I don't believe anyone in the family got charged with anything, but, well . . . I heard the kid was a strong swimmer but still somehow drowned, you know, with no one else but the parents around, and you've got to ask questions in those circumstances, right?'

'Yeah,' I said, tightly. 'I guess people do.'

'But it's three years ago. And a house is a house and that one's as close to a solid investment as you're going to find in this market — they're not making any more lakes, after all. And it's not like you're scared of ghosts, right?'

'No,' I said, and smiled broadly.

Something must have been wrong with the way I did it, however, because the guy pulled his arm back inside the car.

'Little insider information never does any harm,' he said, defensively. 'But you didn't — '

' — hear it from you. Got it.'

'Okay, well, nice meeting you.'

'You too. By the way, one of your tail-lights is out. You might want to get that fixed.'

'Uh-huh,' he said, with a final, curious look at me, and then his window purred back up.

I stood and watched as he drove away. When he had gone around the corner and out of sight I walked back to the gate and climbed over it.

★   ★   ★

I wondered, as I walked up the driveway, whether I'd ever done this before. You don't, as a matter of course. You're driving, naturally, hence the name. And so I hadn't noticed the way it went steadily uphill during the five minutes it took to walk from the gate. When I turned the final bend, however, the view was abruptly almost too familiar, like a scene from a dream I'd had only the night before.

Except things were different.

84

The grass around the house had grown very long indeed, and the birch trees on the far side seemed to have gotten closer, the alder and dogwood amongst them thicker. I walked down the slope to the centre of the lawn, wet grass swishing against my jeans, and then turned toward the house.

It looked like it was asleep. All the windows had been boarded over, and had large stickers warning about the alarm system. Assuming the absent owners had, unlike Ted, kept up the payments, I knew that a break in the house's windows, or disturbance to the contacts of any of the doors, would alert a security company over in Cle Elum. It would be a long way for vandals to come, anyhow. A long way for anyone.

I stood staring up at the triangular silhouette the house made against the trees and fading sky, and my chest suddenly hitched, and my neck tightened, until the tendons stood out like painful cords.

I did not really want to go any closer to the house, but nonetheless I walked toward the steps on the far side of the encompassing deck. Having come this way, I did not wish to find myself back in Oregon wishing I had gone a few more yards. It was foolish, especially as we had lived in the house for three months after the event, but as I trudged up the steps I almost believed I could feel the air move past me, as a younger man ran down the steps in the other direction, looking for his boy. It was a breeze, of course, and nothing more.

I walked slowly back to the other end of the

deck, peering at the boarded-over windows and doors as I passed. Someone had made a good job of securing the house, though presumably that made it far harder to sell. The views from inside were one of its key selling points, and not everyone has the imagination for that when they're standing inside a cathedral-ceilinged coffin. I wondered at the financial reserves of a family who could buy a house like this, move out, and withstand it remaining unsold for a couple of years. Wondered also why they had not remained here. I had loved this house. Every room had something about it — its view, shape, or position in relation to the space where you had just left — that made you content to linger in it.

Perhaps the owner's problem had not been with the place itself, but with the locals, who had evidently started to retro-fit a juicy little scandal over what had taken place, with Scott as their own JonBenét Ramsey and Carol and I as the unconvicted perpetrators of negligence, if not something far worse. Why they would wish to do that I had no idea, but it had been as well that the SUV driver had moved on when he did. A good idea, too, that I not make a nostalgic diversion to Roslyn or Sheffer on the way back, in case I was recognized and someone said something they might regret.

I walked all the way around the house and found only one window, on the far side and at the back, where it looked like someone might have tried to break in. They'd got as far as levering one corner away and then given up. On

86

the other side was a small storeroom at the end of the utility area, and for a moment I remembered it as it had been. Shelves, lined with produce bought from local markets. Backup supplies of batteries and bottled water — Carol had always seemed quietly convinced that the collapse of civilization was only a matter of time, and that it was best to be prepared. The smell of sheets, drying.

When I got back around to the front I paused for a moment at the spot halfway along the deck where I had been accustomed to stand at the end of a day's work, or with my first coffee of the day. The very position, in fact, where I had asked Carol where Scott had gotten to.

Being there should have felt momentous, or unusually horrible, but it did not. Just sad. The lawn below was overgrown and forlorn. The artisan yard furniture was absent, and I couldn't remember whether it had gone with my wife or if we'd left it with the house for the new owners. The latter, I thought. Either way, it was gone.

I looked for a moment into the woods, remembering how on that afternoon I'd noticed the paths were getting a little unkempt. They were completely overgrown now, ferns covering the ground. About sixty yards from the house were the scant remains of a sturdy old cabin, a remnant from pioneering days. I realized that if left long enough the big house behind me might disappear even faster than the cabin was doing, and the thought depressed me.

I went back down the steps and walked down the slope toward the final place I knew I should visit. The remaining light was reflecting off the lake at the bottom, turning it into a strip of blue-white glare. I kept my pace even as I walked out onto the jetty and until I reached the end, and then I stopped. Down here not much had changed. The lake stretched out ahead, the right fork of its L-shape disappearing out of sight at the end. Ours was the only house with direct access to this section. On all other sides trees came right down to the shore, and the shallows were dotted with fallen leaves, sodden scraps of brown and dark green and gold.

As I stood there, I realized that, of all places in the world, this would be the one where I would most expect to lose control. It was, after all, the very last place where my son had spoken, and breathed, and been alive. But it did not happen here either. I felt wretched, but my eyes stayed dry.

⋆　⋆　⋆

I can only ever think about that afternoon in the third person. I do not think 'I' did this, or felt that, and despite the distance I've tried to put between it and me, my recollection is locked in the present tense. From the moment at which I emerge onto the deck, it's as if it's happening again now. Perhaps this is nothing more than another defence mechanism, a way of making it feel like a fantasy, continually fresh-minted in my head, rather than an event with a genuine place in history.

But it has such a place. There was an

afternoon, three years ago, when my son died in front of my eyes, when I'd dived into the water and then stood exactly where I was now, holding something in my arms for which I had made a sandwich four hours before; when I stood knowing that the person for whom I'd slapped cold cuts and cheese between bread, and then sliced the result into the preferred triangular form, had gone away and was no longer there; and that the wet, heavy thing that remained was nothing but a lie.

What is the difference between those two states? Nobody has a clue. The local doctors and the coroner certainly didn't. All they could tell me was that Scott had been dead before he hit the water, and they had no idea how or why.

I'm sorry, Mr Henderson. But he just died.

This difference is why our species makes sacrifices, performs rituals, repeats forms of words to ourselves in the dark watches of the night. Gods are merely foils in this process, an audience for the supplications of metaphor in the face of the intractable monolith of reality. We need *someone* to listen to these prayers because, without a listener, they cannot come true, and therefore there must be gods, and they *must* be kind, else they would never grant our wishes — in which case why would we pray to them in the first place? It is a circular argument, like all neuroses, a hard shell around emptiness.

If gods exist then they are deaf or indifferent. They commit their acts, and then move on.

★ ★ ★

I knew it was time for me to get on to the next thing, whatever that was. Finding something to eat back in Black Ridge, most likely, then a quiet evening in a no-frills motel room before flying back to Portland and finding a ride to Marion Beach. Good friend though he had been, I knew I wasn't in the mood for Bill Raines's offer of a night's drinking and talking up old times, for any number of reasons.

As I turned back from Murdo Pond, however, something made me pause. A wind had picked up, and the leaves on the trees around the house were moving against each other with a sound like the papery breaths of someone not entirely well. The water in the lake was lapping against the jetty supports, like a tongue being moved around inside a dry mouth. The combination of the two sounds was disconcerting, and for a moment the air didn't feel as cold as it should, but then felt very cold indeed. It struck me that no one in the world knew where I was, and though that thought has sometimes been a source of comfort, right then it was not. Though I had owned this jetty, those woods, that house, it did not in that instant feel like a place where I should be.

A stronger wind suddenly came down out of the mountains to the west — presumably the source of the cold blast I had just felt — provoking a long, creaking noise to come out of the woods. A tree that was dry and not long for this world, presumably, bending for the second-to-last time. Still I did not start walking. I found I did not want to go back toward the house or the trees. My feet felt unsecured, too, as if something more than the water's gentle movements was moving the jetty's supports. Gradually this increased in intensity, until it was like a vibration buzzing against one leg, as if . . .

'You moron,' I said, out loud. I stuffed my hand in my jeans pocket. The vibration was just my phone.

I stuck it to my ear. 'Who is this?'

It was Ellen Robertson.

11

I got to the Mountain View a little after eight o'clock. It was the only place in Black Ridge I could bring to mind, and I wanted to sound at least slightly in charge of the situation. I did not suggest my motel because you do not do that with women you do not know. She agreed and did not ask where the bar was. She said she'd be there some time between eight-thirty and ten, but couldn't be more precise and would not be able to stay for long.

I walked back along the jetty, up the lawn, and climbed back over the gate. The house did not look like anything other than an empty dwelling, but I did not walk any slower than necessary.

I did hesitate for a moment at the top of the rise, however, turned and said goodbye, before I walked off down the drive. It did not feel as if I had done anything of consequence.

★   ★   ★

The bar was largely empty when I arrived. Lone drinkers held each corner of the room, like tent pegs. There was no one at the counter, generally the first roosting place of the professional drinker — for ease of access to further alcohol, and the faux-conviviality of shooting it back and forth with the bartender. I guessed I was between shifts, that the place never did that much hardcore business, or that Black Ridge was slowly sinking into the swamp and the drinkers had worked it out first. The Marilyn Manson playing on the jukebox probably wasn't helping either. Not everyone enjoys the company of music that sounds like it means them harm.

I stood waiting for a couple of minutes before I heard someone coming out of the rear area. When I turned I was surprised to see the woman I'd spotted while sitting on the bench opposite, earlier in the afternoon.

She looked at me a moment, raised an eyebrow. 'Am I in trouble?'

'I have no idea,' I said. 'I just want a beer.'

The eyebrow went back down and she slapped each of the pumps in turn and told me what was in them.

'What's popular?' I asked.

'Money and happiness,' she said, quick as a flash. 'We don't have either on draught.'

I nodded at the one in the middle. 'Can I smoke in here?'

'Oh yeah,' she said. 'We are not afraid.'

I watched her as she leaned over to the other side to get me an ashtray. I guessed she was probably in her late twenties. Tall and skinny, with a high forehead and strong features, hair that had been dyed jet black and cut in an artfully scruffy bob. Her skin was pale, her movements quick and assured.

'You want to pay, or run it?' she said.

'For a while,' I said. 'I'm meeting someone.'

'Oh yeah — who?'

I hesitated, and she winked. I wasn't sure I'd

ever seen a woman wink before.

'Okay,' she said. 'I get it.'

'You don't,' I said. 'It's just an old friend.'

'Whatever you say.'

One of the tent pegs came up to buy another beer, and I took the opportunity to walk away. I climbed on a stool at the counter which ran along the bar's street window, got out my cigarettes. It was a long time since I'd smoked or even taken a drink inside, and my associations with the practice were not good. Have you ever set fire to the hair hanging lankly over your face, when very drunk and trying to light yet another cigarette — despite the fact you've already got one burning in the overflowing ashtray? It's not a good look. Nobody's impressed.

But that was then.

★   ★   ★

The drunk period lasted about a year. It began in the way one chooses, without being aware of a conscious decision, to take one route around the supermarket rather than another. The first time, it's happenstance; the second, it's the way you did it before; and then it's just what you do.

I had been someone who didn't drink at home, or alone, or to frequent excess. And then I was. Small differences. Big difference.

Just because.

The advantage of being drunk is not that it helps you forget, though it will keep reality at arm's length. Mainly it conveys a rowdy vainglory to the things you *do* think about,

94

which may seem preferable to their being blunt, hard facts. It wasn't the drinking that was the problem — it didn't make me aggressive or abusive (merely drunk, and maudlin) — as much as the hangovers. I never got to the point of turning pro, where you plane out of the morning-after by starting again bright and early, and so I found myself mired four or five times a week in dehydrated despair, consumed with self-loathing, all too aware I was letting down Scott's memory by failing to be the straight-backed and self-reliant adult I'd hoped he would grow up to be.

When I'm hungover I can only get by if I retreat inside, which basically means I can't listen to other people. Carol needed me to listen. Her way of dealing with the thing we couldn't talk about — it was not subject to interpretation, once we'd established the medical profession didn't have a clue as to what might have caused Scott's brain to blow a fuse, and Carol's hours on the Internet had produced no further clues — was to talk about everything else. As if she felt that by containing life's trivial chaos in words, in obsessive detail, it would become contained, made incapable of doing us further harm. Not only did I disbelieve this, I found it hard to withstand hours of meaningless utterance from someone who had once been so concise and sparing of observation.

As a result I drank even more, to get through the listening periods, and the hangovers got worse and more frequent, and my willingness to listen decreased yet further. It came to the point where she would be talking all the time we were together, knowing I wasn't listening but unwilling to stop, unable to understand that I was coming to hate her for filling the world with noise that made it impossible for me to start healing in silence. Consequently we began to spend less and less time together, and I started missing more and more of her narrative — until I realized I had lost track of whatever story she was trying to tell; and then finally came to understand that I was no longer even a part of it.

I got this, in the end, when she left. Of all the things she tried to say, that was the one that got through. It was four months after Scott had died. I woke one weekend morning, late, in a house that felt empty and too quiet. I lurched around in my robe until it became clear that significant things were missing: principally, my wife and remaining child. Eventually I found a letter propped up on the desk in my study. It boiled down to: The world is broken, you're fucked up, and I'm out of here.

In the next six weeks I did what we should have done long before — something Carol had tried to make me do many times. I sold the house. I sent her three-quarters of the proceeds, once the loan and other expenses had been paid. Half for her, a quarter for Tyler. An odd name for a child, I'd always felt, but it was not my choice. He had been a while in arriving, and was Carol's son from before birth, somehow announcing this to us from the womb. I would have loved him nonetheless, but it was Scott who had been *my* son. I did not feel like a father any more, and had failed at pretending otherwise.

The last time Carol and I met was on the six-month anniversary of what happened. We met in a restaurant equidistant between Renton, where she was living (close to her brother, over on the Seattle side of the Cascades) and Black Ridge, in which I currently had that motel room. Carol looked tired and drawn. Tyler seemed to have no strong reaction to my having been absent, nor to me being there again. I learned that he was sleeping through the night now, however — having started almost immediately after he and his mother left the house. Carol and I had been married for a little under seven years, and apart for only a month. Yet on that afternoon the proportions seemed reversed, and it was clear neither of us was looking for a reconciliation.

'Are you still drinking?' she asked. Her hands were, possibly without her being aware of it, organizing the table's silverware into neat lines.

'No,' I lied. I was actually drinking less concertedly by then, as if the demon knew it had done its job and was ready to go spread hell in someone else's life. But the position felt precarious, and I did not want to endanger my progress by getting into it with Carol. By leaving she had made it my problem, not hers, and it would be another six months before I felt the boss of it again.

She raised her chin, and I knew she understood both what the truth was and what it signified. That was okay. It was even nice, for a moment, to feel married and known. It was about the only thing that made me feel that way. In the old days there would have been a smile in her eyes. Now they looked dark and sad and old.

Twenty minutes later we stood and kissed each other drily on the cheek. I haven't seen her or Tyler since. Maybe there was more she could have done, or said. I fell short in those and other ways too. Though we had been a good couple when times were fair, we had no idea how to deal with each other when they were not. We'd tried therapy. The problem is that marriage is a language — an oral one, with no tradition of writing. Once you begin to codify it, it starts to die. There's a lot of sleight-of-hand in relation-ships, too, and talking excavates all the tricks. It's a hell of a risk, assuming you'll still want to watch the magician, and live that life, once you know how all the gags are done.

It had been a fair-weather partnership, perhaps, and the weather had turned very bad indeed. That evening, in fact, when I sat outside in a plastic chair and did nothing but stare into the motel's empty swimming pool for three hours, getting more and more shit-faced, it seemed like the sky had become a thick blanket of storm cloud that would never, ever lift. I eventually passed out in the chair, waking just after four, when rain started falling on me.

The next day I checked out of the motel. I drove for a couple of months with no destination, trying to overlay the past with sights and sounds. Eventually I wound up in Oregon. It's a place with a loose texture. You can sink into it and live out some kind of life without other

98

people bothering you a great deal. I kept drinking for a while longer. Then I stopped, and had gone to sleep instead.

★ ★ ★

By nine-thirty I was beginning to get irritable. I was drinking slowly but had still sunk enough for it to start to feel like old times, and not in a good way. The street outside looked cold and empty, and the bar wasn't exactly cosy either.

'Another?'

I looked up to see the barwoman leaning on the counter six feet away, looking out of the window with a local's calm indifference.

'I guess,' I said. 'But tell me, where do you have to stand, exactly, to get the mountain view?'

'Outside,' she said, turning to me. I realized there was something cold in her gaze, too, as if reflecting the weather outside. 'Plus you have to crane your neck a little, or else walk down to the crossroads. Why? You going to sue us over the name?'

'I'm John,' I said, and put out my hand.

She shook it, smartly, a single up and down. Her hand was large and dry. 'Kristina. I'll get you that beer. Hey — wait up. This your date?'

I looked out the window. All the businesses on the other side were closed for the night, bar the pizza place, and the streetlamps on Kelly strove for historical authenticity rather than the provision of illumination. A figure stood on the boardwalk under one of these.

'I don't know,' I said, without thinking.

99

'Yeah, it can be that way with old friends.'

'For God's sake.' I shook my head, mortified. 'What *is* this stuff I'm drinking?'

'Truth juice. Beware.' She grinned and headed back to get my beer.

I watched the woman on the opposite side of the street. She didn't move for a couple of minutes, but then started to make her way over.

By the time she made the sidewalk I had no doubt this was the person I'd come to meet.

12

I turned on my stool so she could see my face when she came in. 'Ellen?'

She didn't reply, didn't even look my way, but came straight over to the next stool. Then changed her mind, moved to a table in the centre of the room. I took a deep breath, went over and sat on the other side of it.

'This isn't a good place,' she said.

She didn't unbutton her coat. Her voice was as it had been on the phone, clipped and very precise. She was of medium build, with glossy blonde hair, brown eyes, and the kind of cheekbones and neat, symmetrical features that cosmetics companies like to use to promote their wares. Her own make-up was well applied, and either Black Ridge had a better hair salon than I would have credited or she had it cut elsewhere. She looked maybe thirty.

'Seems pleasant enough,' I said. 'Didn't spot a Hilton anywhere in town, otherwise I would have — '

'For me, I mean,' she said, irritably.

'So let's go somewhere else.'

She shook her head. 'I don't have long.'

Just then Kristina arrived with my beer. 'Getcha?' she asked, with a brief smile. Ellen shook her head.

'So let's start with that,' I said, when we were alone again. 'The I-can't-speak and I-haven't-got-long routine, and sitting away from the window

101

in case a passer-by sees you. What's up with that? You were the one who got in contact with *me*, remember?'

Before she answered, she reached across the table and picked up my beer. Took a sip, and replaced it neatly on the bar mat. I found this annoying.

'I'm in a difficult position,' she said.

'Uh-huh.'

'My husband died four months ago,' she continued, negating all the assumptions I'd just made.

'I'm sorry to hear that.'

She smiled quickly, in the way you do when someone expresses a condolence that, while polite, is too generic to make any difference.

'He was not an unwealthy man.'

'Okay. So?'

'He has family in the area.'

Each moment I spent in this woman's company made me less convinced she had anything of interest to tell me. But I realized she perhaps wasn't doling the information out this slowly for the sake of it, or at least not solely. Her hands were twisted together, the knuckles white. I took a swallow of my beer and put it down in the middle of the table. She noticed this but did not reach for it right away.

'How 'not unwealthy' was your husband, exactly?'

'Eighteen million dollars,' she said, matter-of-fact. 'Not including the house. So it's not like he was Bill Gates. But we had a pre-nup anyway. No one's arguing with how the money was distributed, well, except that I got any *at all*, but that was Gerry's choice and there was nothing they could do about it, and we *were* married for four years.'

'Where are you from?' I asked.

She looked thrown. 'Boston. Why?'

'So how did you meet Mr Robertson?'

'On vacation. What is it to you?'

'I have no idea,' I said. 'Right now it doesn't seem like *any* of this bears relevance to me. So if the money's not the issue, then what is?'

'I think I'm in danger.'

'You said. You also brought up the death of my son, which made me fly a distance to be here. I'd like to believe I didn't waste a few hundred dollars and a lot of time. So far that isn't happening.'

'Something happened,' she said. 'To Gerry.'

'He died.'

'Yes, he *did*,' she said, as if I'd implied otherwise.

'How did it happen?'

'He'd been out for a run. He ran six miles every afternoon, starting around four o'clock. About twenty past five I thought, 'That's strange, he's usually back by now', and so I went out onto the porch and . . . there he was, in the chair he often sat in after he was done. But usually he'd call out, you know, say he was back. I thought 'whatever' and was on my way back inside and then I thought it was strange that he hadn't said something, because he must have heard me come out. We'd had . . . we had a fight, earlier in the day. It was no big deal, but I

103

wanted to make sure things were okay. So I went back to where he was sitting. He was drinking from a bottle of water. He looked hot, and, you know, puffed up, like he'd run further or faster than usual. But he turned and saw me coming, and he started to smile. Then . . . '

She held her hands up in the air in a gesture that reminded me of the one Ted had made, when trying to convey the degree of damage the restaurant had suffered. How much damage? Enough. Too much.

'Heart attack?'

She nodded.

'I'm sorry,' I said.

I was. However irrelevant this woman's problems, there are those who have lost someone they care about, and those who have not. If you have, then you understand that the people who die drag us along for the ride, as if we are tied to the back of their hearse by a rope. Ask someone who has lost their mother how they feel about Thanksgiving. But one day you realize that *you're* still alive, and you pour someone else's gravy over your turkey and are thankful there's any at all. If you want to stay sane, anyhow.

'Are you okay?'

I realized I'd been staring down at my hands, and glanced up to see Ellen looking at me. She seemed a little less tense than she had.

'I'm fine. So . . . '

'Not everyone believes that's what happened.'

'Why?'

'I don't *know*,' she said. 'I *loved* Gerry. We were happy.'

104

'How much did you get?'

She looked annoyed at the question. 'Two million dollars. Is that enough?'

I shrugged. Enough to kill someone for? Yes. But as people will whack each other over sneakers or an iPod, there's an argument that adding zeros doesn't constitute motivation. Money is neither a necessary or sufficient condition for murder, and two million dollars is not as much as it sounds.

'Ellen,' I said, firmly. My beer was almost done and so was I. 'I came up here because — '

'It's the house,' she said.

'The house?' I said, confused. Part of my head was still processing having revisited my own property, and for a moment I thought that's what she was talking about. 'Your house? What about it?'

'It's part of a compound, three houses, around a pond,' she said. 'They're old, but they were remodelled by some big-name architect, I forget who. It's off the road to Roslyn and Sheffer. Gerry and I lived in the second-biggest house. The caretakers have the tiny one, Gerry's children have the other. He was married before. She died ten years ago. I didn't get the house in the will because the place has been in the family forever, but I'm allowed to stay there as long as I wish. Gerry was *very* clear about that. It's there in black and white.'

'Why do you *want* to?'

'Because I like it here,' she said. 'And . . . I've had times in my life when I got pushed around pretty hard. It's not happening again. But since

Gerry died, it's not right any more.'

'What do you mean?'

'Actually, I will have a drink after all.'

I looked up, but Kristina wasn't in view. Just as I got to my feet to go to the bar, my phone started buzzing. I pulled it out, expecting to see Becki's name on the screen. The caller had rung off, however, and I didn't recognize the number in the log.

'Who was that?'

Ellen was looking up at me. I laughed, disconcerted again by her presumptiveness.

'I have no idea.'

Then it rang again. The same number flashed up. I was about to accept the call when Ellen grabbed my hand and twisted it so she could see the screen.

I've never seen someone go white before. Maybe it didn't even happen, in a literal sense. But what happened to her face is what people mean when they use the phrase. She stumbled to her feet, started to say something, but then just left.

She was out of the bar before I really knew what was happening, and by the time I'd got to the street, she was gone away around some corner I couldn't find.

★   ★   ★

When I got back inside the bar the people in the corners were talking to their companions or looking into their beer. Kristina was back behind the counter.

106

'Something you said?'

I glared at her. 'Kind of an obvious joke, wasn't that?'

She stared straight back at me, and I noticed the colour of her eyes properly for the first time, a pale green shading to grey, like mountain rock glimpsed through a layer of lichen.

'You look like someone who's fraternized with a few barkeeps in his time,' she said. 'So you'll know we work from a limited script. You ready to pay?'

'I'm sorry,' I said, though I wasn't. 'It's been a long day, and I'm tired and pissed off. None of these problems are yours, naturally.'

'Best kind,' she said, slightly less frostily. 'You want another beer, or what?'

I nodded and she poured it out.

'So — Ellen just upped and went, huh?'

'You know her?'

'Not really. Used to come in here once in a while, with Gerry Robertson.'

'Her husband.'

'Right.'

'Anybody else?'

'No. Definitely not. They were a cute couple. I mean, kind of a May-to-December deal, well, October maybe, he was early sixties, but they were tight. Gerry wasn't a dumb guy, either.'

She sounded sincere, but there was something she wasn't saying.

'And? But?'

'Are you, like, a private detective or something?'

'No. I'm a waiter.'

107

She laughed. 'Really.'

'Really. You got some plates of food in back, I'll be happy to carry them around to prove it.'

'We don't do food any more. Not since the last few deaths.'

I laughed, and for a moment it seemed like we caught each other's eye, though that sometimes happens when you've had a couple too many beers. 'So what aren't you telling me?'

'Well, just about what you said earlier. Even though it wasn't true. About being an old friend?'

'What about it?'

'I got the impression there *were* no old friends with that one. That where she was before Black Ridge was her business. If you see what I mean.'

I did, though I wasn't sure what difference it made to anything, or whether I cared. I finished my beer and went out into the dark, where it was cold and getting colder, and you could smell the coming rain.

It was only when I was putting my phone on to charge in my motel room that I noticed a new icon on its screen. Someone had left a message.

I'd walked quickly from the Mountain View, and knew — as the phone had been in my coat pocket — it was possible I'd failed to notice an incoming call from Ellen. That didn't mean I wanted to hear what she had to say. It had taken fifteen minutes to walk back, enough to decide that tomorrow was going to find me on a plane back to Portland; perhaps — just perhaps — via a diversion over the mountains to Renton. If Carol would consent to meet, that was, and wasn't freaked out by my suddenly appearing in her near-neighbourhood after three years. Maybe that wouldn't happen, but I was looking for ways to make the trip up here seem less like a dumb idea.

In any event, it seemed unlikely that anything Ellen had to say would derail the decision to cut my losses and go. So I might as well hear it.

I retrieved the message, my thumb ready over the button that would delete it. It wasn't Ellen, though it was a woman's voice.

It said: 'Don't trust her. She lies.'

13

You live in a place, and you create it, and in time it may come to seem like a surrogate child — your responsibility and fate, your joy and cross. The older she got, the more Brooke understood this. She considered it once more as she stood at the back of her sitting room, looking down out of the window toward the black velvet of the forest.

To leave somewhere is hard, especially if claiming that land had already involved upheaval, and hardship; bloody-minded determination of a kind most families dare not hope for in a single generation, much less time after time. It takes strong blood to create somewhere new, to commit a town to life.

Only after generations of winnowing will it be shown who has held the centre, and always will.

★   ★   ★

This was something her grandfather had taught her, back in the good old days of her own childhood. Before bad things happened and the flat plains of adulthood widened out. The word he used was 'omphalos' — from the Greek, apparently, meaning 'navel'. Put another way, a web. Grandpa only lived to see the toddler steps of the Internet, but he understood its principles ahead of time — far better than those who now frittered their hours buying and bragging and networking with individuals who, were their company genuinely worth having, probably wouldn't be spending quite so much time alone in front of a computer.

The truth of the world, as Grandpa taught it, was that everything in it is related, and can be made to pass through the same point. You, yourself. I.

To illustrate this he would hold up an object at random, anything from a matchbook to a doughnut. He'd note how the matchbook was constructed of cardboard, in turn made of wood. This led to discussion of trees and their wide and varied species, the manufacture of paper, and its predecessors, and the importance of logging to the settlement of the Pacific Northwest in general and Black Ridge in particular — a business his own father, Daniel, had been instrumental in setting up. He'd move on to what was printed on the matchbook, the colours, and how these might be traditionally used — red for Christmas, black for death. He'd comment on typography, how this locked the design in time and led off down further side roads, from the use of giveaways in commercial environments back to the development of the printing process, and the prehistory of the written word itself.

Before he even got started on what the matches were actually *for*, the importance of tobacco to the early colonization of America and its ritual deployment by local tribes prior to that . . . an hour would have passed, and then someone would come into the room, breaking the spell.

Brooke would look up, blinking, having been pulled so far into the object, unfolded at the centre of its interlocking web of relationships, that she had forgotten about being herself.

You could do it with anything. Doughnuts led to sugar (growing, refining, importance to the development of Africa and the Caribbean, its chemical nature and allied compounds), and to baking (crucial position of wheat in world markets, genetically modified or otherwise, cultural relevance of unleavened bread), the history of the Krispy Kreme corporation (and its retention of a cool 1950s-styled logo, versus companies like Holiday Inn who'd finally drunk the design Kool-Aid and bowed under the yoke of the rectangle . . .).

At which point her grandpa got up and went over to a drawer where, after a little digging, he pulled out an old matchbook, showing one of the old Holiday Inn signs in Massachusetts, not far from the town where the Robertson family had lived before making the long and pioneering journey out west.

The circles closed, briefly, before the web quickly started to branch out again — a spider scuttling out over the whole of creation.

As she got a little older, her grandfather would encourage *her* to start the process, giving her a nudge only when she temporarily ran out of steam. Once you understand that you're integrated with everything else, you appreciate there is nothing of irrelevance in the universe.

112

That, actually, it *is* all about you.

And in all this time, during the many, many hours they spent in this game, he never touched her. She knew he wanted to — and her growing awareness of this, and the fact he never once submitted to the impulse, led to her loving him very much indeed.

It is impossible to stop yourself feeling things. Feelings are like cats (as he also used to say). You can enjoy them, appreciate them, be annoyed to hell by them — but there ain't nothing you can actually *do* about them. Cats and feelings act outside the realm of human control. With the continued application of will, however, you can do (or not do) anything in the world. This she also learned from him, long before she became familiar with charlatans like Aleister Crowley and their adolescent excuses for pandering to mankind's basest instincts, weary children determinedly playing with their own shit as a way to appal the eternal parent that surrounds us.

A man's job is to provide the backbone, not the blood. To be strong, to be iron, the tree in the forest around which everything else grows. Some people do, others organize. Some have power — unfiltered, prone to excess — and others understand how to direct it, to gain advantage through its use.

The blacksmith makes the sword.

The knight wields it.

Grandpa had been a strong man. His father too. Brooke's own dad . . . Not so much. He had been *nice*, of course, but nice does not build walls that stand for two hundred years. The matter that worried Brooke the most in the middle of these nights was the future course of the bloodline. She had forestalled it going to seed, but that wasn't enough. It was time to set up another meeting on someone's behalf. Her brother always agreed to try, at least.

She couldn't do anything about that right now, however, and so instead she stood and looked out into the forest a little longer, until the difference between her and it shaded away. You live in a place. And once you've been there long enough, the place lives in you.

★   ★   ★

The doorbell rang eventually, and she heard Clarisse downstairs padding across the hallway to answer it. Then a quiet male voice, receding as he was shown into the sitting room. Time for business.

Brooke glanced in her mirror as she passed it, and didn't mind what she saw. Tall, trim and polished, with thick chestnut hair, clear blue eyes and the kind of bone structure that has nothing to fear from age. She looked like the kind of woman who haunts boutiques and gallery openings and sits on the board of the local tennis club — as, in fact, she did. Most people are limited in their perception. What they see is all they understand — and so to look one way, and yet be another, is the most basic magic of all. Nobody needs to know about the damage inside.

She took the main staircase down through the

house — her house, their house, *the* house — and across the hallway to the sitting room. Within it, a man sat perched on the edge of one of the good chairs. He wore glasses, and a coat that looked expensive.

'Richard?'

He nodded quickly. 'Rick. Richard, well, Rick. Yes. I'm a friend of — '

Brooke cut him off. 'I know everything I need to know about you, or you wouldn't be here.'

The man blinked, evidently unused to being spoken to in this way by a woman. Other than his wife, presumably. He looked the kind of slick, confident male to whom his partner would have occasion to use blunt words once in a while.

'Okay. Right. Of course.'

'What can I do for you, Rick?'

'I've been told,' he said, carefully, 'that you can make things happen.'

'Happen?'

'Make . . . people do things. Change their minds.'

'Sometimes, yes.'

He breathed in deeply, eyes dropping away for a moment. Most of them did something like this, on the first occasion, as they considered for the last time whether this was a line they really wanted to cross.

'I've got a problem,' he said, all in a rush.

14

The next morning was bright and clear — unlike my head, having endured a long night in a bed that appeared to alternate excessive softness and hardness on an inch-by-inch basis. It had been windy, too, causing branches to move against the back of the motel, scratching along the shingles. A little after three it got so bad that I considered going around there and snapping them off. I lay motionless in the cold and dark, trying to summon the will to get out of bed, but drifted into a state somewhere between more-or-less asleep and just-about awake, until eventually the walls of the room grew slowly lighter.

A shower didn't make me feel better, nor a long stare in the mirror. It seemed odd not being able to step out of the door straight onto a beach, and I realized for the first time how used I had gotten to my new life. Perhaps you have to try to go home in order to understand that it now lies somewhere else. In the Pacific Northwest you're seldom far from someone willing and able to sell you a cup of decent coffee, and I decided that would have to do instead of surf.

Five minutes' walk away I found someone setting up a latte-from-a-van business in a parking lot. I hung and chatted for a while with the thickset guy who ran it, learning little except that my opinion of humankind, though not universally upbeat, remains more positive than some. In the end the man's views on local politics, gays and Native Americans just got too depressing and I set off back to the motel.

On the way I pulled out my phone and listened to the message on it once more: those two sentences, delivered with conviction. I don't like people leaving that kind of message, whoever the hell they are, and I was no longer sure I'd be leaving town this morning. I called the number back, and kept walking as I heard a phone ring somewhere.

Finally it picked up.

'Robertson residence?' The voice was female, deferential, not the one I'd heard before.

'Sorry, wrong number,' I said.

I cut the connection. I wasn't surprised. It was consistent with Ellen recognizing the number when it came up on my screen. But it also suggested that someone had gained access to her cell phone without her knowing. How else would they have got my number from its call records?

Whatever else might or might not be true about Ellen Robertson, one thing was certain. Someone was fucking with her life.

My problem? Not really.

But.

⋆   ⋆   ⋆

As I walked back into the motel parking lot, I saw a woman heading out on foot the other way. It took a moment for me to recognize her as the motel owner.

'Morning,' she said, smiling broadly. 'Sleep okay?'

'Fine,' I said, disconcerted.

Combined with hair that was now clean and flowing loose over her shoulders, and wearing a cotton dress instead of being stuffed into old jeans and a T-shirt, it was hard to credit her as being the same woman I'd seen the day before. Even her skin looked different, no longer white and dry but tawny and warm-looking, the bridge of her nose stippled with the freckles of the natural redhead.

'You sure I don't know you?' she said, head cocked on one side. 'I mean, you're staying in my motel, of course . . . '

We laughed merrily together.

' . . . but I mean, from somewhere else?'

'I don't think so,' I said.

'Well, that's me,' she smiled. 'Always getting things mixed up. So — did you decide whether you wanted to stay the second night?'

'Not yet,' I said. 'Depends on a couple things. Do you need to know right now?'

'Not at all,' she said cheerfully. 'Got five people leaving all at once, so you're good either way. By midday is fine, just so as I can get Courtney to service the room. Number nine, isn't it?'

'That's me. Can I ask you something?'

'Shoot.'

'I've got an interest in old houses. I heard the Robertson place is quite something.'

'Well, heck, yes,' she said. 'Hazel had the whole place done by that guy, oh, I forget his

118

name, but he was famous. From over east. Wisconsin, maybe?'

'Hazel?'

'Gerry Robertson's first wife.'

'So you know them? The Robertsons?'

'Well, everyone does. Was Henry Robertson who first platted out Black Ridge back in the 1870s.'

'I was wondering about going up there, seeing if they'd let me have a look around. You think that's likely?'

She considered. 'To be truthful, I doubt it. Gerry might have. Hazel, for sure. She was real proud of it — spent years having the work done, and a lot of money too. Was only finished five months before she died, that's the sad thing.'

'What happened to her?'

'Car crash. Up on Snoqualmie Pass, two weeks before Christmas Ninety-eight. Went off the road and down the escarpment. Didn't find the car for nearly two days. They reckon she didn't die straight off, either.'

For a moment then there was something in her eyes. Then she smiled again. 'But there's no harm in trying. You know where to go?'

'Actually, that's what I was going to ask you.'

She got straight to giving me directions, in detail, another contrast to the way she'd been the afternoon before. Evidently yesterday had been a bad day. I was distracted in the closing stages of her instructions by the sight of an animal emerging from behind the motel and ambling toward us.

'That's one hell of a dog,' I said.

119

Marie turned to see, and laughed. 'You got that right. Half wolf, I was told, but I'm sure that can't be. Genetically, I mean. Found him as a puppy, though, and he's always been as good as gold.'

The dog drew level and looked up at me. Standing next to his owner, he looked even bigger. Big and grey and quiet, like a thundercloud.

'Hey,' I said.

I have never been a great fan of dogs. This one's eyes were very dark brown, almost black. He let them rest on me for a moment, then looked away. I felt as though my measure had been taken.

Marie patted his back affectionately. 'Woman living alone, you need something, right?'

'You bet,' I said. 'Well, thank you.'

'Need anything else, just let me know. And holler when you've decided about the extra night.'

She patted the dog on the back once more, and they strode off together toward the road.

★ ★ ★

Fifteen minutes later I drew up outside iron gates that stood a little way off Route 903, halfway between Black Ridge and the turn-off to our old house. It was not yet nine o'clock. The coffee and walk to fetch it had helped a little, but I still felt only about three-quarters awake. I got out and went to press the buzzer on the left side of the gates. After a time a male voice answered.

'Who is it?'

'My name's Ted Wilson,' I said. 'I — '

'What do you want?'

I went through the same spiel I'd used on Marie back at the motel. There was a long pause, and then a whirring sound as the gates started to open.

'Come up,' the voice said.

I left the car and walked up the drive. This led to a wide, grassy area surrounding an ornamental pond, around which were positioned two sturdy but attractive houses, painted white, in something like Georgian Revival style — and another that was more of a glorified cottage. The pond was free of leaves from the trees overhanging it, and the grass had been recently mown. Even the pebbles on the drive looked as if they had been selected and arranged for consistency of size and colour.

I headed straight for the biggest of the houses, stepped up onto the porch and rang the doorbell. Almost immediately it was opened by a thin woman in late middle age, wearing an apron.

I followed her into a wide hallway, at which point she smiled wanly and disappeared through a side door. I stood waiting for something like ten minutes, looking at the pictures on the walls.

When I finally heard footsteps coming down the staircase behind me, I was standing in front of a cream wooden panel on which a short section of a poem had been painted in a flowing calligraphic script.

I turned to see a man of about my own age,

maybe a couple of years younger, and sixty pounds heavier. Wearing an expensive pair of chinos, white button-down shirt and a V-neck sweater in sage green, he looked like he'd been given an interior decorator's advice on how to dress to best suit his surroundings.

He looked me up and down, and appeared not to feel the same way about me.

'Cory Robertson,' he said, offering his hand, which was soft and warm. 'So you're an architecture fan?'

'That's right.'

'How did you come to hear about the house?'

'The woman who runs the motel I'm staying in,' I said. 'I mentioned I was interested in old buildings, and she asked if I'd heard about the Robertson house. Or houses, I guess. So thought I'd come up, see if there was any chance of getting a look around.'

'Is this a professional interest?'

'Oh no,' I said. 'The feature in the *Digest* back in '97 was pretty thorough. My interest is purely personal.'

He gave me a brief tour. I saw a house that was large, well kept, and to which someone had made a number of coherent and unshowy additions. Five minutes in an Internet café on the way out of town had given me enough background on the property to sound like I understood what I was seeing, and to drop the name of the architect in question.

The upstairs was arranged as two separate wings on either side of a wide landing. Ellen had mentioned that Gerry's children lived here, using

122

the plural. Presumably Cory had a sibling who lived in the half he did not show me. Cory's portion was neat and trim, the only evidence of personality being a few framed group pictures of him and similarly patrician buddies in thick jackets and orange hunting caps, standing with postcoital grins over dead examples of God's handiwork. One of the men looked a little familiar.

We went back out to the landing. The window there allowed a partial view of the property at the sides, revealing a covered swimming pool and tennis courts — and the start of the forest behind. From here it was also evident that all of the blinds in the dwelling on the other side of the ornamental pond were drawn.

'There was work done on the other house, too?'

'Yes,' Cory said. 'More extensive, as a matter of fact — quite a substantial addition in the back.'

'Wonderful. Could I have a look?'

'I'm afraid that won't be possible,' he said, smoothly. 'There's a tenant in that part of the property at the moment. She's not home right now, but I wouldn't feel comfortable invading her privacy.'

'Of course,' I said. 'So, you rent it out?'

'Something like that. But she'll be leaving soon.'

'I'm surprised,' I said. 'If I was lucky enough to live here, I think it would take a great deal to make me leave.'

Cory merely smiled.

123

'You've been very kind,' I said, as he led me back down the main staircase.

'My pleasure. When one is fortunate in life, it behoves one to share it round a little.'

'A generous attitude,' I said, though evidently it did not extend to his father's second wife.

When we reached the lower hallway my eye was caught once again by the poem on the wall. Cory saw me looking, and read the lines aloud.

'The ports ye shall not enter/The roads ye shall not tread/Go, make them with your living/And mark them with your dead.'

'*The White Man's Burden*,' I said.

'Very good. My grandfather was a fan.'

'Of Rudyard Kipling, or imperialism in general?'

'Kipling.' He smiled thinly. 'But when his father arrived here with a wife and four young children, you'd better believe the locals needed a little civilizing.'

He stood out on the porch as I walked back down the drive. When I glanced back, however, I saw his eyes were not on me, but the other house.

I thought I saw the curtains in one of the upper windows move, but the sky was full of scudding clouds and it could have been a reflection of them instead.

I got back into my car unsure of what I had learned. Unsure too, of what I thought of Cory Robertson. Possessed of the bland presumption that comes from local note and wealth, but also its gentile politeness, it was hard to imagine him making someone feel they were in danger.

Except, perhaps, when he had been speaking of his tenant's anticipated departure, or when intoning a poem which — though well-meant at the time, and born of a blithe paternalism that was not quite the same as racism — could serve as a defence of the territorial rights of the self-defined 'civilized' over all others.

I wondered, too, whether Cory realized how one of the lines could apply to his own mother, who had left this world alone, tangled in wreckage in a gully below one of the roads that men like his grand-father and great-grandfather had forged through these mountains.

Mark them with your dead.

Something told me that he did.

15

On the way back to the motel I tried calling Ellen Robertson, but got no reply. At the motel I packed, which took less than two minutes. If I drove hard down to Yakima, I might just be able to get to the Pelican in time for the evening service, but I'd be pushing it, and it anyhow seemed wrong not to at least try to see Carol while I was up here, in which case I'd get back to Marion Beach too late — and I needed to warn the restaurant.

It made sense to call my ex-wife first. The prospect made me feel nervous and tired. It had been five months since we'd last spoken. A short and polite exchange of news, of which I had little and she the same, or none she wanted to share. Conversing with people you used to love is very draining on your sense of reality. The gulf between now and then is too deep and bizarre to ignore, and there's little more strange than someone who used to be the opposite of a stranger. Nonetheless I dialled Carol's cell-phone number, rehearsing the breezy tone I'd use to invite myself around for coffee.

'Hey, it's me,' I said, when she picked up. It didn't sound the way it had in my head.

There was a pause, and so I added, 'John.'

'Oh hi,' she said, with bland warmth, as if it had been with her, rather than Ellen, that I'd pretended to be a bookstore manager announcing the arrival of a not-much-anticipated volume. It was precisely this tone of voice, and its payload of considered maturity, that prevented me from dialling her number more often.

'Hi to you too. So, how are things?'

She was fine. Tyler was evidently fine, too. Carol's brother was not quite fine, however, having slipped on a wet supermarket floor and hurt his ankle. The play-by-play on Greg's vacillation over whether to sue the market soon ballooned to occupy more airtime than had been dedicated to my ex-wife and remaining child. I took the phone outside and smoked a cigarette while I withstood it. Is there anything in the world more dull than the lives of the relatives of an ex-partner? It's like being proudly shown a factory-condition Betamax VCR and expected to admire the detailing.

'The thing is,' I said, when the topic eventually ran out of steam, 'I'm in the area. I wondered whether — '

'You're *here*?'

'Yes. Well, not in Renton. I'm in Black Ridge.'

There was a pause. 'What are you doing there?'

'It's been a while. I wanted to see the house.'

'You went to the *house*?'

'Yes. There's no one living there at the moment.'

'But why did you go there?'

'Because it was time.' I was feeling defensive by now, also annoyed, and my voice had become clipped. 'I'm going back south later. But given that I *am* here, I thought I'd come over and see you.'

'I'm on my way to work.'

'Okay, so this afternoon. I can fly out of SeaTac and — '

'This afternoon's not good either.'

'Carol, I have a right to see my son.'

'Oh really? After three years?'

'After three, ten or *twenty* years. What's the problem? Is there something you're not telling me?'

'We're divorced, John. I don't have to tell you anything. I don't have to see you and I don't want to. Just go back to Oregon. And stay there.'

For a moment I didn't know what to say, and then I did. 'Fuck you, Carol.'

I don't think she was even on the line any more.

I stood, my hand squeezing the phone so hard it hurt, for several minutes after she'd cut the connection. Discourse between the married doesn't always bear scrutiny in matters of reason or politeness. Even less so that of the no-longer-married — who will casually say things that would lead to a knife fight in any other situation. This had never been the case between Carol and me, however. I tried to work out if it would bother me if she had a new man in her life, and couldn't decide. At some level, maybe, but I'm a big boy and could have taken the information. She should have known that.

I called her back, but there was no reply. There didn't seem any point leaving a message.

★ ★ ★

128

I was putting my bag in the back of the car when my phone buzzed.

'You were here,' a woman said.

'Yes,' I said. 'And so were you, Ellen. Which wasn't what Cory told me, when I asked if I could have a look in your house.'

'But *why were you here?*'

I was done being talked to this way by women, for one morning at least. 'Because someone left a message on my phone last night,' I snapped, 'after you went nuts and ran off. It was a woman's voice but calling from the Robertson house. It said that I shouldn't trust you. Because you lie.'

There was silence. I'd already put this down to her realizing she'd been caught out, before I realized I could hear the sound of quiet, weary crying. 'Ellen,' I said, 'I'm going home now.'

I heard nothing but more of the same sound. I looked at my watch. Coming up for eleven. It was already going to be touch and go whether I would make it back for the evening shift, but I don't think it was that which changed my mind. I believe two conversations melded in my head — the debacle with Carol, and the present one — and I felt I had to do something about at least one of them. A woman's anger or distress is different than a man's. There is something more critical about it, as if it relates to an underlying condition of the natural world. Depending on the kind of male you are, you will either feel compelled to resolve the situation, or become excited (in a corner of your soul you don't want to know how to find) at the idea of making it interestingly worse.

'Come meet me,' I said. 'Let's talk. Doesn't have to be in Black Ridge. I've got a car and a map.'

There was silence for a moment. 'Can I trust you?'

'Yes,' I said.

★   ★   ★

I put my bag back in the room and stopped by the motel office to tell them I'd be staying the extra night after all. Marie wasn't there, but a young girl with long brown hair was standing behind the desk looking over a list of chores, as if wondering what language it was written in.

'Hey,' I said.

She looked up, slowly. Blinked at me. She seemed to be about sixteen, seventeen, and very pretty. From the housecoat she was wearing I guessed she was the maid. She looked like she'd been awake for about a week. Not partying, just awake.

'Hello?' she said.

I told her what I wanted to do but she just didn't really seem to get it. It didn't appear to be a matter of lack of intelligence so much as the information just not getting through. In the end I leaned over the counter, grabbed a piece of paper and wrote the information there in big letters too. The girl seemed not to take offence. I'm not sure she even noticed. I said goodbye and she watched me back out of the office like someone observing clouds passing overhead.

Outside I called my third woman of the

morning. I was so focused on making sure Becki was okay with covering for an extra night that it wasn't until that was done that I noticed she was sounding distracted.

'Are you okay?'

'Yes,' she said. 'Well, sort of.'

'Don't tell me Kyle's done something dumb again.'

'I don't know,' she admitted, after a beat. 'But he's acting weird, and kinda shouty, and . . . shit, this really isn't your problem, Walking Dude. You okay up there? Where the hell are you at anyway?'

'Washington. A place called Black Ridge.'

'And it's going okay, this family thing?'

'Fine,' I said. 'Look, I'll be back tomorrow night, okay?'

'Be good if you were,' she said, and was gone.

I walked to the car, reflecting that — for a man who'd spent every night of the last three years alone — I suddenly had a whole lot of women in my life.

★　★　★

I had an hour and a half to kill before meeting Ellen, and I used the time to grab something to eat in The Write Sisters. Once you ignored the fact that the food was good for you, it didn't taste too bad. Afterwards I decided to order coffee, experiencing some difficulty in attracting the blue-haired server's attention. In the end I had to stand up and go over to the counter, and she operated the coffee machine as if for the first time.

131

'Are you okay?' I asked, eventually.

She shrugged. 'Bit of tummy pain, that's all.'

'Seen a doctor?'

'They'll just tell me to take a pill.'

'It's how they roll,' I said, and got a very small smile.

As I drank the eventual result of her labours I leafed through a local guidebook on the town. It had been produced a decade back, and the only business I recognized was Marie's Motel. The others had evidently all closed down.

Black Ridge had a background common to many settlements in the area, and it didn't take long to absorb. Originally a site of intermittent use to a variety of Salish-speaking local peoples, it was lost to the white man after a tribal member with no authority was talked into putting his mark on a treaty document. After that, any Indian found on land to which a white person held title was deemed to be squatting, and could legally be moved on.

And so they were. Settlement came in fits and starts, until in 1872 one Henry Robertson subdivided his homestead into lots, laid out the streets and registered the town, together with John Evans, Nikolas Golson, Joshua Kelly and Daniel Hayes, a dairy farmer — the families having arrived from Massachusetts either together, or more or less at the same time. The Kelly family disappeared back east again within months, and Golson was run out of town a year later for petty theft, but the rest of the settlers prospered. Timber gradually became the main focus of business and the place was successful and confident enough to be incorporated in 1903, at which point the couple of blocks where I was sitting constituted the centre of town, a collection of short, angled streets that looked like they had been drawn in the sand with a stick.

I glanced through the window when I reached that point in the narrative, and found it hard to imagine the eleven saloons that had plied noisy and sometimes dangerous business along either side of those muddy tracks, or the mustachioed men and boot-faced women who had frequented them. Either that vitality had seeped into the ground like spilled blood, or their spirits had blown away into the forest long ago.

For a time men and women from local tribes had played a part in the town's history, predominantly helpful, occasionally losing it and whacking some especially annoying white boy, but eventually they faded from the story along with, frankly, pretty much everything else of interest. Black Ridge now felt tired, starved of power and direction, as if its batteries were giving out. The only thing that struck me was why Henry Robertson had chosen to build his house a substantial walk away from the fledgling town, in what remained forest to this day, rather than slap in the middle, as founding fathers (like Henry Yesler, over in Seattle) were prone to do. The Evans house still stood, having been turned into the town's library during the 1970s. The site of the original Hayes property was also nearby, now under the bank in whose parking lot I'd acquired a coffee early that morning. The Kelly family, despite apparently not even lasting six months in the area, got the main street named after them. So why had Henry Robertson chosen to build four miles away? It didn't seem likely that I'd ever know, or that it could matter much.

I added a copy of the book to my tab, paid, and left. The waitress was looking more off-colour, if anything, and I hoped she hadn't taken her lunch at work, and if so, that I hadn't eaten what she'd had.

★   ★   ★

The place Ellen specified was a picnic spot between Cle Elum and Sheffer. Eight tables spread amongst the trees, with a gravelled lot in which one vehicle was already parked. A red sports car. I hoped it was Ellen's, or — given her nervousness about being observed — it seemed unlikely she'd stay when she arrived. When I got out I saw a figure standing at the edge of the trees, a few yards past the furthest table. I realized Ellen wouldn't know what car I drove, or be able to see me clearly, and so I walked into the area slowly.

'Ellen?'

There was no response.

I took a few more steps and realized she must have been deeper into the trees than I'd at first thought, or had then moved, as what I had assumed was her turned out to be just another tree.

'Ellen — it's John Henderson.'

She must be able to see me, wherever she was standing, and so I stopped moving and waited.

After about a minute she came walking out of the woods, from more or less where I'd expected. She looked tired and pale.

'Are you alone?'

'Yes,' I said. 'Why wouldn't I be?'

'Sometimes people aren't.'

'Well, I am,' I said, holding out my arms and turning slowly to encompass the world in general. 'Even the little voices have stopped talking to me.'

She bit her lip, and finally smiled.

16

We sat on opposite sides of a table. She was wearing jeans and a thick maroon sweater, her hair and make-up looked less polished, and I revised her age down a couple of years as a result.

'So where are you really from?' I asked.

'I told you already.'

'You're not from Boston,' I said. 'So let's use the next two minutes as a test. Somebody's tried to convince me you're untrustworthy. I'd like to believe that isn't true. So. Where are you from?'

'How did you know?'

'Got a good ear. Your accent is excellent but the more I hear it the more I realize the vowels are too rounded sometimes, and once in a while your word choice is off. No one around here is going to know the difference but I've spent time talking to someone who really does come from Boston.'

'And you're an expert?'

I waited.

'Romania,' she said, defiantly.

'But you've been here a long time?'

'Eight years. I was in England for a while before that, and France, and now I live here. I too have a good ear. I wanted a good job in America. So I took the trouble to work on my accent. My French isn't so bad either.'

'How old are you?'

136

'Thirty-four. And that's not a polite question in any language.'

I was surprised into a smile. 'Okay,' I said. 'Look. You've been honest, and I'll be the same. I'm sorry if you're having a hard time but this is the last conversation we're going to have unless you give me reason to believe you have information relating to the death of my son.'

'What about you?' she said. 'Where are *you* really from?'

'Newport Beach,' I said, lighting a cigarette. 'California.'

'I don't mean that.' She took one from my pack without asking, and picked my lighter off the table. 'It said in the newspaper you were a lawyer.'

'Yes. I was.'

'But not always, I don't think.'

'And now you're the expert?'

She didn't smile. Just waited, much as I had done, looking me directly in the eye. She didn't seem a whole lot like the woman I'd met in the Mountain View Tavern, and I remembered what Kristina had said.

'I was in the armed forces. Later, I was a lawyer. I did some other things in between.'

'Uh-huh,' she said. 'Like what? Listening closely to the way people spoke, and what they said?'

'It's a long time ago.'

'So was Romania.'

So I told her. My teens were scrappy and I went into the army at twenty to get away from a life I could see tangling badly in front of me. Did

137

five years and came out without having been shot and with only a few stitches here and there. I left soon after I met Carol, and joined the Secret Service instead, which I figured would at least keep me in the country most of the time. The service, despite the flashy, look-at-me name, is somewhere between grunt-level Fed and bodyguard, and basically involves a lot of standing around. I was in it for two years, during which time I at no point met the president, the vice president, or got shot. After that I moved to the side, after being invited to work for an intelligence department tangentially allied to Homeland Security. During those years I additionally studied for a law degree during evenings and at weekends. I started this when my wife got pregnant the first time and I realized there was soon going to come a point where I didn't want to be around guns every day or have my whereabouts and safety governed by forces outside my control.

I left and joined a small, old law firm in Yakima owned by the father of an old army buddy — Bill Raines, also working there by then — and did okay. They had bread-and-butter clients coming out of their ears and it wasn't hard to bill enough hours to get comfortable. I worked mainly in offices, taking depositions and processing other discovery work, support functions for people like Bill, and only occasionally got to stare someone in the eye and dare them to take on me, our client, and the firm. Mostly they didn't rise, and when they did, usually they lost and generally they took it well — though the odd thing was I nearly *did* get shot one afternoon by opposing counsel, who it turned out had a major cocaine problem and was, moreover, a poor loser.

In general, however, it was a decent, quiet, respectable life. It should have stayed that way, with me eventually making partner and becoming fat and excessively knowledgeable about wine. It would have, but for a single afternoon.

I stopped there, having already said far more than I had intended. Ellen listened well, with eyes that laid you open without seeming to pry.

She thought about what I'd said, and then she started to talk.

★   ★   ★

They met in Paris, where they shared a table out of necessity outside the Café de Flore on a busy spring afternoon — two strangers touring the St-Germain hot-spots, ticking the box of one of the places where pioneering existentialists had moodily sipped café crèmes. She was personal assistant to an executive in a bank in Boston. Robertson was on his fourth annual trip outside the US after the death of his wife, and still finding it hard to enjoy himself. Gerry had been a financial director down in Yakima before retiring in his mid-fifties, and so they had things to talk about, kind of. They found things, anyway. They also arranged to meet for coffee the next day, and then dinner that evening, and after that . . .

As I listened, I decided Kristina had probably

been right about something else. When Ellen talked about how she and Gerry kept the relationship going, via phone and email and weekends away, how he'd proposed to her in New Orleans on the fifth anniversary of his wife's death — and his reason for choosing that date, putting his past to bed in open view, rather than denying it — and how it had felt when she'd finally moved in with him to the house I'd seen earlier that morning, I had little doubt this was a woman who had felt deeply, and that the feeling had been reciprocated. Why not? Naturally there are differences between people whose ages differ by ten, twenty or even thirty years (or so one would hope, if the older party has been paying attention to life in the meantime) — but probably far less than those that exist between a child of four and one of two. Being neither old nor young necessarily implies you're a fool.

There followed four years of happy domesticity and platinum club international travel, the only blight on which had been, predictably, Gerry's children. This had not taken the obvious form, however. Cory and Brooke Robertson welcomed the newcomer to the family compound, had been friendly to the point, apparently, of near suffocation. This confused Ellen until she realized they were treating her as if she were another sibling. Of course she didn't expect them to deal with someone of their own age as a meaningful stepmother, but neither was she prepared to accept the role of a late-arrival sister who just happened to share a house (and

140

bed) with their dad.

After a discussion with Brooke in which she'd made it clear that this was not the lay of the land, there had been a distancing, but — Ellen felt — no more than was appropriate. Life went on, with a family dinner together in the big house every Sunday.

'So what was the argument about?' I asked.

She looked confused.

'Last night you said you and Gerry had a fight,' I said. 'The day he died.'

She stubbed the cigarette on the picnic table's surface and flicked it away into the trees. 'Children. But not his children.'

'You wanted a child?'

'It had been going on six months. Actually, nine — since the night of our fourth anniversary, that was the first bust-up. I'm, well, I told you. I'm thirty-four.' She held a finger up and jerked it from side to side. 'Tick tock, tick tock.'

'Could he have produced more children?'

'Oh, I think so. Gerry was a vigorous man.'

'Good for him. But a little old to cheerfully contemplate three a.m. bottle feeds. Especially when he'd been through it all thirty-odd years before.'

She glared at me, in my temporary capacity as representative of all male-kind. 'But he never *said*. When we got married, he never said, 'We can have no children.' We never had *big* fights about it, but . . . it was coming up more and more.'

I could imagine, having been married. I was familiar with the process of relentless female

141

advocacy. Aware too of the male counter-weapons of bluff inattentiveness and circumvention, and how they do nothing but make a situation worse. 'So — that day?'

'It came up, it went the same as always. He went off for his run. I stomped around the house for a while and then got on with something else. It . . . it really wasn't such a big fight.'

Her chin twitched, and she stared down at the table. I had spent many nights telling myself that Scott and I had been on good terms in what had turned out to be his last days, that when I'd read him a bedtime story the night before he died it had been with pleasure, and not a sense of duty, and so I knew what her body language meant.

'Better you were still having the fights,' I offered. 'It gets to the point where you're *not* talking, that's when you're screwed.'

She looked back up, and smiled a little. I smiled back, but sat looking at her like a man who wasn't going to say anything else without incentive.

'It was his face,' she said. 'That's why I called you.'

'What do you mean?'

'He looked like they say your boy did, when he died.'

The coroner's report on Gerry Robertson was straightforward. Being fit for his age and that the family had no prior history of cardiovascular problems didn't, sadly, amount to much.

'Two weeks after he was buried,' Ellen said, 'I was in Sheffer. I don't know why, I can't remember. Probably just to be somewhere. I was trying to eat some lunch. And I heard someone talking about 'the Henderson house'. And what happened there.'

I swore, annoyed that my life had evidently become such a touchstone for local gossip. 'Was it a guy in his fifties? Expensive-looking glasses?'

She frowned. 'No. A woman. Why?'

'Never mind. And?'

'This woman was saying she'd heard it from one of the policemen who was there, a guy called Phil.'

I nodded. I remembered Phil Corliss, from the Black Ridge police department. He and his boss had been first on the scene after Scott died, but eventually ceded control to the larger Cle Elum police department. Of all the cops who'd turned up that day, and over the rest of the week, Corliss was the only one I never thought was trying to work out how or why I'd caused harm to my son. No one asked, and none seemed like they truly felt that I or Carol should be thrown in the back of a police car and worked over in a windowless room, but all except Corliss looked as though the thought had crossed their minds. Corliss and his boss, in fact — who was there too briefly for me to log his name.

'The woman said Phil had told her something about the way . . . look, are you — '

'I'm fine. Just say whatever you've been building up to. My patience is not infinite.'

'The deputy said your boy's face looked strange. When he saw the body. Like he had been scared?'

I didn't say anything.

143

'So . . . I went to the library and I got out the newspapers from back then. I read what happened. And it made me start to think.'

'I still don't get — '

'Gerry didn't have a heart attack,' Ellen said. 'My father, *he* had a heart attack. I was fourteen, I was there. He said he felt strange. Then he was fine for a few hours, but I saw him frowning and touching his arm, like this.' She rubbed her right hand up and down her left arm, quite roughly. 'He stopped, but said he felt sick. He was okay for one more hour. Then he was rubbing his arm again, and he moved it up to his chest. But still he said he was fine. He got up to get some indigestion tablets and it was as if his left leg gave way. He slipped down onto one knee, crooked. He started to say something — and I saw that he knew what was happening. He *knew* he was having a heart attack. With Gerry *it wasn't like that.*'

'So how was it?'

'I said his name. He turned and smiled at me — and it was a lovely smile, and it said the fight didn't matter. I was about to say something nice to him when I realized he wasn't looking at me any more.'

'What do you mean?'

'He was looking through me, back to where the trees start. He looked confused. It was like he smelt funny, too, not like his sweat usually did. And he stared at me like he'd never seen me before in his life, and I made him scared.'

She abruptly reached into her purse and pulled something out. 'I have a picture,' she said.

144

'You took a *photograph*?'

'Later. They left me alone with him.'

She held the picture out. I saw the harshly lit face of a man in his sixties, with soft features and thinning grey hair. His eyes were closed and he looked dead. Nothing more.

'It had changed,' she said, defensively.

I felt furiously let down. 'Well, yeah, Ellen. Facial expressions don't just freeze on people's faces forever. Christ, are you *kidding* me?'

'It wasn't just his face, anyway,' she said quickly. 'It was what he *said*.'

'And what did he *say*, Ellen?'

'He said, 'Who *are* you?' and I turned to see where he was looking. It was sunny and bright and you could see all the way to the trees but there wasn't anything *there*, except you know, the trees behind the main house. And so I turned back to him, to ask what he was talking about, but . . . he was dead.'

'So he had a stroke, or the CVA cut off the blood to his brain, and his vision got skewed.'

'Is that what happened to Scott?'

'I don't know why you think you know what happened to my son,' I said, angered at her use of his name. 'In the newspaper it just reported that he died. So what makes you think — '

'The woman in the café was telling this other person that the policeman had said your son died looking scared. *That's* how Gerry looked. *That's* what disappeared from his face. He saw something, and it made him die. The coroner smoothed his skin out to hide it. So *no one would know*.'

145

I was staring at her now. 'Ellen, that's just . . . nonsense.'

'Someone *did* something to Gerry,' she insisted. 'And now they're trying to do it to me.'

'Do *what*, Ellen?'

'They're watching me all the time. They're in my house at night. They follow me everywhere, and hide when I turn round.'

'*Who?* Cory and Brooke?'

'No. It's not them.'

'Are you sure? Someone from that house called me. How else did they get the number except off your phone — which says they've been snooping around your house. And who else did you mean when you said someone was intercepting your emails?'

'Well, yes,' she said. 'Cory is doing that. They want me to leave the house. But it's not just them. It's someone else. They're trying to punish me for Gerry dying — for something *I didn't do*.'

'Who?' I said. I was close to shouting now. '*Who* do you think is doing this?'

She muttered something, a word I didn't quite catch. It sounded like 'trigger.'

'What did you say?'

She made a noise of angry disgust, got up, and stormed away toward her car. By the time I'd caught up with her she'd already yanked the door open.

'Ellen,' I said. 'Listen to me. You need help. Seriously. The death of someone you love can do strange things to your head. Believe me, I know.'

'You don't know *anything*,' she shouted, eyes

146

bright with anger or tears.

Then she slammed the door and drove away.

$$\star \quad \star \quad \star$$

I walked back to the table to retrieve my cigarettes, and wound up sitting down and smoking another. I was disappointed and relieved. Relieved to have gotten to the bottom of what the woman felt she had to tell me. Disappointed that it was meaningless bullshit.

I was angry with her, too. I hadn't been honest with Carol when we'd spoken. I hadn't chosen to go up to the house. I had many times in the last several years reaffirmed in my head a clear decision to never go anywhere near the house or this area again. I wouldn't have done it at all if Ellen Robertson hadn't got in contact. Ever since I had been back in the Northwest I had felt my new life fading, as if the distance between then and now was being eroded — and the visit to the house had been the start of this. The last twenty-four hours had been a dumb and dangerous waste of time, and it was time to go back to the future.

I slipped my cigarette butt into the pack, as had been my habit even before the health Nazis redefined smoking as akin to mass homicide. In doing so I remembered how Ellen had flicked hers away, and got up to go and look for it. I wasn't really expecting to find it, but moved more by a self-righteous annoyance that took littering as additional evidence of her being a stupid bitch.

147

I traced the likely trajectory across the grass and into the trees, realizing as I did so that this had been the area where I'd first glimpsed her when I arrived. And there, close to a lichen-spangled rock, was a fresh butt. I picked it up and was about to stomp back out again when something caught my eye.

I hesitated, then walked a few yards further into the trees. What covered the ground there — as you would expect, in these kinds of woods at this time of year — was a mixture. Fallen leaves in a hundred shades of brown, grasses turning more grey than green, widely spread rocks with patches of verdant moss.

There was also, however, a collection of twigs and small branches, covering an area approximately three feet square. I looked up, and confirmed that the trees around me were pretty much exclusively firs. Trees of a type, in other words, that would be unlikely to drop material of this kind. There were alders and silver and paper birch within vision, yes, but none just here.

Humans have pattern-forming minds, and this can sometimes be misleading. As I stood looking down at a random collection of fallen objects, I nonetheless thought, for a moment, that they looked almost as if they formed a shape — one which I couldn't quite discern. It just didn't look entirely random.

There was something else, too. A faint odour. Earthy, but with a high, sweeter note, as if some small creature had died in the vicinity.

A bird cawed suddenly nearby, making me

148

jump. I realized I was staring at a scattering of autumn debris, and felt a fool. I swept my foot in an arcing kick through the twigs, spreading them over a ten-foot radius, and walked back to the car. It was time to go home.

17

When you work in a library you often see people who look familiar. The book-hounds who get through two or three novels a day, and are constantly ferrying their treasure troves in and out. The young women who know they're less short-tempered mothers in public, and bring their children to play in the kids' area with its heavily battered plastic toys. Men looking for work, or at least presenting themselves that way, drifting through entire days in the company of newspapers or non-fiction written by people who lucked into financial success and are now compounding their good fortune through best-selling books entitled *Ten Reasons Why You Suck, And I Don't.*

But Carol didn't think the man she had become aware of this morning was any of these things.

He hadn't been there when she'd arrived at ten-thirty, she was pretty sure, though she'd still been flustered by the call from her ex-husband. Talking to John had been the absolute last thing she'd expected that morning, and hearing he was over in Black Ridge had thrown her completely. She'd spent a soothing period tidying — it was amazing how people who employed the classification system to *find* books seemed to believe it dispensable when it came to putting them back — and using the computer to run up a poster for a reading group.

When she looked up from printing out a draft she glimpsed a man in the non-fiction stacks. She noticed he was thickset, with flecks of grey amidst his short dark hair, but no more than that.

She didn't think anything of it until, an hour later and with the phone call largely behind her, she realized the man was still in the library, now over where the new fiction was laid out. Again she saw him only briefly, from behind, as she trundled a cart of returned books over toward the children's section.

An hour was not an exceptional length of time to spend in a library. Many spent longer, but most of these fitted into the recognizable tribes. When she had joined the library Carol had been subjected to a rather long orientation lecture from Miss Williams (currently at the dentist, thank God). Miss Williams's world view was characterized by a high level of mistrust — of pretty much everyone, but notably of those who might be using the library 'inappropriately'. Who used the restrooms without putting in a reasonable stretch perusing books; who were here because it was warm; and most of all the people Miss Williams called 'watchers'. Men who cruised the stacks, pulling out a volume occasionally and leafing through it, but whose gaze always seemed to be somewhere else — on a woman in another section, bending over to get something from a lower shelf; on one of the young mothers, leaning forward to assist her child without considering the effect this might have on the front of her blouse.

151

Or, Miss Williams implied, sometimes on one of the children themselves.

★ ★ ★

This man didn't look like a watcher.

Carol didn't once see his gaze drift. Either he'd sensed someone was keeping an eye on him — though generally when that happened, a watcher would absent himself from the library *very* swiftly — or he was just a regular guy spending an unusual amount of a weekday morning wandering around the books. Unemployed, on vacation, at some other unknowable kind of loose end.

It was now that she was looking at him more closely that Carol began to think she recognized him. She didn't think it was from Renton, however, and for just about the only time since she'd started working there, she began to wish Miss Williams was around. Either she'd already be on the man's case, or Carol could point him out and fade back to watch the fireworks. There was supposed to be two members of staff on duty at all times, but budget cuts blah-blah-blah, and so today this was Carol's problem and hers alone.

Assuming it *was* a problem, and she wasn't just letting her imagination get away from her. She was starting to feel anxious. She didn't want to feel that way. Not in her place of work, an environment in which she'd begun to feel comfortable and valued. She wasn't actually alone, after all. There were three mothers over by

152

the window, a couple of guys over in non-fiction, another sifting dispiritedly through the 'Help Wanted' sections of the local papers.

Carol came out from the desk and headed over to where she'd last seen the man, a cheerful offer of assistance forming confidently on her lips.

He wasn't there.

She turned, confused. Two minutes ago, she'd seen the back of his head and shoulders over here in Art (Oversize). Now he was gone. He couldn't have left the building. That would have meant going past Carol at exactly the time when she'd been turning him over in her mind. She didn't get *that* wrapped up in her own thoughts. Not any more, anyhow. Not usually.

She backed out of Art and looked around. Couldn't see anyone but for the people she'd catalogued before deciding to come over to this side. Except . . .

Yes. Over in the American History section, a pair of feet was visible beneath one of the half-height stacks, stuck out as if the owner was sitting at the table there. Carol was beginning to get irritated with herself now. So some guy had *so* little to do that he was making a meal over visiting the library. Big deal. Maybe Miss Williams had a case against these people, but she didn't, surely? No.

And she wasn't scared of them either.

She walked quickly across the central atrium and into the stack that led to the American History section. The guy was going to get some goddamned help whether he wanted it or not.

She found him sitting to one side of the table and looking down at his large, fleshy hands, which were resting comfortably on his lap. He wasn't holding a book, and as soon as Carol realized this she understood she might have made a mistake.

'Can I help you?'

The man looked up. His eyes were the pale end of blue. He was dressed casually, in jeans, a white shirt and a dark jacket. He looked too large for his clothes, and had the air of someone who was dressing against type.

'Sir, is there anything I can help you with?'

Her voice sounded fine the second time too. Strong, confident — and loud enough to carry to other sections of the library.

'No, Carol, there's nothing I want from you. Not here, anyhow.'

She stared at him. 'How do you know my name?'

He reached into his jacket and pulled out a small envelope, pale cream, the kind that holds greetings cards. He held this out toward Carol, who saw the name 'Carol Henderson' written on the outside in a flowing hand, but did not take it.

'Who the hell *are* you?'

The man stood and walked away — placing the envelope on the table as he left. He strode past the empty front desk (where a young mother stood waiting to check out an armful of books) and through the door to the street, where he turned left and disappeared.

'Um, miss?' said the mother, when she caught sight of Carol. Carol hesitated, then grabbed the

154

envelope from the table and hurried over to process the woman's books.

It was only when the young mother had left that Carol opened the envelope. Inside was a sheet of glossy paper, about six inches by four. When Carol turned it over she realized it was a photograph.

It had been taken from the opposite side of the street to the Renton kindergarten, and showed Tyler going into the building.

★ ★ ★

She arrived at the school twenty minutes later. She'd already called Ms Hackett, immediately, and been told that her son was fine — but when she got to the kindergarten to see her son doggedly colouring by himself in the corner, for a moment she thought she was suffering an optical illusion, so convinced had she become that her son would have disappeared.

Ms Hackett appeared in front of her. 'Is everything okay?'

Carol hadn't explained why she'd called, or why she was here now, red in the face from running.

'Fine,' she said. 'Just fine.'

'So . . . why did you want to check if Tyler was here? When you called?'

Ms Hackett was fourteen, or so it seemed to Carol, and spoke with the surety of someone for whom the world could be contained between the neat, parallel lines of an exercise book. Someone against whom the universe had not yet turned,

155

biting like a pet turned rabid dog, shredding to blood and bone.

'My ex-husband's coming to visit,' Carol lied. 'It's unexpected. I just wanted to check that Rona hadn't already picked him up — you know Rona, right?'

Ms Hackett nodded. Of course she did. Photos of everyone mandated to collect a child — parent and *especially* non-parent — were arrayed in neat lines on the wall in the staff room. As Carol should know.

Carol bulled on regardless. 'She's taking him to a play date this afternoon, and I'm not sure what the address is.'

Way too much information, she knew. Ms Hackett's eyes drifted to the wall clock, which clearly indicated it was some while yet until the time for Tyler's group to be released back into the wild. The teacher would also be thinking, Carol knew, that any competent mother would know *exactly* where her child was going on a play date, would have the GPS coordinates logged with the local police.

'I'm glad you're here, in fact,' the teacher said, turning away and opening a drawer. 'I did want to ask you about something.'

Carol didn't want to be asked about anything. She wanted to grab Tyler in her arms and leave. But that wouldn't look right. 'Fire away.'

The teacher handed Carol a small stack of childish works of art. 'Is this something you've taught him?'

Carol leafed quickly through six or seven drawings, at a loss. What was the teenager in

156

front of her asking? Had Carol taught her son to scrawl randomly over pieces of paper in a variety of colours? Surely that was a standard feature of the under-fives?

She looked more carefully at the last of the sheets and couldn't see much except what could possibly be a badly drawn stick figure of a dog, slashed across with red lines.

'I don't . . . I don't quite get what you mean.'

'Well, look,' the teacher said, earnestly, and started turning some of the sheets of paper around. 'I'm talking about the way that pattern keeps cropping up on other — '

'I actually don't have time for this right now,' Carol said, waving at Tyler — who immediately leapt up and came running over. She handed the sheets back to the teacher. 'Perhaps tomorrow?'

'Sure. Though . . . Tyler's not with us on Fridays, is he? I can check, but . . . '

'Of course not. Silly me. Monday, then.'

Carol smiled glacially at the woman, daring her to come out into the open and say what she was obviously thinking. That Carol was unfit. A crazy person.

The teacher didn't say anything. Carol took Tyler's hand and led him out of the classroom.

★ ★ ★

'I'm fine, honey,' Carol said. It wasn't the first time Tyler had asked, but it was the last time he was going to get a civil answer. 'I just thought it might be fun for us to play at home. Won't that be fun?'

She slowed as they crossed the playground, scanning her eyes over the other side of the street. The man from the library wasn't there, but she didn't know for sure that it was him who'd taken the photograph. When they reached the sidewalk she stopped completely, carefully looking all around. Everybody looked normal. Except for her, of course.

She glanced back and saw that Ms Hackett was standing in the window of the classroom, arms folded. Carol stood her ground, and stared right back.

'Don't you look at me like that,' she said, very quietly.

Ms Hackett watched a moment longer, then turned away and disappeared into the gloom beyond the clouds reflected in the school's windows.

They played a game all the way home, counting their footsteps in sets of eight. As soon as she entered the sitting room Carol noticed a light flashing on the answering machine. She erased the message without listening. When nobody called, nobody listened — and when people pushed their way into your life and handed over threatening photos, nobody listened to that either.

She sanctioned a request for half an hour's DVD-watching, to give herself time to think. As Tyler settled on the floor to watch his favourite section of the ever-popular classic *The Incredibles* (for about the fifty billionth time), she watched the street while she thought it through.

Option 1: Leave.

Option 2: Stay.

The decision didn't take long. She was tired of running. She wasn't going anywhere.

Some time later she became aware she was still by the window, and Tyler was asking if he could watch the DVD again. Which meant she'd been standing there, what? Twenty-five minutes? More? When she tried to think back over that period it felt blank.

She blipped the DVD back to the part where the Incredible family went superhero (her son was volubly bored by the parts where they pretended to be normal, having yet to learn that's what most of life boiled down to) and went to the bathroom to wash her face.

Feeling better, she headed to the kitchen to make some De-Stress herbal tea, which she'd taken to buying from a health store a few doors down from the library. It tasted fairly weird but the nice-looking, capable woman who owned the shop swore by it, and so Carol now drank it several times a day. As she measured out a table-spoon into the strainer she realized she was running low, and so turned to the little blackboard on the wall to add it to the weekend shopping list.

She'd clamped a hand over her mouth before much sound came out.

Someone had written something on the blackboard, in big letters, firm and underlined.

COME HOME NOW

Part 2

[Faith is] the substance of things hoped for, the evidence of things not seen.
Hebrews 11:1

18

By mid-afternoon I was in a truly heinous mood. Phone calls had established I couldn't get on a flight until the next morning. Another attempt to talk to Carol on her cell had failed, resulting in me leaving a message on her home answering machine that I already regretted. I could drive down to Yakima to be early for the airport tomorrow — or reorganize it *again*, and fly out of Seattle instead, or drive the car the seven or so hours down to Marion Beach — but I couldn't imagine why I'd do any of those things.

So I kept heading along empty roads through the forest, until I realized that I was going somewhere in particular after all.

★   ★   ★

When I got back to Black Ridge I drove through town to the eastern side and parked outside the police station, which stood on the busy road that cut through that end of town down toward Yakima. Inside the station, a heavy-set guy of around forty was sitting behind the desk pushing a pen around. His badge said he was Deputy Greene.

'Deputy Corliss around?'

The policeman shook his head without looking up. 'Something I can do for you, sir?'

'I wanted to talk with him specifically,' I said.

'Regarding?'

163

'Keeping his mouth shut.'

The deputy stopped what he was doing. I realized I was breathing more deeply than I should, and that my hands were clenched inside my coat pockets.

'Can I help you?'

A new voice. I turned to see an older man had emerged from an office in the back. He was tall, broad across the shoulders, with short, greying hair. I knew who he was.

'Recognize me?' I asked.

He looked calmly back for a moment. 'Yes.'

'You okay with your men gossiping about dead kids?'

The sheriff raised both eyebrows slowly. Deputy Greene sat back and observed us with the air of someone who'd sensed an average day might be about to become genuinely interesting.

'Was about to go grab a coffee,' the sheriff said. 'Come. Let's talk.'

★   ★   ★

We sat outside a diner down the street. During the two-minute walk there I had got my hands to relax. I knew I was overreacting, frustration making do with the only outlet it could find. Sheriff Pierce listened impassively to what I told him. By the time I'd finished I'd realized it didn't amount to a lot. Nonetheless, the policeman looked pained.

'Phil Corliss is a good man,' he said. 'I'm sure he didn't mean anything by it, probably just assumed that — whoever this woman was

164

— she'd have the sense not to pass it on. Could be his sister. She's a talker, but Phil's too close to realize that. I'll have a word with him.'

'I'd appreciate it,' I said. 'Your deputy was good to us and I don't mean him any ill-will. This probably seems dumb to you. I don't even live here any more. But . . . '

'Doesn't seem dumb at all,' he said, shaking his head with finality. 'The business of law-abiding people is their concern and no one else's. Not even mine, thankfully. So where are you living at now?'

'Oregon,' I said. 'My wife is over in Renton.'

'Separated?'

'Divorced.'

He nodded. 'Terrible thing happened to you people. I'm not surprised it turned out that way.'

For a moment, I suddenly felt very sad. Carol and I had loved each other. Shouldn't we have been better than this? Shouldn't *I* have been, at least? Wasn't there some other track the train wreck of the last three years could have rolled down?

This thought knocked the remaining wind out of my sails and I wished I could just get up and walk away without anything further being said.

Pierce nudged the conversation. 'First time you've been back?'

'Yes.'

'Visiting friends?' I looked at him, and he smiled. 'Sorry. Habit.'

Talking to him, I remembered something else about Pierce: that, in the hours following Scott's death, he had seemed something of a father

165

figure, or the closest thing to one that had been available at the time. Quiet and dependable, the person who might stand in the way of you backing helplessly into the pit an event like this opened up. This in turn made me realize that I hadn't seen my own father since that time. Three years. Nearly a twelfth of my life. How could that be right?

'No,' I said. I hesitated, and then thought . . . *what the hell?* 'Someone contacted me. A woman. The one who overheard the conversation I told you about. She implied she might know something about what happened to my son.'

Pierce frowned. 'And did she?'

'No. She's been bereaved and I think it's made her a little unstable. Do you know the Robertsons?'

'Of course. I grew up right here in town.'

'The woman I'm talking about was Gerry's second wife. Ellen.'

He nodded. 'I'm aware of her.'

'Was there anything weird about her husband's death?'

'Nope. Went on a run, blew his pump. Which is why I take care to never go above a walking pace.'

'Very wise. And that's all she wrote?'

'Just one of those things. You ever get to the bottom of what happened to your boy?'

'No,' I said. 'And I don't suppose I ever will.'

'Could be there's no bottom to be found,' Pierce said. 'Sometimes there isn't. Stuff happens, and that's all there is to it. As police, you learn that.'

I shook his hand and walked away down the street, leaving him to finish his coffee in peace.

★　★　★

I killed a couple of hours walking around town. I hadn't meant to. The truth is, I got lost. That doesn't happen to me often. I have a good sense of direction and Black Ridge is not a large place. Unlike pretty much every other conurbation of its age, however, whoever laid the place out clearly hadn't believed the right-angle was king.

I felt tired and as if whatever energy I had was seeping into the ground as I walked. The whole town felt pretty much the same way. Streetlights flickered. As I passed a tired-looking diner on a side street, all its interior lights went off at once. They came back on again. Through the window I saw the lone customer and a waitress look at each other. It was impossible to tell what the look communicated, if this was business as usual.

By the time I got back to the motel it was fully dark. I sat on the bed and flicked around television stations that seemed to have been conceived with someone else in mind. I couldn't convince myself I was hungry. Instead I found myself cradling my phone in my hands, considering phoning my father but wondering what good could come of it.

Fathers are often portrayed as distant, eyes and attention constantly elsewhere. It wasn't until I'd become a parent myself that I realized this might be because fathers may be tired,

167

bored, and mired in an existence they don't understand. Our culture is rife with parenthood porn, the idea that children are bundles of innocent joy and our love for them should be unconfined — keeping silent about the fact you may occasionally wish to bang their head, or your own, against a wall. Resisting this urge is precisely what makes the bond between the generations so strong, but sometimes you want to do the banging nonetheless.

I knew this, and yet still I found talking to my father hard. It hadn't always been that way. When I was young, he and I used to go for a walk every Saturday morning. We met in the kitchen at ten o'clock sharp. It was our Norman Rockwell moment. I suspect now that the ritual was likely a negotiated concession, driven by a mother's need for a couple of hours' friggin' peace, but regardless of this drab adult insight it remained a slot my dad and I got together. There was a randomness in the way my father chose which streets to cross, and at which points, that made the voyage seem different every time. The last stop was always the same, however: the drugstore, where Dad would order a coffee and Mr Franks would ask how he wanted it and Dad would say 'hot and wet'. Neither ever smiled during this exchange, and it took me a long time to realize it was a weird grown-up joke, not evidence that both were retarded.

Before the drugstore came the penultimate stop, Walter Azara's Ford dealership. My father knew Azara to nod to, but when we paused outside the lot he made no effort to strike up

168

conversation. Quite the opposite. Unless we'd happened to pass Wally earlier, so Dad knew he wasn't on the premises, the time we spent looking at the cars was charged, as though there was something illicit about it. I didn't get why this might be. Weren't they on the front lot precisely so people *could* admire them?

This was the early 1970s and the glamour Fords were Mustangs, which Dad would peer at for some time, conferring judicious attention to every detail except the price banner across the windshield. For me the real draw was the area where Walt displayed a couple of older vehicles, including a 1956 De Luxe in canary yellow and a Crown Victoria from the same era, in tan and cream. Back then you still sometimes saw these finned showboats on the roads, shedding rust and lumbering along as if baffled at the modern world, this cramped universe of straighter lines. The cars on the Azara lot were mint, however, restored by Walt's wizardly chief mechanic, Jim.

I would look them over, week after week, running my hands over bulging fins and smooth panels that were searing hot and shiny in the summer and cold and sleek the rest of the year. I would try to fill in the gap between when all cars looked like this and the way the survivors on the roads looked now, but could not. I did not yet understand about time, or how there could come a point where something bright and sparkling new — a car, job or wife — becomes just another thing you have; then something on the periphery of your vision that you don't think about much

169

any more; and finally the thing that's breaking down the whole time and making your life a living hell. You learn, though. You learn about all that.

We made this walk every Saturday for a number of years. I don't remember the first time, so I can't be sure when it started. I do remember when they stopped. I was twelve. There had been an atmosphere in the house for a few weeks. I didn't know what was behind it. Dad simply seemed distracted. We took our walks as usual but one time he forgot to say 'hot and wet' and Mr Franks just had to get on with pouring him a coffee. I remember the sound of it splashing into the cup, and seeing him glance at my father. Dad remembered his lines the next week, and I didn't think much about it. You don't, when you're a kid.

Then one day we got to Azara's and something changed. It was a cold fall morning and there was no one else in the lot, and I remember feeling relieved because by then I'd begun to sense the tension in my father if there were other people around. We started across the road, me veering straight toward the flashy dinosaurs, but I hadn't made the far kerb before I realized something wasn't right.

I turned to see my father had stopped halfway across the street. He wasn't looking at the lot, or at me, but at some empty space halfway in between.

'Dad?' He didn't say anything. 'You coming?'

He shook his head. At first I thought he was joking. Then I realized from the set of his body, already half turned to head up the street, that he was not.

'Why?' I said. It was inconceivable to me that we would not do this. We *always* did.

'I'm tired of looking at other people's cars.'

He walked toward the drugstore. After a moment, I followed. When he ordered coffee he and Mr Franks did their joke but my father laughed afterwards, too loudly.

The next Saturday I went to go find him in the kitchen at ten o'clock and he wasn't there. I looked through the window and saw him in the yard, raking leaves. I waited a few minutes but it looked as if he was going to be a while over it and so in the end I went back to my room and read a book.

Over the next few years we'd occasionally find ourselves heading into town together on a Saturday, sometimes even covering much of the same ground, but we never really took that walk again. When you're a kid so much changes, all the time, that it's hard to tell what's important and what's not. It was a decade before I came to regret the loss of the walks we did not take, and to wonder why they had stopped.

In your twenties you think you know every damned thing — and are furthermore prone to grand gestures. So I went back home one weekend and tried to get my father to go on the walk again. At first he didn't appear to remember what I was talking about, but finally I got him out of the house.

At the pace of two adults, it only took ten minutes. Walter Azara's lot had become a discount carpet warehouse. At the drugstore — now a Starbucks, naturally — I gave a great big smile and asked for my coffee hot and wet. And both the barista and my dad looked at me as if I was retarded.

I called him, in the end. We spoke for ten minutes, and, as such conversations go, it was fine. Afterwards I walked out to the burger hut on Kelly, bought the last quarter-pounder out of Dodge, walked back with it. Then I watched more television until I fell asleep.

What would we do without TV? Live, I guess. And sometimes you're just not in the mood for it.

★　★　★

I woke with a start, as if someone had slapped me hard across the face. It took me a couple of seconds to realize a phone was ringing.

The sound rang out again, a harsh, jangling noise, and I realized it was the phone next to the bed. I levered myself up, groping for the handset. The room was dark but for a glow from the television screen and red numerals on the bedside clock which told me it was 1.15. It was raining hard on the roof, and the wind was up.

'Yes,' I croaked, into the phone. 'Who is this?'

'You're making a mistake,' said a woman's voice.

'Ellen?' I said, but I already knew it was not. This voice was harder, deep with cigarettes and command.

172

'Bad things have already happened,' it said. 'If you get involved in things that aren't your problem, it will get worse.'

'Who the fuck are you?'

'No one you know,' she said, and laughed, rich and throaty. Then the line went dead.

19

There was no sign of life in the motel office but I kept banging on the door anyway — crowding in close to get out of the rain. After a few minutes a light came on in the back and Marie came into view, wrapping a gown around herself. She opened the inside door and peered up at me through the screen.

'What is it?' Her voice was slurred, befuddled with sleep. Her hair was sticking up at the back. 'Isn't it late?'

'Someone just phoned my room,' I said. 'Is there any way of finding their number from your switchboard?'

'Well, no,' she said, confused. 'They've all got direct lines. From . . . ' she yawned massively, before continuing, 'when you could rent them by the month.'

'How would someone find out the number?'

'It's not hard,' she said. She had the weighed-down look of someone who'd assisted the onset of sleep with either a pill or a sizable glass of something with a kick to it. 'It's listed in the room. Don't you *know* who it was called you?'

'Sorry to disturb you,' I said.

She blinked owlishly, turned around, and trudged away into the gloom.

When I was back in my room I checked and, sure enough, found the direct line handwritten at the bottom of the framed list of things that you weren't allowed to do. That ought to have made things easier, but when I reached the operator I was told the call was from an unlisted number.

I'd been barely awake during the conversation, and found it difficult to recall the exact words, but I had no problem remembering what had been said. It struck me too that whoever had called had been confident I would be there. Since I'd been in Black Ridge I had not mentioned the name of where I was staying to anyone — not even Ellen. Also, though it was late, it was not so very late. I could have been elsewhere. Had the caller just assumed I was at home, or . . . ?

I went back outside. The wind had grown stronger, and was very cold. A plastic bag zigzagged suddenly across the parking lot, as if jerked through the air by an angry hand, momentarily wrapping itself around the solitary lamp before being sucked back into the trees. It felt as if there was no other living human within miles, and I was alone, just outside a town which was itself a thin veneer upon a sheet of tilted and jagged rock.

There were three other vehicles in the lot, but I could not feel the presence of any of these people. The middle of the night makes you feel like you're peeking backstage even if you've not just been woken by a strange phone call. Everything seemed too still, the objects of man standing out unnaturally against the surroundings.

Then, on the far side of the road, I thought I

175

saw something move. A paler patch, just in front of the trees, or a little way inside them.

I remained absolutely still, staring until my eyes started to sparkle, and saw nothing more. Just the plastic bag, perhaps, drifting back to earth?

I walked slowly across the road, feeling the skin on the back of my neck tighten. I headed over the mud on the other side, and into the bushes, feeling cold twigs scrape across my jeans. I trod on something that cracked, loud in the silence.

When I got into the trees I stopped.

There was a damp, rich odour, like water in which flowers have been left too long. Then I saw it.

I don't know what it was, but *something* moved, back in the trees, like a shadow.

It wasn't tall enough to be a man, at least not one standing upright. Some part of my brain threw up a flag of animal fear, but I don't think it was an animal I'd seen either.

Then I saw it again — it or something else — ten yards to the right. A paler movement this time, as if moonlight had fallen upon shifting mist. Maybe that's all it was.

'Who's there?'

I hadn't intended to speak, and my voice didn't sound great. It rebounded weakly against tree trunks and silence and fell to the ground.

A second later I heard a very distant shout, or a cry. It could have come from behind me, from back in town, but I didn't think so. It sounded like it came from deep in the woods.

I stood my ground for another couple of minutes, and saw and heard nothing more. So I slowly backed away, and out of the trees.

When I got back to the road I saw the plastic bag, lying forty yards away. It had come back down to earth, after all, but nowhere near where I'd first thought I'd seen something.

I went back inside my motel room and locked the door and lay awake on my back for what felt like a long time, tensed against the phone ringing again. It did not. The only sound was that of the wind and rain, and of branches once again scratching against the shingles on the back of my room.

★ ★ ★

As I was driving out of the lot early the following morning, my cell buzzed. When I saw who it was I pulled over and took the call.

'Tell me you're coming back today,' Becki said, without waiting for me to speak.

'I don't think so.'

'John, it would be *real* good if you did.'

'You're not that busy, surely? And Eduardo or one of the others can make the pizzas if — '

'The pizzas are not the problem,' she said, dismally. 'It's my *fucking* boyfriend.'

'What's he done now?'

'Fucked up. Is what he's done. He's *fucked up.*'

She sounded close to hysteria, something so hard to imagine in her that I started listening properly. 'I thought it got straightened out.'

177

'So did I. He just . . . went about it a really dumb way.'

'Went about what?'

'He subcontracted. Gave some of the stuff to some guys to try to shift it quicker.'

'Oh for God's sake. Did he *tell* you he was going to do this?'

'Yes. And I told him it was a dumb idea and he did it anyway. He's been . . . he's been dipping into the product a little too much. He's really not thinking straight and he's getting kind of hard to deal with.'

'And these guys stole it?'

'No. They are actual friends of ours, not assholes like Rick and Doug. *But* they tried to sell a couple wraps to the wrong guys outside a gay bar in Portland, who turned out to be fucking Street Crimes Unit, i.e. *cops*, and so they got the shit kicked out of them. And lost the drugs.'

'How much?'

'About four thousand worth. And the guys who lent the money are beginning to get, they're . . . it's not good, John. I really wish you were going to be back today. I'm getting scared. I'd go to Dad but he's always had a huge fucking downer on drugs. And on Kyle, too. There's a ninety-nine per cent chance that Dad would just turn him straight over to the cops.'

'Are the drug guys leaning on Kyle too?'

'Like, seriously. They called last night and Kyle's too freaked to tell them the stuff's actually *gone*, so instead he says he just needs another couple days to close it out. And now he's really panicking. He's . . . he's *losing* it, John. At three

178

o'clock this morning I was having to explain to him how he couldn't go make a complaint against the Street Crimes Unit for stealing his drugs. I swear to God.'

I didn't know what to tell her. It was too late for her to dump Kyle and walk fast in some other direction. Too late for me to state the obvious, which was that his suppliers would have a deal with the Portland police, and Becki and Kyle's friends got rolled because they were not part of this arrangement. Too late to explain to Kyle that his suppliers would have been circling him from day one, biding their time. You don't give a pile of drugs to some numb-nut in the hope of him selling it for you, unless you have a Plan B in place — and a Plan B that might, in fact, have been Plan A all along.

Then I realized Becki was being ominously silent, and my heart sank further. 'What else?' I said.

'Kyle always told me they didn't know where we live. But my neighbour told me she's seen a couple of black guys watching our place. Twice. They . . . they so *do* know where we live.'

'You know for sure it was them?'

'Who the fuck else? What am I going to *do*, John?'

'Text me your bank account details.'

'What?'

'Do it now. I'll talk to you later.'

'I don't understand.'

'Just do it, Becki.'

I closed the phone and drove out onto the road.

Probably I could have gotten rid of her more gracefully, but I wanted to see whether I had got something right.

There was only one person in whose problems I could be said to be getting involved (bar Becki, of course), and that was Ellen. Yesterday I'd met with her and we'd spoken for nearly an hour. If someone actually was spying on her in the way she claimed, that meeting could have provided enough provocation for the Robertson dynasty to get involved. It would not have been hard for that person to follow me to where I was staying, nor to determine the direct line of my room.

Cory had a sister.

I thought it was probably Brooke Robertson who had left the original message on my cell phone, and then called the motel room in the middle of the night.

I was going to go find if this was true, and explain to her — and anyone else who needed to hear it — that threatening me was not a good idea.

★ ★ ★

On a section of road three miles short of the turn, I ran into traffic. At first it was light but after half a mile it slowed to a crawl, and then a standstill for ten minutes.

I used the time to make a phone call, but after that quickly started to get frustrated, and was considering trying to U-turn and find some other way around when the traffic started to move again for no apparent reason. I didn't

180

notice a flashing light behind me until the approaching police motorcycle banged his horn at me to get out of the way. I pulled as far to the right as I could to let him pass — hampered by the wall of rock only a couple of feet away — and suddenly realized why the cop was trying to get by. Moments later I passed the cause of the snarl-up, and I nearly rammed into the car in front of me.

I saw a sports car twisted against the side of the road, and the body of Ellen Robertson being cut from it.

20

They took her to the county hospital, Hope Memorial. I knew it well, having once fretted in a room there while Scott had stitches put in a cut just below his knee, courtesy of a rogue nail sticking up out of the jetty over the lake — an event which had found me that evening crawling the entire length of said jetty on my own hands and knees, with a hammer, making damned sure it wasn't going to happen again. I remembered sitting in the waiting room with a folded cloth held tightly against Scott's leg, listening to my pale son describing how he'd stared down into the cut immediately after feeling the sensation of nail carving through flesh, seen it 'empty', and then watched as blood flooded in from the surrounding tissue to fill the gash until it dripped out onto the jetty. I remember smiling and nodding reassuringly while feeling absolutely certain I was going to throw up — in a way I never had when confronted with far, far worse things while in uniform.

I established that's where Ellen was headed by shouting the question out of the car window to the paramedics, and hoped it was a sign that — despite the blood that had covered most of her face and sweater — she hadn't cracked her head or spine or too obviously mashed up her insides.

The traffic was messed up again on the other side of the accident, and it took me a while to find a way of cutting back around the far side of Cle Elum and then taking the back route past the top end of Black Ridge — passing not far from Bill Raines's house, which made me feel guilty. I checked at the desk in the hospital when I eventually got there, describing myself as a friend, and learned she was being patched up. That was the term used, which reassured me.

I retreated to the parking lot to wait, and was leaning against the hood of my rental when I saw a large car come in from the other end. It parked on the right and both doors opened at once.

Cory Robertson got out of the passenger side. A woman of about his height and not-dissimilar age, wearing a smart black trouser suit, got out of the other. They walked off toward the main doors virtually in step.

I decided I'd go check on Ellen's progress again.

★ ★ ★

When I came out of the elevator on the second floor I saw Cory in imperious discussion with the nurse, presumably having been told the same as me, which was that visitors were not welcome, and unlikely to be for an hour or more.

I hung back to watch, admiring the steely implacability of the woman behind the desk. If our country is ever in danger of invasion, all we need do is man the coastline with medical receptionists, and no one could ever pass. When Cory finally turned and walked away, exasperated, I decided I might as well kill two birds with one stone.

I stepped out of the corridor, giving them plenty of time to see my approach. The woman paid no attention. Cory Robertson glanced away, then quickly back again.

'What are *you* doing here?'

'Visiting a friend,' I said. 'How about you?'

'I thought . . . you were just passing through.'

'Circumstances change.'

I turned to the woman. Though I'd never seen her before their car pulled into the lot outside, the family resemblance was marked. While Cory's face had already started to sag, however, this woman's remained sharp, her body lean with the form that comes from spending a good deal of time on the tennis court you own and swimming in your own pool. There was a tiny key on a thin gold chain around her neck.

'Hi,' I said, holding out my hand. 'I'm John Henderson. But you know that, of course.'

She didn't shake, or make the slightest movement toward doing so. She merely looked at me with what appeared to be mild amusement.

Cory looked confused. 'You said your name was Ted something.'

'I lied.'

'So who the hell *are* you?'

'Aren't you two comparing notes? Your sister seemed to know exactly who I was when she called my motel room in the middle of the night.'

I saw the penny drop.

'You entered our house under false pretences, sir,' Cory said, sounding about three times his age.

184

'Guilty. And you said the other house on your property was empty, whereas the 'tenant' was there all the time.'

'And why would you care?'

A husky voice said: 'Because he's screwing her, of course.'

I stared at Brooke. 'Excuse me?'

She smiled with what appeared to be genuine warmth. 'Well, it's been a few months, Cory. I'm sure our resident Eastern European fuck-bunny must be needing her holes plugged again by now.'

I was incapable of responding to this.

Brooke tilted her head on one side. 'Tell me, Mr Henderson. Does the fact she's a murderess add a certain something? Does it impart a special *frisson?*'

'Not here,' Cory told her, mildly. 'Evidently it will be some time before we can pay a visit on our poor friend. I suggest we come back later.'

'Good idea, little bro,' his sister said. 'I'm sure we'll meet again,' she added, to me, and winked. 'I'll look forward to it, handsome.'

And then the two of them walked away.

★   ★   ★

Forty minutes later a harassed-looking doctor came out to say I could visit Ellen briefly. I was directed to a side room where she lay propped up in bed, staring out of the window at the clouds gathering outside. After I'd stood in the centre of the room for perhaps a minute, she turned her head.

185

'Are they here?'

'No,' I said. 'Assuming you mean Cory and Brooke. They were, but they left.'

'You met her?'

'I guess,' I said. 'We had an encounter, certainly.'

I walked over to the bed. The side of her face was extensively bandaged, heavy bruising already creeping out from underneath it. 'Are you okay?'

She shrugged.

'What's the damage?'

'Twenty stitches.'

'I saw the car. I'm amazed it wasn't a lot worse.'

'Lucky me.'

'You don't seem surprised that I'm here.'

'The nurse told me a man was waiting. Didn't sound like Cory. There's no one else it could be.'

'Were you trying to do something this morning?'

She glanced down at her hands. 'No,' she said. I wasn't sure I believed her. 'Though maybe I should have been. Maybe it would just be quicker that way.'

'Ellen, what's going on?'

'I told you. I tried to.'

I went around the bed to the window side and sat down in the chair.

'Tell me again,' I said.

★ ★ ★

It had started, she said, the day after the funeral. Until then the Robertsons had appeared to treat

186

her with compassion, as if she were one of them. Of course they hadn't been aware until that point that their father's will stipulated Ellen be allowed to remain on the property for as long as she wanted. Once that wish had become known, things changed.

At first, Brooke and Cory had simply stopped talking to her, or registering her existence. If they passed her in the grounds, or on the streets of Black Ridge, they behaved as if she wasn't there — and it was this that had caused Ellen to start spending time in other places, like Sheffer, where she had eventually overheard the conversation relating to Scott's death. The maid who'd previously cleaned Ellen's house stopped doing so. The Wi-Fi, which had extended across the property, stopped working, suddenly requiring a password that Ellen did not know — but then, twenty-four hours later, worked without one again; around the time she began to suspect that Cory (whose business concerns included IT installations in local firms) was in a position to spy on her communications with the outside world. If Ellen tried to phone the Robertsons, the call was not answered. When she knocked on the door of the house, apparently no one was ever in.

When it became clear that a freeze-out was not going to be enough to dislodge her, matters began to escalate. Mail stopped arriving at her house. There had never been much, but her mother wrote once in a while, and these letters stopped arriving — along with the bills and mail-order catalogues that make you feel connected to the world. After trouble with a credit card company over non-payment of a bill that had never arrived, she had to switch to paying everything online.

'I know it doesn't sound like a big deal,' Ellen said.

But I could imagine. The trivial supports us. You think you're withstanding the crisis and then one morning you discover there's no bread in the kitchen or you don't like your shoes and next thing you're smashing your forehead against the wall and crying as if you'll never stop.

Meanwhile, other things started to happen.

There would be knocks on her door in the middle of the night. The first few times, she went down — to find no one there. By the fifth or sixth occasion she began to find this ridiculous, and stopped going down — until she noticed one morning that things seemed to be missing from the downstairs rooms, or at least to have been moved, as if whoever had knocked and received no answer had then used a key to enter the premises. The missing objects weren't even things you might believe they would wish to regain possession of, or not always. A couple of minor heirlooms went, certainly, but also a side table that Ellen had bought for five bucks at a yard sale, and a battered saucepan, and finally all of the soaps from the main bathroom — which was on the same level as the bedroom in which Ellen slept.

So she started getting up again when she heard the knocks, and running downstairs, shouting furiously at whichever Robertson must

be playing this stupid game.

But still they were never there, and still things continued to disappear.

One night Ellen tested it. She watched television until eleven, and then switched the TV off — along with all of the house lights. She didn't go to bed, however, but sat on the floor in the hallway, wrapped in a blanket, and waited. She kept watch throughout the night, using coffees and cigarettes and magazines.

At nearly two a.m., there was a sudden banging on the door — terrifyingly loud, with no warning and coming from nowhere. She didn't answer it. She stayed crouched on the floor, a kitchen knife ready in her hand, waiting for it to be unlocked and opened.

It was not, however, and she stayed that way until finally it began to get light again outside.

She trudged upstairs just after seven, feeling obscurely triumphant, as if she had managed to turn the tide in her direction.

Her toothbrush was missing, however, and though she spent two hours turning the house upside down, it never turned up.

You can always buy a new toothbrush, and she did. But when she locked the door of her house that night she no longer felt the place was hers, or that she lived there alone. The fact that all windows and other points of access were secured only made the feeling more acute.

The knocks on the front door continued. After a time sounds began to come from the window of her bedroom, too. And from inside her closet, and underneath the bed, or so she thought.

189

Never loud enough to be provably more than the shifting of fittings or floorboards in response to fluctuations in temperature — which the house seemed increasingly prone to — but enough to keep her awake night after night. Milk bought from the market in the afternoon seemed to turn brackish and sour by mid-evening — unless it was the water that was at fault, or the new brand of coffee she drank in order that every cup not remind her of the specific brew that she and Gerry had always favoured.

Then had come the night when, just before going to bed, she had momentarily lifted one of the bedroom blinds, which she now kept permanently drawn, and seen a large black bird hanging over the pond.

It had seemed to hover in place, unmoved by the strong winds swirling down and around, whistling through the trees. It was gone, but then she heard the sound of something moving away into the trees. Something larger.

Ellen had yanked the blinds shut, and spent the night perched on the end of her bed. That's when, according to her, she knew.

'Knew what?' I asked.

'It was a *strige*,' she whispered, not sounding like she was from Boston at all.

'A *what?*'

She turned to stare out of the window.

★   ★   ★

The thing about grief is that there is no telling what it will do to you. It comes from so deep a

190

well that it is capable of bending reality — or, at least, of mangling how the afflicted perceive the world. I had felt or heard or seen things that I knew full well I could not have done. A face glimpsed in the street or playground, a happy shout from two streets away that sounds so familiar you cannot believe it might have come from a stranger — until you run desperately to see, and find that it has issued from a child who looks nothing like yours. Death opens a wound that is so raw that you may find yourself jamming the squarest of pegs into the roundest of holes, attempting to heal the breach in a universe that now feels horrific and broken.

I had heard Scott's shout. I had seen the face of my mother, who had been dead for ten years. But, of course, I actually had heard or seen neither.

Now was not the time to tell Ellen this. She would work it out soon enough, I hoped, and I know from experience that you will never alter someone's belief system by direct confrontation with contrary evidence. Faith is the opposite of proof.

So I asked her a question instead. 'Brooke called you a murderer,' I said. 'Why would she say that?'

'She says I hurt their father. That he died because of me. That's why they're punishing me.'

'The coroner's report was black and white. A heart attack, like you said.'

'How do you know that?'

'I get around. So why are they harassing you?'

'They don't believe it.'

191

'How do you know, if they're not talking to you?'

'Because three weeks ago, she *did*. I was on Kelly Street, I was . . . I was thinking of going into that bar, the Mountain View. Just to be somewhere, you know, to have someone to talk to. But then suddenly Brooke's there in front of me, and she just *lost* it.'

'How?'

'She started shouting at me in front of the other people — people I used to know, who used to talk to me when Gerry was alive, and who just walked around us as if it wasn't happening. How I'd pay for what I'd done. And since then everything has felt even worse. I can't think straight. Everything's getting louder, all the time.'

'Ellen, there's nothing *left* for you here. So why don't you leave? Start again somewhere else.'

'Like you did? After what happened to your son?'

I didn't say anything.

'Did that work? You ran away. What did *you* find? You can't just leave. If you try, it just comes with you. It comes with you inside.'

'This 'strige', this is something from home? A Romanian thing?'

She nodded irritably.

'So how could it be here? In America?'

She looked at me as if I was very stupid indeed. 'In Romania we also have things called *abore*,' she said. 'And *munte*, and also *noapte*. It's very strange, but it turns out you have them here too.'

'And what are they?'

'Trees. Mountains. And night.'

I was losing patience. 'Your English is very good, Ellen. So what would we call a strige here? The nearest equivalent?'

She cocked her head and looked straight back at me. 'A witch. Okay?'

I breathed out heavily and leaned back in the chair, considered again telling her about faces glimpsed and sounds heard, but knew it wouldn't work. In her position my grip on reality might be tenuous too — assuming I would be sober enough to have views on anything at all.

'You think I'm crazy, yes?'

'No,' I said. 'I think it's a great shame that Gerry Robertson should die so soon after finding a woman who loved him as much as you did. And still do.'

'You think that's all this is? Everything I've told you?'

'I'm going now,' I said, standing. 'But I've got to ask one thing. If what you think is happening is real, what bearing does it have on me, or on Scott? Why would anyone have wanted to harm me?'

'I don't know,' she said. 'Unless you're being punished too.'

'What for?'

She smiled coldly. 'That's for you to know, right? So, what did *you* do?'

I told her to get some rest, and walked out of the room. When I was halfway down the corridor I heard her shout after me.

'*What did you do?*'

21

I told the nurse at the station that Ms Robertson had requested no further visitors be admitted without checking with her first. The woman agreed with the confidence of one who knew this was a function she could perform, and take satisfaction in.

On my way to the elevator I passed a door that was half open, and glimpsed a girl sitting on the edge of a bed. It was the blue-haired waitress from The Write Sisters. Her face was wet, and she was staring down at the floor. I hesitated, decided it was none of my business. Then took a step toward the door anyway.

'Are you okay?'

Either she didn't hear me or agreed that her problems were not my concern.

Cory and Brooke's car was gone from the parking lot. I was tempted to drive straight to their house to continue our conversation. I knew it wasn't a good idea, however, and once in a while that's enough to stop me doing something.

There was a police car sitting in the same row as mine, and as I drew closer I saw that Deputy Greene, the cop I'd encountered behind the desk at the department in Black Ridge, was sitting inside. He wound down his window.

'What are you doing here, sir?'

'Visiting a friend.'

'I don't think the sheriff would appreciate you

interfering in other people's business.'

I walked over to his car. 'Is that message from you, or from him?'

'Does that matter?' He looked up at me, his calm, bland eyes striking against the pale fleshiness of his face. 'I'd just listen, is all.'

He started up his car, and drove slowly out of the lot, probably not realizing that I'd dismissed him from my mind before he even made it to the road.

When I turned my phone back on I saw I had voice mail. I listened to it, forced into a smile by a combination of gratitude, bewilderment and foul language I would have believed impossible within the constraints of the English language.

I sent an SMS message in return, saying:

We'll talk repayment later. Meantime, make sure it gets to whom it's supposed to. TODAY. And keep your boyfriend on a tight fucking leash until I get back.

I sent it to Becki's cell phone, then got in the car and headed back toward Black Ridge. As I turned out of the lot onto the main road I passed a car I recognized, heading into the hospital lot — the dark green SUV which had pulled up alongside me on my first day in town, just before I visited my old house. The same man was inside.

My mind, however, was elsewhere.

It was mid-afternoon by then and I realized I was hungry. I thought I was, anyhow, though when I started looking for somewhere to eat I

195

found none held any appeal. In the end I came to rest in the street opposite the motel in which I had spent several weeks holed up, trying to drink my way through pain and unhappiness. After two nights' bad sleep my eyes and brain felt desiccated, and for half an hour I did nothing but sit.

People meanwhile came and went from the motel. Others walked past on the street. Cars went by, and clouds moved overhead. It rained for a little while, stopped, and then started again. Slowly it began to get colder. I finally realized that the feeling in my guts was the beginnings of low-level panic. Over what, I wasn't sure. I found myself staring at the door to Room 4 of the motel, and after a time it almost felt as if I was trapped inside, that the world outside that room had become a vast room in itself, one from which I might not find an escape. I knew what this feeling meant, though it had been a long time since I had felt overwhelmed by it. I knew what it signified when your body begins to feel it is locked inside a place where there are no doors, as if you are being buried alive. I knew also that the Mountain View Tavern was comfortable, and that they had a beer on draught that I liked.

Instead I drove to the coffee shop on Kelly and sat staring out of the window, trying to work out what there was to learn from what else she had told me, if anything. I was confident that Ellen's toothbrush was somewhere in her house, and that a distracted mind — she had been clinically distracted every time I'd met her — could lose track of how quickly she was getting through a bar of soap. The other objects would have been taken by the Robertsons, as she initially thought, or simply lost in the undertow of domestic life.

What she needed was counselling, to move away and start again. To find her own Marion Beach.

Instead she had Cory and Brooke, and that made me angry. I was beginning to see in her something of the person who — a similar length of time after someone he cared about had died — had battened himself into a motel room and made a decent attempt at driving at the wall. Despite her denial, I suspected the incident on the pass this morning had not been wholly accidental, and that Ellen was close to walking off the edge of her own cliff. If someone had been around to push *me* at the time, it was likely I wouldn't still be alive.

There was a quiet knocking sound, and I looked up to see Kristina standing outside the coffee shop, tapping on the window. Though just as black and semi-kempt, her hair looked longer, inexplicably.

She winked, waved hello and goodbye in one motion, and then turned to walk across the road toward where she worked. I made my coffee last as long as I could, but eventually I paid for it, went outside, and headed in the same direction.

★ ★ ★

The bar was pretty crowded and I was served by some other guy. It was half an hour before

197

Kristina swung by my seat at the window to clean up my ashtray. She made a face as she dumped the butts into the can she was carrying.

'You don't smoke?'

She shook her head.

'Funny. You look like a smoker. And I mean that as a compliment.'

'Used to,' she said. 'When I lived here before. I gave it up when I left. With other things.'

'Drugs? Alcohol? Polite conversation?'

'All of the above. I heard about Ellen. She okay?'

'Banged up some. Though why would you be assuming I'd know?'

'I just heard you were kind of close, that's all. I didn't — '

'But you saw us in here together the other night,' I persisted. 'Did we *look* like an item?'

'Not really.'

'Yet forty-eight hours later we're picking out china and booking a string quartet?'

'Look, whatever, okay? It's really none of my business. You want another beer, or what?'

I said I did, and stared out of the window until she returned with it. She was set to leave straight away, but I held up my hand.

'I'm sorry,' I said. 'But I would like to know why you think there's something going on.'

'I don't, necessarily,' she said. 'And I honestly don't give a crap. I mean, really, truly. But I was having extensions done across the road this afternoon and I heard someone saying how it was nice that Ellen was turning the corner. Finding someone new to hang with, that kind of

198

thing. Even though it's only been four months, blah-blah-blah.'

I kept my voice level. 'Was it Brooke Robertson?'

'I don't want to get involved. It's a small town, people talk. Other people listen. That's all.'

'By all means listen to what that woman says,' I told her. 'But don't believe it. I think there's something wrong with her.'

'Could be, could be. But I'm wondering if the whole you-and-me-talking thing is really working out. Ratings are mixed.'

'I'm sorry about before. Again.'

'Copy that. But I'm going to leave now. Find a customer with more polished social skills.'

'Shouldn't be hard, even in here.' I waited until she'd started to turn, and added, 'You actually *pay* someone to make your hair look that way?'

She stuck her tongue out at me and walked off.

★ ★ ★

Four beers later I had an idea — which is seldom a good way to start a sentence — and stepped outside the bar to make a call. I got the number from directory assistance and asked to be put through.

'Pierce,' said a voice, after a short interval.

'It's John Henderson.'

'You in a bar?'

'No, outside one. You've got good hearing.'

'Yes, I do. I talked to Corliss, if that's why

you're calling. He won't do it again. He's also been asked to instruct his sister to be more discreet.'

'Thank you. But that's not it. I wanted to ask you a favour.'

'Uh-huh.'

'The woman I told you about — Gerry Robertson's ex-wife? She was involved in an accident today.'

'I heard.'

'I visited her in the hospital. It sounds like Brooke and Cory Robertson are making life tough for her. I wondered whether someone in local law enforcement might have a conversation with them, expressing a hope that a bereaved woman is getting the support she needs at this time.'

'I'm not sure that's the kind of thing that falls within our remit,' Pierce said. 'Sorry.'

'Me too. Would it be easier if the Robertsons weren't such a big deal around here?'

'I don't like the implications of that question.'

'Then I apologize. And I guess I'll have that conversation with them instead.'

'I don't think that would be wise.'

'A polite discussion between responsible adults wouldn't be any of your business, thankfully.'

'Mr Henderson . . . ' he sighed. 'Look, I spoke with someone who witnessed the accident this morning. He was talking it up all over Harry's, and I asked him to keep it down.'

'People have a real impulse to share information around here,' I said. 'Almost a compulsion.'

'That's because it's a real place. You want

stony silence and nobody-gives-a-shit, go over the mountains. This old guy — and I've known him for a long time, he was a friend of my father and he's not a person prone to exaggeration — was headed in the opposite direction and saw the whole thing. He said Ellen's car was veering erratically as it came up the hill, so much so that he slowed and pulled over as far as he could. The car kept coming, not fast but all over the place, and he saw Ms Robertson inside, gripping the wheel, shaking her head back and forth. Like she was on drugs, he said.'

'I'm sure the admitting ER doctor has a toxicology report that you should have no problem getting — '

'Jesus, I know that,' Pierce said testily. 'I made the call, and she was clean. Chemically. But mentally? Does that sound normal to you? Driving a wet mountain road throwing your head all over the place?'

'No,' I admitted.

'Then she suddenly stared straight ahead, and the car went off the road and into the mountainside.'

I didn't say anything. Through the window of the bar I saw Kristina hove in view, register I was absent but still had beer in my glass, and wander off again.

'So yes, could be your friend needs a little help — '

'She's not my 'friend', for the love of God. That's something *else* that — '

He overrode me. '*But* I don't think the Robertsons are her real problem, and anyone

201

who tried to take it up with them would be causing a nuisance that *would* come under my jurisdiction. As a misdemeanour. You understand what I'm saying?'

'Loud and clear.'

'Excellent. Good night, and safe flight home.'

I snapped the phone shut and shoved it into my pocket. I stayed where I was for a few minutes, realizing it was mid-evening and cold and I still hadn't eaten that day.

I went back inside and ordered another beer, though the fire in my head had gone out. I drank it slowly, as the bar started to empty, sitting at the counter and knocking it back and forth with Kristina.

Miraculously, we managed not to argue about anything.

22

I left the car on Kelly and made my way back to the motel on foot. I would have done this wherever I was, but as I walked through the town I recognized I was also doing it for another reason. I wondered whether someone might have observed me in the bar, counted the beers, and when they saw me get in a car, make a call to Pierce or one of his deputies. Who would have done that? I had no idea. Neither Robertson had been propping up the counter alongside me, keeping a tally, waiting for me to go over the limit. I didn't think the bar staff were in their thrall either; certainly not Kristina, who didn't give the impression of being easy to boss around. The whole idea was dumb, and it annoyed me to be giving head space to it. I walked all the same.

The streets were quiet and, though it was only ten o'clock, pretty much every dwelling I passed was dark enough to seem like it housed the dead. It wasn't raining, for once, and the sky was clear and blue-black, but the wind was beginning to pick up.

When I opened the door to my motel room I found something had been pushed underneath. A thin brown package.

I picked it up, turning to look back across the lot. I'd seen no one on the way in, but would there really be no one on hand, to check I'd received this message, whatever it turned out to be?

I went inside and opened the envelope. It contained a single sheet of paper, two-thirds covered with type, a low-quality photograph reproduced at the bottom. The text concerned the murder in Berlin in October 1995 of a man called Peter Ridenhauer, found dead in his apartment from multiple stab wounds. Ridenhauer had been under long-term investigation for sex trafficking: enticing or coercing women with promises of reputable and highly paid work in upmarket European countries, then taking possession of their passports before forcing the girls to become involved in prostitution — usually easing the transition by causing them to be addicted to heroin, which he supplied. Some eventually limped home years later, many overdosed or disappeared; all could be expected to have to endure twelve or more clients a day, many of whom had tastes that could not be slaked in the company of more voluntary working girls. The primary suspect in Ridenhauer's death — a girl formerly under his control, glimpsed entering his apartment with him on the evening of the murder — disappeared from Germany very soon afterward, and though the case remained open it didn't seem anyone was in a great hurry to solve it.

The suspect's name was Ilena Zaituc. The attached photograph showed, without much doubt, a younger version of the woman I'd visited in the hospital that morning.

My hands were trembling as I opened the

door and walked back out into the parking lot. I stood in the middle and held the piece of paper up.

'Mistake,' I said, getting my lighter out.

I didn't shout, but I said it loud and clear, and though my voice felt guttural in my throat I knew the sound would carry. 'If this is supposed to make me think worse of her, it doesn't.'

I held the lighter up to the document, and set fire to it. When it had caught, I let go, and the wind took it, flipping it away and up into the air. The flame dodged and jerked like some tiny, fierce spirit.

I thought I heard a noise then, back in the trees on the other side of the road. It could have been a laugh, or a bird, or perhaps just a branch cracking in the gathering wind. I took a few paces in its direction, and held my arms out wide and to my side.

'Be my guest,' I said, and my voice did not sound like my own. But nothing happened.

★   ★   ★

I considered calling Pierce but knew no good would come of it. I thought about going to pay a visit to the Robertsons, but knew that now — full of alcohol — was not the time. Who knows how long they'd been saving this information about Ellen, without doing the obvious thing. If they'd simply wanted to be rid of her, they could have turned her in. Therefore they wanted something else. This wasn't about the shortest route to a desired conclusion. Ellen was right. This was about punishment, delivered slowly, and only when they considered the time was right. Harassment, in other words. Making the most of discomfort. Extracting the full value from pulling out the pins of someone's life, one by one. I felt they should be dealt with in the same way.

But then, when I realized what I was thinking, I tried to turn from the idea as you would try to turn from reaching for that next drink, the one you know will jam the cellar door so wide you'll have all the excuse you need to fall right in. So instead I sat in the motel room in the dark, working through pot after pot of bad coffee, past the point where I hoped I would not be too hungover the next day, until I eventually fell asleep.

★ ★ ★

And woke again, three or four hours later.

The room was pitch black. My head was thick and throbbing with caffeine and waning alcohol, and I felt rusty with dehydration. I seemed stuck to the chair, turned to wood or stone, unable to move.

Eventually I dragged myself to the bed but there was too much noise to get back to sleep. The wind was howling outside now, the roof drumming with rain. These sounds were at least constant, however, something that might in time slip below the threshold of awareness. What I could not ignore was the branches once again clacking and scraping against the back of the motel.

I got up and stumbled to the door. When I unlocked it and turned the handle, the wind blew it back in at me, wrenching my wrist hard enough to make me cry out.

I went outside and made my way down to the end of the block, then around the corner, keeping under the eave as much as possible, but still getting quickly soaked. I made the turn around the back of the hotel, knowing the irrational fury I was feeling had little to do with windblown branches, but there was nothing else I could take it out on right now — that there were some motherfucking twigs that had scratched their last tonight.

I hunched my way along until I was close to where the back of my room should be. I was only going to tackle that stretch. Other residents could do their own brute-force horticulture. But when I raised my head, I stopped.

I was standing with one foot braced on the concrete base that ran the length of the building, the other on the muddy grass. Ahead of me, on my left, was the run of the back of the motel block. To the right was the beginnings of the woods.

In between was a distance of about five feet.

I stood staring at this until I was absolutely sure I was seeing what I thought I was. Though the wind *was* whipping them back and forth, and was at least as strong as it had been at any time since I'd been in Black Ridge, branches from these trees could not have been scraping against the back of my room. They couldn't reach.

Not tonight, nor on any other night.

And yet, I saw as I bent closer, *something* had evidently made contact with the shingle cladding. There were marks in the wood there. Evidently fresh, from the last few days, as the inner wood they had revealed remained bright and clean. Scratch marks. Some short, others a foot or so long and going every which way. There was no actual shape to them that I could make out, but they reminded me of the arrangement of twigs and branches I'd seen on the forest floor the day before.

I turned and looked into the woods. With only the dim lights from the top of the motel roof shining on them, you couldn't see past the first ranks of trees. This turned the forest into something like a black mirror, into which it seemed all too possible you might be able to step.

Then I heard the sound of a phone ringing through the motel wall. The phone in my room.

I hesitated, but turned from the forest and hurried back around to the front side of the motel, slipping and nearly falling in the puddles. The phone stopped ringing just as I got back into my room.

It rang again, however, two minutes later. I grabbed the handset.

'Brooke,' I said, thickly. 'You don't want to do this.'

But there was no one there. The phone rang again at hourly intervals throughout the night, and there was no one there then either, just a fault on the line that sounded like someone shouting short words from a very long distance.

23

Sixty-two times. Sixty-three.

Sixty-four.

Standing in the freezing hallway, wearing only panties and a bra. Shivering, her feet moving back and forward in little steps, Carol knew exactly where she'd seen movement like this before. In a zoo, in the long-ago late 1970s, a poor zoo, a Guantanamo for mammals. A lone bear, its coat matted, in a cage that was too small and didn't look as though it had been cleaned in a long, long while.

On the way out, her dad had complained. He'd given the people at the gate merry hell. He might even have written a letter when they'd got home — he had said he would, and he generally carried through. But it was too late by then. Carol had already seen the bear, up on its hind legs, hanging on to the rusted chain-link fence, its feet moving back and forth in small, old-person shuffles, back and forward, forward and back. A bear lost in internal darkness, a bear having an endless, slow-motion panic attack.

She had stared at it, gripping her father's hand, knowing she was seeing something wrong, that animals shouldn't look like that.

No animal.

Not even her.

Nearly thirty years later, but feeling no older, she pushed herself back from the door lock.

209

Again. It was just before two in the morning. She had been there an hour and a half.

Because it wasn't even the first set of sixty-four.

★   ★   ★

There had been nothing since the man in the library. No more calls. No more notes. She didn't think that meant they had gone away. She had not called the police. A non-threatening phone call and a photo she could have taken herself would add up to squat in their eyes, and generate nothing but scorn or, even worse, pity. You'd think a single parent would evoke concern as a first reaction, but that's not the way it goes. Especially not a woman.

Why would a woman in her thirties be living alone in the first place, unless there was something wrong with her? Unless she'd proven too difficult and strange for a man to live with?

The letters on the chalk board wouldn't have made any difference, even if she hadn't furiously scrubbed them off — before realizing that was an unbelievably dumb thing to do.

As soon as she had something concrete then *of course* she'd go to the cops. But for now it was a case of hanging tough. Not panicking. Holding the chaos at bay, as she had for nearly three years with no help from anyone. Staying put and asking nothing of anyone other than herself. Sometimes help from others comes at too high a cost.

She of all people knew that.

She forced herself to walk backwards down the hallway. She was only able to do this by promising the gods she wasn't pretending to believe the door was actually locked, just taking time out before restarting the process. Beginning again, with renewed dedication and rigor. It seemed like the light bulb in the ceiling was flickering as she passed beneath it, but that was just tiredness. Just the headache that stretched from ear to ear. Just . . .

. . . oh, who was she *kidding?*

The fucking bulb was flickering.

Even Tyler had noticed it, on the way to bed, hours before. She'd told him it just meant the bulb was about to blow, which caused some confusion as he was only familiar with the concept of blowing in relation to birthday candles. So their bedtime story was all about a lucky light bulb called Leroy, who lived in a *lovely* house with a mummy and her *little* boy, whose birthday it was tonight and so he was getting ready to blow out all the candles on his cake, and tra-la-la.

Tyler was sleeping now, but judging by the last couple of nights he'd wake up sooner rather than later. Her normally sound sleeper was suddenly all over the place again. And what could *that* mean, if not . . .

The bulb was flickering. The drawers in the kitchen felt stiff, and a little too hard to pull out. It was darker under the chairs than it should be.

Were these things true anywhere except in her own mind? She'd never been sure. Except for the

211

bulb. That *had* to be real, unless Tyler was only in her mind too, and that was a road she wasn't going down, not now, not tonight, not ever.

Of course, it could be that the bulb really *was* just about to give up the ghost. Could be.

But that didn't make any difference. The last days had been like falling into a shaft whose infinite depth — the better for falling down, my dear — did not negate the certain knowledge of sharpened stakes at the bottom. The only way to stop yourself toppling is to dig yourself in. Anyway, anyhow.

She stood in the kitchen and knew her feet were still moving but didn't know how to stop them. Movement was now their natural state, as a heart knew nothing but how to beat. Unless you stopped it, of course, but all the knives in the kitchen had been wrapped tightly in a towel and stowed way in back of the yard, as of yesterday afternoon. There had been a time when . . . but that time wasn't now. She'd got through that period and it wasn't her fault it was happening again. She'd done everything she could, built her walls, and then John had fucked things up. By calling her? Or merely by going there, going back?

She didn't know. Rationally, she believed the former. You could sit and chew that one over with a therapist (assuming you could afford one) and he'd nod sagely and make notes, and say he could see how it could have redirected her attention to a bottomless grief she'd never expunged, and charge you a hundred bucks, happy he'd been of service.

But she knew what *she* believed. What her faith told her. After all, hadn't this all started *before* John called? She thought it had, that things had stopped being where she expected them to be in the supermarket, that she had woken feeling as if she had been half smothered in the night . . . *before* he called. When he was already up there, but she hadn't even known about it.

Because of course, there had been the *other* phone call, from a woman Carol had known since she was small. She could blame John all she liked, but that game was getting old. She could hate him for what happened then, but not for what was happening now.

Either way, it had to stop.

It had to stop for good and all. No running, no hiding, and certainly no doing what other people wanted her to do. In the meantime, the lock could go fuck itself. If she stayed up all night, then it didn't have to be locked, did it?

Ha.

★ ★ ★

Ten minutes later, armed with a warm robe and a large pot of strong coffee, she sat at the kitchen table with a big book of very difficult Sudoku puzzles. All she had to do was wait until the sunlight, look sane when Rona came to collect Tyler, and work out what to do next. Everything is easier when it's light. Rays of light are bars in the cage which protects us from what's outside. A little, anyway. Most of the time.

Anything else she had to do?

Oh yes — *not lose her mind*. That's right.

She was halfway through the third puzzle when she heard the soft sound of a window being broken at the back of the house.

24

The first thing I did next morning was go to the office. The owner was in place, behind the counter.

'Looks like you're a keeper,' she said.

'Excuse me?'

'Unless you're headed out today? I just meant you're staying longer than you thought.'

I was watching her face, and looked for — but did not find — signs that this observation was loaded.

'It's a nice town,' I said.

'It surely is.'

'You been here long?'

'All my life.'

I nodded, keen to get back to my real reason for being here. 'Your dog,' I said.

'Yes?'

'Where does he sleep? At night. Does he have a kennel?'

She laughed. 'Hell, no. I tried it, when he was a puppy. Used to howl like, well, I already said I was told he was half wolf. That's what he sounded like then, for sure.'

'So now?'

She jerked her head, indicating the area behind the office. 'Takes up three-quarters of my bed — on a good night. Why?'

'Thought I heard something around the back last night. Wondered if it could have been him.'

215

'Hmm,' she said. 'Well, can't think what that might have been. Years back, a bear, maybe. *Maybe*. But no one's seen one of those near town in a coon's age. I mean, like, forever.'

'Probably just the wind, I guess.'

'Most likely. Got up fierce as hell last night. Keep you awake?'

'Something did.'

★ ★ ★

The car wouldn't start.

I walked over to Kelly Street right after talking to Marie, with a simple goal — driving straight to the Robertson house — but when I got in the car and turned the key, nothing happened.

I got back out and stared at it furiously, which is about the sharpest tool in my car-fixing armoury. My father had known how to do that stuff but I'd failed to pick up any of those skills, and modern vehicles are in any event less responsive to being optimistically tackled with a monkey wrench. I did open the hood to see if there was any obvious sign of tampering, but saw nothing I could understand (like, say, a missing engine), and felt dumb for even looking.

In the end I stomped across to The Write Sisters, thinking I may as well be warm while I waited for someone to come fix the fucking car. A server I hadn't seen before was watching me as I walked in.

'Problem with your car?'

'Won't start.'

'Funny. Melanie had the same thing. Personally

216

I don't drive,' she added. 'It's bad for the planet.'

'Right. I keep forgetting. Though, given I live in Oregon, I guess I've got a little more carbon to burn this week, realistically.'

'But that's the thing,' she told me, earnestly. 'People shouldn't do all this moving around. We're meant to live as part of our environment — love it, nurture it, return to it. That's how we should live.'

'Oh yes?' I said, tightly. 'And what would happen then? How would it change things?'

'I don't know. I just think it's a good idea.'

'Americano,' I said. 'With milk.'

While she brought my drink into being — using, presumably, coffee beans from the plantation out back and milk from the cow hunkered upstairs — I talked to the rental company and eventually got the sense something might happen about my car at some point.

When the coffee arrived I looked up.

'Wait a second,' I said. 'You said someone had the same problem with their car? It wouldn't start?'

'Melanie. From the salon? She actually lives only two minutes away so she leaves her car on the street here virtually the entire time. She was here, first thing, supposed to go off and sort out a cake for her daughter's birthday, she's twelve in a couple days, unbelievably, but the thing wouldn't start. She's waiting for Brian Jackson to arrive, if you need someone to look at yours.'

'Brian being a mechanic?'

She nodded, looking disapproving.

'Can I have this to go?'

As she poured the coffee into a disposable cup I remembered something. 'The other girl who works here. Blue hair?'

'Jassie?'

'Is she okay?'

The girl looked at me quizzically.

'She didn't look so good last time I saw her.'

'Well, funny thing,' the girl admitted. 'I wasn't even supposed to be working this morning, but she didn't show up yet.'

'Maybe her car punked out on her too.'

'Yeah, right. Like she'd drive. She's a hardcore vegan.'

I smiled as if she had said something I could understand, took the cardboard cup and went back outside onto the street.

Fifteen minutes later a guy arrived in a white truck and parked close to the hair salon. He went in and came back out a minute later holding some keys.

I sat on the bench and watched the guy — Brian, I assumed — climb into a blue Ford and fiddle around for a while, then get back out and pop the hood. Meanwhile I worked through most of a granola bar from the café, which this morning tasted stale and bitter. The mechanic spent quite a while bent over the car's innards without provoking anything that sounded like a harbinger of successful internal combustion.

In the end I went over.

'Any idea what the problem is?'

'Not a clue.' He looked round, still bent over the engine. 'I know you?'

218

'Got a car on the other side of the street, won't start either.'

'One of those days. You got someone coming for it?'

'I do.'

'Huh.' He straightened, looking pained. 'Hope he has better luck. Maybe the immobilizer's blitzed or something. Guess I'm going to have to tow it back to the shop.'

He went back and climbed in the car to let the brake off. Stuck the key back in the ignition, and gave it a turn for the sake of it. The car started.

He switched it off, turned the key again. The engine fired back into life immediately.

He and I looked at each other. 'Huh,' he said, again.

I waited until he'd delivered the news that Melanie's vehicle seemed to be working once more, declined payment, and driven away in his truck. Then I walked over to my own car, unlocked the door, and got in. I put the key in the ignition and turned it. The car started.

'Huh,' I said.

★ ★ ★

It began three or four hundred yards from the turn-off. At first I didn't notice except to think that whichever local business sponsored the tidy-up of this stretch of mountain highway wasn't getting their PR dollars' worth. Once it grew from occasional scraps of paper to include a few widely spread items of clothing, I realized something in particular must have happened.

219

Perhaps a suitcase coming loose from a roof rack, spreading its cargo to the winds, unnoticed by the driver.

And then I saw a flash of purple, and pulled over.

I left the engine running as I walked across the road to what I'd seen caught in a strip of crimson dogwood on the other side. I knew what it was before I'd even picked it up, recognizing it from a couple of days before. The sweater was sodden, soaked by the overnight rains. There was something odd about the way it smelt, over and above the unattractive odour of wet wool. Something sweet. Further articles of clothing were dotted down the slope toward the creek far below, caught in the branches of trees.

As I drove the remainder of the distance I saw other objects, including two small, battered suitcases, but I no longer believed they or the rest of the debris had fallen from a car. No one would have packed a small wooden table in a suitcase, and yet one was strewn along the side of the road, smashed to matchwood, along with fragments of several ornaments and the remains of a framed wedding photograph.

I parked outside the gate and leant on the entry buzzer, hard. After a pause, the gates opened. I probably should have thought about the fact that no one tried to stop me entering, but I was angry, and I did not.

Brooke Robertson was standing outside the main house. She was dressed again in a black trouser suit, the legs flapping noisily in the wind.

'Good morning, Mr Henderson,' she said.

'What a pleasant surprise.'

'It may not stay that way.'

'How thrilling.'

Pieces of clothing lay strewn around the lawn, including a blouse I recognized from the first time I'd met Ellen, in the Mountain View. The door of her house was hanging open.

I turned back to the woman in front of me. 'What the hell is wrong with you?'

'I have no idea what you're talking about.'

'Really.'

She smiled. 'You look tired. Problems sleeping? I find a bout of moderately savage sex is the best solution. Doubtless you're familiar with that approach?'

'Not having someone call your motel room through the night would help.'

'I'm sure I have — '

' — no idea what I mean. You bet. You're kind of limited, aren't you, when it comes to understanding what other people say.'

'I don't listen much of the time. One so seldom hears anything of interest. Especially from men of your type. Action is your forte, I should have thought.'

She said this in a way I did not care for, and I took a step toward her, knowing and not caring that I was close to behaving in ways I should not.

'How about you concentrate just this once, Brooke, and — '

I heard someone call my name, and saw Brooke was looking calmly over my shoulder toward Ellen's house. I turned to see Cory Robertson walking across the lawn toward us.

221

Beside him was Sheriff Pierce, holding a pale blue shirt in one hand.

'Standing kind of close there,' the sheriff said to me when they reached us. 'Wouldn't like to think there was an altercation taking place. Especially after the conversation you and I had last night.'

'What the hell are you doing here?'

'My job.'

'Did Ellen call you?'

He looked puzzled. 'Well, no. Of course not.'

'Something strange occurred here last night,' Cory said. 'The sheriff is here to investigate.'

'Odd? Yeah. You let yourself into Ellen's house and trashed her belongings. Spread them half a mile down the road. Why? Do you think she deserves that?'

'That's not what happened,' Cory said.

I turned to Pierce. 'Are you really going to let these people get away with this?'

'I think you've got the wrong end of the stick,' he said. 'Not all the stuff you see belongs to Ellen.' He held up a man's striped business shirt.

'Not that it's any of your business,' Cory said, taking his shirt from the policeman, 'but my sister and I spent last night with friends in Yakima. When we returned this morning, the doors to both houses were open, and, well . . . '

He gestured around the lawn.

'Bullshit,' I said. The three of them looked at me like parents and a teacher who had all just witnessed inappropriate behaviour, and weren't sure whose responsibility it was to upbraid me for it.

'So who's supposed to have done this?' I said. 'Ellen? By mind control, from the hospital?'

'Much closer than that,' Brooke said.

I could almost feel her smile on the back of my neck, but didn't give her the satisfaction of turning.

'Ellen's not *in* the hospital any more,' Pierce said, after a pause. 'She checked herself out yesterday evening. Nobody knows where she is right now.'

'Unless, of course . . . you do,' Brooke murmured.

I stared at Pierce.

'The door to the house she has been living in was opened with a key,' he said. 'Cory and Brooke's place was forced.'

'A subterfuge the average eight-year-old could have dreamed up,' I said. 'And given what's happened here, shouldn't you care just a little bit about where Ellen Robertson is?'

He ignored me. 'I'll get this logged,' he told Cory. 'Anything else, you phone me.'

Cory nodded. He looked so calm, so magnanimous in his forgiveness of the regrettable behaviour of others, that I wanted to punch him in the face.

The sheriff evidently caught this. 'Does Mr Henderson have business here?'

'Not that I'm aware,' Cory said.

'Maybe you'd like to walk with me back down to the gate,' Pierce said, taking me lightly by the elbow.

'Yes,' Brooke added. 'Run along. We've tidying to do.'

223

I pulled my arm away from the policeman and started walking. When we reached the road I saw a police car was already there waiting for the sheriff, with Deputy Greene behind the wheel.

The gate swung shut behind us. Pierce and I hadn't spoken on the way down the drive, but before he got in the car, he turned to me.

'I'm not going to have a problem with you, am I?'

'That depends on whether you start doing any police work.'

He looked down the road. 'Mr Henderson, what happened to your son was a sad thing but it doesn't give you a free pass. Neither does the service you used to perform for your country.'

'Somebody thought I ought to see a piece of paper last night,' I said. 'You should hear about it too.'

'What are you talking about?'

'It related to a Romanian woman called Ilena, suspected in the murder of a sex trafficker in Europe ten years ago, her whereabouts currently unknown. It was pushed under my motel door. Then somebody called my room at hourly intervals throughout the night. You think either of those are things Ellen Robertson might do? If not, then she isn't the problem here.'

The sheriff looked away at the trees for a moment, then back at me. 'Remember what I said.'

He and his deputy spoke for a moment once the car door was shut, and then they pulled away.

★ ★ ★

I'd opened my own car and was about to get in when I heard a woman's voice, slowly reciting numbers.

Brooke was standing about a foot the other side of the gate. Her arms were folded, and the warm smile was back. Once she saw she'd got my attention, she said the numbers again, three separate series of digits.

'So what's that?' I asked.

'Our house phone. My cell, Cory's cell. Write them down. That way you'll be able to establish that none of them were involved in any alleged persecution of you last night.'

I nodded. 'Probably you feel that makes you smart, Brooke. In fact it's additional evidence of premeditation.'

'I don't know who called you last night, Mr Henderson, but it honestly wasn't me.'

I knew I was playing into her hands, but I didn't care. 'What's the real problem here, Brooke?'

'Nothing that won't be resolved. And actually I should probably thank you, as your arrival seems to have helped matters along. Your presence has unbalanced Ellen somewhat, don't you think? Perhaps your raw masculinity simply turned her pretty head.'

'No, seriously,' I persisted. 'Is it that she's prettier than you? I mean, I'm sure you've noticed. Probably Cory has too. Has it been trying, having a more attractive woman around?'

She laughed.

225

'And younger too, which is worse. Is that what makes it difficult?'

I reached into the car, grabbed something from the passenger seat, and walked over to the gate. She made no move to step back. I stood in front of her, opened the neck of the sweater and checked the label.

'Dior,' I said. 'Expensive, right? I assume you'd know. I guess your father probably bought a lot of that kind of thing for you in the past. Did he stop, once Ellen came along? Did it slip his mind, once he had a life of his own again? After all, just because we get older — and you *are* getting older, Brooke, no matter how much exercise you do — it doesn't stop us all being about ten years old inside, does it? Not when it comes to the people who gave birth to us.'

Her face was blank now.

'Is it that simple? Is Ellen the little sister who came along and stole Daddy's love?'

'You're a very dull and stupid man.'

'I've heard it said. So — what should I do with this sweater? Find Ellen and give it to her, or do you believe it belongs to you? Like Black Ridge and everything else in a fifty-mile radius?'

'Perhaps the sledgehammer approach used to work in your old profession, but it means nothing here.'

I let that one go, the easiest way of hiding that it had thrown me to have this kind of thing dropped into the conversation twice in five minutes. Now she was not smiling, Brooke's face had become more handsome, hinting at the black-and-white photographs one sometimes comes across of pioneer women, sitting fierce and implacable alongside men who stood in the picture to prove their dominance, but who could not have survived a week without their wives. She would even have been very attractive, were it not for her eyes, which were dark and flat, as if painted on pieces of old stone.

As I turned to go, she spoke again. 'She caused the death of my father.'

'I don't believe you,' I said, though her voice did not sound as it had before. The sun was out and it seemed a little warmer, suddenly. Also as though the odour I'd caught off the sweater had intensified. It was a dry smell, but still sweet.

'You don't know people like I do,' she said. 'Or understand how everything links to everything else.'

'I think you meet the people you deserve.'

'Very deep. I like that. And so tell me. What did your poor wife do, to deserve you?'

She turned and walked away up the drive, toward where her brother stood watching us.

25

'Where the hell are you?'

'I don't know.'

It had taken Ellen Robertson nearly two hours to answer her phone, and I wasn't in the mood for being screwed around. 'What do you mean, *you don't know?*'

'I . . . I'm just not sure.'

I established that when she'd checked herself out of the hospital, a little after eight the previous evening, she'd arranged for a cab from town to come pick her up. At first she'd intended to go back to her house, but on the way home she'd realized she simply couldn't face the Robertsons, and told the driver to drop her in Black Ridge instead.

'You could have come to me.'

'I didn't know where you were staying.'

'You have my cell number.'

'I didn't think it would be a good idea.'

When she arrived in town she wound up walking into a bar, at the opposite end of town to Kelly Street and the Mountain View. She got rather more to drink than to eat and soon realized she wasn't feeling right. A man sitting at the bar became attentive. This culminated in a dispute that required the intervention of a bartender. After the man had been encouraged out into the night, Ellen had a few more drinks before finally making her way to a motel. This

228

morning she'd woken early and checked out on autopilot. She didn't sound at all clear on where she'd been since then.

'Well, what can you see right now?' I asked.

'Some places.'

'What are they *called?*'

She listlessly read out a couple of business names.

'What? Did you just say 'The Write Sisters'?'

'Yes,' she mumbled.

'Turn around. The coffee shop is right opposite the bar where you and I met. The bar you used to go to with Gerry, remember?'

She didn't say anything.

'I think you may have left the hospital just a little prematurely, Ellen. I'm going to come take you back.'

'I'm not safe there.'

'Trust me,' I said, without thinking. 'You're better there than at home right now.'

Vague though she was, she was onto that fast enough. 'Why? What do you mean?'

I had little choice but to tell her what had happened at her house.

'So *now* do you believe I'm in danger?'

'I never had any problem believing Brooke and Cory meant you harm,' I said. 'Not after I'd met them. Look, will you go get a coffee, wait for me?'

'I'm *not* going back to the hospital.'

'Ilena, please just do as I ask.'

There was silence. When she finally replied, she sounded very far away. 'So. You know.'

'It makes no difference to me.'

'It will. It always does.'

When I parked on Kelly Street I spotted a female figure slumped over one of the tables in the window of the coffee shop. I parked and walked quickly inside. The place was pretty full. I passed the mechanic guy, sitting by himself with the local paper, who gave me a cursory nod.

When I got to her table, it seemed to take Ellen a moment to recognize me. 'I waited,' she said, eventually. 'But I'm still not going.'

'You want something to drink?'

She shook her head. I went to order coffee at the counter. The blue-haired girl had evidently turned up for work after all, and was fiddling with the coffee machine. Her shoulders looked bowed. I had to order twice before she mumbled that she'd bring it over.

Back at the table I looked Ellen up and down. 'You actually don't look so good.'

'How charming.'

'I don't mean on the outside. Are you getting headaches?'

She shook her head. 'Feel a bit dizzy. That's all. I need something to eat, maybe.'

'No, you've got a concussion,' I said firmly. 'You need to go back to the hospital.'

'What did I say when you first got here?'

'I'm not going to drag you there,' I said. 'I'm not your dad. I'm just telling you what I think. It's up to you what you do with the information.'

'How was I when you saw me in the hospital?'

'Fine. Pretty much. You were saying some weird shit, but that seems to be how you roll.'

'But now you think I have a concussion?'

'Onset can be delayed, which is why they keep people in for observation, and why you should still be there. You've got to get yourself feeling strong enough to take on Brooke and Cory.'

'Take them on?'

'They didn't just mess with your stuff this time. They've involved the police.'

'I can't fight them. Don't you understand yet? It's not just them.'

'I know that. The sheriff is looking for you right now, convinced or pretending to be convinced that you're responsible for acts of vandalism against people he feels honour-bound to protect. And he knows your real name now too.'

She hadn't appeared to be concentrating, but the last sentence got through to her. She stared at me, looking miserable. 'How? *How* does he know?'

'He needed to understand that you're being — '

'You told him.'

'Yes.'

'And so everyone knows now. *You* know, *he* knows . . . '

'He won't spread it around,' I said. 'He's basically a good — '

'Everybody knows,' she repeated, dismally. 'No more Ellen. Welcome back, Ilena.'

'Ellen . . . '

It felt colder, suddenly, as if a breeze had come down the street and made its way in through the cracks around the door to come sit with us at the table. Ellen wouldn't look me in the eye.

231

There was no sign of my coffee. I glanced round at the counter but the girl there didn't seem to have moved since I came in. I assumed she must be doing something, however, as I could smell something sweet in the air, presumably a syrup, oddly strong. I heard a very faint sound and turned back.

'Ellen — *stop* that, for God's sake.'

'Stop what?'

'Your *hands*.'

She glanced down, apparently mystified, to see she was slowly raking the fingernails of one hand across the back of the other, hard enough to draw blood.

She moved her fingers away, and looked at the scratch marks, a pattern of long lines, crossing each other at crooked angles. I didn't know what to say and I couldn't read the expression on her face. It seemed like simple curiosity.

'You need to get back to the hospital, Ellen.'

She shook her head. 'This is nothing to do with me.'

'What are you saying? That this is Ilena, making you do this? You still need — '

'*I'm* Ilena, you *asshole*,' she said loudly. 'What, you think she was some stupid bitch, into self-harm? Poor little Romanian slut, couldn't protect herself from the bad men, so she cuts herself instead?'

Around the café, a few of the other patrons were not being very subtle about lifting their eyes above the level of the local paper.

'Keep your voice down,' I said, calmly. 'Did Gerry know?'

She breathed out heavily. 'Not in the beginning.'

'Not information you're going to lead with. I can see that.'

'But I told him later. Before we were married.'

'Everything?'

'Things nobody should have to tell anyone. Especially a man they love.'

'He didn't care?'

'Of course he cared. He wanted to go back in time and find the men who'd done bad things to me. I told him time doesn't work like that, and I didn't need protecting, but . . . from him I didn't mind. He did it without making it feel like he was taking anything away from me. And the thing that happened in Berlin? He said he was proud of me.'

'I would be too.'

'You shouldn't,' she said, suddenly distant again. 'Lately, I have not been so strong. Or so good.'

'What do you mean?'

'People always look after number one, right?'

It seemed for a moment as if she was going to say something else, but she clammed up.

'This feeling you've had,' I said. 'Of being watched, in danger. Did you ever feel it before Gerry died?'

She shook her head. 'I felt very sad sometimes, for no reason. It's why we had quite such a bad argument about the children thing, on that day. I just . . . everything seemed to be going wrong. To feel as if it was dying. And for a few days beforehand I also didn't sleep very well. But

233

that's not the same.'

She hesitated for a moment. 'Did you understand those things I was telling you in the hospital?'

'What do you mean, 'understand'?'

'Did you understand that none of it really happened?'

I stared at her. 'What do you mean? I thought you said it was a witch.'

'Yes, that's what I'm saying. They make you believe things that aren't true. See things that aren't there. Those things I said — they didn't really happen. None of them.'

I felt wrong-footed and dumb. If you've privately decided someone's deluded, then you want to be the person to tell them that. 'So . . . '

'It was in my head.' She hesitated, and then seemed to come to a decision. 'It was supposed to stop. But it hasn't. I was stupid to believe it would *ever* be taken off. That it even *could*. And yesterday evening . . . I heard tapping on my window at the hospital.'

'Tapping?' I said, thinking of the scratching sounds against the back of my motel room. 'What was it?'

'Gerry,' she said.

'Gerry?'

'He was perched on my windowsill. Outside. Like a big bird.'

I felt the skin on the back of my neck tighten.

'You know he wasn't really there, right? And that you were on the second floor of the building?'

She shrugged.

'What . . . was he doing?'

'He was looking in at me as if he had never loved me.' She glanced away. 'It's why I had to leave the hospital. But it's too late.'

'The day he died,' I said, trying to steer us back toward matters I could comprehend. 'Do you think he'd changed his mind about something? You said that — '

But then there was a scream from behind us.

I turned to see a woman was backing away from the counter, staring at the server behind it. The blue-haired girl was standing exactly as she had been, hunched over the big coffee machine. But billows of steam were coming out of it now. Far too much steam.

As the customer kept screaming, the girl slowly turned from the machine. Her face was pure white. Her hands were bright red, held out in front. When she came out from behind the counter you could see the steam coming off them.

She looked sluggishly over at me as I got up and started toward her.

I stopped, held up my hands to show I meant no harm. I remembered her name — Jassie — and said it. She looked at me again, confused, with a look of dislocation from everything around her.

'Why haven't you got a *face?*' she said, suddenly, backing away.

I don't see how she could have mistaken my intentions, which were simply to help, but her own features stretched into something that must have been appalling to feel from within: her mouth falling slack as if melting, eyes wide with utter distrust and horror, as though suddenly remembering that no one around her was real and that everyone meant her harm.

She tried to get away from me, not even in the direction of the door, but stumbling toward the big picture window.

I want to believe that she tripped, but I don't think that's what happened. She did collide heavily with one of the empty chairs — but it wasn't that which pitched her forward. She did it herself. She got to within a yard of the big window and then threw herself headfirst into the glass. It shattered.

As her throat was borne down onto the jagged edge below, driven by her momentum and weight, the window above collapsed into large, vicious shards that sheered down into her back and neck and head and smashed to oblivion into the floor around her.

It sounded like most of the world's noises happening at once, and then there was utter silence.

★   ★   ★

A few people got up immediately and ran out of the café. The rest were frozen in place, staring at the remains of the window, the beached shape straddling across the inside and outside, blood pooling underneath it so fast it looked like film speeded up. One arm and a leg twitched briefly, and for a moment it looked as though the girl was trying to roll sideways, but then stillness

236

came upon her body like a rock sinking into water.

I've seen the moment of death often enough to know it — but evidently you can recognize it first time around. People started to cry out then, to talk and shout. A couple got on their cell phones and started barking at emergency operators.

Ellen meanwhile stared at the prone body with nothing more than a look of blank resignation.

The woman who'd screamed was mired just outside on the sidewalk, hands fluttering by her sides, evidently unable to move.

I walked quickly out to her. 'What *happened?*'

The woman didn't seem to grasp what I was asking until I gently took hold of her shoulders and asked again. 'What *happened in there?*'

'I was just asking her if she was okay,' the woman said, defensively, staring back into the café, studiously keeping her eyes away from the broken window. 'I hadn't been in for a couple days and Jassie's usually so friendly and everything, and I thought she looked tired, or like she'd lost weight or something, so I just asked if she was okay and she didn't say anything and then I saw that she was . . . '

She stopped, and looked at me. 'Who are you? Do I even *know* you?'

I could hear the sound of a police siren, approaching fast. People were starting to come out of other businesses and onto the sidewalk now, slowly, heads tilted, as if approaching a box they'd been told they should not open but were unable to resist. More people were coming out of the café now, too, milling around outside. On the opposite side of the street I saw two people come out of the Mountain View, a young bartender and an older man in a dark roll-neck sweater — whom I recognized.

The bartender acted like most of the other people did. The other guy, however, jerked forward, as if he was going to throw up right there on the street. Then he turned and walked stiff-legged and fast in the opposite direction, not looking back, his hands held up in front of his face.

By the time I'd got back into the café, Ellen had disappeared. A cop car came swinging round the corner and into Kelly Street. It stopped with a screech outside and the sheriff and Deputy Greene got out.

The deputy stared at the window of the coffee shop with distaste. 'Holy crap.'

The sheriff assessed the situation with a long sweep of his eyes, and then spotted me. As Greene started to clear people out of the way, Pierce strode over to where I was standing.

He spoke clearly and quietly. 'I want you to get out of here, now. Otherwise I'm going to arrest you. Do you understand?'

'Are you kidding me?'

'Does it look like it?'

It did not. 'I saw that girl at the hospital,' I said, nonetheless. 'Jassie. The day Ellen Robertson had her accident. She was sitting by herself in a room, with tears running down her face.'

Another police car came tearing around the corner. Pierce glanced outside as two more cops jumped out. I recognized one of them as the

238

deputy, Phil Corliss, I'd briefly met three years before. I could hear another siren in the distance now, presumably paramedics.

'Your observation is noted,' he said. 'Now get out of this town or I swear to God you'll regret it.'

I stepped back. 'You're welcome to it.'

He glared at me a moment longer, as if considering saying something else, but then turned to deal with the chaos unfolding behind him in the street.

26

All I had to go on was the man's throwaway line about living a mile up the road. I rejected a turning half a mile past our old house, and paused at another a little further along on the other side of the road, but didn't see the vehicle I was looking for. A delayed reaction to what had just happened in the coffee shop was making my movements strange and jerky.

Two minutes later I came upon a driveway on the right, and turned straight up it past a mailbox with the name 'Collins' neatly stencilled on the side. It occurred to me we'd never driven up the road this far in all the time we had lived here, and I couldn't imagine why. Sure, the area was full of interesting stuff to look at and all of it lay in other directions, but it still seemed odd. I guess there are some roads you don't go down until something outside your control takes you there.

The drive curled around to the right before eventually leading to a circle outside a recently constructed house, twice as large and half as appealing as ours had been. Lined up in front of a small, faux-barn-like structure were a compact, a station wagon and the dark green SUV. A car for every occasion. I parked where I was blocking all three.

I rang the bell and the front door opened after a couple of minutes.

The man I'd seen outside the Mountain View had managed to pull it together in the last forty minutes, and probably looked fine to the outside world, including the wife and kids I could hear hooting and laughing in some room beyond the hallway.

He was halfway into a good-neighbourly smile before his face froze.

'Hey,' I said. 'Don't know if you remember me?' I left a beat before continuing. 'We met a few days ago, outside that house for sale, a mile down the road?'

'Right,' he said, stiffly, knowing this was not the last time he'd seen me, and that I knew it too. 'Of course.'

'Richard, who is it?'

A woman came out of the kitchen and beamed in our direction. She was whip-thin, around the same age as her husband, and looked like someone who was well disposed to the world in general.

'Beginning to think I might be taking the property down the road seriously,' I said, smiling at her but still talking to him. 'Wanted to ask a couple of questions about the area, before I get the family up to take a look.'

'What kind of questions?' Collins said.

'Come in, come in,' his wife insisted, coming closer. 'Coffee's just made.'

'That's very kind, ma'am, but I'm real short on time. Just a quick word is all I need.'

She rolled her eyes as if this was another of those funny things that happened to her all the time, and retreated cheerfully back into the house.

241

I stepped back from the front door and indicated for the man to follow me.

'What do you want?' the man said, quietly.

'A word with you. And I'm not leaving without it.'

He followed me halfway to where my car was parked, and then stopped. 'This is far enough.'

'You want to tell me what happened back in Black Ridge?'

'I don't know what you're talking about.'

'I saw you on Kelly Street. You come out of the bar when you hear a commotion — and you're close enough to see the colour of the hair of the girl who's just smashed her head through a plate-glass window. Instead of staring or turning away, you *run*, run exactly like a guy who's trying to look like that's not what he's doing. *That's* what I'm talking about.'

'It was . . . well, it was very upsetting.'

'Generically, or personally? Did you know Jassie?'

'No. Well, I knew her by sight, of course. I've had coffee in there a hundred times.'

'Didn't know her any better than that?'

'No, of course not.' He was trying to bluster but there wasn't enough force behind it.

'Do you normally drink alcohol at that time of the morning? You don't look the type.'

'I . . . I've got a lot on my mind right now. Business matters.'

'I see. Was it business matters that took you to Hope Memorial yesterday?'

He stared at me. 'What?'

'I was visiting someone there. As I was driving

242

out, I noticed you driving in. Odd thing is I saw Jassie Cornell in the hospital a few minutes before.'

'I'd like you to go now.'

'I'm sure. But one more thing. Before Jassie killed herself, she did something else. You know what that was?'

He looked at me, his face strained. 'I really don't know why you think — '

'She put her hands into the outlet from the coffee machine. She put them under a jet of super-heated steam and held them there until they started to blister. I was fifteen feet away and I swear I could smell the skin burning. Strange, huh?'

He swallowed heavily, eyes turning glassy.

'You've got a nice wife,' I said. 'Maybe too nice. I know how that goes.'

'You need to get off my property,' he said. 'Now. Or I'm calling the police.'

'They're still busy back at the coffee shop. Could be a while before they get to you. Whereas I'm already here.' I let that settle for a moment. 'But you're right. I'm imposing on your time.'

Just before I got into my car I looked back. He hadn't moved.

'One more thing,' I said. 'The family that used to live in that house down the road?'

He waited, and said nothing.

'That was me. It was my son who died.'

I could see him swallow from ten feet away.

'I'd appreciate it if you didn't spread any more rumours,' I said. 'Because that kind of thing cuts both ways. Do you understand what I'm saying?'

He nodded, barely.

★　★　★

I was sitting at the end of the jetty over Murdo Pond when it began to rain, starting as a mist that coalesced between the trees, seeping down out of the higher ground, gradually solidifying into droplets. When these fell on the surface of the lake they seemed to disappear, as if the water was so heavy and thick it absorbed them.

I had been in the grounds of our old house for over an hour, smoking one cigarette after another. It was late afternoon now. The temperature had already dropped five degrees and showed no sign of stopping. It wasn't going to rain for long. If this kept up, it would turn to snow. My coat was in the car. I was shivering. Little of this was due to the cold, however, though I could feel it seeping up through the jetty from the water, could almost see it gathering across the lake's surface.

As I sat there, I had been thinking about faces.

First, the face I had watched in the rear-view mirror as I'd driven away from the house further up the road from our old house.

Then Jassie's, just before she threw herself toward the window and out of this world.

I know that if you fasten upon a mental image for too long, especially a memory, you can start to believe strange things about it. The image can morph, reshaped by the mind considering it, creating something that feels like reality but lies somewhere outside, straddling the grey zone between the world and what you believe about it. I know too that we find patterns where there are none. Nonetheless I believed I knew what I had seen.

In the face of the man, pure fear. The horror of a man who has done something wrong, and knows it.

In the face of the girl who was now lying on a table somewhere, coldly indifferent to the desultory conversation of men and women whose job it was to deface her body in preparation for stowing it safely underground, I had seen something that was far harder to name. I knew, however, where I had seen it before, and I no longer felt dismissive of the things Ellen had tried to tell me concerning how Gerry had looked when he died.

I knew that what I'd seen in Jassie Cornell's face was similar to the memory of Scott's last expression, an image I had turned over in my mind so many, many times in the nights of the last three years.

We can never get inside the heads of others. The best we can do is read what's on the outside. I believed nonetheless that whatever had been going through the waitress's mind in her last moments had been very similar to what must have been going through Scott's, when he stood very close to where I now sat, when he had stared over my shoulder as if everything he felt he'd learned in four years had suddenly been undermined and he had glimpsed some vile truth about creation and everyone in it.

I didn't know what tied these three things together. It could have been coincidence that Gerry Robertson had a heart attack, just before it seemed likely he was going to acquiesce to his wife's desire for a family. It might not.

The detail of what had occurred between the blue-haired barista and the man with the big house and three cars was occluded to me too, and the cause of Scott's death was as much a mystery to me as it ever had been — except for the fact that I now thought I knew of two other people who had died in similar circumstances, and except for the fact that a word Ellen had used more than once kept running through my head.

Punishment.

Punishment for a man who might have been about to compromise the financial position of his children. Punishment for a slick, middle-aged guy who had been taking a drink alone in the middle of the morning.

And maybe punishment for someone else too.

I stood up, hearing my joints creak against the cold, feeling old and alone. There were other things I wanted to ask Ellen now, but I couldn't raise her on the phone. I had sat for as long as I could without doing something. The sight of the lake had become oppressive, and I walked quickly past my old house without even giving it a second glance.

There were two men I needed to talk to.

★   ★   ★

As I strapped myself into the driver's seat, my phone rang. I hoped it would be Ellen finally returning a call. It wasn't.

246

'Hey,' I said, briskly. 'This really isn't a good time.'

She was crying. Hard, with the hitching notes you rarely hear in someone who isn't a child.

'Becki, slow down. What's the problem?'

In the twenty-four hours since we'd spoken, and since I'd wired her ten thousand dollars out of my divorce settlement, Kyle had managed to excel himself. Some guys are always prone to open the doors that others are too smart to even find. Kyle seemed like he aspired to actually kick them down.

Instead of using the cash to pay his debt and bring his life back to earth, he had tried to double up by buying *more* drugs, this time from a crew up in Astoria. They sold him the drugs. They followed him down an alley. They took the drugs back. Since then Kyle had been drowning his sorrows in a series of local bars, fuelled by the remains of his original drug stake, bankrolled by the last of my money. He was beginning to show signs of unpredictability and violence. At the present time he hadn't slept for three days, and Becki presented this state of mind as a mitigating factor for the decisions he'd made.

I listened to this and didn't feel much about it. Everyone always thinks they're bigger than drugs — rock stars with training wheels, hard-eyed corner boys or homemakers with a scrip from their physician. Drugs watches for a while with amused indulgence, then takes them outside and kicks their ass. Angry though I was with Kyle, it was not my job to stand in the way of the appointment he was making with fate. There's a

247

point past which you're no longer talking to the person, but the drug, and everyone sounds the same in that state because the drug is eerie and vicious and amoral and utterly beyond human ken.

Then I caught another sound in amongst the sniffles, and started paying attention again.

'Becki, are you okay?'

'Yeah,' she said, quickly, but I knew what I'd heard. The wince of someone in physical discomfort.

She didn't want to tell me, but I got it out. Last night, probably about the time I'd been around the back of the motel staring at scratch marks on the wall, Becki had been woken from anxious sleep by the sound of someone ringing the entry buzzer. She assumed it was Kyle finally coming back to earth, and jumped out of bed to give him plenty of grief and a hug, in that order, or most probably at the same time.

But it wasn't her boyfriend.

They wanted Kyle to get the message as soon as he eventually walked in the door, which is why the main attention had been to Becki's face. They hadn't done the obvious thing two men could have done, but only, by the sound of it, because they were professionals. In the longer term this would be a bad thing.

I found myself calm, but not in a good way. Calm like a sheet of ice forming across a cold, deep lake.

'Does Kyle know about this?'

'I told him on the phone this morning.'

'So why isn't he home with you right now?'

She didn't say anything.

'Pack a bag and go stay with your father,' I said.

'Are you crazy? I can't let him see me like this.'

'You don't go today, he may not see you again.'

'John, I look like I fell down the stairs on my face. Dad sees this, and *he's* going to break Kyle's neck himself.'

'That's his right.'

'John, I can't let him see — '

'Becki, just *do it*.' She was crying again now. 'I'm stunned these people gave you a pass last night. It won't happen again. Go. Take anything you value. Do *not* leave anything with your parents' address, their phone number, or yours. Make sure you're not being followed when you leave. Do not go back.'

'I . . . I just don't know . . . '

'Becki, I can only help you if you let me. Tell me you're going to do what I say. Promise me.'

She said she would.

'When you get to your dad's house, call Kyle.'

'He's not picking up since this morning. Since I told him about . . . what happened.'

'So leave him a message. Say you've spoken to me. Tell him the money can be straightened out, but I regard you as a friend I would do a great deal to protect. Explain that if he doesn't call me right away, then I'll be talking to him more seriously than he can possibly imagine. Make sure you stress the word 'talking'. He will understand what I mean.'

249

I could hear her sniffing, rubbing her eyes, trying to get her shit together. I could almost see her looking around the apartment and taking inventory of what she cared enough about to take.

'I'll tell him. Okay.'

'Get out of that place,' I repeated, more gently. 'Now. You don't live there any more.'

'I will.' She hesitated. 'Do you mean that? That you would do a lot to — '

'Becki, I've got to go.'

I closed the phone and drove out onto the road.

* * *

The first thing I did was drive back to Black Ridge and the sheriff's department. He kept me waiting forty minutes.

He listened to my account of Jassie's death without making any notes, then thanked me for my time. I asked him if he knew anything about the current whereabouts of Ellen Robertson. He said that he did not. I asked him what he thought *he* would do, where he would go, if he had just suffered a car accident and the people who were supposed to care about him had meanwhile turned his house upside down. He informed me that I was incorrect in my interpretation of the events.

'What do those people actually have to do, to get the cops to stop turning a blind eye?'

'Something concrete,' he said. 'Something that can be investigated.'

'The sheet on Ellen's past, the past they've evidently been torturing her over. Not enough?'

'I'll remind you that I never saw it.'

'I hope you're not calling me a liar.'

'No, though it would be within my rights to consider it. With no piece of paper, there's nothing I can do. You burned it. And you could argue, given Ms Zaituc — assuming that's who she is — is under suspicion of murder in Europe, the Robertsons are exercising kindness by not turning her in.'

'I guess you could argue that. Assuming your tongue wasn't so far up that family's ass that you could still use it for intelligible speech.'

'Mr Henderson, I'm going to make this simple for you.' He pulled a sheet of paper out of the tray of the inkjet printer that sat in a stand to one side of his desk. 'Let's call this Black Ridge.'

He took a pen and drew a black cross bang in the middle. 'That's the family,' he said. Then he made a smaller cross down by the bottom edge of the paper. 'That's me.' He set the lid of the pen upright on the paper, almost halfway between the two crosses. 'And that's you.'

'You lost me.'

He lifted one side of the piece of paper with his finger. The lid toppled, slid off the piece of paper, across the desk and onto the floor. 'Any clearer?'

'You missed your vocation,' I said. 'Schools all over the country are crying out for that kind of expositional talent.'

'This is precisely what my job is about. Explaining things. Over and over. To people who don't seem capable of getting it the first time.' He looked coldly at me. 'There's a community here, Mr Henderson. You're not a part of it — which I know you get was the point of the little demonstration. I am. The Robertsons too, along with a bunch of other people, many of whose families have been here a very long time. The *right* thing is sometimes about maintaining the status quo, especially if it's been in place for a lot longer than any one person within it has been alive. As a policeman I have to work in straight lines, and there's nothing here points in the direction of action against Brooke or Cory.'

He shrugged. I looked back at him, knowing that ultimately he was right.

'And perhaps, at the risk of stretching the metaphor a little far, you should now consider ways of voluntarily taking yourself off the local desktop. Now. Air travel, for example.'

I stood. 'Two things for you to consider in turn. First, if your son dies in a place, you stop being a tourist there.'

'I didn't mean . . . '

I picked up the piece of paper on his desk, tore it in half, and dropped the pieces in the trash.

'And I'll leave the interpretation of that as an exercise for the student.'

27

She banged on the back door. Banged hard. Then, though she knew there'd be no point, went back around the front and hollered and hammered again. Nothing. Either out, or not answering to anyone.

Kristina gave it two more minutes and then walked backward across the lot. Looked back toward the building, just in case a curtain twitched. It didn't, and it wouldn't. Her mother wouldn't be hiding from her. She just wasn't there.

She turned and stormed away down the road. She had to go to work. The faces of the people she passed on the street were turned away. From her, from each other, from everything. It was getting dark and the cold was coming out of the woods like a rolling mist. Some of Black Ridge's residents were hurrying home merely to get warm — but that wasn't all it was. People understood it was coming time to be indoors. People know these things.

And in a way, so what, she'd witnessed this kind of bullshit all her life — the portion spent in Black Ridge, at least. But that had felt different. It had been business as usual, the ways things had just always been. Maybe she only felt guilty now because she'd thought cruel thoughts about the dead girl's waistline, but if so, that was enough.

People are real, and what you do to them is real too. *Whoever* you think you are.

She'd heard it happen, felt it all the way from her apartment on the other side of town. She'd been trying to read a novel, as a distraction from the nice-but-dumb thoughts she'd found herself annoyingly prey to over the last forty-eight hours.

Then, suddenly — bang. The sensation was so violent that she'd reared back from the book as if someone had shouted at her.

And it was gone.

She'd blinked, looked around the room. The music on the stereo seemed distant for two seconds, went silent, and then popped back up, as if she'd swallowed and cleared her ears in a plane coming down to land.

Half an hour later she heard the report on the local radio news. The coffee shop on Kelly Street. A girl. Dead. The sheriff interviewed, saying she had an accident with the Gaggia machine, then tripped, out of her mind with pain, and took a bad fall.

Kristina knew it was more than that. There is meaning in all circumstance, and the things we dismiss as accidents are sometimes merely the actions of things we don't understand. Life is a long downhill slalom around these events, in the dark, before you suddenly hit the wall at the bottom. The things we call tragedies are when the forces around us really get off a good one.

And when they do, it's *loud*.

★ ★ ★

The talk on the radio rolled straight over Jassie Cornell's death to other local concerns — another strip mall closing, cuts in road maintenance budgets, job losses, the usual Black Ridge dirge — sealing the event in the past, where it needn't bother anyone any more. That was the way it went, and it was seeing and understanding this that had eventually sent Kristina halfway around the world — to find, of course, that it was exactly the same everywhere else.

People turned their backs on the truth, even if it meant walking around in circles all their lives. In any real town, a place with a heart, people know what's happening without having to vocalize it. No one points out the elephant in the room. There must be deniability, lest you wind up with little local difficulties. Outsiders point the finger once in a while, open the box, and towns-people who've tolerated the arrangement (and benefited from it in their secret, impulse-driven lives) suddenly decide that having schlepped all this way from the old countries, they don't want to be under the thumb again. Things are said. Accusations made. People hang, burn or drown. So . . . *shh*. But everybody knows, just as they know which parts of town to avoid after dark, which noises in the night you get out of bed to investigate, and which you steadfastly ignore.

John knew it too, she believed.

She thought that at some level he was beginning to sense things did not work here like they did elsewhere. Hence him still being here, and she knew he *was* still here in town, because she'd heard about his car breaking down across

255

from the salon that morning. Plus, she just knew. Hence the dumb thoughts.

She worried that he might be starting to think he was understanding the lay of the land, but getting it the wrong way around. She was adept at reading people — it came with the territory, whether you liked it or not — and she already knew he was a man who was not going to back down, even if that meant marching hard and fast in the wrong direction. It wasn't good for him here, and yet here he still was.

Here *she* was, too — and she was beginning to wonder if she knew why. You can fight turning into your mom all you like, but in the end you discover it may never have been negotiable.

$$\star \quad \star \quad \star$$

Later, in between her shifts, she went out onto the street and tried her mother's cell again. There was no reply. It was kind of fucked up, she realized, that it didn't occur to her to be concerned by this.

It's a strange position to grow up in, knowing you never have to worry about your mother's wellbeing. You carry these things with you. If there was anything she had managed to learn in her time away, it was that *you're never away.* Wherever you are, you're there, as the poor blue-haired corpse would doubtless have said. The soil you run over as a child becomes a part of you just as much as it does that of any plant. Jassie Cornell doubtless never consumed any-thing that wasn't USDA-certified organic, in case some badness got uploaded into her pristine (albeit pudgy) frame. Why should it be any different with less tangible taints, like the qualities that floated over the earth and in between the trees, which gave the winds their colour and determined how people felt when they woke in the shade of these mountains? Why would anyone — apart from brittle-brained scientists — imagine that you don't absorb those too?

Kristina believed she knew the answer to one question now, at least, and it was making her feel sick and heavy and weary and sad. *This* was why she was back here. She'd never been away. Never had, never could, never would.

The trees in these woods were not trees. They were bars in a cell.

The evening shift started in half an hour. Was there anything she could achieve in that time? Probably not. So she should just head back over to Kelly, try to use the walk to calm down.

Was there anything she could do *after* that?

She felt suddenly anxious and afraid, bowed over with the realization that she was a girl who really should have listened in class; stricken with the knowledge that the only person who could help was the one she absolutely couldn't ask, the same woman who'd wanted nothing more than to teach her all of these things in the first place. Who'd started the process, taken her daughter on a drive, and then been firmly shoved away.

For a few months before she came home to Black Ridge, Kristina had been plagued by terrible dreams, and a therapist had told her they

257

were driven by denial, and that no matter how much you try not to think of, say, a red cross, that's what you see in the back of your head. The only solution is to think positively of something else. Fine advice unless the red crosses run in your blood.

When you start to feel afraid for no reason, it is a sure sign that things you cannot see are on the move. When they begin to stir, all you can do is run.

The only question is whether you run away, or toward.

28

I parked thirty yards down the street, a long residential curve on the north side of town. Though the houses were of a good size the area looked sparse: one of several Black Ridge residential developments from the 1970s and 80s that never really took off. I chose a position that was distant from a streetlight, so as to look like just another slumbering vehicle. It was getting even colder, but I sat it out.

After two hours I saw a car sweep up the road and park a little way ahead. A large figure emerged with an armful of files. He went inside the house and I gave it another ten minutes.

Then I walked over, up the path, and rang the doorbell. After a minute or so the door was opened.

'Hey, Bill,' I said.

'Jesus, hey,' he said. He grinned, but it looked tired. 'Come on in.'

★　★　★

A few minutes later I had a beer in my hand and so did he. It appeared to be his second since he'd gotten home, which was going some. The counter top and table in the kitchen were covered in open files. The sink was empty and clean but for a lone spatula. A garbage bag near the back door looked to be full of the former

259

cardboard homes of takeout pizza. This reminded me I hadn't had a call from Kyle in the several hours since I'd spoken to Becki, but that was low on my priorities right now.

'Busy?'

'Always,' he said. 'You know the law — she's a demanding mistress. But what was that you always used to say? Without love and work there is neurosis?'

'Koestler,' I said, thinking it was odd the things people remembered about you, that however much you tried to be someone in particular you might always be defined by acts that had been unintentional.

I followed Bill into the living room. There were files all over the place here, too, even on the lid of the piano up against the wall. Otherwise it was tidy, though there was dust on the bookshelves. Guys are good with tidy. Dust always seems to elude them.

'Tonight's not good,' Bill said, apologetically, 'if heading out for that drink was what you had in mind. Got a big case on Monday, medical, expert witnesses up the wazzoo. Need a clear head tomorrow to prepare, not least because I still have no real clue what my client's problem is.'

'That's fine,' I said, watching him take a large swallow of his beer. 'I'm really just stopping by.'

'How come you're even still in the area? Thought it was a fly-by.'

'Turning out more complicated than I thought.'

'You going to tell me how?'

'Maybe.'

260

'Mysterious.'

Though we'd mainly socialized in bars down in Yakima, near the office, I'd been to Bill's house often enough in the past. I knew the house rules. I got out my cigarettes and pointed in the direction of the French windows.

He nodded. 'Sure. You ready for another?'

He joined me outside a few minutes later, holding two more bottles. We drank for a while in silence.

'You've lived around here a long time, right?'

'Spent some years here as a kid,' he said. 'Been here pretty much since the army. Why?'

'You know the Robertsons?'

'Well, yeah. I met Gerry a few times, on business. We used to represent his firm.'

'What about the current generation?'

'Sure. Brooke and Cory. Why?'

'Gerry's second wife was in an accident yesterday,' I said.

He frowned. 'Really? What was her name, Helen?'

'Ellen.'

'What happened?'

'I'm not sure.'

'What's it to you?'

'I don't really know that either,' I said.

It was full dark now and the light coming out of the house lit Bill's face harshly, revealing lines where there had been nothing but fine young skin when I had first known him, ten years before Scott had been born. I'm sure he saw the same thing in me.

'You going to explain that?'

'Do I need to?'

He took a long swallow and looked away down the yard, a space that was open about not being the haunt of children. 'Depends what you want from me,' he said. 'If it's legal advice, then yeah, kinda.'

'Probably not legal,' I said.

'Then what?'

'I met with Ellen a couple times over the last few days. That's who I was hoping to hook up with, the day I ran into you down in Black Ridge.'

'Met with her . . . why?'

'Long story. She got in contact with me. The point is she's convinced she's in some kind of danger.'

'From whom?'

'Brooke. Cory too, probably.'

'Cory's the kind of guy you could lay out with one slap. Brooke . . . yeah, I could see her unnerving someone.'

'She's unnerved Ellen pretty bad.'

'I'm kinda not following you,' Bill said, and downed the rest of his beer. 'They should make this shit in bigger bottles. One more?'

While he was gone I stepped back into the living room. There was a pair of shoes under one of the side tables. A tie, too, hanging over the back of a chair. There would come a point, not soon, but eventually, when files and folders would be the dominant furnishing.

Bill wandered back into view, two bottles in one of his large hands. He paused to glance down at a file on the table. I took a deep breath.

262

'Jen really out of town?'

He looked up. 'She's really out of town.'

'How far out?'

'What's it to you, John?'

'House just feels a little empty, is all.'

He looked at the floor. 'Things have been a little rocky lately, since you ask. We're undergoing a period of domestic reorganization right now.'

'I'd probably better not drink that beer after all,' I said. 'I'm driving.'

'Responsible guy. Well, next time you're passing through town, give me a little more notice, okay?'

'I will.'

He walked me out into the hallway. A couple of yards short of his front door, I half turned.

'She's okay, though, right?'

'Who?'

'Jenny.'

'She's fine, John. Nice of you to ask. But she's fine. Right as Raines.'

'That's good,' I said, but I could not smile at another of his habitual jokes. I looked at him and something hooded and flat in his eyes made me fear that Bill's wife was not fine, and that harm might have been done to her.

Unfortunately, whatever channel opened in the ether evidently operated in both directions. He blinked, just once, otherwise standing very still.

The first punch nearly took me out of the game right there. It came up low and hard and though I started to turn it landed heavily and it was all I could do not to go straight over onto my back. Instead I staggered sideways into the wall.

I crouched just in time, getting under Bill's second lunge and managing to partially turn him toward the door.

I stepped back up the hallway, but not far. I didn't want to get backed in that direction, further into the house. I didn't want Bill to be able to get around me either, because I was sure somewhere in the building would be a gun. So when he came charging toward me I went hard straight back at him. I got his shirt in my hand and he hit me in the gut so hard I lost all my breath. He put his hands up around my neck, and I snapped my head forward to hammer down onto his nose. There were smashing sounds, as arms and shoulders and heads cracked into things on the walls, pictures coming down along with an ornamental bookcase, spreading glass and broken pottery over the floor and our clothes. He looked like he was going down but then came up even stronger and knocked my head back against the wall so hard that for an instant everything was white.

He was trying to shout something, and so was I, but I didn't have any idea what it was. He tagged me again and again in the stomach, up under the ribs on my left side, close-up work I couldn't seem to turn away from and I knew I couldn't take for much longer. He started trying to drag me down, to drop me round his leg so he could get to the footwork, the real business, from which I knew I'd never get up.

I wrenched away and took a lurching step

back, saw him coming after me again. I ducked low and to the side and drove up under him, turning and pulling his shoulder down at the same time, sending him barrelling past awkwardly enough for me to drive my knee into his chest as he fell past. He tried to recover his balance but his right leg went out from underneath as he slipped on a piece of glass and his head went smack into the bottom of the staircase.

I was over him immediately, foot drawn back, but after he'd crashed to the ground he didn't move.

I stayed there, panting, and waited.

He was out.

I rolled him onto his back and made sure he could breathe, then hauled myself up the stairs. It was less tidy up here, though still far from bad. Men living on their own make at least as good a job as women do of holding back the chaos.

There were four sections to the closets in the bedroom. Two were full of suits and shirts. One was empty, the other held a couple of dresses on hangers.

I went back down to the kitchen. Quickly washed my face with cold water from the tap, and dried it with a hand-towel that smelled of mildew.

And then, before I sat down and was unable to get back up again, I left.

★   ★   ★

'What the *hell* happened to you?'

'Nothing,' I said. I was sitting in the window

of the Mountain View, turned away from the rest of the bar. It wasn't very full, but though I knew from the bathroom mirror that the bruising hadn't really taken colour yet, I didn't much want to look at people anyhow. The only reason I was here was because I was freezing cold and my hands and ribs hurt, and being inside anywhere seemed like a good idea.

On the opposite side of the street I saw The Write Sisters now had a piece of hardboard up over the broken window. Quick work.

Kristina set down the beer she'd brought without my asking for it. 'Your face have anything to do with the Robertsons? Or Ellen?'

'No,' I said.

She left me alone, coming back twenty minutes later with another beer. I thanked her and turned pointedly back to the window. The boarding over The Write Sisters looked wrong to me, as if it had been nailed up over something that was still broken, as if beyond it a body still lay.

Kristina didn't leave, however, and eventually I looked back at her. 'What?'

'I'm worried about you.'

'I'm good,' I said, breezily. 'Just a trying day.'

She shook her head. 'I was concerned before you even arrived tonight. You . . . I've been hearing things.'

I saw the other bartender, a young guy in a black T-shirt, looking our way. 'From who?'

'I just don't think this is a good place for you to be.'

'Why? The beer's great and the service is

266

friendly, sometimes,' I said, trying to make a joke.

She didn't go for it. I was jittery, finding it hard to look at anything, but my eyes found her face and stayed there. Her grey/green eyes, pale skin and black hair. She looked like the opposite of every woman I'd ever known.

'So what *did* you hear? On the barkeep grapevine?'

I was trying to be offensive. I don't know why. Either side of her nose there were a couple of faint things that must have been freckles. I felt uncomfortable under her gaze.

I lit a cigarette, and focused on that, trying to hide the trembling in my fingers.

'You need to give up,' she said.

'Yeah. But not tonight.'

'Not that. Smoke yourself to death, be my guest. I mean give up, get away from here.'

She handed me my check.

★ ★ ★

I stood on the sidewalk outside, not knowing what to do. I still didn't want to go back to my motel room. Those places are like a living death when you're in a certain state of mind.

In the end I crossed the street and went into the pizza place, where the AC was up unnecessarily high and the music plumbed the forgotten depths of the 1980s as if in a deliberate attempt to keep the clientele moving through. If so, it was working. The place was virtually empty and the waitress had no problem with me

267

ordering coffee and sitting at a booth in the window, out of everyone's way.

As I sat I realized first that one member of the family of three in the far corner was watching me, and then that it was Deputy Greene.

He was seated with a woman of around his own age and easily his own weight, her ass crammed into a pair of blue velour pants and threatening to seep off either side of her chair. Sitting opposite them was someone I also recognized — Courtney, the waif-like teenager who cleaned the rooms at my motel.

Greene and his wife ate in silence, methodically pushing slices of pizza into their faces as if engaged in a competition where fortune favoured the steady and consistent performer. The girl, whom I assumed must be their daughter, had either finished already or was not hungry.

I worked through my coffee and accepted a refill when the waitress silently reappeared. It was a reassuringly old-school brew, without froth, syrup or environmental attitude. Just a big cup of something hot and wet, and I sat there with my hands around it for warmth and comfort, watching nothing happen in the street outside, wondering if my head was actually going to burst. I was not hungry, could not imagine being so, but the pizza smelled good.

Perhaps just because it reminded me of a time, a very few days ago, when life had seemed simpler.

Eventually Greene and his companions left, still in silence. As they walked by the window,

Courtney's eyes passed vaguely across over mine, but not in a way that suggested she had any idea what she was looking at, or that she recognized me at all.

At some point after that my phone buzzed in my pocket but I couldn't imagine anyone I might want to talk to. I assumed Becki had given Kyle my message, in which case not being able to contact me might work even better than hearing my voice.

I didn't notice anyone coming into the restaurant until I heard the sound of cloth swishing as she slipped into the seat opposite me.

I looked up to see Kristina, sitting very upright, with her arms folded.

'Tell me,' she said.

29

There was a stage in Scott's development when he'd begun to understand that making coherent sounds with his mouth was regarded as a good and clever thing, and he was keen to show he was getting with the programme. In addition to his more straightforward declarations, he'd sometimes regale us with monologues in which he'd announce something about an object or situation, say the word 'because', add another clause, then another 'because' — and keep going until he'd delivered a (somewhat surreal) sentence about two minutes long. He didn't yet understand what 'because' meant, but he'd got that it could be used to connect things, to form a bridge between states of affairs.

After he was dead I came to believe this insight had not merely concerned language. He would have forgotten it in time, as we do, but back then he knew everything there was to know.

★   ★   ★

I had an affair, basically.

There was this woman and something happened and by and by it became a situation, by which time it was too late. I tried to do The Right Thing. The Right Thing came for long walks with me, but was just too even-handed in his approach. I wanted The Right Thing to be tough as nails, a track coach crazy to win and willing to kick ass. I wanted him to be Jesus, arms out in front of me, obscuring the road to wrong-headedness and shining with the pure golden light of everything that was good and sensible and true.

Instead he came on like an old drinking buddy who'd seen too much of life to take a hard line on anything.

'Well, yeah,' he'd say. 'I hear you. I *am* what you should be doing. But, you don't *want* to, do you?'

And I'd remind him of his duties, pointing out that what was in my head was *dumb* and *dangerous* and made *no sense*. That Carol deserved better. That I had a family. That I was being that cartoon asshole, the married man having an affair, and the correct thing to do was sever contact, be grateful I hadn't yet fucked up the important things — and think about something else until the whole thing faded into something mildly interesting and long-ago, like the first moon landing.

And he'd shrug again, and say: 'Sure, I get all that. You make a good case. But . . . we're still having the same conversation, right? And you *still* can't forget the smell of the skin on her neck, where her jaw curves up toward her ear. That's something I can't touch. With the neck thing, you're on your own.'

In the end I stopped inviting The Right Thing to come on walks with me. He was no help at all.

★   ★   ★

In the meantime I became distant and strange. I was prone to lapses of concentration and a cramp in my stomach that made food uninteresting and my temper shorter than it should have been.

I knew how much I loved my wife, my *family*, how lucky I was. I didn't perhaps *understand*, didn't get it in the way I did after it was all gone, but I knew well enough. You realize what makes sense is to consign your emotions to a moment in time with no forward momentum. You may even fantasize about having this conversation with the other party, both accepting — with sadness, but a straight-backed sense of what's right — a course of action that would have God nodding in approval, picking you up in his big warm hand and moving you back to a more acceptable part of the moral landscape.

But you never get to the closing sentence of this discussion, because what this fantasy is really about, if you only had the sense left to know, is conjuring a situation in which the two of you are together again.

We did the right thing, several times.

We said, in words or via email or text, that it was over — and behaved that way. But it's *hard*. After years in which your life has melded with that of your partner, suddenly you've spent a period as an individual again. An affair is such an *active* circumstance. You make choices about how/when to be in contact, whether/how to lie, what words to say and how much to expose; searching reality for interstices in which you can pursue this thing. Dealing with someone new makes *you* new again, too, shaken awake by trivial differences. Carol seldom wore perfume, for example. This other person did. Carol almost never wore jewellery, whereas the other woman even made a few pieces of her own from time to time (including a silver bracelet which she gave to me, and which I lost track of, toward the end).

To be drunk on adrenaline and then dropped back into the daze is to die before your time. Suddenly the charge of the future is switched off, and life feels like the rusty skeleton of an abandoned amusement park. No longer does it echo with the sounds of glee and chatter, no more is it filled with the smell of sun lotion and ice cream and lit by neon and cotton candy so pink it hurts your eyes. Now it is empty and silent. You keep trying to find your way out, to locate the parking lot where you know there remains only one vehicle now — your own. As you search, you keep your head down, trying not to glimpse the swooping rides that only a few days before were making your heart dip and soar, and which are now dark and dead and creaking in the wind. You don't want to leave — you never *wanted* the place closed down, however much money it was losing, however dangerous it had become. You want this place to still be vibrant and alive, you want to climb back on the ride — and you do not want to be here to watch the whole edifice crumble to dust.

When you finally find your car, lonely under a solitary lamp-post in the vast and empty lot, you want to drive away into the night leaving *something* to which you can return in your

273

dreams and in the wistful watches of long afternoons. You want to be able to hear the echo of your own heart, when it last laughed and shouted on the roller coaster of a summer afternoon.

You want to think that maybe, if you were to run back here on the right night, and at the right time, you might find that person still standing waiting after all, smiling that smile and holding two tickets for one last ride — one that might last forever this time.

★   ★   ★

You get through those times, trying to take contentment from the fact that the experience was had. But that's a poor kind of reward and speaks from a soul growing older and less vital, more inclined to settle for retrospective comfort than risk a future that seems too uncertain, too hard, or simply too short. It seems this way especially when you're old enough to realize the memories you're cherishing will degrade, fading from the intensity of a just-woken dream into a dusty book of old photographs; to finally become little more than words — nothing remaining vibrant except, perhaps, a split-second memory of someone looking at you with greedy glee, the bottomless gaze of someone who, just for that instant, wants to be nowhere else in the world.

Which is why, however firmly it had been finished — and episodes of non-contact went on for weeks and even months — sooner or later one of us would be unable to resist adding some

274

coda that wasn't really a coda. There would be a coda to the coda. Finally another meeting would take place. It would be somewhere public, where two adults could legitimately encounter each other under the auspices of friendship; but after a few drinks we'd catch each other's eye and know that, just for this evening, neither of us cared if we caused the universe to crack in half.

I tried not to be bad. A lot of the time it worked. Some of the time it did not.

We saw each other, on and off, for thirteen months. It started, in other words, when Carol was five months pregnant with Tyler. You can ask how I'd let myself get into that situation, but I have no answer for you. It would be like asking a ghost why they stepped in front of the car. Because they didn't see it coming. Because they didn't know what would happen until it was happening, and then they couldn't stop.

Just because.

Something happens, and other things happen as a result. If you believe heaven and hell have more complex roots than this, then you're either a more subtle man than me, which is entirely plausible, or you have a lot to learn.

Here's the bottom line. I could have been out on the deck of the house that Carol and I shared, drinking that beer and spotting that my son wasn't in vision, twenty minutes earlier. I could perhaps have got to him before he reached the end of the jetty, before whatever happened had gone too far.

I wasn't and didn't because I spent those twenty minutes in my study, enjoying a phone conversation with Jenny Raines. Bill was out, she was bored, so she called. It was the first time we'd spoken in weeks, and we lingered over it, and my boy died.

Things happen because.

Scott knew that, and he was only four years old.

★   ★   ★

Kristina listened while I told her these things, or a heavily truncated version of them. It took maybe ten minutes. It is instructive to discover how compact your history becomes when you verbalize it to someone else, how small your big deals can seem.

She sipped her own coffee for a while after I'd finished, her eyes elsewhere. 'What exactly happened to your son?' she asked, eventually.

I had alluded to Scott only once. 'He died.'

'How?'

I gave her the bones of that, realizing that she was the first person I had ever told about this, too, except for my father. She closed her eyes.

'I'm so sorry,' she said.

She had ignored or seen past everything I had said about my behaviour, and gone straight to what was real about my life now, things I had spent the last three years dealing with alone. While I wasn't sure I deserved that kind of consideration, I was grateful for it.

'Thank you,' I said.

She shook her head, as if I had missed her point. Her hands were laid out on the glass

276

covering the table top, and I noticed the long, pale fingers were trembling slightly. Knowing what I was doing, but not why, I placed one of my hands on top of one of hers.

She opened her eyes and looked down at it, but did not move. I felt I ought to say something, but knew the placing of my hand already had. My mind hadn't caught up with what my body was trying to communicate. I was aware that my heart was thudding, hard, as if each beat stood alone.

'No,' she said, and moved her hand.

I smiled crookedly, not very hurt, or not yet. 'After everything I just told you, I'm not surprised.'

'Nothing to do with that,' she said. 'I'm not hearing that this woman means anything to you now.'

'No. I guess I'd like to hear she's still alive, but other than that . . . I haven't spoken to her since the day Scott died. I look back and it's as if a crazy person did what I did. Or it's a story I heard about someone else. Someone really dumb.'

'You're not the only human who's been an asshole. Get over it.'

I laughed. 'You cut right to it, don't you?'

'It's been said.'

I looked her in the eyes. 'So?'

A curt shake of her head. 'You just don't want to get involved, chum.'

'Okay,' I said, though I realized that this was not true, and that she hadn't actually moved her hand very far; but also that the one I'd put on hers had grazes from the fight with Bill, and that if there was ever going to be a time for this conversation, it probably wasn't now. 'You want another coffee?'

'No,' she said. Then, more gently, 'I should get back to the bar.'

'Didn't seem too busy in there.'

'No,' she said, and smiled, a little. 'But . . . '

She stopped talking because she saw I was staring out of the window. 'What?'

I stood. A car had just driven past, not fast. I thought I recognized it. 'Wait here a second.'

I headed quickly out onto the street. The car was still moving toward the intersection, but losing momentum, as if the person in charge had taken their foot off the gas. It took me a moment to be sure, because I'd always seen the vehicle with the roof up and music pumping out of it, but yes — I knew this car. I ran along the sidewalk and caught up with it just as it finally came to a halt.

I ducked down and saw Becki was driving, and that Kyle was strapped into the passenger side, asleep or crashed out, head lolling forward.

Becki's hands were clamped to the wheel, and she was staring straight ahead.

'Becki?'

She turned to look up at me, as if in disbelief. Her left eye was half shut, the cheek beneath it swollen.

'John?'

'What are you *doing* here?'

But I couldn't hear what she said next.

30

I squatted down by the side of the car, awkwardly reaching my arms through the open window to put them around Becki's shoulders. When she'd stopped crying — which didn't take long — I retreated to let her rub her face dry and push the hair out of her eyes.

'I'm sorry,' she said. 'I didn't know what else to do.'

'Call me, maybe?'

'John, I've just driven all the way up here from fucking Oregon. Does that sound to you like a phone call kind of situation?'

I heard the door to the pizza place open, and turned to see Kristina coming out onto the sidewalk.

'We're paid up in there,' she said.

'Kristina,' I said, but I didn't know what to follow her name with. She walked away.

Becki watched her go. 'Who's that?'

I ignored the question. 'What's going on here, Becki?'

'What's going on is we're in deep shit,' she said, with a terrible little smile.

★   ★   ★

I drove to the motel, with Becki following. The office was shut but I eventually roused Marie from her television and got the keys to the room next to the one I had. It took a while to get her

279

to understand that friends of mine had arrived and I was getting the room on their behalf, but I didn't want her to see Becki's face. Partly because motel keepers can be funny about renting to women with facial bruising. Also because such things are memorable.

When I got back out Becki was standing leaning against the side of her car, smoking. Her idiot boyfriend was still passed out in the passenger seat.

'What's the deal with Kyle?'

'He'd been awake seventy-two hours straight.'

'Wake him up and move him inside.'

She managed to get Kyle out of the car and more or less on his feet. When he saw me he looked vaguely relieved for a moment, but then his eyes slid away.

As Becki shuffled him over to their door I went into my own room and washed my face and hands and stared at my reflection for a while. Much of me had yet to catch up with the fight I'd been in, never mind what had happened since. I realized Bill would be on his feet again by now, and that if he wanted to find me, it wouldn't be hard. So be it. I was done running from that situation. Telling Kristina about it had proved this to me, if nothing else. If Bill needed a pound of flesh, he was welcome to come and take it. He was owed.

⋆ ⋆ ⋆

Next door I found Becki apparently alone in the room.

'Where is he?'

'I told him to take a shower. It was overdue.'

I heard that they'd been in town for forty minutes when I found them, ploughing methodically up and down each street in turn. Becki had decided on the way across the mountains that was the only thing she could do, given I wasn't answering my phone. This meant they must have made it here from Marion Beach in not much over six hours, which required driving at speeds I didn't even like to think about.

'I told you to go to your father's,' I said.

'I did exactly like you said. I packed a bag and I was out of there in under fifteen minutes. I didn't go *straight* to my dad's because . . . I needed to think, work out how to explain the whole bag of shit to him. Also I knew if I waited an hour he'd have left for the restaurant already. Otherwise he'd have stayed at home going nuclear on me over Kyle and I just didn't need that. You've only ever been a positive thing in Dad's world, John, and so you haven't seen all sides of him. When he goes to war, the collateral damage can be significant.'

'I can believe that.'

'So I drove around, trying to get hold of Kyle to tell him what you said, but I couldn't raise him so in the end I decided I'd left it long enough, and went over to my dad's place. And Kyle's right fucking *there*, sitting on the doorstep. He'd said he'd finally gone back to our apartment, must have missed me by ten minutes. He'd guessed where I'd go.'

'Did you tell him to go away?'

281

'No, John. I did not. He's my *boyfriend*. He only hadn't been answering my calls because his battery ran out, and then he lost his phone someplace. He broke down when he saw what had happened to me.'

'Though he hadn't come earlier, when you told him on the phone?'

'He wanted to get a gun from somewhere and go talk to these people.'

'Christ,' I said. 'Which evidently didn't happen, thankfully.'

'No. So we talked, and I got some sense out of him for the first time in days. I told him we had to find a way of making everything okay. He asked me . . . I agreed to go back to our apartment with him, talk things through, try to work something out.'

'What was that going to be? The solution?'

'I don't *know*, John.'

'So what happened?'

'We went home. Kyle had been up for, like, days, and I'd told him a shower would be a good thing on several levels. Then I realized he was taking a *really* long time about it and when I get to the bathroom and find him bright and perky I of course understand just how *fucking* dumb I've been.'

'Because that's where the remains of the original stash was, which is why he wanted you to come back with him. He'd already been home to find you weren't there and he'd lost his keys along with his phone and didn't feel quite up to the task of breaking into a second-storey apartment.'

Becki's face went blank, and her chin trembled for a moment, but her eyes stayed dry. 'Yep.'

'I'm sure that's not the only reason he wanted to see you,' I added, feeling old and cruel.

'I'm glad *you* are,' she said. 'Because I've been back and forth on the subject. So I'm screaming at him and he's shouting too and it's close to getting out of hand, when I see something out of the window. A huge black GMC coming up the way, one of those things that looks like it wants to be a Hummer when it grows up. The people who live on our street don't own that kind of vehicle.'

I rubbed my temples with my fingers. 'Christ.'

'Right,' she said bitterly. 'So we split. Down the fire escape and over the fence into next-door's yard. Thank fuck, I had parked around the corner instead of right outside, *but* there's no way out of there except down that same street, and they saw us leave.'

'They came after you?'

'First I thought I'd just tear around for a while, and they'd fall off and we'd get a chance to work out what to do next. But no. Up the coast, through Astoria, they're still on us. Dude can fucking drive, too. I am no stranger to red on the speed dial, as you know, but this guy's pedal to the metal all the way. And Kyle's just lolling there in the passenger scat smoking and has nothing useful to suggest, and there was only one thing I could think of, so I spun out over to Portland and up the interstate to Seattle, and . . . well, here we are.'

'When did you last see them?'

'I'm not sure. On the highway, that kind of car's not so distinctive as in Marion Beach. I *thought* I saw it behind us on 90 just before we started over the mountains. But it could just have been another car, right? They could have given up?'

'They could,' I said. I put my hand out.

'What?'

'Your car keys.'

I went outside and drove her car out of the lot. I went a couple of blocks until I found a tangle of residential streets and stowed the car at the end of it, on the far side of a high-sided truck. It wasn't perfect but short of driving it thirty miles and sending it off the road it was never going to be, and the night was going to be complicated enough without me having to explain to Becki why I'd trashed her beloved car.

I found what I expected to find under the passenger seat, and took it with me. I picked up a six-pack from a liquor store on the corner and walked back to the motel through the drizzle, feeling like I was on autopilot.

When I got back I knocked on Room 10 and said my name. Becki locked the door again behind me.

'I still don't hear any movement from in the bathroom.'

'Whatever,' she said. 'Maybe he fucking drowned.'

I set the beers on the bedside table and handed one to Becki, who twisted the cap and drank a third of it in one swallow. She was too tired to stand but too wired to sit, and she looked young and unhappy, too, like a child who'd realized she'd wandered into a playground game that little kids didn't win.

'We'll work it out,' I said.

'Glad to hear it. So what's up in your life?' she said. 'Who was that chick? What happened to *your* face and hands? We going to cover that in the debriefing?'

'No,' I said.

'Shame. I could do with some light relief.'

'Then you've come to the wrong place.'

'Are you pissed at me for coming up here?'

'No. I just don't know what I can do for you. Kyle's dug his own grave and he's still digging.' I reached into my coat and took out the package I'd removed from her car. I held it up in front of her.

Becki smacked her hands up against the sides of her face, and turned toward the bathroom.

'You ASSHOLE!' she shouted. 'I swear,' she said, turning back to me, 'I didn't know he'd brought it.'

'I believe you. But there's lots you don't know about him now. Like that he would manipulate you back to your apartment, against all common sense, just because he wanted his drugs. Like there's not just cocaine in this bag, but crystal meth.'

'No fucking way,' she said, angrily. 'He's never . . . '

But she wasn't sure. She sat down heavily on the edge of the bed. 'What am I going to do?'

I shrugged, put the package back in my jacket.

'I'm sorry I came,' she said, miserably. 'I was just *so* fucking scared and I didn't know where

285

else to go. Once I got the idea of you in my head it was like there was something to aim for. It was dumb.'

'You did fine,' I said. 'It's what I would have done.'

'Really?'

'I wouldn't lie to you.'

I walked through the room and opened the bathroom door. Kyle was slumped on the floor, head back against the wall. His mouth was open and he was snoring quietly. I noticed that the bathroom door, like the one in my own room, had a key. I dropped my pack of cigarettes in his lap, removed the key from his side and left the bathroom. Then I locked the door and put the key in my pocket.

'Get some sleep,' I told Becki.

'You going to give me that key?'

'No,' I said.

★   ★   ★

Back in my own room I lay on my bed and stared up at the ceiling. My head was full of things I did not want to revisit. The sight of what had happened to Jassie that afternoon. The memory of Bill's face, as he looked at me in his hallway, realizing what I was implying and what he was going to do about it. What I had not managed to do in that whole fiasco was to get a sense of whether Bill had known about me and Jenny, and thus if Ellen's harping on about punishment was likely to have a bearing on my life. Even if I had been sure about that, the next

286

step required believing in things that I did not.

I could not get my thoughts to go in straight lines, and unless I concentrated they all ended up collecting in the same cul-de-sac: the image of my hand resting on a woman's, on a table in an empty pizza restaurant; how large and three-dimensional that hand had felt, and how warm. That and the fact that when Kristina left, she'd said 'we' were paid up, rather than 'I'. Big deal, and probably I had achieved nothing except complicate the only positive relationship I had left in this town, but as I drifted toward sleep I did not regret what I had done. Sometimes the things you do without thinking are the closest to the truth you'll ever come.

Just before I went under I reached into my pocket, took out my phone, and laid it on the bedside table where I would be sure to hear it if anybody called. I wasn't thinking anyone necessarily would.

⋆ ⋆ ⋆

Nobody called, but I did dream.

In the dream it was the middle of the night and I was walking alone through the streets of Black Ridge. There was something about the way the main East — West drag curved through the town that was working at me, and I didn't realize I was close to the motel in which I used to meet Jenny Raines until I was upon it.

The entire building was dark, no cars in the lot. As I stood looking, feeling bitter regret for the things I had done in those rooms, I saw the curtains of one move aside.

It was too dark to see who or what might have opened them, but I thought I saw a pale oval shape reflecting moonlight, just above the level of the sill.

I turned stiffly away and walked through town in a series of jump cuts, ending up on Kelly Street. The window in The Write Sisters was whole again, though badly cracked — lines jagging across the middle in a pattern I nearly recognized, a blood splatter across the middle in a shape that looked a little like an animal. When I got back to Marie's I stood for a while in the road. Here every light was on, every curtain open, though all the rooms beyond were empty.

I heard something behind me, and turned.

When I saw nothing I walked across the road and into the forest, as I had in reality a few nights before. The further I went into the trees the more I felt I could hear noises from between them, the murmur of distant conversation.

This scared me but I started to run, heading in the direction of the sounds.

I ran faster and faster, threading between the trunks, convinced that I could not now only hear voices ahead, but smell wood smoke or something like it. Something strong.

I missed the shape of a large tree root in the darkness, tripped and went sprawling on the ground. All the air was knocked out of me and for a moment my vision went white, as if I was about to lose consciousness. I don't know what would have happened if I had. Would I have woken? Died?

I rolled onto my back, and pushed myself upright.

There were people standing back in the trees, looking at me. Two tall, and three smaller.

I couldn't see their faces, or tell how far away they were. I tried to push myself backwards, pathetically, getting no purchase on the floor, feet scraping and scrabbling.

Suddenly the group was spread out, with the two taller figures much nearer to me. A man and a woman, exhausted, bony, wearing clothes that were dirty and worn and old-fashioned. The man was closest, only a few feet away, and as he pushed his face closer down to mine, like a dog scenting a stranger, I saw it was scarred across the cheeks and forehead with a pattern of freshly slashed cuts that I knew was the same as the marks I'd seen on the back of my motel room — and that his face was my own.

Then they were all gone.

There was no sound, no wind. I panned my vision across the hundred and eighty degrees in front of me, until my eyes began to prickle and my ears roar, and finally saw something coming through the undergrowth toward me.

I turned slowly around, as afraid as I ever have been in my life.

And woke up.

31

She could have stolen a car. She possessed that skill, assuming the vehicle was of a certain type — a legacy of the bad old days. But she didn't want to leave town like that, a thief skulking away in the night. She wanted to leave as Ellen.

Not Ilena.

So she'd gone to the place on Brooker and took the only car they had left, an anonymous compact. The guy behind the desk told her many things about mileage and insurance and filling the car up before reaching her (unspecified) destination, but she was unable to take it in. She didn't think John was right, that she had a concussion, but her head definitely wasn't working right. She couldn't remember when she'd last eaten — before the hospital, certainly — so it could be that was it. Could be, but probably wasn't. It was the town, the trees. They were all in her head.

After a while the rental clerk stopped trying to tell her stuff she clearly wasn't taking in, and gave her the keys. He gave her body a good looking over at the same time, until she stared at him, and he stopped.

She went to the lot around the side of the office and stood in the dark looking at the cheapest car she'd driven in a long time. Since before Gerry. Might as well get used to it. The money she had wouldn't last long. She would need a job and an apartment and many other things, to walk around the world's shelves and try to find objects and situations to care about, if she could.

Time to start again.

Again.

★   ★   ★

Only when she was behind the wheel did it begin to feel completely real; only then did she get her aching, cloudy head around what she was planning to do: leave the only place she'd ever been genuinely happy. The cause of that happiness was gone, of course, dead and gone, but still we put our faith in places. We think that if we just lived somewhere different, everything would be okay. We believe that if we paint the stairway a bright new colour, and clear out the closets, our minds will follow. We'll take just about any ray of hope rather than accept that ninety-five per cent of the world we inhabit exists within the confines of our own skulls.

She wished she had something to bring with her, but it couldn't be. She had brought a few objects from the house the morning before, the morning of the crash, but they were in a bag in the trunk of her car and she had no idea where that was. Towed somewhere after the accident, presumably, but either she hadn't been told where or she'd forgotten. It would have been nice to have those things, small though they were. A couple of items of clothing, bought in special places. A book in which he'd written a

291

loving message. A napkin from a café in Paris, from that first weekend. She had secretly put it in her pocket when he went to the bathroom. She had known it was the start of something. Sometimes, you just do, and keeping souvenirs is the only way we have of pinning those moments down before the world takes them away.

But really, what would she do with those objects? Take them out once in a while and shed dry tears over them? Use them to remind herself of the way things no longer were? She wasn't twenty-one any more, either, and no amount of wailing would bring that back either.

There's only one piece of baggage you can never really do without. Ellen lifted the right arm of hers and turned the key in the ignition.

$$\star \quad \star \quad \star$$

As she drove out through the quiet town she heard her phone beeping in her pocket. John Henderson, perhaps, trying again, as he had several times that afternoon. She had nothing to say to him. Seeing him in the coffee shop, after Jassie Cornell had killed herself, had been like watching a child getting ready to march off to war clutching a stick as a pretend rifle. She'd told him as much as she could without coming right out and saying it. If he didn't get it, there wasn't anything more she could do. She regretted getting in contact with him, pulling him up here, trying to deflect her doom into him with the pattern she'd been taught. There was nothing she could do about those things either.

292

As Gerry said, on one of the long nights where they had talked through her bad times, his arms around her and her face running with tears: *The past is like an asshole ex-boyfriend, Ilena. Change your number, and just don't ever talk to him again.*

If it wasn't John calling, then it was one of the others, and she certainly had nothing left to say to them. She put some music on the radio instead.

She drove past the end of Kelly Street without a second glance. A couple of hundred yards further up the road, about half a mile short of the beginning of the real forest, the radio faded, and then cut out. Soon afterwards the car started to cough, too, and judder, and then died. She steered calmly onto the side of the road.

She waited patiently, turning the key once every three minutes. Eventually it started again. Things got like this sometimes, around here. Little things, never big enough to make a fuss about. Signs that the place itself was shifting in its sleep, and might be about to wake up. All the more reason to get the hell out.

As she pulled back onto the road she thought she heard something in the back seat of the car. She knew that if she looked around, it would very likely be Gerry sitting in the back there, or the thing that looked like him. He had followed her from the hospital. She had seen him on the street after the horror with the girl in the coffee shop. He had been walking slowly along the other side, his head turning to keep his eyes on her.

293

If she looked in the back seat now the face she would see would have the same look in its eyes, and she knew the story it told wasn't true. Gerry hadn't hated her. He had loved her.

That knowledge was the one thing she was determined to take with her out of this place. It was the sole possession they couldn't take from her.

And so she didn't turn around, but put her foot firmly down on the pedal, and set off down the road into the forest.

★ ★ ★

She got less than twenty miles.

She didn't notice the headlights behind her. She had been crying, and it had taken all her concentration to keep herself going straight and safe along the dark forest road.

There was the sound of a car accelerating past her, in the other lane.

She jumped, startled, and wiped her sleeve across her eyes. It was a long way to Seattle. She had to keep her shit together. Probably just as well the other car had given her a little shock. She'd concentrate better now, put the radio back on, try to think forward. There was no need to think about the past tonight. She would have plenty of time to regret it at leisure.

But once the car had gone forty yards past, it suddenly cut back into her lane.

She jammed her foot on the brakes, skidding thirty feet. She was thrown hard into the belt, and then thudded back into her seat.

294

She moved fast, shifting the car into reverse, but as she wrenched around in her seat she realized another car had come up behind and was blocking that way too.

There was nowhere to go, and so she turned back around and took her hands off the wheel.

A man got out of the car in front, a silhouette in her headlights. She watched as he walked back along the road.

When he reached her car he rapped gently on her window.

She lowered it. The policeman looked gravely down at her.

'What's up, Ellen?'

'I'm leaving.'

'I don't think so.'

'I did what I was asked.'

'Yeah, kinda. But this afternoon you were saying things that you shouldn't have.'

She looked up at him. He shrugged. 'Someone heard you. You knew what the deal was.'

'But I did what I was told,' she said. 'I'm done. You have to let me go now.'

He didn't say anything.

'She was never going to let me leave, was she?'

He still didn't answer, just opened her car door. Before his hand fell on her, Ilena managed to turn her head to look into the back seat of the car.

Gerry wasn't there. There was nothing there. Nothing left anywhere any more.

Part 3

Once we have taken Evil into ourselves, it no longer insists that we believe in it.
Franz Kafka
The Zurau Aphorisms

32

Brooke swam from seven until seven-thirty, fast, methodical laps up and down the covered pool at the rear of the house. Then dressed in her suite, blow-dried her hair and selected a pair of good shoes. Carefully, as if the day ahead held a wedding, or a funeral. Because one never knows — it might.

Cory was already at the breakfast table when she arrived, halfway through an Eggs Benedict. He rarely ate more than cereal. He must be hungry. She realized, as she sat, that she was hungry too. The air felt very thin today, short on sustenance, as if the land had exhaled overnight and was waiting for a reason to breathe in again.

When Clarisse appeared at her elbow with a pot of Earl Grey tea, Brooke asked for the same as her brother. Who meanwhile kept eating. Small, neat mouthfuls.

'Good evening?' she asked, eventually.

Another mouthful went in, was chewed, swallowed.

'Very pleasant,' he said. 'She's very . . . nice.'

'And?'

He shook his head.

★ ★ ★

Her plate arrived and they ate in silence. In between mouthfuls she looked out of the window, watching the trees sway at the edge of the property. The house was warm, but it looked cold outside. The sky above was a weather report with only one story to tell.

'I'm sorry,' he said quietly.

'Upwards and onwards.'

'So what are your plans for the day?'

'As yet unfinalized. You?'

'Yakima for lunch.'

'Business or pleasure?'

'Business.'

She didn't believe him, and he knew it. 'One of the pumps in the pool isn't working properly.'

'I'll give Randy a call.'

Clarisse reappeared to freshen their teapots, and to dispense further portions of silence. Brooke ate hers slowly. Cory moved on to toast, spreading it thinly with butter, back and forth, forth and back.

'Cory?'

'Yes?'

'It can't be left any longer.'

'I said I'll call him, Brooke. This morning. Before I go out.'

'I'm not talking about the pool.'

He put his knife down. 'I've told you. I'm not going to — '

'I meant on a larger scale.'

'Are you sure?'

'Yes.'

He finally raised his head to look at her. 'Do you have something in particular in mind?'

'It's already under way.'

He nodded slowly, distantly, reminding her

forcibly of their father. Cory never mentioned him now, nor the manner of his demise. They had been close, or at least closer than Gerry and Brooke had ever been. His death was the first thing that had ever come between them, and sat there like another silence, but one that didn't seem to erode.

'You know I trust you in these matters,' he said, dabbing at his mouth with a napkin.

'Yes.'

Trust, or hand over all responsibility to? For a moment Brooke missed her grandfather so much that it hurt like toothache. Her mother, too. Even Dad, that silly, fond old man. Anyone whose presence would take some of the weight off her shoulders, prevent the world from always being so very quiet: another body to warm a house now home only to the faint clatter of silverware, and china, the mutter of non-fiction television in this tidy lair of the nearly middle-aged, forward movement all but stopped. Like everything else in this town, running out of steam, turning into a photograph.

Unless someone did something.

Her brother stood, hesitated for a moment, looking out at the woods.

'Yes,' he said, more firmly. 'Yes, I can feel you're right. You'll tell me what you want me to do?'

'I will. Don't go far today. See if your friend will take lunch here instead.'

Cory walked slowly out into the hallway, leaving her alone at the table with a plate of congealed hollandaise.

When Clarisse came to clear the dishes, Brooke looked up. 'I think you could take this afternoon off,' she told her. 'And tomorrow morning. In fact, why not stay with your daughter for a couple of days? Take a little break. You deserve it.'

'Yes, Miss Brooke.'

★ ★ ★

After breakfast she went back up to her private sitting room. She sat on the couch and considered the web of things. She thought through how matters would need to be done, working the web of and-then-and-then-if-then. You can plan all you like, however, and she had, but still you had to be open to the moment, to leave space for the gods to walk through the room.

Eventually she got up and went to the middle section of the drawers that lined the side of the room. She used the key on the chain around her neck to open one of them, and withdraw evidence.

Then she picked up the phone, and called a policeman.

'It's today,' she said.

★ ★ ★

Afterwards she went down to the kitchen and picked a few things out of the fridge. She put them in a small plastic lunchbox — where it had come from, she had no idea — and carried this

302

with her as she left the house.

After a short drive she parked, got out, walked to a house and unlocked a door. She opened it a little, squatted down, and slid the lunchbox across the floor into the darkness beyond.

'We're going to move you a little later,' she said. 'After that there will be no more food.'

The people in the dark said nothing, though Brooke heard the sound of quiet crying.

'I'm sorry it had to be this way. You were invited to make it easier, after all.'

'Fuck you, Brooke,' said a weary voice, in the dark.

Brooke relocked the door, and walked back to her car. She did not turn when a sudden breeze ran through the trees, causing a harsh whisper of leaves as loud as a human voice.

But she knew what caused it, and was glad.

33

Next morning I walked back into the motel parking lot to see Becki banging on my room door.

'Where the fuck have you been?' she said, furiously, as soon as I was within earshot. 'I need the bathroom key, and I need it *now*.'

'Use mine,' I said, handing her one of the coffees I had bought, along with a small paper bag. She looked inside and saw the toothbrush, shampoo and other toiletries I'd picked up, and her face softened.

'We can't just leave him in there,' she said.

I unlocked my door. 'Right now I can't think of a better place for him to be. He has access to water. Sooner or later he'll get hungry, at which point we may be able to talk sensibly with him. Until then I'm in no hurry for him to become an active factor in my life.'

I reached into my jeans pocket, pulled out her bathroom key and dropped it into the paper bag. 'It's your call.'

She thought a moment.

'It can wait,' she said, with half a smile. 'Not sure he's ever seen this time in the morning anyhow.'

★　★　★

I told her to stay indoors once she'd showered, and went and got in my car. It was time to leave town. Ellen still wasn't returning my calls, but there were two other things I wanted to do before I left.

I turned out of the lot and headed toward the main road through town. I found myself slowing outside the motel I'd seen in my dream: the one I'd lived in for a while, and also the place I used to meet Jenny Raines. That's all Black Ridge had been to me before a few days ago. The place of assignations. Charged with a toxic blend of pleasure and guilt, therefore — guilt that had writhed and reproduced after Scott's death, forging a fake connection in my head to the worst thing that had ever happened to me.

Since I'd woken that morning, my thoughts had kept coming back to Bill. A good guy, an old friend, next to whom I'd walked in uniform, patrolling towns and deserts in a place where no one wanted us and where being someone's friend meant being their shield. Who'd invited me into his life again years afterward, encouraging his father to find me a position and a salary that a very recently qualified attorney would have never received otherwise. I have a feeling Bill even introduced us to the realtor from whom we bought our house, though I'm not sure.

And how had I repaid him? By becoming as bad a thing in his life as anyone or anything had ever been to me. I never did anything to him directly, of course — but that's not how bad things work. They're dark and slippery, always just out of sight, operating at a remove that's hard to foresee and impossible to fight.

I called Bill's office and was told he wasn't

there. I remembered him saying he had a big case coming up, and seeing the number of files spread around his house, and considered it likely he was working from home. I did a U-turn and drove back the way I'd come.

Bill wasn't at home either. I waited, then knocked again and walked back halfway down the path to look for evidence he was inside and electing not to see me. There was none. I turned away, unsure what to do. It was too cold to hang around on the porch.

I went back to the car and sat in it. I tried the old cell-phone number I had for him, but it dead-ended in silence. It struck me that, despite talking up the notion of a drink when we'd met on the street on my first day here, Bill hadn't gone out of his way to ensure we could actually get in contact. I'd been too caught up in avoiding a further meeting to realize he might have been doing the same. Might the kinder and more adult thing just be to leave the guy alone, rather than assuaging my own guilt by forcing him to look once more inside a box he'd tried to glue shut? Kristina had told me to just get over it, and it could be she was right.

Or was that sloping away from my responsibilities, as I'd turned my back on Tyler and most everything else? Didn't I owe Bill the opportunity to call me an asshole to my face? Would it ever be over without that? I remembered evenings soon after Carol and I had moved to the area. Bluff, pleasant gatherings with the Raineses and their neighbours, dinner parties where the men are in good shape but pompous, the women mild and thickening, and both are far duller than they have any need to be; which start with the guests paying court to the hosts' most extroverted child, last a couple of hours with each couple gently carping at each other (except for the pair whose problems are too serious for such sport, and who therefore appear to be basking in rather formal perfection) — and eventually dissolve, abruptly, when someone has to leave early because their babysitter has exploded.

Except Bill and Jenny never had any kids. And now, neither did I. Lives get tangled, until you look down in your hands and cannot follow the string for all the knots. I decided I'd wait it out a little longer in the hope of loosening at least one of them.

★ ★ ★

Some time later I heard a knocking on the window, and looked up to see Bill standing by the car. He had a fat lip and a mild black eye. He looked tired.

I wound the window down.

'You planning some kind of ninja stealth attack?' he asked. 'If so, you suck.'

'I came to apologize.'

'For what? Sleeping with my wife or fucking up my house? Not to mention face. Nothing a client likes more than a lawyer who looks like he lost a bar fight.'

'All of the above.'

He looked down at me for a moment, then turned and walked slowly toward his house.

The walls of his hallway looked more bare than they had, but the mess had been tidied away. I leant against one of the kitchen counters while Bill made coffee, feeling about as awkward as I had in my life.

'She's in Boulder,' he said, eventually.

'Back home?'

'Sure you two must have done at least *some* talking,' he said, drily. 'Which case, you know she was from Philadelphia.'

I didn't know what to say to that.

'Left five months ago,' he said, handing me a coffee. 'Which was frankly a relief. She'd gotten to the point of being hard to live with.'

'Hard how?'

'Down all the time. I mean, really, *really* down. Stopped going out, stopped making her jewellery, stopped doing anything except staring out the window at the woods. Running around some inner wheel, tidying the house and then tidying it again. She's with some guy now. I hope he's doing a better job than me, though Christ knows I tried.'

'When did you find out?'

'About you two? Only a couple weeks before she left. Things had been getting brittle. Eventually you came up in conversation, mostly as further evidence that I was so dumb and preoccupied with work that I couldn't see what was happening right under my own nose. Which I guess is fair, as I'd had no clue what you'd been up to. Of course I *did* think of you as a friend, so I wasn't braced for it coming from your direction.'

'Bill, I didn't do it to you.'

'Yeah, you did,' he said. He was looking me straight in the eye and for a moment the air between us was tense and clear. 'Who *else* did you think she was married to?'

'I'm sorry,' I said, subsiding. 'I did a very bad thing, and I'm sorry.'

'Okay.'

'That's it?'

'What do you want from me? If you'd been here the day I found out, then yeah, I might have gone old school on you. Now? I have slept on it many times, John. It's done. It's your problem, not mine.'

'You seemed less sanguine about it last night.'

'Yeah, and look what that got me.' He sighed. 'That only happened because you were implying that I might have hurt her, which was too fucking much.'

'I was kind of mixed up.'

'Understood. But I'm *not* any more, John. And I don't want to burst your bubble but you weren't the only one, okay? After you left town there was at least one other guy. Not that it seemed to make her any happier.'

For an instant this information actually stung, and I realized that if you have woken up next to someone but once, you are never truly disconnected again. Then I laughed, briefly, and shook my head.

'My point exactly,' Bill said.

We didn't say anything for a few minutes, but stood drinking coffee in vague attitudes of cautious affability.

'So what are you doing these days?'

'I'm a waiter,' I said, daring him to make something of it.

'Good deal. The world needs waiters. I imagine you carry a very efficient plate. That what you're going back to?'

'Yes.'

'Today?'

'That's the plan.'

'Sounds like a good one.'

'I'm very glad you approve.'

He raised an eyebrow. 'We're not going down that road again, are we? It's just, my fists hurt enough as it is.'

I smiled. 'No, we're not.'

And that seemed to be that. Bill turned toward the hallway, and I understood that this was over.

★   ★   ★

Outside the sky was low and hard and cold, with a matt texture I recognized from when I'd lived around here. The weather was considering getting serious. As I stepped into the wind, Bill spoke again.

'That other thing get straightened out?'

'What thing?'

'Something about Ellen Robertson. It got lost in the undertow last night.'

'It's done with,' I said. 'Or at least, I'm walking away from it. Ellen's gone AWOL anyhow.'

'Sounds wise to let it go.'

'Yep. I'm growing up all over the place.'

'Let me give you a piece of advice, John. Okay?'

310

'I'm listening,' I said, assuming it would be along the lines of letting the past be the past, letting go and moving on, stepping on the stones of tarnished yesterdays toward brighter tomorrows. I was prepared to hear him out. It was counsel I needed to hear, as many times as necessary.

'Don't fuck with Brooke Robertson.'

Not what I was expecting. 'I'm leaving today,' I said. 'But as a matter of interest, why?'

'Back at school, I knew those two passing well. I even stepped out with Brooke for a few weeks, back when we were, like, fourteen. But you know me — I'm just a big, straightforward lunk.'

'No one thinks that.'

'Yeah they do, and they're pretty much right and I don't mind the hand I got dealt in terms of personality. There are worse guys to be, most of the time. I'm just saying Brooke got her cards from a whole different deck.'

'I don't understand.'

'She's real smart, but broken. We stopped hanging out and it was me who ended it, though she was cute, gave every indication she might put out, and was actually interesting to talk to. A couple years later there was a rumour of something between her and one of the English teachers. She got a huge crush, he wouldn't play along, something like that.'

'And?'

'He died.'

I laughed. 'What, with Brooke's hairbrush found stabbed through his heart? Come on, Bill.'

'He got sick. One day he's the fittest guy in the

place and second in command of the basketball team. Six weeks later, he's dead from a stroke. Brain just blew his lights out.'

'Which happens. And what would Brooke possibly have to do with it? Jesus, Bill.'

'I guess you're right. But what was that other thing you always used to say? Dots freak people out. So they join them with lines that aren't there.'

'I was right.'

'Statistically *everyone's* bound to be right, once in a while. Even a fuck-wad like you.'

I smiled. 'You were Brooke Robertson's sweetheart? Really?'

'No,' he said, patiently. 'That's my point, John. I don't see her often these days, and when I do, I don't enjoy it. I don't know if there was ever a heart there to be sweet over, but there sure as hell isn't now. She's got it into her head that she has to hold the fort against the Mongol hordes, and whatever girl once lived in her head has been taken out and buried in the woods — by Brooke herself. She's a Robertson now. *The* Robertson. Nothing else.'

'It's certainly clear who wears the pants in that household.'

'Yes and no. Cory may like it round the back, but he's not a complete pushover either.'

'Cory's gay?'

'Christ, John, ain't no closet deep enough,' Bill said, as if pained. 'I admit, he's kept a tight lid on it, and you'd need your ear close to the ground to have heard anything, but . . . well, yeah. Funny you didn't get that. You're normally pretty sharp.'

'I try not to make simplistic judgements on people these days. Especially over matters as trivial as where they hang their sexual hat.'

'One day we may all be so evolved,' Bill said. 'Until then, well, fuck you, Gandhi.'

I laughed, looked at his big, open face and wished a lot of things had not happened.

He stuck out his hand, and I shook it.

'You take care,' he said, went back inside.

34

About halfway back to the motel I became aware
that I was being followed. In the rear-view mirror
I saw a large black SUV maintaining a consistent
distance about eighty yards behind me.

I cut my speed in half. It did the same.

I took a turn off the road into Black Ridge,
onto one that ran by itself with forest either side.
The black car followed.

So I took my foot off the pedal and let my car
roll to a halt, right in the middle of the lane. The
SUV dropped its speed too, stopping twenty
yards behind me. I gave it a minute for the driver
to start leaning on the horn, but it didn't
happen. Whoever was in the vehicle was not on
his way anywhere other than to a conversation
with me.

I got out of the car, leaving the engine
running, both hands out and empty by my sides.

The windows of what I now confirmed was a
large GMC were heavily tinted, giving no clue as
to who or how many were inside. I walked round
to the rear end of my own car, leaned back
against it and lit a cigarette, looking straight at
the windshield.

After about two minutes the doors opened.

A guy got out either side. Both black. One had
the bunched shoulders and neck of someone
who'd punched a lot of bag, and a wide,
impassive face. The other was wiry, his skin a

little paler and his hair sticking up. Their Nikes were very clean indeed.

'Boy, are *you* lost,' I said.

They came and stood at the front of their car. The big guy glanced me up and down. The thinner one just looked me in the eye.

'Know who we are?'

'I can guess.'

'So don't fuck with us, yo.'

'Not considering it. You're serious people, I can see that. Soldiers, right? Professionals.'

Both watched me without saying anything.

'Otherwise you wouldn't have stopped at beating up on the girl. That was you two, yes? Righteous job you did. You beat up a woman, she looks beat.'

Something flickered across the face of the heavier one, and for maybe a nanosecond he looked uncomfortable. Most of these people have declared boundaries, however flimsy and/or subject to negotiation. For some it's refusing to kill on a Sunday, for others it's not breaking the limbs of anyone over seventy. It's how the ones that still care prove to themselves they have their actions under control, that they're not animals who do whatever they're told. For the bigger guy, it looked like beating up a woman wasn't business as usual. The thinner guy's face didn't change at all.

'You know how she be, means you seen her since.'

'Sharp,' I said. 'Your boss evidently put this matter in good hands.'

'No doubt. So where they at?'

'Even assuming I knew where they were, I'm not just going to hand them both up to you.'

'Don't care about the girl. It's your boy we have to talk to.'

'He's not my boy.'

'Whatever. We talking to him one way or another.'

'Your boss — ' I started to ask.

'He ain't our boss.'

'The man who contracted you. What does he want? The money, or to show the world he's tough?'

The larger one spoke. 'You a cop?'

I shook my head. 'Don't give a shit about you or your business, except how it relates to my girl. Whom you have mistreated. But ten thousand isn't shit, and so basically you're set to drop Kyle, right?'

The smaller guy moved his shoulders about a quarter of an inch, looking back at me with the calm surety of someone who'd committed all his worst deeds on purpose.

'In which case I can't help you,' I said. 'If it was just about the cash, maybe we could do something. Maybe *I* could do something. But if you're going to whack the kid regardless, there's nothing in it for me.'

The smaller guy started to reach a hand around his back, presumably to where he had a weapon stashed down the back of his jeans, under his baggy shirt.

'There's something in it for you,' he said, tightly. 'Like you could not get your fucking — '

'You're not from Portland, right? He hired you from over East?'

The guy kept his hand where it was, but nodded.

'And what are you getting? A couple thousand each? Five between you?' No response, which meant I was in the ball park. 'There's another way of handling this. Call your boss, tell him you got the money off the kid, how about you just leave it at that. See what he says.'

'He's — '

'Still going to want him dead. Right. So instead you say you couldn't find him, and you don't take the man's money, but you split ten thousand dollars between you.'

'Where's the ten come from?'

'Me.'

The two guys glanced at each other.

'That ain't going to play,' said the small guy, when he looked back. 'Our job is to drop people, yo. We don't do it, where we at?'

'So, what? Guy who hired you — he pay enough for you to be the Terminator? Are you supposed to drive around the whole of the United fucking States until you find this kid? For how long? A week? Two weeks? A month?'

The smaller guy kept looking at me.

'Right. So instead you tell him he disappeared in the woods up here, maybe he got some friends or something, he's gone. You scared the crap out of his white ass anyway, and he isn't coming back. You tell your boss that if the kid ever *does* show his face in Portland, you'll come back and do it for free. Otherwise . . . you're soldiers and grown-ups and you got other business to attend to.'

317

A thoughtful head-shake. 'The guy's real pissed behind this boy. He ain't going to let it go at that.'

'He's pissed this week. Next week something else will mess with his head and he'll be all over that instead. You know what these people are like.'

The larger guy sniffed. 'What if the kid talks up how he got away with this shit, when he back at the beach?'

'He won't. There's a line to teach that little asshole how to behave, and I'm way ahead of you. Ten thousand ahead, which the fuck will now owe *me*.'

The smaller guy finally brought his hand back out from behind his back, and folded his arms.

'I'm thinking,' he said.

'Do that. I'm leaving town in about an hour,' I said. 'Call me before then and we'll organize how you get the money. You don't, I'll assume you want to take the loss.' I reeled off my cell number. 'And now,' I said, 'it would be necessary for you guys to leave first.'

'You run out on us, and we'll come for *you*,' the thinner guy said. 'And we'll sure as shit be doing *that* for free.'

'Understood. Matter of interest,' I asked, 'who pointed you in my direction?'

'A police.' The guy smiled. 'Who else?'

They walked away and got into their car.

Right, I thought. *Who else.*

★ ★ ★

318

On the way back through town I made my final stop, parking outside the Mountain View. I hadn't banked on it being open, but it was, so I went inside.

The young bartender I'd seen before was behind the counter, cleaning down the surface in a tight white T-shirt and covertly enjoying the way this made his biceps move. I asked him if Kristina was in, and he shook his head.

'Supposed to be, but she hasn't arrived yet.'

'Any chance of you giving me a phone number for her?'

He looked at me with both eyebrows raised, and I realized from the skin around his eyes that he was a little older than I'd thought. 'Yeah, right.'

I found a scrap of paper in my wallet, wrote my name and number on it. I folded this over and held it out. 'Will you give this to her instead?'

'Look, sir, aren't you kind of — '

I stepped up to the counter and smiled.

'Here's the thing, muscles. I don't know Kristina that well, but I suspect if she wanted to be dating you then she already would be. I also believe that if it came to a fight, she could absolutely kick your ass. I *know* I could.'

He blinked at me.

'So how about you drop the attitude and answer my question in two words or less? Will you give her this note, or what?'

'Yes.'

'Good man. Something else. Yesterday morning, when the thing happened opposite? There was a guy drinking in here. In his fifties. You came out together.'

319

The man nodded cautiously.

'He a regular?'

'Never seen him in here before.'

'See him talking with anyone?'

'Not in the bar.' He hesitated. 'But I noticed him up the other end of the street, fifteen minutes before, about. Talking with Jassie.'

'You're sure it was her?'

'Her hair was kind of blue, dude.'

'Did it look friendly? The conversation?'

'Too far away to tell. Guy drank two large Bushmills in half an hour afterward, though.'

'You mention this to the police?'

He shrugged, and I realized he probably wasn't so bad a bartender after all.

'Remember to pass on that note,' I said.

Back in my car I sat for five minutes and watched two men replacing the window of The Write Sisters. By lunchtime it would be open for business again, though you could still make out a stain on the sidewalk where repeated cleanings had not yet removed all vestiges of the blood of someone who had formerly worked there. Eventually it would disappear, soaking down into the paving stones and then into the earth beneath, and life in Black Ridge would go on as it always had.

Wouldn't most places think about shutting for a few days, after something like that happened? Wouldn't most towns *feel* different, in the wake of an event like that, whereas Black Ridge felt exactly the same? I didn't know why it picked at me, and there was nothing I could do about it.

I drove away, making sure there was no sign of any large, black SUVs in the rear-view mirror.

★ ★ ★

I parked in the bank lot where the coffee guy plied his bad-tempered trade, stashing the car on the far side of a large, white truck, and walked the rest of the way. The motel parking lot was empty, and there was no one in the office, though the presence of the maid's cart, run aground outside Room 2 like an abandoned ship, said I could probably deal with her when it came to checking out, arduous though the transaction would likely be.

When I knocked on the door to Room 10 there was silence for a moment. Then the door was yanked open.

'Becki,' I said. 'You're supposed to — '

I saw the wreckage of the bathroom door behind her, and pushed past.

'Oh, crap. When did this happen?'

'Half an hour ago. He'd been banging for like, two hours, saying how he was okay and stuff and he just wanted something to eat. I didn't know what to do, but I thought you'd probably say to leave him there until he calmed down.'

'Yes, I would have.'

'But eventually he just, fucking, *kicks the door out*. I had no idea he'd even be able to do that. And he's all 'Where's the fucking car?' and I know what he's really asking, but I don't even *know* where the car is, and . . . '

I realized she was standing with her back not

321

quite straight, one hand over her ribs on the lower left side. 'Did he *hit* you?'

'No. No. He just — it was an accident.'

'Bullshit.'

'It *was*. We were shouting, and there was kind of a pushing thing . . . John, he's not who he used to be. I'm serious. He's been fucked up the last few days, for sure, but it was like a whole new level. He came out that bathroom like he'd been fucking *possessed*.'

'Do you have any idea where he is?'

She laughed, a short jagged sound. 'I was lying on the floor at the time, and he was not in a plan-discussing place. He just booked. He's probably running around town like a fucking dog, sniffing for the car and his fucking dope.'

'Okay,' I said. 'That's not good. I ran into the guys who're looking for you.'

'No,' she said. 'Please no. They're *here*?'

'I have them half interested in taking a deal but if they happen to see Kyle on the streets then their life will be a lot simpler — and they will go back to Plan A. You have to stay here.'

'Fuck that,' she said. 'I'm not just — '

'You want to give these people two shots at recognizing someone? I have to find Kyle, knock the asshole out or feed him drugs if that's what it takes to get him in a car. Then I'm paying the guys who're looking for him, and we're out of here.'

'I can't stay,' she said. '*I cannot just sit here.* What if Kyle comes back when you're out looking for him? What if he leads the *other* guys back here?'

322

I realized there was some sense in this, and also that she was telling the truth either way. She could not just stay here by herself.

'If there's anything in here you need to bring with you, get it now,' I said. 'I'm going next door and then to get my car. I'll be ten minutes. When I knock, come out quickly and get straight in the back seat. Okay?'

She nodded, and handed over my room key.

I let myself in next door, already wondering if there was anything I really needed to take, but thinking it would just confuse the maid if I left stuff behind. I was moving so quickly that I didn't even notice that there was someone lying on the bed before I was halfway across the room.

'Who the hell . . . '

As my eyes accommodated to the darkness I realized I couldn't see anything of the person's face, because it was obscured by the large manila envelope lying over it.

I took a step closer and recognized Ellen Robertson's hair spread over the counterpane around her head, amidst the blood.

And then I saw the nail which had been driven through the envelope to hold it in place, sticking straight up from her forehead.

35

For a moment I couldn't do anything. Couldn't move, couldn't even seem to breathe.

I finally took a step forward and saw that the envelope had my name written on it, as if Ellen had been labelled with me. I took the end and moved it. There was initial resistance from where it had become stuck to her forehead with blood, but then I was able to swivel it around the fixed point of the nail.

Ellen's eyes were open.

She was dead, though. Someone had cut right across her throat with a knife that had been big but not very sharp. Although blood was smeared down her neck and onto the bedspread, it was clear she hadn't been killed in the room — or there would have been a far worse mess. Much, much worse. Someone had murdered her and brought her here. Judging by the lack of blood around the other wound, in the centre of her forehead, the nail had been banged in well after her death, after she'd been laid in place.

I found myself stepping backwards and sitting on the other bed, suddenly and heavily. Ellen's arms lay down by her side. From what I could see of her hands there didn't seem to be any cuts or broken nails, any signs of a struggle.

Had she been drugged? Caught unaware, from behind? When I'd last seen her, yesterday afternoon, she'd been pretty vague. Concussed,

324

I'd assumed, though I was beginning to wonder about anything that happened in this town. Maybe she'd just given up.

What I did next depended on what I was going to do after that, so I did nothing. Thinking two steps ahead was beyond me for a little while.

Eventually I checked in the bathroom, which I should have done straight away. There was no one there.

I went back and stood over Ellen's body, as she stared up past me, toward the ceiling and beyond. I leaned over and gently tore the top of the envelope, down to where it was fixed by the nail, being careful not to brush against the protruding end, in the probably vain hope that there might be fingerprints on it, or that anyone would care that they happened not to be mine.

When I'd got it away from Ellen's face the envelope felt unevenly bulky, as if there was more than paper inside, but that would have to wait. I carried it to the door with me and took off the 'DO NOT DISTURB' sign.

I slipped outside and hung the sign on the handle, then walked stiff-legged to where the maid's cart now stood, outside Room 5.

The door was ajar. I knocked on it. I heard the sound of shuffling feet from within, and then Courtney was standing peering up at me.

'Hello,' she said.

She looked mild and ethereal and harmless, and it was hard to conceive how she could exist in the same world as the thing lying on a bed four doors along.

'Hey,' I smiled. 'I'm in Room Nine?'

She nodded slowly. 'Okay.'

'Thing is, I'm going to be here another night, and I've got papers spread all over the room. Work stuff. I just want to make sure they're not disturbed.'

'Okay,' she said, again. 'I'll be careful.'

'Great. Thank you.' I pretended to leave, but then stopped and turned back. 'Actually, you know what? Maybe you should just forget my room for today.'

She looked doubtful. 'But what about your sheets?'

'That's okay. I'll use the other bed.'

'You'll need fresh towels, though.'

'I'll just grab a couple from the cart, okay?'

Courtney still didn't look happy. 'I don't know. I've had people ask before, and Marie was really bugged when she found out, because, like, it turned out they'd made a total mess.'

'It's nothing like that. It's just important these documents don't get moved around, that's all.'

Everything seemed to take a very long time to be processed in this girl's mind. 'I just don't want Marie pissed at me. I mean, really, really.'

'I won't tell if you won't. Promise.'

Something happened to her face then, and it was not good. She blinked, several times, rapidly, her cheeks creasing, face turning slightly away.

I didn't know how much longer I could stand there doing this, and so I got out my wallet and pulled out a twenty. 'It would just make my life easier, that's all,' I said, holding the bill out to her.

She stared at it, her face still and cold.

'I'll leave your precious room alone, cock-sucker,' she said. Then she turned on her heel and stormed back into Room 5, slamming the door in my face, leaving me standing there with the twenty still in my hand.

I walked back to 10 and knocked. Becki opened it immediately, clutching a brown paper bag and raring to go.

'Change of plan,' I said, and gently pushed her back indoors.

★　★　★

Becki perched on the end of the bed.

'But . . . but . . . Are you *kidding* me? But . . . *what the fuck*? Why would someone *do* that?'

It had taken a while to get her to accept there was a dead woman next door, and to understand that it was not the woman she'd seen talking to me on Kelly Street the previous night, but a whole different one. I did not fill in the back story and I wouldn't have told her about Ellen's body at all, except there was no other way of convincing her that going out to find her boyfriend was no longer my foremost concern.

'You didn't hear anyone going in there?'

'No, nothing. I mean, Kyle was shouting and banging like crazy, for a long time. So it could have been when . . . What are you going to *do*, John? Are you going to call the cops?'

'No.'

'Why?' She looked up at me earnestly, as if she'd suddenly worked out the solution to everything. 'You've got to call the cops. That's what you do when this kind of shit happens, right?'

'Not this time. The sheriff distrusts me and whoever put Ellen's body there knows that. The sheriff may even be . . . '

I stopped.

'What? May be *what*?'

'I'm just not calling the police.'

Becki dropped her face into her hands. 'So then we just *go*, right? We find Kyle and bug out of here.'

I didn't answer. Since finding Ellen's body I'd felt as if I was terribly behind. The more I tried to catch up with events the more it seemed like I was sliding to the side and getting lost in the trees.

'*Right?* John? That's what we do?'

'The room is booked under my name and with my credit card,' I said, distantly. I could hear the clank of the maid's trolley moving along the walkway of the motel, and I realized I should have asked the girl to leave this room alone too. 'Even if I moved the body, the blood may have seeped straight through to the mattress.'

'So?'

'So there's no running away from this.'

'There's got to be.'

I shook my head. No way of running from this or anything else.

'Aren't you going to open that?'

She was looking at the thing I still held in my hand.

'I don't know.' I knew I had to look in the

envelope but I did not want to. What information was worth delivering this way?

But I slipped my thumb into the gap caused by tearing it away from the nail in Ellen's forehead. There may or may not have been saliva evidence from whoever sealed it but I didn't think it would ever come to that.

When the envelope was open right across the top I held it over the bed and turned it upside down. An old, grey T-shirt fell out. It was made of thin cotton and had been folded several times. I picked it up carefully. It smelt fusty, as if it had lain somewhere undisturbed for quite a while.

'The hell's that?'

I wasn't completely sure until I checked the label and confirmed that the shirt had come from The Human Race, a store near Pioneer Square in Seattle that I'd used once in a while, back in the old days.

'I think,' I said, 'that it's mine. When I lived here I used to go for runs in the woods. This looks like something I used to wear.'

I realized there was something inside the shirt. Something hard and unyielding. I put the T-shirt back down on the bed and carefully unfolded it.

In the middle was a piece of jewellery, a sturdy silver bracelet half an inch wide, with small pieces of turquoise inset at regular intervals. I recognized it immediately, though it had become very tarnished, and though I had thought it was lost.

'Oh, Christ,' I said.

I moved it to one side, to get to the final object. A piece of thick paper, about four inches square. I turned it over. It was a Polaroid, taken somewhere with very low light. Someone had held a torch and shone it straight at a face, while taking the picture. A photograph of Carol.

'Who's that woman?' Becki said, her voice not far from hysteria. 'John, what the fuck *is* all this?'

'That's my ex-wife,' I said.

'You've got *a wife*?'

'I did.'

I picked up the bangle again, turning it over in my fingers. On the inside, hidden amidst the mottled greys of discoloration, was an inscription I knew would be there, and which I recognized well: J^2

'John? There's something else in here.'

I turned sluggishly to see that Becki was peering inside the T-shirt.

'You want me to get it?'

The truth was I didn't know whether I did, but she went ahead anyway, pulling out a piece of paper that had been neatly folded over twice.

She handed it to me and I unfolded it. At the top were the standard log-lines of an email, with a date from three years ago. The message said:

Yes, it's me. I *know* we're not suposed to be in contact but I've had WAY to much wiine withstanding Bill's clients (still yakking it up downstairs) and I wish I was somewher being touched by you instead. I'm goig to feel crap about this tomorow but I'm pressing the button anyway. Don't reply because I won't answer. And *fuck you* for making me feel like this, you asshole :-) xox

I'd never seen the message before. But I knew who it was from, and to.

'What is it? What's it say?'

'Nothing,' I said, folding it again. I grabbed the shirt and the bracelet and the picture and stuffed it all back into the envelope.

'It didn't look like nothing. You look like you've seen a fucking ghost.'

'Becki, *shut up.*'

She reared back as if I'd slapped her. I hadn't meant it the way it sounded. I just couldn't think, couldn't put the pieces together in my head. 'I'm sorry,' I said.

Our heads turned together then, at the sound of a door opening. But it was not the door to the room we were in. 'What the hell was that?'

'Sounded like . . . John, it sounded like someone going into your room.'

I opened the door and stepped out. There were no cars in the lot. The maid's cart was right where it had been, back down near Room 5. The door to my room was open about an inch, however.

I gently pushed it. It swung open slowly to reveal someone standing in the room, close to the desk. Courtney.

I walked in, not knowing what I was going to do about this. I heard Becki enter the room behind me, then the sharp intake of her breath.

The maid heard it too, and turned her head.

331

'Oh, hi,' she said, and returned to what she'd been doing.

Her voice was back to the way I'd heard it every time before, as if she was on a heavy dose of meds. She held a dusting cloth in her hand. The wastebasket from under the desk had been moved to the middle of the floor, ready to be emptied.

I took another step toward her. Becki was becalmed in the doorway, staring at the body on the bed.

'I asked you not to come in here,' I said.

'Oh, I know,' the maid said. 'But, you know, I thought about it? And I really don't want to get on Marie's bad side. I need this job.' She paused. 'And anyway — there's no papers here.'

'What?'

'You said I wasn't supposed to disturb anything. But there's nothing here. Which is kind of weird.'

'*That's* weird?'

'Well, yeah,' she said, going back to wiping the desk in slow, pointless circles. 'Was it like, a joke, or something? I don't always get jokes.'

'I was concerned,' I said, pointing toward the bed, 'about what you might think about what's lying over there.'

'Oh, that,' she said, glancing over at Ellen's body. 'I already knew about that.'

'You knew about it?'

'Of course.' She looked at me as if I was being obtuse. 'How do you think he got it in here?' She reached in the pocket of her housecoat and pulled out a large ring of keys. 'Duh.'

332

'But . . . '

'Don't worry. It'll be our little secret,' she said, and went back to dusting.

'Who was it? Who put her in here?'

'I don't know,' she said, apologetically. 'I'm sorry. He didn't have a face.'

Becki was no longer looking at the body, but staring at the maid.

'We're leaving now,' I told her.

'You got it.'

Courtney held up her hand. 'Oh, wait,' she said. 'I was supposed to give you this. Sorry. I don't think very clearly sometimes.'

She fished in her coat pocket again and held something out toward me. I took it.

It was another Polaroid. This time it showed a jetty stretching out over a lake, in fading light. It was the jetty near our old house. A house in which it would now be very dark, and where, should you wish to photograph someone, you would need to shine a flash lamp at their face.

'Oh no,' I said, and started to run.

★ ★ ★

Becki tried to follow but I'd left her behind before I even got to the road. I heard her calling after me for a while but then it was drowned out by the sound of my panting, and the thudding of blood in my ears.

I fumbled the keys out as I ran across the bank's parking lot and headed straight for my car, and I didn't hear the men coming out from behind the blue truck until it was far too late.

333

36

When Kristina had got back to her apartment just before dawn, she trudged straight to the shower and stood under it, staying there long after the hot water had run out. It finally got too cold to bear and she turned it off, but remained huddled in the corner of the tiled cubicle, her face in her hands.

She didn't feel any cleaner.

She felt as if she had remembered every bad thing she had ever done, every bad thing *anyone* had ever done. She felt as if they were in her hair, under her fingernails, coating the lining of her stomach and crawling through her veins. She felt as if, were she to spit, or throw up, or bleed, then particles of these deeds would be there, like tiny, twisting worms.

And the worst of it all was that she couldn't be sure that feeling this way was unpleasant.

She had known this potential all her life, and running around the world had not made any difference in the end. Suddenly, last night, she had undone decades of resistance — like deliberately stepping in front of a car. A story told to her over coffee in a pizza restaurant — by a man she really barely knew — had flipped a switch she'd had her finger hovering over ever since she'd been back in Black Ridge.

No. It wasn't that simple.

Of course not. And she ought to know better

than to blame others for what she'd done. Nobody forced people to behave in the ways they did. With a few sad exceptions, most people did what they did. They chose their paths through the woods, even if those choices were sometimes shaped by who they were, and what had been done to them.

★ ★ ★

Done to Kristina, for example, on the night her parents had brought her to the turn-off on Route 61 a little after nine-thirty in the evening. It was very dark, and cold. Her mother was in the passenger seat, not speaking. Her father was driving, doing — as usual — what he was told.

Kristina was in the back, by herself, and she was already afraid. Though no one had said what was about to occur, she was beginning to get an inkling. Why else bring her out all this way into the forest, this late, on a school night? Why had the neighbours been told she was away, staying with friends?

Her dad took the forestry track which skirted close to the Robertsons' land, driving deeper and deeper into the woods. Eventually he stopped the car and got out. He walked a few yards from the vehicle, until he was invisible in the darkness except for the firefly light at the end of his cigarette. Five years later he'd be dead of lung cancer.

Her mother turned and looked at her.

'I want you to get out of the car now, honey,' she said.

335

★ ★ ★

Eventually Kristina got out of the shower. She dressed, feeling as if it was for the first time. The first time after kissing someone you should not have kissed, a kiss that led nowhere but to broken lives. The first time after shoplifting and getting away with it, after telling a lie that would break someone's heart. The first time after slipping into someone's room in the dead of night and doing things that are not allowed under law or by any other measure of human kindness.

Good things never change the world. Nothing is different after you drop coins into a charity box, lend your arm to an old lady, or help build a school in some doomed Third World disaster area. You may get a fleeting kick out of these deeds but nothing in you is actually altered. You can never define yourself through actions you know witnesses would find admirable. They're too easy. They don't count.

After you do a bad thing, however, everything is altered. When you sin, you become an active force. You step through a veil and start to shape the world. Why else would people keep doing it? After bad things your universe is never the same, and as Kristina had walked into the forest the previous evening, she had been all too aware of the permanence of what she was about to do.

★ ★ ★

And almost as afraid, she thought, as on the night when she had stood by the side of the dead-end

336

track and watched her father reverse the car back away down the road. She waited until its headlights had disappeared, then until she could no longer hear the car's engine. Until she was utterly alone.

Then she turned to face the trees.

She has been told nothing about what was to happen now. At first it's okay. She's just standing in the forest, after all. If you live in these mountains, you know the woods. You go for hikes, walks, picnics, school trips to peer at the barely discernible ghosts of rotted cabins and long-ago roads. The forest is there all the time, at the periphery of your vision. It's where you are. It's who this place is.

But of course . . . it's different at night. You think it's just the noises, but it's not. You think it's the rare sensation of being utterly alone, fully adrift from human contact, but it's not that either. You may think it's the cold, or a concern about animals, or any number of explicable fears. They all play a part, naturally. But they're not the thing.

They're not the bad things.

And it is they whom you will sense for the first time that evening, the long, terrible and horrifying night. The night on which you are abandoned in the forest with no promise that you will ever come out — because the possibility of bottomless descent is the point of this exercise. The point is that you become so scared, so deep-in-every-cell terrified, that for a time you lose your mind. You find it again at some point during the procedure, but it's never entirely clear

337

(even years later) if it's the same mind that you lost, or whether part of you has become host to something else. This night will shatter you into tiny bloody pieces, and a different young woman will emerge on the other side.

Whatever mind it is she ends up with, it is sane enough at least to stop her howling and crying, and from biting her own skin, and to help her find a stream in which to wash away the excrement that has run down her legs. It is even enough to help her track down her clothes, so when she is discovered standing neatly by the side of the road, later that morning, it will look as though everything is alright, and nothing has changed.

It has, though.

When she gets back home, her father — whom she loves, very much — won't even look at her. Her mother gives her a long, warm hug. She is proud. The next generation has been corrupted, inducted, had her legs spread wide. There is much to learn, but it has begun. Kristina has become the newest of a long line, stretching back into history.

Slowly, with the fear only just beginning to build in her breast, the long-ago fourteen year old turned from the track, and started to walk into the forest.

In every way that counts, she never came back.

★   ★   ★

After that, there are supposed to be years of becoming accustomed, tuition, practice. Kristina

338

never had those. When her father died her mother came into even sharper focus, and Kristina decided she did not want to be like her, a peasant with power, her life controlled by someone else. The rich own the farm, the peasants till the soil. It works that way with this as everything else.

Kristina rejected everything, all at once, as children do. Just as adults sometimes change their minds.

Was her decision to drive into the forest the night before, after the bar closed, entirely to do with a man she had met? Was it honestly centred on the idea of helping him, trying to stand in the way of what was heading his way? She doubted it. Nothing could happen there, after all. Especially, she realized dismally, now she'd allowed herself to accept the mantle that had been waiting for her all her life. If you like someone, you do not cast them into that role, make them a spear carrier to a town's dirty little secret.

Perhaps it was just like taking the drink you know will send you off the wagon. Lifting the phone and making that drunken call. Scratching that burning itch to do wrong, to allow the bad things out, and by doing so, become alive.

★　★　★

She had driven into the woods and found the place from that night. It should have been hard to find, but it was not. It was like swirling down a drain to the centre of the world, and she could have driven there with her eyes shut.

She left the keys in the ignition and got out and, as an afterthought, took off her coat and left that in the car as well. Then she closed the door and walked straight into the forest. She did not feel cold. After a few hundred yards she unbuttoned her dress and let that fall behind her. In the patchy moonlight, by the glow that seeped in and around the snow which managed to make it down through the trees, her skin already looked blotchy and blue. But on the inside she felt very warm.

After a while she found the trunk of a tree which, though now fallen, she recognized. An important tree, and one which she had spent a portion of a long-ago night clinging to. She stood by it, head lowered, for a period of time it was hard to measure.

Then suddenly she raised her head.

Slowly she turned around.

Out of the darkness between the trees she saw a shape approaching. The shape itself was limitless, unbounded, but it chose to coalesce a tiny portion of itself into a form she could understand.

She watched the big, dark dog as it came toward her. And it felt like coming home.

★ ★ ★

As she sits in her alien apartment the next morning, she doesn't know how much the night will have changed. She doesn't know what she'll now be able to do. But amidst the feelings of

340

nausea, and guilt, and self-hatred, is a massive dose of relief.

So strong that it almost feels sexual.

When she finally stands up to get her shit together and go to work — she still has to function in the real world, after all — she realizes something else.

She wants a cigarette.

37

I was lying on my side. The back of my head hurt and the inside felt black and twisted. My face was pressed into something that smelled dusty and scratched against my cheek.

When I opened my eyes it made no difference, so I closed them again.

$$\star \quad \star \quad \star$$

A little while later I became aware once more. I was on my back, and my neck hurt. My head now felt merely brittle instead of broken, and so I opened my eyes and kept them that way. It still didn't change anything. I gingerly slid my hands up toward my shoulders and used them to lever my upper body away from the floor. This took longer than I would have expected. When it was almost done I pulled my feet back until I was sitting in a hunched position. I reached behind my head and found a bump there which hurt to touch. So I stopped touching it.

I gave my eyes a few minutes to adjust to the light but there appeared to be nothing for them to adjust to. My vision stayed milky black, the only variation coming from the waves and mists of chemicals firing in my retinas as they tried to find something to grab on to. I rubbed them and my face with my hands, hard, but that only made things worse.

342

I made a slow check of my pockets, and found that although I no longer had my cell phone, I retained my wallet and cigarettes. I stuck one of the latter in my mouth and sparked the lighter in front of my face. The cigarette was half lit before I realized I could see someone.

Sitting three or four yards away, cross-legged on the floor, was Scott.

'*Christ*,' I shouted, the cigarette falling out of my mouth. The world went black again, all the darker for the moment of light.

'Hey, John,' said a female voice. 'Welcome home.'

★ ★ ★

I was on my feet without being aware of doing it. The back of my head still hurt and I nearly fell straight back down but I held the lighter up in front of me and flicked it again, three times before I got a light.

Carol was sitting on the floor close to the boy. She looked a lot thinner than when I'd last seen her, and older. I took a step forward and looked at the other person, as he looked up at me.

It wasn't Scott, of course.

After a couple of seconds I realized the planes of his face were different, and his eyes. The resemblance was strong, but whereas people always said Scott looked like me, this boy without question took after his mother.

'Is that Tyler?'

He kept staring up at me as if I was a monster, and he'd been told that if he stayed real still, I might not attack immediately.

343

'Yep,' Carol said. 'Tyler, this is your dad.'

The lighter got too hot to hold and I let it go out. For a moment I was glad of darkness.

I took another pace forward and carefully lowered myself back down to the floor. I held the lighter in my other hand and lit it again, and looked with incomprehension into the face of the woman who had been my wife.

'Carol — what the hell is going on?'

★ ★ ★

She told me that they had been snatched from her rented house in Renton, in the middle of the night before last. Two men had come for them, one of whom she recognized from having delivered a message at the library where she worked. Since then they had been stashed here, inside our old house. She had already tried to find a way out, but whoever sealed the house had done a good job.

'That's not what I meant,' I said. 'I meant *what is going on?*'

She didn't reply. I could hear the sound of her and Tyler breathing in the darkness, almost in unison. Now that I understood where I was, I could feel the shape of the place where we had lived for several years. The lighter got too hot again and I reached behind on the floor and found the cigarette I'd dropped.

I lit it, and each time I took a drag it glowed just enough to show their faces looking at me.

'You shouldn't have come back here,' Carol said.

'Why?'

'You just shouldn't.'

'I only came because someone told me they might know what had happened to Scott.'

'And did they?'

'I don't know,' I admitted. 'A lot of the time it seemed like she wasn't altogether there.'

'She?'

'Her name was Ellen Robertson. She was Gerry Robertson's wife.'

'Was? What happened to him?'

'He died, a few months back. How come you even know the name?'

'I grew up not so far from here, remember?'

'You knew him?'

'Not really. I knew Brooke.'

'You know *Brooke?* How?'

'We went to school together.'

'Were you friends?'

'Brooke's not anyone's friend. She's just Brooke. She's a Robertson.'

'Funny. Bill Raines said something similar to me this morning. I still don't understand what it's supposed to mean.'

'You've seen Bill?'

'Yeah.'

'How is he?'

Now it was my turn to be silent. I took another pull on my cigarette and saw Carol's pinched face, six feet away from me in the darkness.

'Have you got something to tell me?' I asked.

'I don't know what you mean.'

'Bullshit.'

345

'That a naughty word,' Tyler said, quietly.

'I'm sorry,' I said. I knew I should probably be reaching out to him, giving him a hug, doing something father-like. In the glimpses I got of his small face I could see the ghost of a baby I had held, and fed. I also knew that he hadn't seen me in nearly three years and that I had no idea how much time we had, and that there were things I needed to know.

'Ellen's dead,' I said. 'Someone murdered her and left her with a message to me.'

Silence.

'You want to know what the message was?'

Silence.

'A shirt I ran in when we lived in this house. A piece of jewellery I was given. And an email. An email to me, from Jenny, which I never saw.'

Another drag on the cigarette, and I saw a tear rolling down Carol's cheeks, one from each eye.

'Tell me,' I said. 'Carol, it's been long enough. I have a right to know.'

★　★　★

She said she'd had no prior suspicion and maybe that was true, but it wasn't clear what else would have made her go into my study one morning after I'd gone to work, nor to go look at my computer. There shouldn't have been anything on there anyway. Jenny and I were not in contact at the time, and even when we had been, emails had been removed immediately: this is Having an Affair 101, as I'm sure you know.

I had my software set to automatically check

for mail on schedule, however. Once at midday, and prior to that at nine a.m. When I was working from home I tried to stick to this routine, to avoid the day clogging up with the constant back and forth of replying to people and then replying to their replies. When things were on between me and Bill Raines's wife, I disabled this schedule and collected emails manually. On the day in question things were *not* on between us, and hadn't been for several months, and so it was enabled again.

The point is the nine a.m. sweep had done its thing that morning, and downloaded an email sent in the middle of the night. It was sitting right there in my inbox when Carol looked at the screen. Pure bad luck, though you make your own luck, I've been told.

Carol read it, the message I had now seen printed out. She stood over the desk light-headed with emotions for which there are no names, and considered what to do. In the end she printed the email and then deleted it from my machine.

She spent most of the day on the lawn with the baby, reading and rereading the email, turning it over in her head. It was only open to one interpretation. Strength of emotion was evident, as was a prior history of indeterminate length. Carol eventually also put together that the inscription on a bracelet another man's wife had made, and then given me for my birthday, could be interpreted as a way of connecting two Js: Jenny and John.

In a court the jury wouldn't even bother to

leave the room. The question was: what happened in real life?

It was evident from the email that whatever had happened between this woman and her husband was over, or at least in abeyance. Carol was a lot wiser than she ever gave herself credit for, and knew straight away that one option would be to simply let it go. Swallow the pain, let matters take their course. People do things, after all. Not all of them last, or change the world forever. A single hurricane doesn't mean you have to dismantle your house and spend the rest of your life living underground. Carol also understood that just because Person A might be — or might have been — intermittently fucking Person C, that didn't mean they didn't still owe their heart and life to Person B.

But it hurt. It hurt in the way that it hurts when people die. It hurts how it can only hurt when the world is redefined in an instant, when countless moments implode, when memories are undermined and smiles turned into lies.

'How could you, John? I mean, how could you *do* it? When I was *pregnant*? And afterwards? Tell me, because I have spent three years trying to understand and still I just don't.'

'I don't know either,' I said.

When I returned from work that evening, I was by all accounts sweet to her. I'd picked up a novel I knew she had her eye on, from the Yakima Borders, and brought something easy for dinner. As we lay together in bed that night — only about forty feet from where Carol now sat in the darkness telling me these things, her

348

voice low and dry — she knew the grown-up thing was to just let it go.

That this was the way to deal with me, anyhow. But Jenny? That was something else.

This was a woman she'd cooked supper for, gone shopping with, chatted over coffee to. Who'd been at her house. Often. Before, during and since.

Carol couldn't let that go.

★   ★   ★

My cigarette was long finished, and we sat in blackness now. Tyler had kept quiet throughout, but I'd noticed Carol using long or adult words to make it unlikely he'd understand much of what was being said. And he was only three and a half, after all. You have to get a lot older before you realize how much you can fuck things up just by being stupid, that living in the moment can be a fine way of screwing up an infinite queue of later moments.

'What did you do?'

I heard her swallow.

'What did you *do*, Carol?'

She said she'd tried to let it go. That she'd told herself that Jenny Raines was no more to blame than I was. But she couldn't get the idea to take. She kept remembering an afternoon a month or so after Tyler was born, when she ran into Jenny in Roslyn. They wound up having a pastry together. Jenny held Tyler for a little while. Carol didn't know whether we were actually having sex at the time or not. It didn't much matter. The

349

woman shouldn't have been able to be that easy with her either way.

I hung my head. I knew how she would have felt. I once made the mistake of staging a surprise party for Carol. She hated it. The fact of friends turning up to wish her well was utterly outweighed by the knowledge that she'd talked to many of them in the preceding weeks, and not one had let anything slip. They'd all lied to her, in effect, distorted her world through omission, making her feel that the reality she perceived was not to be trusted.

'So I put a sadness on her.'

'What's a 'sadness', Carol?'

'What it sounds like,' she said.

'In words of one syllable?'

'Getting up and not being happy. Not being able to see the point. Looking around at the things you're supposed to value and supposed to care about and not being able to remember a single reason why.'

I recalled how Bill had described Jenny in the months before she left town. 'You mean, depressed.'

'No. It's real. It's something you can do.'

I shook my head, pointless though that was in the darkness. 'Carol, this just sounds like nonsense. Please tell me. What did you actually *do* to Jenny?'

'I'm *telling* you, John. I didn't actually do anything. I went to someone who could.'

'Who?'

'Brooke.'

'Brooke *Robertson?* And she did what?'

'She directed it. At Jenny.'

'Are you saying Brooke is a *witch*?'

'Not her. You're not from around here, John. You wouldn't understand how it works.'

'Oh screw this, Carol.'

She spoke in a strange, singsong voice. 'I went to Brooke. I paid the fee. I gave her the things you need. She did what I asked. It . . . '

She ran out of words, and started crying again, hard.

'It *what*, Carol?'

'It went wrong.'

'Mommy?' Tyler had become discomforted by the sound of his mother being upset. I had too, but I couldn't stop.

'What are you — '

'*It was just supposed to be a sadness.*'

'Carol . . . '

'*Listen*, you asshole. You asked, so fucking *listen*. Didn't you feel *anything*?'

'When?'

'The day that it happened. Didn't you?'

I stood up and walked away, but I didn't have anywhere to go — and whatever Carol was doing, I didn't think she was lying to me.

I turned back toward her.

'Tell me.'

38

She said she had felt uneasy since lunchtime that day, but put it down to tiredness, Tyler's continual crying in the night, an oncoming stomach upset. She said I'd made her a sandwich — which I did not recall, though I remembered everything that had gone into Scott's — and she had left most of it, blaming its dry, stale taste on the way she felt.

Afterwards I had gone back to my study, and she took the baby outside, hoping fresh air might make her feel better and maybe help the little guy sleep. He grizzled for a time, but slowly his crying softened, and then from nowhere she realized he wasn't making noises any more and his eyes were shut and all was good.

So she sat looking down toward the lake, idly wondering — not for the first time — why it was called Murdo Pond. She was a Roslyn girl, a town only twenty miles distant, but around here that was far enough for things to be a mystery and remain that way. Gradually she started to feel her own breathing growing more measured, her eyelids getting heavy. She thought that, for a few moments, she might even have drifted off to sleep, but she wasn't sure.

If she had, it would have explained why the light looked altered, the sun's change in position causing it to fall in slightly different ways. The breeze had died, too, and a heavy stillness came over everything.

She began to feel hot, clammy, but the one piece of advice her mother had passed down was 'Never wake a sleeping baby', and if that isn't in the Bible, it should be. She heard gentle rustling in the trees over on the left, where the ornamental paths and the remains of the settler's cabin lay, but it wasn't reaching where she sat; nor the breeze that must have been moving over the water of the pond, causing the long ripples across its surface. There was an odd smell from somewhere. Perspiration began to stand out on her brow, and even her insides began to feel warm, as if her kidneys or liver were overheating, something at her core running too fast. *I hope I'm not about to throw up*, she thought.

And that's when I had said, from the deck: 'Where's Scott?'

Our memories of what happened next were different. She believed the air had become yet more still as I hurried along the paths at the start of the woods. She says I called out when I saw Scott at the end of the jetty looking out into the pond, though I don't think I did. She heard *something*, anyway, or perhaps felt it, some jagged sound of urgency and danger, and assumed it was me.

When we were down at the base of the jetty she remembered being compelled to turn and look back, by the expression on the boy's face, as he stared past me up toward the house and woods — and seeing nothing. By which she meant . . . that *nothing* was there. As if the

353

power had gone down, everywhere and for good. No sense, or reason, none of the intangible and unconscious ties that bind the world together. The sound of no voice, shouting so loud as to drown out everything else. She could see trees, the bottom of our lawn, the boat dock, slivers of the house, the sky. But none of it seemed to mean anything, to be connected to each other or to her. In that instant she saw everything in creation as a jumble of refuse, strewn upon the abandoned earth like a midnight rock fall discovered the next morning: meaningless, silent, dead. *This* was what she saw in Scott's face, an utter horror of everything, the expression of a child who had seen his parents suddenly become eerie strangers and the world flipped into a reeking void populated only by faceless monsters.

Then Scott had shouted in denial, called my name as if to save me, and it was all done.

★   ★   ★

I recognized something of the feeling she'd described, from when I'd stood at the jetty on my first afternoon back in Black Ridge. But I knew her talking was precarious, and didn't say anything to derail her.

'Brooke did what I asked, and a bad thing came,' she said, again. 'But it didn't go away. It stayed around. It was what made you start to drink, what kept pulling you down to that *fucking* lake.'

'No.' Much though I might have been happy

354

for the blame to go elsewhere, I knew whose fault those things had been. 'That was just — '

'I know you *think* it was you,' she interrupted. 'But you never drank before — why start then?'

'My son had just *died*.'

'So? Is that how you handled your mom dropping dead of a heart attack two days before Christmas? Did you grab a bottle in Iraq every time a guy you knew got blown to pieces by some asshole with a rusty claymore?'

'No,' I said, not wanting to add that, on those occasions, my actions had not been exaggerated by carefully concealed feelings of guilt. 'But — '

'Everything started being wrong. That's why I kept pushing you to sell the place. I *knew* we needed to get out. That's *why I left* — I couldn't wait any longer for you to get the message. I needed us out of that house before anything else happened.'

'You wanted out of *everything*,' I said, only then realizing how much it had hurt. I'd been so consumed by knowing her actions were reasonable, that my drinking and distance and uselessness were sufficient cause to convict, that I hadn't allowed myself to hate her for the abandonment nonetheless.

'*No*. I just wanted to be somewhere else before it was too late.'

'Carol, Scott just d — '

'No, he *didn't*. Scott was killed.'

'Oh Carol, by *what?*'

'One of the things that live out there.'

She jerked her head backwards, presumably indicating the forest that surrounded the boarded-up house. 'They've always been here. Across America, Europe, caves in Afghanistan. I have researched *so much* into this, John. You have no idea. Every culture has a different word for them. They're everything about a place except the concrete and physical. They're the spirits we've feared and make sacrifice to, the things we've always *known* live between us. They're what magicians encountered when they thought they were summoning the devil. They're *everywhere*, but they're most powerful in the wild, which is why the wild scares us. We started living in towns in the first place to try to swamp them with numbers, to blanket them with noise and light, but even in cities we feel lost and empty and sad and it's because *they're still there* — behind the buildings and underneath our streets and living in the parks. We cut down the forests and we gouge holes in the earth to make it harder for them to hide — but they can still get inside us. They still ruin everything.'

She started to cry again, soundlessly.

'Carol,' I said. I felt terribly sad for her, and knew I should have been better at keeping in contact, before this mania had time to get such a hold.

'It's with me all the time now,' she said, her voice barely above a whisper. 'Sometimes I can hear it walking around us. Waiting outside the house.'

'In Renton?' But how would that — '

'They crawl inside, find carriers. That's why you haven't felt it. You may just have been running away from everything, but actually you did the right thing. I didn't get far enough, and now I can't.'

'Why?' I said, though I was reminded of something Ellen had started to tell me in the coffee shop, about how there were some things you could not get away from.

'I'm dirty inside. Everything I touch turns to shit. I don't trust anything. I can't . . . I can't even believe that I've locked a *door* properly.'

She broke down then, fully. Unable to speak coherently, barely able to breathe.

I shuffled over in the dark, knelt down and put my arms around her shoulders, let her sob into my neck. She felt bony and hot and not like any woman I had ever held. She was saying that she had set this thing on Jenny, and that it had gleefully overstepped its bounds — and instead hurt the thing that had mattered most to the man who had mattered most to the other woman at the time. That she hadn't meant to, but that it was her. That she had done it.

'What do you think you did, Carol?'

She looked up at me, her face so pulled by grief that it was barely recognizable.

'I killed Scott.'

⋆   ⋆   ⋆

Nothing I said seemed to get through. In the end I stood up and left her to it. She had wrapped her arms around her knees and was rocking back and forth in a tight ball, whispering to herself.

I went over to where Tyler was, and squatted down. I could hear him shifting away as I approached, and sparked the lighter so he could see my face.

'It's okay,' I said.

'My mommy's sad.'

'Yeah.'

'Why?'

'She's just sad,' I said. 'Sometimes that's how it is. Will you stay and look after her?'

'Where are you going?'

'I need to look around.'

'But it's too dark.'

'I know. But I used to live here. You . . . you did too. You won't remember.'

'Mommy said I did. I was very smaller.'

'That's right. Much smaller.' Looking down at this face, at the face of someone who should have been my boy, was making me feel dead. 'Give your mom a hug now, okay?'

'Okay.'

I started by confirming which room we were in. I'd assumed it was the main living area, and I'd been correct. The much-vaunted cathedral ceiling towered over where we'd been sitting. I believed Carol when she said she'd already checked out the building, but I knew she must have done it with a child in tow, and I thought there was no harm in me looking again.

I didn't know what to think about what Carol had said, and I didn't know how much longer we were going to be left here. I just wanted to be doing. I needed to do something other than deal with the fact I was in a house where I used to live, with a boy who was half mine and a woman I had loved but now barely recognized — and

358

who was either crazy or telling me things I found hard to fit into the world.

I started by tracing my way around all the walls along the front of the building. I moved quickly and did not linger in any room, especially not my study. Every window was sealed tight, as I knew having seen it from the outside on the first day I'd been in Black Ridge. I was soon back in the main area.

'Carol — how many of them are there?'

She didn't say anything.

'Carol, I need to know.'

Her voice floated to me out of the dark, muffled by her arms. 'You really don't get it, do you?'

I went back, feeling my way along the walls. My point had been that yes, I could break the glass of one of these windows, and then try kicking out the boards. But they'd been nailed on hard, and it could take a while and make a lot of noise. If there were people with weapons outside, I'd get shot. I had no idea how many people had taken me in the parking lot. Carol had said two guys had come for them in Renton, but that didn't mean that's all there was.

It randomly struck me that without my phone I couldn't receive a call from the two guys looking for Kyle and Becki, and realized it would have made sense to have got one of *their* numbers, had I not been too preoccupied with hiding the fact I was half convinced they were going to drop me right there in the road. Wasn't anything I could do about that now. About that or much else.

Everything was pretty fucked up.

I'd gone almost the whole way around the ground level, moving more quickly as I realized what a waste of time it was, when I remembered something I'd noticed from the outside, on my first visit to the house after coming up to Black Ridge.

I left the outside wall and felt my way across the middle toward the side of the house that faced the driveway. This took me through the area I'd once thought of as Scott's domain, the non-space in the hall he used to colonize. I was glad it was dark. In the weeks in which we'd remained in the house after he died, I'd gone to some trouble to avoid passing through here. I didn't want to be able to see it now.

'Carol, I'm going to go try something.'

There was no reply.

I went down the stairs to the lower level. It can't actually have been darker down there, but it seemed so. I felt my way past the room that had served as Carol's office, then one that had been earmarked as a den for the boys when they got big enough, and took a left off the corridor into the utility area.

I knew this had been emptied and swept and scrubbed before we left, but when I lit my lighter I still expected to see what I'd recalled on my first visit, shelves stacked with slices of life.

I let it go out again and saw something else, however — a very faint sliver of light, coming from the corner of the window in the small storage area at the end of the utility room. It

360

would still take a while, but at least this window had been started from the outside.

I navigated my way back up to the main room.

'I'm going to try to make a way out,' I told Carol.

'Rah rah for you.'

'Carol . . . '

Truth was I didn't feel I had much to say to her. With every minute that passed the things she'd told me were sinking in a little further, and while that didn't mean I believed she'd done anything that had caused Scott to die . . . I didn't know what I felt for her, or about her.

I went back downstairs.

★   ★   ★

I took off my jacket and wrapped it around my arm. Planted my feet and jabbed my elbow into the bottom of the windowpane. Nothing happened the first time, but on the second it broke. I froze, putting my head close to the window and listening for sounds outside. I could hear the wind, but nothing more.

I tapped my elbow again a couple of times higher up the pane, using my foot to sweep the fallen glass to one side. Even in the dark I felt as if I could almost see the fresher air seeping into the room. I realized I had no idea what time it was, but from the shade of the line of light at the bottom of the window, I guessed it was getting dark.

I couldn't see where the nails had been banged into the frame, so I just rapped my elbow around

361

at regular intervals. Not much happened in the way of movement. I couldn't remember, hadn't noticed when I'd been outside, whether it had been secured with nails or screws. If it was the latter then the boards weren't going anywhere without being broken.

I grabbed hold of the frame on either side and placed my heel into the bottom corner. I pushed against it. I thought it gave, a little.

There was still no noise from the outside apart from something that sounded like rain.

I kept pushing with my foot, methodically.

39

Finally, just when she believed her head was going to burst, when she felt like she was *actually going to go nuts*, Becki caught sight of somewhere she recognized.

She didn't know how long she'd been running, lost in the streets and the rain. Couldn't understand how it had even *happened*. Okay, the roads were at weird angles to each other, like no one had a ruler when they built this place and just slashed out a design with a knife, but it was a small town, hardly bigger than Marion Beach. She'd driven up and down it the night before and she *knew* what a sorry-ass little place it was and more or less how it fitted together.

So how the hell couldn't she find her way?

How come every turn she took seemed to lead her down a street of houses that looked exactly the same as one she'd just left, but somehow wasn't? She was wasted, she knew that, exhausted and freaked out like never before in her life, and maybe the dead woman on the bed and the psycho maid had been a little too much — but it seemed like once you were tangled in this place, it didn't want you to get out again.

Plus now John was gone.

The one guy who'd had her back through all the crap of the last week had disappeared. She didn't know for sure, but she feared that the white truck she'd seen hammering out of the bank parking lot might have had something to do with that.

She'd tried calling his cell phone, had tried again about every ten minutes since, but there was no reply and that scared her even more. Except for last night, when she gathered he'd had shit to deal with, John *always* answered when she called. He was always there. For her, for her dad, for whoever. If he wasn't there now, it could only mean bad things.

And there was the emptiness. It was only late afternoon, for God's sake, but it was like everyone had decided to call it a day already. There was hardly *anyone* on the streets, on foot or in cars, and those few who remained seemed to be scurrying home as if jerked there on long ropes. She tried calling out to a couple of them. Either they didn't hear, or they ignored her. Went inside, shut the door, goodbye. The town hadn't looked like a bundle of laughs the night before, but at least it had seemed *open*. Right now it was as if it was going into hibernation, forever — as if Becki was some pet that had been caught outside with a bad storm coming, whose owners had decided that being safe indoors was more important and, hell, they could always get a new dog.

She tried John's phone, again. Once more it just rang and rang. She shoved her cell back into her jeans and started to walk, taking one turn and then another onto a street she was *sure* she'd been down before, but that's when she saw the strip of familiar lights ahead, and started to run.

As she came into the top of Kelly Street she was dismayed to see that pretty much everything seemed to be shut here, too. An Irish bar — shut. Burger place — shut. What was going *on?* Was it some local fucking holiday she didn't know about?

Where the hell *was* everybody?

Then finally she spotted someone. A real live person, halfway down the street, near the pizza restaurant where John had materialized the night before. Someone was standing under an awning there by themselves, smoking, not looking as if they were right about to go hide someplace. For a wonderful moment Becki thought it might even *be* John, but quickly realized the silhouette was far too thin, and had long hair.

She kept running anyway, and called out. Anyone was better than nobody. The figure heard her shouting, and looked in her direction. Becki recognized who it was, and called out again.

'Wait,' she said, when she got closer, and saw that the woman was looking at her as though she was a lunatic. 'Please, I saw you last night. You were in the restaurant with him, right? You came out, and said you'd paid, or something, and then went away? Remember?'

'You mean . . . John?'

'Yes! They've got him,' Becki said. 'They've *got John.*'

'Who has?'

'I don't *know.*' She started crying. Didn't want to, but couldn't stop. 'I DON'T KNOW ABOUT ANYTHING.'

The woman put a cold hand on her shoulder.

'It's okay. Just tell — '

'It's *not* okay. There's a dead person in his room. Someone put it there and there's this maid who doesn't seem to care, and is, just like, *insane*, and they left an envelope full of stuff and John saw it and then *he just took off*. I tried to keep up with him but I couldn't, but I saw where he was headed and before I got there this truck came out and when I got there he just wasn't *there*.'

The woman didn't look right. Not shocked, or freaked out. She just looked sad. And odd.

'Look — are you *hearing* this?'

'Who was the dead person?'

'The dead . . . How the fuck would I know? I think . . . I think I heard him say the name Ellen.' Becki wiped her eyes savagely with the back of her fists, and looked properly at the woman's pale, bony face and sharp eyes. 'Why don't you look even *surprised*?'

'Forget about what's back at the motel,' the woman said, dropping her cigarette to the sidewalk. 'Courtney's lost. She won't tell anyone.'

'Lost? What are you talking about? She's the maid. She's right fucking *there*.'

'I meant it differently. She won't say anything. She can't. Don't worry.'

'Are you *nuts*?'

The woman pulled a folded-up piece of paper out of her purse and glanced at it.

'Have you tried to call John?'

'Yes, of course.'

The woman tried anyway, and got the same result as Becki had, and *finally* started to look

366

like the gravity of the situation was getting into her head.

She put her phone back into her jacket, her eyes over Becki's shoulder.

'Friends of yours?'

Becki turned, and saw that things had, unbelievably, got even worse.

She started to back away, then realized she didn't have it in her to run any more, especially when she saw there was someone already in the back of the large, black GMC idling up the street toward them.

'No,' she said, dully. 'But they've got my boyfriend.'

The car pulled over to the kerb and the passenger door opened. A wiry black guy got out, a man Becki recognized all too well. The last time she'd seen him he'd been delivering a series of sharp, clinical blows to her face and body, while another man kept an eye on the road out of the window and appeared as if, all in all, he'd rather be somewhere else.

'S'up, girl,' the man said, smiling at her in the way you smile at a plate of food that's exactly what you ordered. 'Got your boy in here.'

'Is . . . is he okay?'

'Everything's cool. Just want you to come for a ride, is all.'

'That's not going to happen,' the tall woman said.

The man laughed. 'The fuck are you going to — '

But then he saw the woman's face.

And shut up.

367

40

Ten minutes later I ran back upstairs. By now it was raining much harder outside. I could hear it drumming on the roof of the high, vaulted space.

'I think we can get out of here.'

'How?' Her voice sounded flat, uninterested.

'Window.'

'You've got it open?'

'Not yet. But a few more kicks will do it.'

'Rah rah for you.' There was silence in the darkness for a moment.

'And then what?'

'What do you mean?'

'Like you said. Who knows who's out there? So you stick your head out and get — '

'Carol, it's either that or we stay here and suffer whatever they've got in mind.'

She picked Tyler up, and followed me downstairs.

'I'm going to have to go first,' I said, when we were back by the window. I flicked the lighter and showed her what we would be dealing with. A window around three feet square. 'Carol . . . '

She wasn't looking at the window, but at the empty shelves back in the utility room.

'I can still smell it,' she said.

'Smell what?'

'Wild strawberry and something. Some other berry. That weird woman, remember, who set up a stall one Saturday down by the market in Roslyn?'

'Carol . . . '

'And you liked it so much and you don't even *eat* that kind of stuff, and she wasn't there again for months and so when she finally turned up again we . . . '

She tailed off. I couldn't smell anything but dust and I doubted that she could either, in reality. But I recalled the day the woman had reappeared with her ramshackle stall, me slapping down a handful of bills and buying every damned jar she had — and us carrying the box back to the car together and how all the way home we were laughing about how we were jam millionaires now, this was the start of a preserve monopoly the like of which the Pacific Northwest had never known. I remembered, too, how when it came to clearing out the house after we'd sold it there was not a single jar left, though I didn't recall finishing it, or anything like.

'What happened to it?'

'I threw it all away,' she said. 'A week after I found out about you and Jenny. Put the jars in a bag and carried them into the forest and threw every single one against a tree.'

I didn't know what to say to that, but for just a moment then, I thought I could smell it too. Not in the house, but in my head. A sweetness.

'Did you hear that?'

'Hear what?'

'Shh.'

I shut up, and heard what she'd heard. It was hard to make out against the rain, but it sounded

369

like a vehicle heading up the drive toward the front door, round the corner of the house from where we stood.

'Take him,' Carol said.

'What?'

'Take Tyler with you.' She held him out toward me. 'There's no point me leaving. *Just take him!*'

'I'm not leaving you here.'

'Then we'll die together,' she said.

'Die? Carol, what is it that you think is going on here? Why won't you *tell* me?'

She put Tyler gently down on the ground, kissed him on the forehead, and ran back upstairs into the house. Tyler tried to follow her, but I grabbed him. He started to cry louder, to call out for his mother.

'Tyler, *shh.*'

But he wouldn't, of course. Left in the dark with a man who meant nothing to him, what else was he going to do but cry?

I pulled him further up my chest and clamped my hand over his mouth. He kicked, and tried to strike out, surprisingly strong and heavy, as boy children are. I heard the vehicle come to a halt outside, the sound of doors opening.

I tried to whisper into Tyler's ear, but he was having none of it. I waited until I heard the sound of at least two sets of footprints head around toward the front door.

'Tyler,' I said firmly. 'Listen to me. Your mom's gone outside. We're going to go find her. But we have to go through this window, okay? We're *going to find your mom.* Do you understand?'

He stopped struggling. I felt him nod.

370

'I've got to put you down. You stand right here, okay? Stand *right* here, and I'm going to open the window and get out and then get you out too, okay?'

Another nod. I could feel his breath hot and wet against the palm of my hand. I put him down, removing my hand from his face as the last thing.

He stood there, not moving.

I knew this was only going to work if it happened fast, so I pushed straight out with my foot, planting it hard and square in the middle of the window.

It gave six inches, and I did it again, and then stopped and planted both my palms on it and gave it a slow, steady shove. The bottom half came away, letting in a sudden blast of cold air and revealing blue fading light outside — but the top portion didn't budge. 'Fuck,' I said.

Tyler watched, his head tilted slightly back, apparently transfixed by the sight of light.

I put one leg over the sill and lowered it to the ground outside, pushing up against the board with my back. It gave, a little. I pulled my other foot up onto the sill, stayed bunched up there.

'We're going to have to do this very quickly, okay? Come closer.'

'You're not my daddy,' he said.

'Yes, Tyler, I am.'

'You don't smell right.' He raised one hand and pointed to the window. 'My daddy's out there. In the woods.'

I heard the sound of footsteps entering the house above, and then Carol's voice carrying

371

from the main room.

'He went upstairs,' she said, far more loudly than necessary. 'God knows how he thought he was going to get us out from up there, but that's guys for you, right? All action, no thought.'

I knew there was no time left, and shoved my foot as hard as I could against the sill. The board came away, all at once, dropping me flat on my back into long, wet grass.

I jumped straight back up and went back to the window. 'Tyler,' I said. 'Come to — '

But he was gone.

Gone back to his mother. He hadn't believed a word I'd told him, just waited until he could get away from the stranger, and back to the woman he loved.

I swore but knew it made no sense to go back in, so I turned from the window and made my way toward the front of the house, keeping tight up against its side. When I got close to the corner I dropped low, and ducked my head around.

A small white truck was parked outside the front door. There was a man standing by the side of it. I realized I knew him. He was Brian Jackson, the mechanic who'd tried to fix the salon woman's car the other morning on Kelly Street.

I saw also that he had a gun, at about the exact same moment that he caught sight of me.

⋆ ⋆ ⋆

He shouted. I turned and ran, trying to lift my feet high enough to clear the grass and get up

372

speed. I headed straight down the side of the house at first, then realized I should try to bank out toward where the woods started, on the left-hand side.

Meanwhile he kept shouting. I didn't know how many men had gone into the house, or if they were armed too. It seemed likely, which meant there wasn't any other option but to keep running through the rain.

I made it into the trees about thirty seconds later, heading for the area where the path had started. Three years had all but erased it, tangling the ways with ferns and dogwood. I ploughed along the ghost of it nonetheless, not bothering to glance behind. It only slows you down.

After fifty yards I saw the slanted shadow of the abandoned homestead, and broke from the path to head over to it. I dropped around the far side, chest thumping. When we'd lived here I'd entertained ideas about renovating this structure, putting a new roof on it and using it as a study or den or summerhouse. Like a lot of things I'd assumed the future held, it didn't happen. I was glad it was here now, though, and pulled myself up the side and stuck my head over the top.

The man from the truck was advancing down the slope of the lawn, still outside the trees, gun held out in front of him. I saw the shape of another man joining him from the direction of the house. It was too far, and getting too dark, to see who this man might be. I still couldn't understand what the hell the mechanic might have against me, or how he could be a part of this, whatever it was. It didn't matter. He was a guy with a gun coming in my direction, which put him on the wrong side of all useful alliances I could imagine.

A shot cracked out.

I wasn't sure whether it was the mechanic or the other man, but whoever it was had some idea of where I was. A beat after the flat slap of the gun, a bullet swacked through foliage only ten feet to the side of me.

Someone shouted out, to me or about me I couldn't tell.

I turned, looked into the forest. From my current position it stretched into the growing dark, for mile after mile into the mountains. If I headed that way, nothingness was all there was to find. No houses, no roads, no logging tracks, just trees and rocks.

If I pulled *up* the slope then I'd be coming back around to the point where the driveway looped in front of the house. Maybe I could get to their vehicle first and derail whatever they were supposed to be doing next — but I doubted they'd have left the keys in it, or that I'd have time to start it before they got to me. If they had two people looking, it likely meant at least two more were back up at the house. With nothing in my hand there was nothing I could achieve against four guys. I hated the idea of leaving Carol behind, but getting off the field of play was the only plan that made sense right now.

Which meant going *down* the slope, trying to cut across the bottom there and make it out to the road. It was only fifty yards across the base

374

of the lawn to where the other copse of trees started, and another hundred or so up to the fence. If I could send the two visible men in the wrong direction, just a little, I should be able to do it.

They were now at the tree line, walking ten feet apart, advancing slowly. I bent low and headed away from the ruined wooden cabin, banking into the trees in the hope that the trunks would obfuscate what I was doing. It seemed to work, as no one shot at me. When I'd put a little more distance between us I altered course radically and headed down toward the lake instead, moving faster until I was twenty yards from where the trees ran out.

The lake was long and grey and pocked with falling slices of white. I was going to stand out against it, even in this light. That just meant I had to do it fast. There was nowhere else for me to go.

I couldn't see the men now. They were back in the trees somewhere. I heard one of them call out to the other, and got an impression of where and how far away they were. It sounded like they were acting on the assumption I was heading deeper into the woods.

I gave it another minute to commit them a little further, and then broke cover.

My foot slipped as I kicked off, and I didn't get up to speed as fast as I'd hoped. The grass was just as long here, too, and wet. But I ran, upright, selling caution to get up as much pace as I could. Halfway across I heard a shout. I kept going.

I was just yards from the trees when there was a distant clap, and it felt like someone had punched me in the side from behind. It knocked me off balance and I spun into the copse and crashed into a tree.

I was back on my feet quickly, albeit in an involuntary crouch. The stinging high in my side told me it hadn't been a punch. Didn't mean anything except I had to keep going, and fast. There was distant shouting behind, and it sounded angry now.

Once I was into the trees I straightened up and ran as fast as I could. I knew exactly where I was going because this used to be on my jogging trail, wearing a vest that was now in the manila envelope I'd lost when I'd been taken out in the bank parking lot. I scrambled up the slope and finally had to break out of the trees again and into the pounding rain for the final stretch.

Nobody shot at me again before I made it to the fence and swung myself over, grunting at the way this made my side feel.

I landed more or less on my feet on the other side, and finally looked back. One of the men was down by the lake. I couldn't see the other and didn't wait to find out where he was. There was no way I could make it all the way back to town on foot, and there was only one alternative I could think of.

I took a couple of big breaths, and started to run up the road.

41

When I made it to the end of the driveway I saw there was a light on over the door of the house. Didn't necessarily mean anyone was in, but all three cars were still parked by the barn and I was soaked and hurt and was determined to try regardless.

I stumbled up to the door and leaned on the bell, peering in through the cobbled glass panel in the top half. It was murky beyond, but after a few minutes I saw an interior light go on and a figure approaching.

The door was opened. When Collins saw who it was he tried to shut the door again immediately.

'Nope,' I said, and pushed my way in.

'You've got no right,' he said, keeping his voice down. 'This is my . . . '

He stopped, apparently staring at my stomach. I looked down and saw all the clothing on my right side was soaked red.

I pulled my coat aside and only then saw how lucky I'd been to get away with only a ragged gash along the side of my ribs. A couple of degrees the other way and I would now be lying face down in the woods.

'What . . . ? what . . . ?'

'I've been shot,' I said. 'The guys who did it are out there looking for me. Maybe they'll guess I ran this way. The less time I'm here, the better it is for you.'

'I'm going to call the cops.'

'No, you're not.'

'Who is it?' called a female voice.

It was Collins's wife, a few rooms away, probably curled up in front of whatever television show the man had been happily watching before a rain-soaked and bleeding stranger pushed his way into his life.

'Someone needing directions,' I said. 'Do it, or I'm going to fuck you up.'

'Just some guy who got lost,' the man called out, closing the front door. 'You . . . you want a coffee?'

'Sure,' she said, sounding touched. 'Thank you, honey.'

I followed him down a corridor and into a large kitchen, safely away from the entrance hallway. It was the cleanest kitchen I'd ever seen.

'I need two things from you,' I said. 'First is to use your phone.' I spotted one over on the counter, and went over to it, dripping second-hand rain all over the pale limestone floor. Some of the water had red in it.

'Who shot you?'

'I actually don't know. Funny old world, right?'

I dialled directory assistance and asked to be put through to the Black Ridge Sheriff's Department. While I waited I went to the window and watched the top of the driveway. It wouldn't be long now before it was full dark, but I could still see if anyone appeared at the top of it looking for me. If they did, I had no idea what I was going to do.

I heard ringing down the line and then the phone was picked up. 'Black Ridge Sheriff's Department.'

'I need to talk to Sheriff Pierce,' I said.

'Who's calling?'

'John Henderson.'

The person at the other end put the phone down. The line went dead, just like that. I stared at the handset.

Collins was looking at me with wide eyes. 'You're John Henderson?'

'What's it to you?'

'Nothing. I've heard the name, that's all.'

'I told you. I used to live down the road.'

'I . . . I wasn't really listening this morning.'

'You're supposed to be making coffee,' I said.

He jerked, as if waking from a shallow dream, and started to get coffee stuff together.

'The machine's not working,' he said. 'The light's not coming on.'

My head had started to ache badly, from being knocked out, or the running, or shock from the blood loss. It made it hard to focus. My side was finally beginning to hurt, a lot.

I dialled another number, taking three tries to get it right, and then listened to it ring and ring. There was a strange crackling on the line, as if the power was cutting in and out.

Finally I heard a slurred voice say: 'Bill Raines.'

'Thank Christ,' I said. 'Bill, it's John.'

'Hey! You back on the beach, carrying plates?'

'No. I'm still here. I need your help.'

He laughed merrily. He sounded like he'd had

more than a couple of beers. 'You're a piece of work, my friend. You know that?'

'They've got Carol. And Tyler.'

'*What?*' Bill sounded suddenly very sober. 'Who has?'

'I don't know. I got away but they've still got Carol and Tyler.'

'What the hell's going on?'

'I don't know that either, but Carol was saying some strange things and it's evidently serious enough for some asshole to have shot me.'

'You been *shot?*'

'Yes. It's fine, but . . . '

'What do you need?'

'I'm coming over to your place, soon as I can. I'll work it out then. But step one is going to be some guns.'

'You got it,' he said.

I put the phone down and turned to Collins. He was still hunched over the coffee machine, and it reminded me of events that had happened the previous morning. Except this guy was still alive, in his big, beautiful kitchen and his wonderful house, with his wife and kids and life.

'Other thing I need is keys,' I said. 'To the SUV.'

'I'm not giving — '

'Mr Collins, I'm leaving here with them whether you give them to me or not.'

'You cannot *do* this to me,' he said, turning suddenly. I realized hc was now holding a large kitchen knife.

'You're kidding me, right?'

He took a step forward, waved the knife at me.

380

'This is *my home*. I have . . . I have friends.'

I knocked the knife out of his hand and stepped in tight to hit him very hard in the stomach, driving my fist up under the ribs. We were close enough that I could see his eyes bulge with the impact, and then he went down, banging his head on a kitchen cabinet on the way.

'Let's talk about these 'friends',' I said.

He looked as though he was going to throw up.

'Or why don't we talk about Jassie Cornell instead? What happened to her?' I grabbed him by the collar and pulled him up to a sitting position, putting my face in close to his. 'What *the hell happened to her*?'

His face was full of panic now.

'First time I saw that girl she was full of the joys of organic living,' I said. 'Three days later, she kills herself in front of thirty people. Explain that transition to me or I'm going to hit you again.'

Tears started to roll down his face, as if they'd been trapped inside his head for days and now couldn't be held there any longer.

'I *liked* her. I did, but, Christ, I've got a *family*.'

'Yeah, and?'

'She was pregnant,' he said. 'She *told* me she was on contraception. She *did*. And then, I mean, *Christ*, you know? What else am I going to do? I told her to get rid of it. She wouldn't *do* it. She *wouldn't get rid of it*. I didn't want anything to happen to *her*. I really didn't. I lo . . . I *liked* her.'

I dropped him. 'What did you do?'

He buried his face in his hands. I kicked him in the side. He muttered something that I couldn't hear.

'*What* did you just say?'

He said it again, the words little more than coughed breaths, but this time enough of it escaped through his fingers for me to make out a word.

Sadness.

He was slumped against the cabinet, rubbing his face with his hands feverishly, smearing tears and snot all over his cheeks. His eyes were open, staring straight ahead. Maybe he was seeing a pool of blood spreading over the sidewalk on Kelly Street. Maybe the soft, plump stomach of a young girl who had lain on motel beds beside him, but who was now dead. I ought to have felt some compassion for him, but all I wanted to do was kick him and then kick him again.

'Keys.'

I followed the movement of his eyes and found a wicker basket with three sets of keys. I took all of them.

When I turned to the door I saw the man's wife. She was leaning against the door frame, her arms folded, face composed.

'My husband was quite correct,' she said. 'You had no right to do this.'

'How much did you hear?'

Her husband was staring at her, with the flat, blank gaze of someone who knew their world was never going to be the same.

She glanced coldly at him, then back at me.

'Nothing that was any of your business,' she said, and slapped me hard across the face.

★ ★ ★

It was still pouring down. The SUV opened with the second set of keys I tried. I dropped the other two to the ground and climbed in the car. Reaching around for the seat belt sent a spasm up the whole of my right side, but when I turned on the reading light and checked, it didn't seem to be bleeding too much any more.

It took six tries to get the engine started. I drove down to the road with the headlights off, and stopped. It was dark in both directions. I didn't have any choice. If I wanted to go anywhere but deeper into the woods, I had to go left.

I drove to our old house and pulled over. I had to check. I got out of the car and ran up the drive and round to the front of the house, covering the last of the distance close up to the house.

The truck was gone.

The front door was hanging open.

I went inside, but there was no one there. I ran back up to the road, got in the car, and started to drive fast back toward Black Ridge.

42

Bill was waiting on his porch when I pulled up, and trotted straight down the steps to the car.

'Christ,' he said, when I got out. 'You look like shit. Is it serious?'

'No. Though I wouldn't want it happening twice.'

Indoors it was warm and there was music playing and he led me straight into the kitchen, poured a big cup of coffee from the waiting pot and handed it to me. He noticed that my hands were shaking and asked if I wanted something in my drink.

I shook my head. 'Where are you on that?'

'Few beers. Don't worry. Not like it used to be.'

I knew what he was talking about, how in the army it'd be a strange old day when most of us weren't at least a joint and a few beers to the wind when something kicked off, and Bill had always taken it further than most.

'Long time ago,' I said. 'Younger heads.'

'I'm fine, Dad.'

I looked him in the eyes and saw that was true, so I quickly told him what I knew. That someone had murdered Ellen and was trying to pin it on me — an attempt that might yet be successful, given her body was presumably still in my motel room. That someone — maybe the same person or people, maybe not — had abducted my ex-wife and child and held them in my old house until they could round me up to go with them. That they'd been taken somewhere after I got away.

And that Carol had known about Jenny and me.

'Huh,' he muttered. 'She could have told *me*.'

'Carol said some very weird things while I was with her,' I said. 'Okay, she'd been locked in a dark house for a while and seemed kind of odd in general but . . . she claimed . . . ' I didn't really know how to put it.

'What?'

'She said she'd done something to Jenny.'

'Done what?'

'I'm just — look, this is what she told me, and I don't know if it means anything. She said she'd had something called a 'sadness' put on her. Half an hour later the guy I took that SUV from used the exact same word, and far as I know the two have never met. Carol said . . . she said that it was this thing gone wrong that led to Scott's death.'

Bill was looking down at the floor, chewing his lip. 'So, what — like a 'spell' or something?'

'I know how it sounds.'

'Who was the person Carol said did this thing for her?'

'Brooke Robertson. Bill, if you know anything about this, now's the time to tell me.'

'I don't,' he said, quietly. 'Not specifically. Thing is, I'm from here, but also not. My parents aren't local. They moved here in the Nineteen-sixties and when I was a kid we lived down in

385

Yakima. I was at school with the Robertsons for a few years, like I told you, but then I transferred, and at eighteen I was hell and gone out of here and into the army. I lost track of all these people until I got back, and never became close after that — because I was spending most of my time down in Yakima again, working my ass off.'

'But?'

He shrugged. 'I've heard stuff, over the years. You know how it goes.'

I did. Snippets, tangential information. Things that bore no direct relevance to the case you were working, that are muttered by the guilty as mitigation or misinformation or time-fillers, and that collect like dust in the far recesses of your head.

'And what did you hear?'

'That there were people who you could go to if you had a problem, or a need. That things could be done, sometimes, people could be made to do stuff. I didn't take it seriously. You know how small towns are. It's like staying in high school your whole life. A lot of people talking a lot of bullshit. Walking the same halls, using the same locker room and cafeteria. People build their own little spooky stories out of nothing, right? Join the dots?'

'I'm not sure that's all this is. And you said yourself that people whispered things about Brooke a long time ago.'

'Yeah,' he admitted. 'And actually I talked to Jenny about that this afternoon.'

'You did?'

'After you left, I thought shit, call and see how the woman is. We got on to the Robertsons because I mentioned Ellen was having problems — she and Jenny had got to know each other a little, it turns out — and we didn't really get into it, but I received the impression there was more to that story about Brooke and the teacher than I ever got to hear.'

Brooke's ancient history was not something I cared about at that moment, and I suddenly remembered other things that might be happening in the world. 'I need to use your phone.'

'Sure,' he said, heading out of the room. 'I'll find you a dry shirt too.'

'Another thing,' I told his back. 'I tried to talk to the sheriff after I got away from these people. Whoever answered hung up on me.'

'Huh,' he said.

I couldn't remember Becki's cell-phone number, even after numerous tries that landed me in dead-ends or irritable wrong numbers and a conversation where neither I nor the person on the other end appeared able to hear the other. My head was throbbing badly now. I took a look through the kitchen drawers and eventually turned up a bottle of Advil. I took four.

Bill came back with a grey sweatshirt that you could have squeezed two of me into. I couldn't help laughing.

'Yeah, yeah,' he said. 'I'm built for comfort these days. But it's dry and has no bullet holes and is not covered in blood. Your call, Mr Armani.'

As I was reaching out for it I had another idea,

and called directory assistance for the number of the Mountain View. The bartender guy answered and put me through to Kristina quickly enough.

'Where the hell *are* you?' she said. There was a strong crackle on this line too. 'Are you okay?'

'I need you to do me a big favour.'

'Okay, but — '

'Friend of mine, that girl who arrived in the car last night? She's — '

'Right here,' Kristina said.

'*What?*'

'But it's complicated.'

'How — ' I started, but she was gone, and another voice came on the line.

'Been calling you,' it said, angrily. 'You ain't fucking answer.'

'I lost my phone. Who is this?'

'Little D. We got your boy.'

'Shit,' I said. 'Look — '

'No, *you* listen. Only reason we ain't long gone with the job done is your woman.'

'What woman? I don't have a woman.'

'Skinny bitch here with the black hair.'

'She's not . . . look, okay, what?'

The timbre of the man's voice changed, as if he'd turned away from the others and brought his face closer to the phone.

'Listen, yo. We find your boy on the street and we're on the way to do the thing, when we see his girl. The blonde one. Switch pulls over, gets out to grab her, do two for one and make it all clean. That's how he be. But she's with your woman here, and the tall girl just looks at Switch like he's a little 'un and starts talking. Switch don't listen to *nobody* once he's started, but now . . . now he got some whole other idea from her.'

'Which is?'

'We ain't whack your boy yet.'

'Thank — '

'But we double on the price. Because now we got him in the hand, yo.'

For a second I considered telling the guy to fuck himself, and his friend, and to fuck Kyle while he was at it.

Then I caught Bill's eye, and realized what was playing on the stereo in the living room. An old Creedence song, 'Have You Ever Seen the Rain?' One of the tracks Bill always used to play on his Walkman in the bad old days, another little joke about his name. And off the back of that, and flash memories of those times, I had another thought entirely.

'Okay,' I said, slowly. 'Deal. But I have a better one if you want to hear it.'

'What is?'

'I've got another problem right now, and I need some soldiers. Tonight. Twenty-five each.'

'You *shitting* me?'

The anger or fear bubbled up out of me. 'Do I sound like I am? When you're already holding two friends of mine? You met me. Did I *look* like someone who fucks around?'

'Wait up,' he said.

The line went muffled for a full thirty seconds. Bill looked at me with a raised eyebrow.

A different voice came on the line. The matter had evidently been handed up the ladder.

389

'Fifty between us?'

'Yes.'

'Up front.'

'Can't be. You think I'm holding that much right now?'

'Up front or no deal.'

'Have it your way, asshole. You *do* this, you get paid what I just said. You don't, you can drop the little shithead right there in the bar and I don't give a fuck.'

There was silence, then a chuckle. 'You a cold motherfucker.'

'That a yes?'

'Where you at?'

I told him and asked to be put back to Kristina.

'What have you just done?' she asked.

'Somebody killed Ellen.'

'I know. Becki told me.'

'You sound pretty calm about it.' She didn't say anything, so I went on. 'They've got Carol and Tyler and the sheriff's department hung up on me half an hour ago. I cannot see anyone except the Robertsons being behind this, and I am done being fucked with by that family.'

'John . . . '

'*What?*'

'You'd do better to walk away.'

'Are you *listening*, Kristina? Someone shot me. They've got Carol and my kid and I don't know what's going to happen to them.'

'They're going to die.'

I was speechless. Then suddenly I remembered what Kristina had said, when I told her what had happened to Scott. *I'm so sorry.* It had struck me at the time but I hadn't known why. I'd chosen to believe that she'd selected that particular form of words because she was feeling close to me.

Perhaps instead it had been because . . . 'Did you *know* about this?'

'I do now.'

'About what happened to Scott?'

'Not when you told me.'

'But what do you know about it *now*?'

'John, I think you're too late.'

'Is there anything you can do to help me?'

'What's going to happen is going to happen. It was started a long time ago. I can't — '

'Then goodbye.'

'Joh — '

I put the phone down. Tried to catch up with what Kristina had just said but couldn't get near understanding any of it and so closed the door on it in my head.

Instead I looked at Bill, who was leaning against the table with his arms folded. I felt dry and wired and like everything was getting away from me.

'We've got additional numbers coming.'

'I gather. Who?'

'Couple of gang hitters who were supposed to be whacking someone I know.'

'Great. They sound nice. Then what?'

'We're going to go find Carol and Tyler,' I said, putting my head in my hands. Most of all I felt exhausted, as if the earth was trying to pull my body and soul down into it to lie still forever.

391

'And if anyone gets in our way, we're going to fuck up their shit.'

'That the whole plan?'

'Pretty much.'

* * *

'Okay,' I said, ten minutes later. 'So, when were you actually planning on taking the government by force?'

He'd laid out what he had in the guest bedroom. A Glock, a couple of Beretta 92s, a shotgun and a serious hunting rifle, plus enough bullets to make a lot of big holes in many things.

Bill shrugged. 'You complaining?'

I took one of the Berettas because it was what we'd had back in the day and I was used to holding one, plus the shotgun, and went downstairs to load up on the kitchen table. Both guns were good and clean. I tried not to imagine Bill sitting here at some point in the last few months, gun in his hand and thinking about me and Jenny, and largely succeeded.

When that was done I finally took my shirt off and grabbed a towel.

There was a knock on the door.

Bill quickly reappeared down the staircase, looked at me with a question mark. I pointed toward the front door, grabbed the handgun off the table and slipped through into the living room, where I could get an angle on the hallway.

After a moment I heard Bill open the door.

'Who are you?' he said.

'Looking for John. He here?'

'You Little D?'

'Switch.'

'Yeah, he's here.'

I heard feet go down the steps outside, and then a group returning back up them. I stepped out into the corridor as four people entered in line.

The two black guys, with Becki and Kyle between them. I'd known Kristina wouldn't be with them, but for some reason it still hurt.

Becki ran straight over and hugged me. Over her shoulder I saw Kyle. He looked pale and wrung out and kept his eyes steadfastly on the floor, and he reminded me of the way Tyler had looked when I first saw him in my old house — as if he was keeping a low profile to avoid catching the attention of darkness.

Becki meanwhile had leaned back and was staring at me. I realized I had a gun in my hand and my shirt off and was liberally blood-spattered and bruised.

'I'm fine,' I said.

'The fuck. What the hell *happened* to you?'

'No big deal.'

Switch glanced at the wound with a professional eye. 'Could have gone bad, where that shit hit.'

'Yeah. But it didn't. Let's move on.'

He nodded, with something that looked like mild respect. 'What up?'

I took out my wallet and threw it to him. 'Best I can do right now.'

'Not what I'm asking.'

'People who did this to me have my ex-wife

and kid. I don't know how many there are, or what they want.'

'You know where they *at*, at least?'

'Not for sure. But I have a good idea where to start looking.'

He threw my wallet back to me. 'You serious, I can see that.'

Ignored by everyone, Kyle had wandered over to a chair at the kitchen table and sat perched on the edge. His arms were wrapped around his body, and he was moving gently back and forth.

'Are you hurting?' I asked. 'If so you're out of luck, because I don't have your drugs any more.'

'It's this place,' he muttered. 'It's not right.'

'True that,' said Little D. 'Town is like a morgue, yo. Like everybody go indoors and lock in. What's with that shit?'

'Don't know and I don't care,' I said, grabbing my guns off the table. 'Let's go.'

43

I'd been for leaving Becki and Kyle at Bill's, obviously, but Kyle wouldn't do it. I couldn't have cared less but Becki was scared too, and very freaked out. I took her to one side in the hallway. I knew she'd had a rough day, rough week, but this was not shaping up as an evening with room for passengers.

'Becki,' I started.

'Forget it, John. No *way* are you leaving me here,' she said. 'Kyle's right. There's something dead wrong about this place. Even those scary-ass guys feel it.'

'They're just not used to small mountain towns. Winter comes, and it's like humans were never here.'

'Bullshit. It's more than that. You think these are the kind of people who normally make deals? Those dudes *beat me up*, John. They came in my apartment and hit me. A *lot*. A girl. And the small one was digging it, believe me. But you know what? On the way over here, the other one *actually says sorry*. And even before that, when I'm on the street freaking at Kristina and they jump out of the car, she takes one look at the small one and he just stops talking. I mean, she's got a real scary energy about her, no doubt, but with *these* guys? Ten minutes later we're sitting in the bar, waiting for you to call like we're a bunch of jerks ready to party and waiting on our ride. What's *that* about?'

'Money,' I said.

She shook her head. 'No, it's not. You ask them. You ask *them* if they're feeling — '

'That's the last thing I'm going to do. You ever *met* any male humans, Becki?'

She sort of smiled. 'Yeah, funny. But you're not leaving me here. Build a bridge and get over it, work on Plan B.'

Plan B turned out to be them coming in the SUV with Bill and me, while the other guys followed in their own vehicle. I put Bill's sweatshirt on, picked up the guns and looked around at the other people holding weapons.

'You up for this?'

The two black guys nodded.

Bill shook his head. 'Never a dull moment with you, Henderson.'

He waited until we were outside and in the car before asking the obvious question. 'What happens if we're going in the wrong direction?'

'We . . . ' I realized he had a point. 'Get me a number for the Robertson house, then hand me the phone.'

He dialled and then handed his phone to me. 'Signal's not great,' he said.

There was no answer for a long time. Then it was picked up, to silence. I could hear someone breathing.

'Brooke?'

'No,' a female voice said, rich and strangely sexual. 'I'm afraid she's not at home.'

'I know that's you.'

'You're mistaken. This is the Seattle Public

396

Library. Who's calling, please?'

'Brooke, listen to me. If anything happens to Carol or my son, then yours will be the last generation of Robertsons to walk the earth. Do you understand me?'

She laughed, so suddenly and so loudly it was painful over the phone.

'You're a funny guy,' she said, and hung up.

I started the car.

'We're going in the right direction.'

★   ★   ★

The rain had slackened a little, but only because it was heading fast toward sleet. I wanted to jam my foot down and drive hard, but I knew these roads well enough to understand that dropping ten miles off your speed in this weather made it half as likely you'd end up spinning off the road. It also made it easier for the other guys to follow.

The car was very quiet. Bill stared straight ahead out of the windshield. I had no idea what he was thinking. I wanted to thank him for being there, for coming, but didn't know how to start. In the rear-view mirror I could see Becki and Kyle sitting well apart. Becki was also staring into space. Kyle appeared to be watching the forest as we passed.

'It's cold,' he said, suddenly.

'Always there with the weather report,' I said.

'I mean, *really* cold. And . . . it smells weird.'

I was about to dismiss this just as flippantly but realized he was right. The heater had been left on in the SUV when I took it from Collins's driveway, and I hadn't changed it, but the hot air it was blowing didn't seem to make any difference. And there definitely was an odour, too. Sweet, spicy, but a little sickly — something like cinnamon. I looked around for evidence of an air freshener in the car, but there wasn't one, and so I cracked the window open an inch. The car didn't seem to get any colder, but the smell lifted a notch.

'Is that coming from the woods?' Becki asked.

'No idea,' I said, but I knew I'd smelled it, or something like it, more than once since being in Black Ridge.

We drove in silence for another five minutes, before Kyle spoke again.

'Something's out there,' he said.

'Shut *up*,' Becki snapped.

'You actually see something?' Bill asked.

Kyle was silent for a moment, his face pressed up close to his window. 'No,' he said, eventually.

'So there's probably nothing to worry about,' Bill said. And maybe he was right, but the further we drove the more a low nausea in my stomach seemed to warn me otherwise. Partly it was simple fear, or anticipation. I don't care who you are or what you've done, when you're in the company of weapons you know you're stepping closer to the veil between being alive and dead. I had been in that situation before, strapped on a gun as a matter of course for years of my adult life. It's never a trivial matter.

I was afraid for Carol, too, and for Tyler, but the feeling I had wasn't merely these things. There was something else. I didn't know whether it was out there, or inside me, but there was something else.

A sense of bad things close at hand, and getting closer.

★ ★ ★

From fifty yards down the road we could see that the gates to the Robertson compound had been left open.

'Not sure that's a great sign,' Bill said.

'They snatched me for a reason,' I said, tapping on the brakes to indicate to the car behind that we were stopping. 'I got away. They let me in, they get me back.'

'And how is that a good thing?' Becki asked.

I pulled over, got out and walked back to the other car. Little D rolled down his window. His face looked grey and pinched.

'This is it,' I said. 'You okay?'

'Just cold, yo.'

He looked convincing, but something told me he was feeling what I had as we got closer to this place: a strong impression that turning round and heading in the opposite direction would be a safer idea.

Switch killed the engine, pulled a nine out from under his seat. 'How's this going to be?'

'Follow me.'

I went back to the SUV and stuck my head in the open door. 'You two are staying here,' I said. Becki started to protest but I talked straight over her. 'I mean it this time.'

She looked down at her hands.

399

'I'd like you to get in front, though. Lock the doors. Anyone approaches who you don't recognize, drive away and drive fast, okay?'

Bill got out the other side, holding the shotgun. He looked up as thunder broke somewhere over the mountains. The rain/sleet gusted harder, chilling cold.

'Harsh fucking night.'

'Better cover for us.'

'Never figured you for an optimist.'

We shut our doors and walked toward the gates, the two other guys in step behind, their guns already out and in their hands. Bill held them back as we approached the bottom of the drive, and I crouched low and trotted through the gates and up toward a soft white glow up ahead.

When I crested the rise I saw the lights in both houses were on, as if someone was trying to attract the attention of overflying aliens. I kept close to the right side of the drive, staying amongst the small trees and bushes, looking for signs of movement. Couldn't see anything, so I crept back and waved the other guys forward. We collected at the left side of the drive.

'Bill and I will take the main house,' I said, having to lift my voice against the rain. 'You check that other one.'

Switch looked across at the building where Ellen had once lived. 'And what if?'

'You find a woman and a boy, get them out and come find us right away. Once we've got them we're out of here, right away, nothing else to do. You see anyone else, be very suspicious.

And if anyone draws down on you, just shoot. We hear noise, we'll come running.'

A single upwards nod, and he and Little D loped off into the rain. Bill and I got our handguns out.

'Never seen something that looked more like a set-up,' he said cheerfully as we ran toward the house. The closer we got, the better lit we were. 'You got someone with a rifle and a sight a hundred yards away, we're toast.'

Half the lights in the house flicked off at once, then, before coming straight back on again.

Nothing else happened before we ran up the steps onto the porch, however. We went low and cased the front of the building, peering in windows. Each room appeared deserted. We returned to the front door and took a side each. I reached around with my hand and turned the knob. It was unlocked.

The door opened. We gave it twenty seconds, then Bill nodded at me and we turned and kicked it in together, guns in front.

Inside, a clock was ticking.

We turned in slow half-circles in the hallway, hearing nothing else. Bill winced. You got it as soon as you stepped in the building. The heating was up full blast in here, and the air smelt bad. Like we'd noticed on the way, but more curdled, sickly rich, as if cloves had been boiled in fat for many hours over a smoky fire, in the company of ingredients normal people are not supposed to eat.

I gestured Bill toward the right-hand side of the house, and took the left, quickly moving through areas that Cory had shown me during a visit that felt as if it had taken place weeks before.

The big sitting room with the kind of straight-backed chairs that are meant to be looked at rather than sat on. Magazines spread across glass-topped coffee tables. A fireplace that had burned at some point during the day, but had been let run down. Every single ceiling light, lamp and wall sconce was turned on.

I went through the door at the back that opened into the library, the major addition on this property, and then through the door on the side that led to the breakfast room. Clean, silent, empty. A window at the back, but it was too dark to see much beyond glass smeared and pattered with driving rain.

The clock was on a mantelpiece in here. It was the loudest clock I'd ever heard, unless something was going wrong with my hearing. I didn't remember it being anything like this loud the previous time I'd been here — didn't even recall noticing it at all.

A door at the other end of the breakfast room led to the large kitchen. It felt mothballed, like everything else in this house, as if the occupants never did more than stand in a corner of each room, in suffocating silence; as if it was a monument to a family rather than anywhere people might actually live.

I emerged into the hallway at the same time Bill arrived back from the other side. He shook his head — pointed at the staircase with a questioning look. I nodded, and he went up first.

We took the sweeping curve slowly, guns ready, but reached the top in silence. The lights flickered again, twice, but then steadied. We searched the right side together first, Cory's side. Nothing and no one in there, though when I passed the photos of him with his hunting buddies, this time I knew I'd seen at least one of them since.

I picked up one of the frames and looked closer, and I got it. Got *them*, in fact.

Richard Collins, on the far left.

And right next to Cory, arm slung around his shoulders, was Deputy Greene.

We went back out across the hallway and toward the door that led to Brooke's half, the first uncharted territory in the house. Bill put up his hand to hold me back for a second, and leaned toward the window to look down over the front lawns.

He turned back at me and shrugged — evidently no sign of the other two guys.

I reached out and carefully undid the door.

Beyond was a mirror image of Cory's half, at least at first. A short corridor on the left, leading to a master suite. The bedroom beyond was immaculate, done up in neutral colours and muted shades. It looked like a hotel room designed for someone who needed everything just so. There was no one in there or in the bathroom off the side.

I rejoined Bill and let him turn the handle of the door at the other end of the hallway. It was locked — the first barrier we'd encountered the entire time we'd been in the house.

I threw my shoulder at it, suddenly irrationally convinced that Carol and Tyler were the other side. The door took the impact without noticing.

Bill moved me to one side and took his turn, dropping his shoulder and jogging it up at the last moment. He had more weight and a much better technique. The frame still wasn't budging, but the panels in the middle splintered, and another two tries had it broken.

When it was open, you could see immediately how this side of the house differed from the other. The addition below had been extended up on this level, making Brooke's sitting room perhaps twice as long as Cory's, in an L-shape with a wide window at the end. There was a fireplace, cold. Three seating areas, and two long walls lined with drawers from floor to ceiling.

Hundreds of them.

44

'Christ,' Bill said, quietly. 'What's all this?'

We split to opposite sides and went along the walls. The units that held the drawers looked as though they'd been constructed over a very long period. Many were as you might expect to find in an old-style apothecary, or museum storeroom, hand-crafted in dark wood, varnished and revarnished time and again. Others looked more recently built, but as though they'd been designed to remain in keeping with what had come before. As you progressed further toward the large window at the back of the room, however, the final two columns of drawers were made of metal, more like safety deposit boxes.

They were about eighteen inches across, four inches tall, and designed to be opened with a small key. All had small recessed handles, and brass plates holding little labels. Each of these had what appeared to be a surname on it, written by hand, some in ballpoint, some in ink; those on the oldest-looking drawers were very faded and in a script that looked like copperplate.

Bill went up to one of the modern portions and yanked on a handle. It didn't budge. He tried a couple in other sections. Even the ones in the oldest part had clearly been built to last. I started looking through the names. The wall wasn't arranged alphabetically, which didn't help. There was no obvious order at all, in fact, and some of the oldest drawers bore labels in new-looking writing.

'What's up?' Bill asked.

I shook my head, not really sure what I was looking for. We both turned at the sound of footsteps running up the stairs, and had our guns trained on the doorway in time to see Little D and Switch come in. Both were soaked to the skin and looked spooked.

'Empty,' Switch said. 'Like, cleaned out. No furniture, carpets, nothing.'

I returned to the wall of drawers, started looking randomly amongst them again. And finally I found a name I recognized.

Cornell.

'And what the fuck is this smell everywhere?' Little D added, shivering. 'Something died?'

'Maybe. You got game with locks?'

'For sure.'

'See if you can open this,' I said, pointing at the drawer I'd just found. He pulled out a ring of slim pieces of metal from his designer jeans, looked closely at the small lock on the drawer.

'I think you got the wrong place after all,' Bill said to me. 'There's nobody here, John. They sold you down the wrong road. What do you want to do now?'

I shook my head, knowing we should be moving in some direction or other, and moving fast, but not knowing where it lay.

I looked at Switch. 'You said it was a police pointed you in my direction, right?' He nodded. 'What did he look like?'

406

'Big guy.'

'Tall, or bulky?'

'Bulky.'

Not Pierce, then, which had been my immediate assumption. More likely Greene, the deputy I'd just seen in the photo in Cory's room — who, I now remembered, had also been hanging around the hospital the morning after Ellen had her accident. Whose daughter was the maid at my motel, and who might (just) conceivably have let him into a room to deposit a body there. What could she do about it, after all? Call the police?

'What actually happened? How did it go?'

'He pull us over, wants to see my licence, registration. I got those, no doubt. So he's, what you around here for, nigger? I tell him we looking for a friend of ours, gone missing. He ask where he missing from, and I say Oregon, young boy name of Kyle. I say what he look like and that.'

'You told all this to a cop?'

Switch shrugged. 'It all true. Just didn't say we were here to kill him. So the police gets helpful, says to look out for an older guy, might know something, tells us what your car look like. He rolls out, have a nice day. That's all.'

'Try calling the Black Ridge Sheriff's Department,' I told Bill. 'See if you can get hold of Pierce. Make like it's trivial.'

'Thought he hung up on you already.'

'Maybe not.'

There was a click from the drawer Little D was fiddling with. I pulled the drawer open. It was empty. Then I spotted another name two columns away.

Collins.

'Try that one instead.'

D moved over and used the same tool, but couldn't get anywhere with it. I heard Bill talking to someone in the background. D switched to another shim and eventually got the drawer open. He stepped back. There was a manila envelope inside.

'Pierce is out,' Bill said. 'Allegedly a message will be passed to him.'

'Who'd you speak to?'

'Deputy Phil Corliss.'

'Then it probably will be. What did you tell him?'

'Not much. I didn't get the sense I'd got the guy's full attention.'

I took the envelope out and opened it. Inside was a second envelope, the kind you'd use to send a greetings card. It had been sealed, opened, and then Scotch-taped shut again. I opened it. Inside was a single hair. Held against the pure white of the envelope, you could just tell it was blue at one end.

When I looked in the drawer again I saw I'd missed a piece of paper that had been lying under the envelope. The sheet looked fresh and new, as did the single line of text written on it:

2009 / sadness / directed at ~~Jess C~~

'Jesus,' I said, softly, looking at the line through the letters at the end. 'Bill — look for the name Ransom.'

408

'Who?'

'Carol's maiden name.'

He went hunting down the rows. I did the same, until I happened upon one with the name 'Greene' on it. I got Little D to open it.

'There going to be money in any of these?'

'I don't think so,' I said.

This drawer was hard to slide open, so stuffed was it with envelopes. Items of clothing. A watch. Photos, some recent, some much older looking. On top of these lay three pieces of paper, stapled together, with perhaps thirty separate entries on each. Whoever kept these records — Brooke, I assumed, though some of the older ones were in a different hand — would be needing to start a new sheet soon. Each line appeared to have a reference to a person, in the distinctive style of two or more letters of a first name, and then a single initial for the last.

Near the top of the last page was an entry dated five years before:

2004 / Lost / directed at Co. G

'Got it,' Bill said. 'Ransom, C.'

I heard Little D move over to Bill and start fiddling with the lock, but I was fixated by the piece of paper already in my hands. 'Co. G' — Courtney Greene? The daughter of the man whose drawer this presumably was? The girl could certainly be said to seem 'lost', but not in the usual ways. Not merely vague or doped or teenaged, but as if she was barely there at all. Plus there had been the bizarre reaction when I

409

told her that I wouldn't tell if she wouldn't, when a different personality had seemed to surface momentarily, as if the phrase had cut through the fog she normally moved through to someone trapped inside, who might have been offered little raises in her allowance, down the years, to keep her mouth shut. Not to mention her apparent acceptance of the unacceptable — a dead body in a motel room with a nail sticking up out of its head.

If you really could visit a sadness upon someone, could you also make another person lose themselves, become occluded to events in the past or present? Could you make them forget things that had happened in the night, and perhaps still continued? Could you cause someone to become lost amidst internal corridors to protect yourself?

Were there men who could do that to their own daughter, and what might they owe the person who made it happen for them?

I was distracted by the lights in the room flickering. All of them. A couple of quick blinks, then a second of blackness, and then all were on again. I put the piece of paper back and moved over to the drawer where Bill was standing. There was an envelope here too. Inside it was an old ballpoint pen with a clear plastic shaft, on which someone had once written the name 'Paul' in correction fluid, and something that looked like the cover of a long-ago exercise book.

There was a piece of the notepaper, with four lines written on it in two different hands:

1989: Mania (passion) / at Paul B.
1991: ditto / at Robert S.
2004: Quickening / at self
2005: Sadness / at JR

Personal effects. Things that another human being's hand or mind had once touched, which could be made to stand in for them. The pen looked as if it had been lying in the drawer for a long, long time — from 1989, presumably. The property, presumably, of a long-ago Paul, whose eye a much younger Carol Ransom had wished to attract; and had the exercise book likely belonged to another teenage boy three years later? Boys now middle-aged and married to other women, who probably didn't even remember the girl who'd once gone to these lengths in the hope of snaring their attention.

Unless, of course, they'd been doing the same thing themselves. There were a lot of drawers in this room, after all.

Underneath the four entry lines, by itself, was something else. A series of marks made on the paper, in pencil, almost random. Lines I'd seen before and in more than one place since I'd been in Black Ridge. I realized for the first time, perhaps because whoever had put them on this piece of paper had more of an understanding of what they were doing, that three of the lines did look like a recognizable shape — like the stick figure of a large, crooked man, or a dog, slashed across with lines.

Beneath that was another line written in ink:

411

Scott H ~~*[+++]*~~

It took me a moment to realize the first part must refer to a boy called Scott Henderson.

'John — are you okay?'

I held out the piece of paper. He read it, and looked up slowly. 'That mean what I think it does?'

'The only other crossing out I've seen seems to refer to the girl who died in Black Ridge yesterday.'

'No. I meant the pluses.'

I shrugged. It was hard to see them as meaning anything other than one down, three to go. The idea was making it hard for me to breathe.

'Something out there,' Little D said suddenly.

He was standing down at the end, by the window that stretched across nearly the room's full width.

Bill went to see. 'What?'

'Thought I saw something way back. A light or something.'

I went over too, and stuck my face close to the glass, shielding the light out with my hands. 'Bill — any idea what's back there?'

'Never been here before. Woods, I'm guessing.'

We tramped quickly down the stairs together and back out the front door.

'Is this snow?'

The rain had now gone through sleet and into something else. Whether it was snow I wasn't actually sure, but it was white and falling slowly and the world now sounded deadened. The

412

awful smell had abated somewhat with it, but it was still there, underneath.

I heard a shout and saw someone was running up the driveway.

'Becki,' I said. 'What the *hell* are you doing?'

'People,' she said, panting, when she reached us. 'I had to tell you.'

'What do you mean?'

'A bunch of cars. We're sitting there, and nothing passes, for ten minutes. Then suddenly all these cars go by, and keep coming. Ten, twenty of them?'

'Are they outside now?'

'No. They went straight by.'

That didn't make any sense to me. If you continued on up the road there was nothing until the turn-off that led to my old house, a couple of miles away. Past that, another twenty miles to Roslyn or Sheffer.

'Where's Kyle?'

'He wouldn't get out of the car.'

Then we all heard it together. A scream, far distant, muffled. But I knew where it had come from — the other side of the house. I also knew who had cried out. Even if you have never before heard the scream of someone you were married to, you recognize the sound.

And I had, of course. The day Scott died.

I started to run, heading for the left side of the building because it was closest. I heard Bill shouting to me as they started to follow but paid no attention. He'd been correct before, though in not quite the right way. This hadn't been a set-up, but they'd left the house open and lit it

413

up to pull me in the wrong direction again and waste time.

That wasn't going to happen now.

I came around the back of the house into a wide, deep lawn, beyond which the trees started in a rough semi-circle. I slowed, trying to see if there was any indication which direction would be best to go in, some sign of a path, or the light that Little D thought he'd seen from upstairs.

There wasn't anything. The woods merely looked like a wall of darkness into which you'd have to be out of your mind to run.

I was dimly aware of the sound of the others following around the side of the house, but then I heard the flat crack of a rifle shot and threw myself down onto the ground.

I heard the sound of pain immediately afterwards, but this time the bullet hadn't hit me.

Becki screamed.

At least one of the people behind me started shooting immediately.

'John — stay down!'

I ignored Bill's advice, got to my feet and zigzagged back. I'd been way out in front, isolated in the middle of the lawn. If whoever had fired had me in mind, I would have been an easy drop.

The others were hunkered down at the back of the house, to one side where they were covered by shadow. Bill was letting spaced shots off into the trees, from a steady double-handed grip. Becki had most of her right hand in her mouth and was biting on it, her eyes bulging. But she wasn't the person who'd been hit.

Little D was lying sprawled on the ground, the small of his back curving up, hands around his own throat. Blood was pulsing from between his fingers in thick, dark globs. He was blinking fast, his eyes trying to find something to fasten on beyond what was happening to him.

'Fuck,' I said, kneeling at his side, unconsciously reaching for a service backpack that wasn't there, trying to remember how you were supposed to respond in these circumstances. 'Where's the other guy?'

'Went running off into the trees,' Bill said. He stopped shooting, reloaded, listened. Silence for a moment, then the sound of shots in the distance.

Little D coughed, spraying blood.

I told him to keep his hands where they were, but I wasn't sure he was hearing me. I tried to turn him on his side, to keep the blood from flooding straight down into his lungs. His arms started to spasm, and it was hard to hold him still.

'Bill, you remember what to do?'

'Find a medic. Call for a chopper. Run away.'

'Apart from that?'

'No.'

'He's dead,' Becki said, dully.

He wasn't. But he'd stopped blinking and his hands were no longer gripping as tightly. A couple of minutes later he did die. His last cough sounded like a man deep under water. Snow dropped onto his face, falling harder now.

'This is a nightmare,' Becki said, to herself.

'Go back to the car,' I told her. 'Drive back to Black Ridge, find the sheriff's department. Get anybody you can find to come out here.'

'Screw that. If they're not going to come when you call, why would they just because some chick turns up?'

'Because you're covered in blood.'

Becki looked down at her hands and arms and seemed to realize for the first time that this was true.

Bill turned his head back toward the front of the house. 'Incoming,' he said, already moving.

I grabbed Becki's arm and pulled her with me, as Bill went wide. He hadn't made it to a viable position before we realized it was Kyle, running toward us. He saw Little D's body and stopped so fast he skidded, staring down at it.

'Kyle, go back to the — '

'Something's coming,' he said.

'You mean 'someone'?'

'I guess,' he said, uncertainly. 'I'm sure I saw people in the trees, or *something* in there, on the other side of the road. I mean, I couldn't really see properly because it was so dark over there. But I know something was coming. Some people or . . . shit, I don't *know*, okay?'

I realized that Kyle was terrified, his eyes and hands in constant movement, as if his body was panicking even worse than his mind.

'We need to rethink,' Bill said. 'Go back to the car, regroup.'

'No way,' I said, pointing toward the woods. 'Whatever's going down is happening in that direction and it's happening *now*.'

416

'With who knows how many assholes in the trees with guns pointing at us. Come on, John. You know it makes no sense to just go running in there.'

'I *heard Carol*.'

'Maybe. Point still holds. We run into there and they'll take us one by one. Though I guess . . . maybe it's everyone except you, right?'

'What?'

He was looking at me steadily. 'They grab you out of a parking lot, but don't kill you. They don't do it when they've got you in a secluded house with no one around, either, and they make a half-assed job of it when you *escape*. Five minutes ago you're in the middle of the lawn, with the house lights full on you. But they shoot the guy over there instead, who means nothing to them.'

'We can't go back to the car,' Kyle said, urgently, near tears. 'I'm *not going back there*.'

Bill ignored him. 'They aren't looking to kill you, John, at least not like that. The rest of us . . . '

'You're right,' I said. 'Get these people out of here.'

And I broke from the house and ran straight across the lawn and into the woods.

45

As soon as I got amongst the trees I dodged over to the biggest trunk I could find and got around the far side of it, crouching low to the ground.

To the right and left of me lay blackness, undifferentiated but for a few grey lines where moonlight caught jagged bark. Straight ahead, however, there was a different quality to the darkness, as though there might be a clearing in the distance. I guessed that was where I was headed.

I left it a beat, panning my eyes back and forth, listening. I heard something that could have been two rapid shots from a handgun, but it was a long way from where I was and could equally have been a branch brought down by the wind. It was beginning to pick up again, twitching the tops of the trees back and forth.

I was just about to move when I heard a noise behind me and whirled around. It was Bill.

'You asshole,' he said, coming up to me in a running crouch.

'Fuck are you doing here?'

He hunkered down next to me, his back to the tree trunk. 'I said we needed to rethink — not that you should come in here by yourself.'

'What about the other two?'

'Told them to stay where they are.'

'They going to?'

'If that girl has anything to do with it, yes. The

418

other kid hasn't got the balls to do anything by himself.'

'So — '

Another scream, from somewhere ahead.

We set off toward it.

★   ★   ★

There was no shape or structure to the forest we were entering. The woods around our old house had paths through it, a couple of scenic vista points, even a bench dragged nearly half a mile from the house by some former owner with more dedication than me. This was just trees, growing every which way. Generations of Robertsons had evidently elected to leave these woods exactly as they were, despite choosing to build their house here instead of in the centre of the town they'd created.

Bill kept pace to the side of me, his shotgun held at port arms. 'This place feel right to you?' he asked, after a while.

'No.'

I knew what he meant. The trees were getting thicker and within a hundred yards there was no snow on the ground. The forest floor barely seemed wet, despite hours of rain. It was easy to run, harder to decide where to run to. The air was heavy and dead with darkness, and for a bizarre moment it was like being fifteen years back in time, two young guns running through the night in another country, on missions we didn't understand.

I'm not sure I ever felt that afraid there,

though. You can, to a degree, keep yourself out of the way of bullets and shells. What we were running toward now felt like it started inside.

Bill suddenly stopped dead in his tracks, his hand held up. 'Hang on.'

'What?'

He was swallowing compulsively. 'I heard something.'

At first I could hear nothing but pregnant silence, so oppressive that it made the sound of my own blood loud and unnatural. Then we heard another shout, from far over toward the left.

We changed course and ran in this new direction. The forest floor was declining now, and rockier, and more moonlight was making it down through the trees.

'There's something up there,' Bill panted.

I could see it too, a change in the pattern of the trunks, confirming that something other than forest lay ahead. It seemed to be getting a little warmer, too. It wasn't just because we were running. It was as though the air itself had been trapped here since the height of summer, or before that; as if the air in this part of the woods had lived here forever and didn't travel anywhere else, and never had. Suddenly what Carol had said about things living in the wilderness didn't sound so dumb. Did air count as a thing? What did it think? What did it want?

I started to speed up, leaving Bill behind, until after a few hundred yards I could barely hear him. I wasn't even sure I was running in the right direction any longer. I was simply running.

The trees thinned out all at once, snow once more on the ground, and then there were no more ahead. Instead there was openness, and beyond that, a lake.

I skidded to a halt.

It looked alien in this light and with a thin layer of white all around. I'd never seen it from this side before, either — nor with the body of a black man sprawled on its shore, an arm and a leg under its surface, trying in vain to sit up.

But I knew immediately what this place was, what it had to be. I knew the name of the only lake in the area of anything like this size.

★ ★ ★

The water was absolutely still. Patches close to the shore had started to freeze and gather snow, sticks pushing from beneath the surface like tiny bones.

Bill arrived behind me breathing hard, then went over to pull Switch up onto the shore. The guy had taken a bullet high up in the leg, but looked as though he'd live. He was swearing to himself, in a low and insistent tone.

'Where the hell is this?' Bill asked.

'It's Murdo Pond.'

I was standing close to the lake's edge, craning my head around to the left. Our old house had to be up that way, a mile or two past a long, wide bend in the shore that would have hidden it even in daylight. I had never been to the Robertson place, of course, and never took a boat out on 'our' part of the pond, and so had simply never

421

put it together that their house, assuming deep enough access to the woods, could have had frontage on the same lake, at the other end from where we'd lived.

The odour came from here. It did right now, at any rate, though I'd never noticed it when we lived on the lake. The thing we'd smelled in the Robertson house, and coming through the forest beforehand: it started here.

I turned the other way and saw that trees came right down to the waterline on either side of where we were standing. But about a third of a mile away I could make out an open section of rocky shore, and a jetty. Someone was standing on it.

Bill saw it too. 'There, look, John.'

The person at the end of the jetty looked as if they had two heads, one smaller than the other.

I could hear the distant crying of a child, and the ragged sound of a woman shouting, Carol gone way past the edge of hysteria, screaming as if trying to break someone's mind.

'Going to have to leave you here,' I told Switch. He nodded, his face pulled tight with pain.

'Fuck them up bad,' he said.

Bill and I plunged back into the trees and ran.

⋆   ⋆   ⋆

We tried to, anyway, but the trees stood even closer together, the ground between them uneven and rocky and plagued with small gullies where spring thaws would trickle down toward

422

the lake. Moonlight struggled to reach the ground here, and cast strange shadows, and for a moment I thought I saw a small group of people running with us, over to the right, but it couldn't have been. There was no way anyone could have got to that side, or be running that fast without making any sound, and a few of the shapes had seemed no bigger than children.

The wind was really starting to pick up, high in the trees, making the branches move constantly against each other. Rustling, whispering sounds, and a harsh crack, a feeling like someone was behind us, or to the side, or perhaps even all around.

Then we were out the other side of the thicket and all was still like a tableau. I saw Carol standing on the shore, pleading. I realized with horror that the double-headed creature on the jetty had not been her and Tyler, but Brooke and Tyler.

The walkway went forty feet out into the lake, and she was close to the very end, holding Tyler fast in her arms. He was struggling, but she was strong.

Carol turned when she heard me running out of the woods. Her face was broken with grief, red and wet with tears. She didn't look like anyone I'd ever met.

'John,' she screamed. 'Get him back!'

I started toward the jetty, but Brooke held up her hand.

'One more step and I'll throw him in,' she said.

'Two steps,' said another voice, 'and I'll blow

his mother's head off.'

Cory Robertson was stationed past the other side of the promontory, standing in shadow and braced against a tree. He had a hunting rifle trained straight on Carol. I'd used a gun like it in the past, and knew it could stop a deer from over half a mile. At this range it would punch a hole in a car door.

I turned, looking for Bill. I thought he'd been right behind me in the trees, but now he was nowhere to be seen. So I kept my head turning smoothly in an arc, as if all I'd been doing was scoping out the terrain, establishing the degree to which I'd become surrounded.

'Anybody else I should know about?' I asked.

'Just us,' Brooke said. 'But Cory's an excellent shot.'

'I believe you,' I said. 'I've seen the picture gallery.'

I knew, however, that I'd just seen the shadow of at least one more person amidst the trees, staying close. A fairly hefty someone. 'Bet Deputy Greene isn't too shabby either.'

'Bravo. Well, yes, I did lie just a little. A few friends have been kind enough to assist us. I'm not going to tell you how many, though, or where they are.'

'Okay then,' I said, slowly raising my hands. 'In which case I'm not going anywhere. You win.'

'Drop the gun.'

I dropped it.

'*Get Tyler*,' Carol shouted at me, her voice cracked. 'She's *going to kill him*.'

I turned to face the jetty. 'What's this about,

Brooke? Why have you got my son?'

'He isn't yours.'

'That's not what his birth certificate said.'

'You want a prize for having screwed your own wife for a change? You wouldn't even have that boy if it weren't for me.'

'Quickening, 2004.'

'Very good.'

'I didn't know anything about that until twenty minutes ago. I don't understand it now either.'

'Of course you don't. Darling Carol already *had* a child but that's just not enough for some people, is it? She was *so* worried that number two was being a little sloooow in arriving and so she came visiting her old friend Brooke. She didn't tell *you* about this, naturally. It's astounding how much of life is invisible, don't you find? That's not the only favour Carol's asked down the years, either, or the only lie she's told.'

'We all lie, Brooke. Big deal. Tell me — how much does it cost? For someone who wants a boy to fall in love with her, or another child? What do you take from people like that? Is it just money? What else do you demand for pretending you can do these things?'

'I don't claim to be able to do anything. But I know someone who can.'

'Right, yes, a witch. And why would a witch need a broker for her services? What does she gain from that?'

'Do you know who she is?'

'I don't even believe there is one.'

Brooke grinned, cold and knowing. 'Precisely. A few hundred years ago that could save your life.'

'And in return you take a cut of the money?'

'And keep the dog on its lead. People with that kind of power tend to be unstable. They need a steadying hand. A patron. Someone with an overview.'

'Just sounds like bullshit to me, Brooke.'

'Luckily I don't give a damn whether you believe in it or not.'

What was Bill doing? Where was he? Would a few extra seconds help?

I turned to Carol. 'Did you tell Tyler about this? Is this why he said to me I wasn't really his father?'

Carol just glared at me with open hatred, as if I was something that had come into her life from underneath the bed in the middle of the night, a thing that had brought only badness into her life.

'Oh, Cory,' Brooke said, lightly, as you might alert someone to the fact you're ready for another cocktail. There was a beat, and then a rifle shot.

I heard Bill cry out, and knew then that whatever happened next, it was very likely to be going Brooke Robertson's way.

A moment later this became even clearer, when people started coming toward us out of the trees.

★　★　★

Bill had evidently frozen deep in the forest when he saw what happened to me, and had tried cutting across the back to get around the other side of Cory. But something — moonlight, the bulk of his passing against the snow — had given him away.

Cory shot him in the upper right side of the chest, out of mercy or more likely from swinging the rifle around too fast. Either way, it was enough. You could smell the blood from where I stood, unless that was merely a different note in the odour coming in waves off the lake. Bill was knocked flat on his back, just inside the trees. He was moving as if trying to stand up in the wrong direction, and his gun had fallen some distance away.

Meanwhile, shadows kept coming toward me.

Initially I'd assumed it was just Cory's buddies, the guys I'd seen in his photograph. It quickly became clear there were more people than that. At first just ten or so of them, then more, and still they kept coming.

Deputy Greene was the first. Then I saw the man who ran the coffee truck in the bank parking lot, and the woman who ran the hair salon on Kelly Street. I saw the guy who owned a market where I'd bought cigarettes a couple of times in the last few days, and people I'd seen sitting reading the paper in The Write Sisters, and talking together in the Mountain View, or passing me on the street.

I saw Courtney.

And I saw Marie, the woman who ran my motel.

Most stopped only as far from the trees as was needed to accommodate those still coming up from behind. But Marie came further, halfway to where I stood. Her eyes were closed and her lips were moving constantly.

Then finally she opened her eyes.

The trees suddenly shook up in their highest branches, as another cold and vicious wind came down out of the mountains, or perhaps from deeper in the trees. This wind whipped Marie's hair up around her face in a cloud, as she turned her head to look at me. She looked very, very different here. She seemed both younger and very old, dreadful with power, as if the movement in her hands could provoke movement in objects she was not in contact with.

She also looked, bathed in a moonlight that found harsher planes buried in her face, a little like someone I knew.

I realized that none of the other people was looking my way, or even seemed aware that I was here. They all seemed to be gazing at the lake, or perhaps at the other side of it, and none was dressed for the weather. One of the nearest to me was the hair salon woman. Her face was blank, cloudy, like Courtney's had been every time I'd seen her. Almost as if she didn't even have a real face, or I was seeing beyond it to an emptiness within, to the truth that there was nothing inside anyone that could be depended upon.

'You first,' Brooke said to Carol.

'*Fuck you*,' Carol said.

I turned as Brooke took a step backward, bringing her even closer to the end of the jetty.

She moved her arms so that the child wriggling in her grasp was hanging fully out over the lake.

'This water here is always very cold,' she said. 'How good a swimmer is your little boy?'

Carol looked at me, helpless now. The anger was gone from her eyes and I saw only the girl I'd met long ago, someone who'd convinced me to come live in these mountains because she loved them and they had always been her home — perhaps not realizing that it was also a case of never being able to get away.

I didn't know what to tell her. Death hung in the air with nothing left to do but fall. If we didn't do what Brooke said then she was going to go through with what she intended anyhow. So far as I could tell, half of Black Ridge was here to see this, or to witness it. To avoid this moment we needed to have started three or four years back, or longer; perhaps on the days we were born. We needed not to have met each other, to be different people, to have always been dead and never tried to be alive. All we could do now was slow it down.

'Do what she says,' I said.

Carol didn't move. I started walking.

'No,' Brooke said, her voice cracking just a little. 'Carol first.'

Carol still wouldn't budge. Perhaps she thought she could create an impasse by refusing to move. Maybe she too was playing for time. I didn't think either was going to work. There was only one way I could see out of this.

'Carol, listen to me.'

'Why would I listen to you?' Carol said. 'Why

should I believe you care about him?'

'Because he's my son,' I said. 'You and I are done. But he and I can never be. Unless there's something else you haven't told me.'

'No. Screwing other people was *your* department. Don't worry. He's your son.'

'And yours. So go to him. You want him alone out there, whatever's going to happen next?'

Carol hesitated, and then abruptly started toward the jetty. Climbed up the three steps, and began to walk out over the water.

I glanced over at Cory. He was holding his position. Evidently whatever Brooke planned had to happen out over the lake, but I didn't know whether it needed the three of us to be there together at the same time, or if her brother was just going to shoot Carol on her way to the end.

He had the rifle in place, but didn't look as though he was sighting on her with immediate intent. And why would they have waited to do all this, and planned it this way, unless they needed all three of us at once?

I heard Carol's feet on the jetty. A few more steps. Then Cory abruptly turned and fired.

Carol flinched, but the shot had been for Bill, who'd been trying to get to his gun. This time he was hit high up in the left thigh.

Cory swivelled back to sight on Carol once again.

The whole forest seemed to exhale.

The warmth I'd felt earlier was suddenly gone, and it was utterly cold. Bill was making the kind of noises men find in their throats when all they want is for an angel to come and take them away.

Everybody else stood still, hair and clothes flapping in a growing wind. Only Marie looked truly real, her and the indistinct shape that now stood by her side.

Carol was halfway along the jetty now. Something seemed to be rising out of the surface of the lake beneath her, like a faint haze. Her back was straight and she was staring directly at the woman at the other end, meeting her eye coldly, and I was proud of her for this.

It felt like there was a point, minutes or seconds from now, beyond which all was pitch black, and as though this darkness had always been present in my life, and that everything I had ever done or dreamed had been a lie. As if my father had never cared for me, nor my mother, nor Scott, nor anyone else on this earth. So what did it matter what happened next?

Carol was nearly at the end of the jetty now. Brooke would want me to follow, after which she would presumably leave us there for Cory to finish this thing off, to drop three bodies, the remainder of a family, into Murdo Pond.

But then, for just a moment, Brooke's view of me was obscured by Carol's back — as I hoped it might be.

I heard a voice whisper from just behind me, a voice I hadn't heard in a long time.

'Run, Daddy,' he said. '*Run*.'

46

I kicked off with everything I had. As I reached the steps and leapt straight up them, I heard a rifle shot. I dodged left as I hit the jetty, but I knew it was going to come down to how good a marksman Cory really was, and how much of a risk he was prepared to take, given that his sister stood beyond me.

Carol heard or felt me coming, turned, tried to move out of the way, stumbled and fell back.

There was the flat crack of another shot. This missed by a foot and took a chunk out of the left handrail. I went back right, gathering speed now that I was on a level surface.

Brooke saw me coming, and tightened her grip on Tyler. Cory fired again, too hurried, missed once more.

Everything you ever do is a risk.

I threw myself straight at Brooke.

★   ★   ★

I hit her hard and fast and smashed her straight back into the rail at the end of the jetty. It broke and then we were falling, Tyler between us, my face so close to Brooke's that we could have kissed.

I punched out at her as hard as I could, and we hit the water hard, heads first.

It was like being kicked in the heart and

432

temples at the same time, so cold that my whole body went into shocked spasm, throwing me backward from Brooke.

I glimpsed Tyler's hand in front of my face, and grabbed at it, pulling him toward me, jerking his head closer to mine. His eyes were full of terror. I didn't even know if he could swim.

Brooke's foot came jackknifing down, kicking at Tyler's head. Her brain evidently worked fast enough to have decided this would do as a backup plan.

I kept hold of Tyler's wrist and used my other arm and both legs to drive us deeper, away from her and down into the dark. As he came closer toward me I saw his cheeks bulging, and hoped that meant he had air stored inside.

Brooke's foot lashed into my face across the bridge of my nose, and then we were down and out of reach. I felt the blood pouring out of my face as a sudden warmth and a metallic taste.

I pulled Tyler closer toward me until I had him fast under one arm, still kicking, driving us as far from the jetty as I could, back into the lake.

Suddenly my head was above water. Tyler's came up with it, and I shouted at him to breathe. His mouth opened just before I sank again, his weight and floundering pulling me back under.

My vision was obscured by the blood clouding up out of my nose, but as I tried to right us both and claw back up it seemed as though areas of shadow and light swirled within the water, as if it was disturbed more than could be accounted for by my movement. It was the coldest thing I have ever felt in my life; cold and hopeless; cold with the heavy resignation of those who have already left. I felt as if the centre of the earth was pulling us down toward it, or as if we were being pushed from above, and as we floated deeper it was as if others fell alongside us. But I did not want to go deeper with them. Not now, not ever. I kicked viciously down with both feet, feeling as if I was fighting sleep, as if hands were grasping and pulling at my face, their nails scoring lines in my cheeks. I kicked again, and kept kicking, lashing out with my free arm, pushing up.

Then we broke the surface again, and this time I was ready for it and already kicking toward the jetty. Brooke was well ahead of me, pulling herself up onto the shore, shouting at Cory — who turned smartly and pointed the rifle at my head.

I dropped quickly under the surface again, kicked to the side, and then pulled us up to break the surface once more.

Carol seemed frozen on the jetty, unable to move in any direction at all.

'Cory, do it now!'

Brooke was jabbing her finger in my direction, her voice barely audible against the wind that was pulling the snow around like a whirlwind. It would have been beautiful but for the likelihood I was about to die, and were it not that the movement of the air contained within it the source of the smell that had been at the back of my head for the last two days. I realized it was not cinnamon nor anything like it, but an odour so rank that the brain was forced to try to invent a new category, to call it anything but what it was.

I desperately kicked out again with both feet and lunged toward the end of the jetty, trying to put a physical barrier between us and the gun. Cory was meanwhile moving the rifle around, panning it, trying to get a clear line of sight through the snow.

Brooke kept screaming, telling him to do it, do it now.

Tyler was clinging on to me, his head over my shoulder, and I felt him stiffen at the same time as I heard a clear, flat, cracking sound.

Carol screamed.

★　★　★

I kept pushing forward, not knowing what else to do, and finally got one hand onto the lowest rung of the remains of the ladder at the end of the jetty. Tyler was kicking and crying now, and all I could tell was that it wasn't his head that had been hit, because he was holding it bolt upright and no blood was flowing from it, or parts missing — at least that I could see.

I tried to find something down below to brace my feet against, but I was losing the feeling in my legs and there didn't seem to be anything beneath us in the water. I shifted Tyler higher up my chest so his weight kept him on me, and grabbed the other rail with my left hand, feeling the muscles in both arms howl as I used everything I had left to pull us up out of the water.

Tyler was screaming now too, but they didn't seem to be sounds of pain. His fingers were digging into my back, and when I turned my head I saw he was staring at something over my shoulder.

I pulled us up another rung and tried to blank out everything except the idea of getting up a further step after that; tried to fade out the wind and the sound the trees were making; tried most of all to blank out the smell. I couldn't tell now whether it was coming from the lake, the trees, or out of the earth, or out of myself. It was what envelops your soul as it lies in the grave, the odour of your own body rotting around you. It was what would remain if you killed every living thing, and left behind only what lay between the trees in these mountains, and swam in its lakes, and could not be seen.

One more rung and finally I was able to get a foothold, and push myself up the last few steps.

As my head drew above the level of the jetty floor, I saw Cory lying flat on his face on the snowy ground, a couple of yards from where he'd been holding his position. Brooke was crouched over him, cradling his head in her arms, making a sound I cannot describe. Beyond them stood Marie, shouting furiously at another figure that had appeared at the other end of the jetty.

It was Kristina. She was holding Bill's gun.

As I fell down onto the planking I saw Carol backing away, toward the land. I thought at first she was looking at me, but then I realized she was staring at whatever Tyler had been screaming at, something that still lay behind me.

I gently prised Tyler's fingers from my neck,

and bent down to put him down on the deck.

'Go to Mommy,' I said.

He stared at me, too scared to do anything. I remembered how to smile at someone that small.

'Go on,' I said, finally loving him. 'Go to her. *Now.*'

He hesitated, took a step backward, and then turned and ran down the jetty like a memory fading.

When he'd made it to Carol, Kristina came walking past them toward me. She looked exhausted and nauseous, and I realized far too late that, although she was much thinner and taller and had dyed her hair to cover the red, it was Kristina that Marie had just reminded me of: and that she now looked as bowed over and spent as the motel owner had the day I checked in.

'Don't look around,' Kristina said, as she approached. 'Don't do it yet.'

My back felt burning hot now. My face was so cold it had lost all feeling, but the other side of my body and head felt as though I was inches from the sun.

Kristina stopped when she was a couple of feet away. She reached up and ran a fingernail along each of the scratches that I could now feel throbbing over my face.

'It's the best I can do,' she said, her voice full of sorrow. 'I'm sorry. I'm new to this.'

She started walking backwards, and she too looked like she was being pulled away, back into a dream of which I was no longer a part.

'Look now,' she said, finally.

★ ★ ★

I turned.

I felt a thing that had been here for a long, long time, for whom this was both home and body, something that was in every tree, in the wind and mud, which sounded in every echo and which fell with every flake of snow, something that informed every deed done, every secret hidden, each act untaken and every word said beneath these skies.

I knew I'd heard its voice before on bad mornings, and muttering in my ears in the dead parts of the worst nights. I know it had helped my finger pull triggers years ago, moved my mouth when I had said 'yes' on evenings when I should not have — or perhaps that the relationship ran in two directions, and that when I had done these things, I had been feeding it.

I knew it smelled my blood now and recognized it, and I understood that I had perceived it as a smell only because my senses did not know what else to do with their shocked knowledge of this creature's presence, because it was a thing I could not see or touch and that was always beyond hitting or fighting or pushing away. So I didn't try.

I let it come in through my mouth and nose, breathed it deep, knowing that was the only way to stop it getting past me to reach those who stood behind. Everything under the sun follows the path of least resistance. Water flows down. People commit easy sins. And this thing came into the person that was closest to it, in space and character, and that person was me.

For an instant everything around me seemed darker, as if all difference had faded away and everything in creation overlapped to occupy the same space. I realized that events that could have happened a hundred years ago were still very close, and also that this present night would remain here, a heartbeat away from every night, for all time: that if any future person stood on this jetty, I would be right here by their side, and they would turn away, disturbed.

I heard the noise of bears and mountain lions and creatures that had lived in these woods much longer ago and whose bones we had still not even found. I heard the sound of horses and logging and settlers banging nails to make walls in cabins that were now rotted and fallen away. And I saw once again the figures that I had dreamt of meeting in the woods the night before, but now they seemed to be standing at the very end of the jetty, their backs to me.

Two adult-sized, and three small, dripping wet.

Behind me, in what remained of the here and now, I was dimly aware of the sound of Brooke Robertson, of her screams of grief, and felt bitter triumph. Otherwise there was only the wood beneath my feet and the smell now sunk deep into my bones.

★　★　★

And then the figures at the end were gone.

The lake seemed to fade back behind the

439

curtain of falling snow, to flatten down from being a wall into its usual horizontal position. I found I could turn from it, as if it was no longer pulling me, and looked back along the jetty instead, toward the land.

All the people who had stood in front of the trees had disappeared — so completely that I wondered if they'd ever really been there at all, or if they were merely the souls who were in thrall to the Robertsons and the power they somehow brokered on the town's behalf. Carol was holding Tyler in her arms, their heads so close together that they seemed fused into one.

Marie had gone. Kristina was sitting by the side of the lake, vomiting, her head in her hands, looking as if her back was broken.

The only person looking at me was Brooke.

She pulled herself away from her brother's body, and straightened up, a pistol in her hand. Something about the ease with which she gripped it told me that she was the better shot of the family.

She walked onto the jetty until she was halfway along. Her stride was steady and her head held high, and I could see in her face every good, strong quality that had pulled men and women across thousands of miles to live in places like these. I also saw there everything that had subsequently been given up, and lost, and sacrificed, to keep on living in the face of the cold and the mountains and rain and the bad things that wanted only to live here in solitude, and which dreamt long, slow dreams of wiping our kind from the face of the earth.

As she started to raise the gun, I heard a voice. 'That's enough, Brooke.'

She and I turned our heads together, to see Sheriff Pierce coming out of the woods alone. The rifle he held was not pointed at me, but at her.

'That's enough,' he repeated. 'We're not doing this again.'

She lowered the gun slowly. Seemed to glance at Carol for a moment, or perhaps not at her, but at the child she held in her arms.

She turned back to me and smiled what appeared to be an utterly genuine smile, for a moment looking like a teenager, a young girl with things to do and every happiness to hold, the beautiful new generation of a family that had always been blessed.

Then she tucked the barrel of the gun under her chin, and pulled the trigger.

47

A year ago, before any of this happened, I remembered something from my childhood. I was in my mid-teens and my mother was doing stuff in the kitchen in the ordered and correct way she had, while I sat at the table and cranked through homework. Dad was doing something outside. The radio was playing, serving up this song and that, and eventually one I didn't recognize came on and it wasn't my kind of thing and so I reached out to change the station.

I stopped when I saw my mother. She was standing by the sink, staring unseeingly out into the yard. She had turned away, but only by a few degrees, as if she'd done what she could before being turned to stone by whatever force had gripped her. The veins were standing out on the side of her temples. She swallowed every two seconds, and kept blinking, as if fighting to keep this thing inside.

As I stared at her, bewildered, I realized she was listening to the radio. The song got to the final chorus and I knew I couldn't be found watching. I dragged my gaze back to the homework on the table, and waited it out.

I kept my eyes down after it had finished, when my mother walked out of the kitchen into the hallway for a few seconds. I heard her cough several times, as if clearing her throat, and the sound of a blouse sleeve wiped hard across her eyes.

Then she was back in the room, doing whatever she'd been doing before. When I eventually did look up, it was as if none of it had ever happened; though the next time our eyes met, what took place on her face was the flattest and emptiest thing I think I've ever seen. It looked like a dead person's smile.

I was young and so by the next day it was history. I never asked her what that had been about, and I'm sure she wouldn't have told me — but I had something similar happen to me last year when I was sitting alone in a bar in Portland, eight years after she'd died. A song came on the bar's jukebox, a song I'd listened to with Jenny Raines, and I suddenly had an inkling of what my father might have been weathering when our walks ended; what had accidentally caused a distancing between him and me that culminated in me running with bad kids, joining the army, and perhaps everything that happened in my life after that.

I sensed a presence in the shadows of my life, and I believe a song grabbed my mother by the heart that afternoon and yanked her back to a period she never allowed herself to think about, to emotions walled away but still alive — that it took her into that parking lot in the back of all our heads and kicked her in the guts until she bled.

When it happened to me I did exactly what she had done. I coughed, and wiped my eyes, and carried on.

* * *

I live in New York now, in a small apartment in a pocket of the East Village that is sturdily resisting becoming fashionable, and remains home to people who are old and do not speak English as a first language — and some of whom, I have heard it said, do not own a single iPod. It has narrow streets and trees that are bare, now that it is winter, and it feels like a place should. I have a job ten minutes' walk away at a restaurant and bar called The Adriatico, a few turns off MacDougal. I earn even less than I did in Marion Beach, but at least I am the official pizza guy, so don't let anyone tell you there's no hope of progress in the world.

When the bar shuts at the end of the night I hang out with the other staff for a while, and then walk home through streets in which there's generally something still happening and our light and sound and chatter makes it impossible to believe that this area, like all others, was once a wilderness.

I'll sit out on the stoop and smoke a last cigarette, enjoying the feeling of cold stone and the sound of distant traffic, before finally going upstairs.

To my continual surprise, I do not live here alone.

* * *

From what I hear, the restaurant in Marion Beach is very quiet now. I know Ted toys with

444

the idea of shutting down completely for the off-season, but the cost of that pizza oven still pecks away at him, and so he does not.

I returned to Oregon with Becki and Kyle to find a state of crisis. The night I wound up in Murdo Pond had seen the local police being called out to the Pelican, to try to catch someone who was attempting to set fire to it. On the back of this, Ted found out what Kyle had done, and went biblical, forbidding him from seeing his daughter. I expected Becki to put up a fight but it seemed she'd had enough of Kyle too. Turns out when Bill had left them at the Robertson house to follow me into the woods that night, Kyle just ran away, abandoning her.

She threw him out, but Kyle didn't get it. He didn't seem to get any of it. He didn't understand that Becki was no longer his girl, that he no longer had a job. He tried once more to get into the drugs industry. He quickly found his level, that of consumer.

The situation has since been resolved. The restaurant ticks over during the quiet season, and Ted is letting Eduardo have his head with a few novel items on the menu, as an experiment. Becki has a new boyfriend and is now emailing me convincingly about going back to college, this time to study for an MBA — so she can come back and franchise the living daylights out of the Pelican.

Stranger things have happened.

★   ★   ★

I have also been in regular contact with Carol, by email and once by phone. She put Tyler on the line, at my request. We did not have a lot to say to each other, but I tried, and will keep doing so. Whether I'll ever be a real father to him, I have no idea. You do what you do and wait and see how it turns out, and by then it's all but done.

Carol still swears that the service she paid Brooke Robertson to broker wasn't supposed to act against me, and I believe her. She wanted no more than to make Jenny uncomfortable and sad, but as soon as you unleash bad things into the world you lose control. They have their own agendas and demands, bigger and more powerful than any individual can comprehend. The last thing Carol wanted was for harm to come to Scott, but he was the most valued thing in the life of the man with whom another woman had committed her punishable sin.

And so something happened, because.

We try to blame others for our misfortunes, point fingers, to seek mitigation for our actions in the behaviour, creed or colour of strangers, but two plus two never equals five. Sometimes it doesn't even make four. Often you've just got two of one thing, and two of another, and they cannot be combined to create anything meaningful at all.

I cannot explain all of the things that happened while I was in Black Ridge, but I know why they occurred.

They happened because of me.

Carol is lighter as a result of this calculation. I am heavier. That is fair.

⋆　⋆　⋆

I understand some of the rest a little better now too. Have parts of a story, at least, put together from talking to Carol and one other person.

I believe Brooke caused something to be set upon her father, after he confided in her that he was going to accede to Ellen's wishes and start a new family. I'm sure she told herself she was doing it to preserve the legacy of her forefathers, and that Ellen's demands were forcing her hand, but I suspect the real reason was far more personal than that. For I have also been told how the story about Brooke got mangled in its way into school legend: that she came to this teacher one night, brimful of adolescent love, and he had sex with her against her will, and the secret and incompetent abortion that followed destroyed any chance of her ever having children — that she might even have died were it not for the intervention of Marie Hayes.

Cory had been the Robertsons' last chance of continuing their bloodline at Black Ridge, but he was no longer capable of that or anything else by the end of the night at Murdo Pond. Their influence is over, unless what his sister did to herself at the end completed the fate begun by the deaths of their father and mother. Brooke knew what she was doing, and her will was strong. What she felt for Black Ridge was, I suspect, as close to love as she was capable of, and it is possible that enough blood has been spilt, for the time being, to remark the forest's tracks with the dead.

447

The Robertsons were a family too, after all, and now they are gone.

★   ★   ★

Every time I think of the name 'Murdo Pond' now, I kick myself for not realizing what it had come from, but they had hidden the history well. Soon after arriving in NYC I managed to find a one-line reference to a woman called Bridget Hayes, in Fort & Reznikoff's *History of Witchcraft in New England*, acquired through The Strand Bookstore's rare books service. She was tried in Murraytown, Massachusetts in 1693 — and acquitted on the basis of character references from key locals, including the Evans and Kelly clans. The Robertsons were not cited in the court reports, though records demonstrate that there was a prominent family of that name in town at that time. They also show these four families leaving together for the West nearly two hundred years later. This event is noted in the slim volume of Murraytown history I subsequently found through AbeBooks, though the author doesn't speculate as to why three prosperous families should leave for the unpredictable frontier, taking with them a lowly dairy farmer and his red-haired wife, whose surname was also Hayes.

The book was creditably thorough in most other ways, including specifying the number of children in each family. The Kellys had two when they left Massachusetts. It is possible they had another en route, I suppose, but unlikely it

448

would have had time to grow to the size of the third child I believe I glimpsed with them.

I think, or perhaps I hope, that was Scott.

I do not like to think of him being lonely in those woods, and while Ellen could have made the pattern of branches and twigs on the forest floor near the picnic area, I don't think she made the marks on the back of my motel room. I like to believe that Scott's spirit was attempting to deflect the forces that live in those woods, not onto me, but *away*: making signs that I have come to realize bear a strong resemblance to the arrangement of the streets in Black Ridge. I have subsequently seen the pattern in other places, too, or something like it, including in photographs I found online of cave paintings and ceremonial designs in Europe. I have wondered whether some of those prehistoric engravings were not maps after all, but attempts to ward off creatures our ancestors could feel but not see.

Or perhaps, in some cases, to pay homage to them.

To tap into their power.

I've also wondered whether Brooke was telling the truth about one thing, at least, and that it was not her who had called my motel room during the night after I found the marks on the back of the motel. When I think back now, it seems to me that the noise I heard on the line could have been that of a child, trying to call out from a very long distance.

Naturally I have no explanation for how that could be, but one morning recently I took down the small pottery vase that had been on my shelf and walked over to the East River Park. I waited until there was no one in sight and then poured Scott's remains into the water. In a vase — or a lake — you can become trapped. From here I hoped his ashes would make it to the sea.

★ ★ ★

Switch survived. He refused to accept his colleague's portion of the money I had promised them, though he did take twenty-five.

Two weeks before I left Marion Beach, I took a drive over to Portland early one evening. Kyle was in the passenger seat. I had tracked him down in Astoria, crashed out on the couch of one of his remaining friends. In previous weeks he had made persistent attempts to visit Becki, accosting her on the street, increasingly aggressively. He simply wouldn't leave her alone, seeming to believe that if he could bend her to his will, then the rest of the world would fall back into place too.

So I made a deal with him. I told him that he was going to come with me to Portland. There I would straighten out his problems, using more of my money if necessary, after which I would drive him to the airport and pay for a ticket to anywhere in the USA. In return, he'd leave Ted's daughter the fuck alone.

He perched on the couch and twitched and sniffed and eventually agreed, perhaps sensing that the deal I was offering was the best the world had left to give.

When we got to Portland I left him in a bar

450

sucking back Bacardi and walked a couple of blocks to where I'd agreed to meet representatives of the gang from whom he'd originally bought his drugs — guys I'd made contact with through a number Switch had given me. There were three men waiting. I explained I would like them to no longer pose a threat to Ted, his business, or his daughter, and outlined the nature of the deal I was proposing.

They stepped back to discuss it, and then the shortest of them — it generally is, for some reason — came forward again.

'Okay,' he said.

'And then it's finished?'

'Said okay. Don't push it.'

I smiled. He eye-fucked me hard but then blinked, and turned his head away, as if he had caught a faint but potent smell coming down the street, or in the air, or from the man he was facing.

Something dry and sweet.

'Yeah,' he said, more quietly. 'We're good.'

So I told them which bar Kyle was sitting in, and went back to my car and drove home.

★   ★   ★

Bill also survived — though it was touch and go for a while — and is now as hale as ever. Apparently Black Ridge has seen a small upswing in its fortunes recently, with three new businesses opening in the last few months. Bill dropped by on a lay-over a few months ago and we went out and got world-changingly drunk on

451

his client's tab. He brought the news that he'd spoken to Jenny again, and she seemed happier. He has even lent her a little money to start her own jewellery business down in Colorado.

The capacity of some people for goodness never ceases to astound me, though I hope some day it will.

⋆　⋆　⋆

A few weeks later I had another visitor.

It was supposed to just be dinner. It had become impossible for her to remain in her home town, and she already had an airline ticket for Europe. She wound up not using it, and Kristina Hayes now holds down the bar at The Adriatico instead. Fights and bad language have declined to zero since she took charge, and the owner thinks she's the best thing since sliced bread. He may be right.

Some nights I lie in bed next to her and wait for sleep, fitting together the missing parts. I try to work out whether Brooke put Ellen up to contacting me in the first place, with the promise of deflecting her doom and burying her past, and then reneged on the deal. Something Ellen said the last time I saw her alive — a remark about how she had not been good — makes me suspect that might have been the case. If so, I don't blame her. You do what you have to protect those you love, including yourself.

I try also to guess at what point Brooke decided to put in place the sacrifice of another family into what had afterward been dubbed

Murder Pond. The gap between Scott's death and what happened five months ago makes me hope his death at least was accidental, and only recently did Brooke conceive of finishing what his death had started, thus recharging the town that the original sacrifice of the Kelly family had brought into life, over a hundred years before.

Kristina says she doesn't know, and it probably doesn't matter. Every day we die a little, and that is one form of sacrifice, but our worlds and situations demand more of us than that. That's part of why I made the deal over Kyle, but the truth is that time only moves in one direction. You cannot go back and un-make your actions or un-say your words. The best you can do is try to make sure the bad things push you in better directions in the future.

Or failing that, pass them on.

* * *

One last memory I have of Scott is this. He must have been about three, and he was trying to climb onto the kitchen counter, something he had been instructed not to do. It was high enough that he could have hurt himself badly if he fell to the floor, which was tiled. Carol and I sometimes left knives in the sink, too, and he would easily have been able to reach them from up there.

The counter was forbidden territory, therefore, but Scott was at an age when there are no such places — especially if a cookie jar awaits the intrepid and the brave. I was doing something at the time, most likely making coffee, and though I was vaguely aware of him using a chair to scale his way upwards, I hadn't yet gotten round to telling him to stop.

I heard a smashing sound. I turned to see a glass was now on the floor, broken into many pieces. I knew the glass had been standing on the counter, just where Scott's hand now lay. Scott knew that too, but he did what we all do.

'Daddy,' he said, earnestly, 'it wasn't me.'

★ ★ ★

A week ago I returned from trawling bookstores in the afternoon to find Kristina on the sidewalk, a few doors down from our building. She was carrying a brown paper bag and had evidently been returning from a groceries run when she got buttonholed by an elderly neighbour. That happens from time to time in our street, and it's one of the nice things about living here, assuming you have a high tolerance for repetition.

But as I got closer I realized this didn't look like a case of being told how much better/worse/largely the same it had been around here in days of yore. The woman was white-haired, small and thin, and we'd exchanged cagey nods in the street before. She was Polish, I think. Many of the older residents of the neighbourhood seem a little wary of Kristina, but not this one. She was standing right up close, and speaking quickly, in a low tone.

When she saw me approaching she suddenly stopped talking.

'It's okay,' Kristina said. 'He knows.'

The old woman glared dubiously at me, then back up at Kristina.

'I know where it lives,' she whispered. 'Not far from here. I can show you.'

Kristina was polite, and in the end the woman walked away. But I know she's been back.

Will Kristina be able to resist forever? I doubt it. You are who you are, and you'll end up doing what you do.

That's just the way it is.

We do hope that you have enjoyed reading
this large print book.

Did you know that all of our titles
are available for purchase?

We publish a wide range of high quality
large print books including:
**Romances, Mysteries, Classics
General Fiction
Non Fiction and Westerns**

Special interest titles available in
large print are:
**The Little Oxford Dictionary
Music Book
Song Book
Hymn Book
Service Book**

Also available from us courtesy of
Oxford University Press:
**Young Readers' Dictionary
(large print edition)
Young Readers' Thesaurus
(large print edition)**

For further information or a free
brochure, please contact us at:
**Ulverscroft Large Print Books Ltd.,
The Green, Bradgate Road, Anstey,
Leicester, LE7 7FU, England.
Tel:** (00 44) 0116 236 4325
Fax: (00 44) 0116 234 0205

THE INTRUDERS

Michael Marshall

Jack Whalen was an LAPD patrol cop for almost a decade. He left under a cloud and now he's not really sure *what* he is. One thing he does know is that he loves his wife, Amy. So when she goes missing on a routine business trip to Seattle, his world is shaken. Jack sets out to find her, only to discover that there is something far more mysterious going on . . . Meanwhile, a young girl disappears from her family's holiday home after an encounter with a sinister stranger. However, it would seem that she is far from defenceless . . . From the shadowy secrets of a past that still haunts him, Jack discovers that the truth has roots deeper and darker than he ever feared.

BLOOD OF ANGELS

Michael Marshall

Ward Hopkins' past comes back to haunt him with a vengeance when an ex-CIA colleague tracks him down, desperate for help in solving a bizarre series of events. Meanwhile, Ward's brother, the serial killer known as the Upright Man, has escaped from prison — where he was awaiting trial for murders beyond number. And Hopkins' erstwhile ally, former homicide cop John Zandt, is still on the trail of the organization which killed his daughter and Ward's parents. The further John investigates, the more extraordinary the secrets he uncovers. Across America, sinister forces are stirring. Only Ward, John and FBI agent Nina Baynam stand against this tide, and against the Upright Man . . .

THE LONELY DEAD

Michael Marshall

A guilty man walks alone into the cold mountain forests of Washington State, aiming never to return. What he finds there starts a chain of events that will quickly spiral out of control. Meanwhile, in Los Angeles, a woman's body is discovered, sitting bolt upright in a motel bedroom. She is dead, and her killer has left his mark. It soon becomes clear he has something to say, and a lot more work to do. And Ward Hopkins, an ex-CIA agent recovering from the recent shocking death of his parents, is on the trail of his past, tracking down the men who destroyed everything he once held dear, and the murderer whose face he sees every time he looks in the mirror.

THE STRAW MEN

Michael Marshall

Sarah tries to struggle, but the man holds her. The scream never makes it out of her throat . . . Sarah is the fifth girl to be abducted by this maniac. Her long hair will be hacked off and she will be tortured. She has about a week to live . . . Former LA homicide detective John Zandt has an inside track on the perpetrator — his own daughter was one of his victims. But the key to Sarah's whereabouts lies with Ward Hopkins, a man with a past so secret not even he knows about it. As he investigates his past, Ward finds himself drawn into the sinister world of the Straw Men — and into the desperate race to find Sarah, before her time runs out . . .